a reason to breathe
cp smith

https://www.facebook.com/pages/Author-CP-Smith/739842239363610

Copyright © 2014 by C.P. Smith
First paperback edition: February 2014

Information address: cpsmith74135@gmail.com

ISBN-13: 978-1495261992
ISBN-10: 1495261999

ACKNOWLEDGMENTS

To Amanda, Amy, Erin, Jackie, Jennifer, Joanne, Kelly, Kellyann, Lisette, Marscha, Melinda, Suzy, my beta Leah Schultz, and all the kickass and supporting women on AAKA. You ladies gave me strength to follow this dream, and I love you all. To Kristen Ashley, whose books helped me through a tough time and inspired me to write; thank you for being you, and writing books I'll never grow tired of. To my family who I ignored to write this book, you may now ask me what's for dinner... and finally to Jess Savage, who I met on this road to publishing, thank you!

As a moth to a flame, my eyes cannot turn from you. Your brilliant light, the power you hold, weaken my defenses and hold my heart. Fighting is no option; you bewitch me body and soul. Like a tempest, you draw me in, never, I'm afraid, to release me. And like a newborn babe, I take my first breath and begin to live.

Prologue

Slamming down the trunk on my car, the last of my belongings loaded, I turned to the house I'd spent the last fifteen years lovingly returning to its former beauty. It was an Arts and Crafts gem that had been neglected for over twenty-five years, now owned by someone else. Not because I wanted to give her up, no, but because I had no choice. Doug and I bought the house when Bailey, our daughter, was five. Now a widow at the ripe-old age of thirty-nine and with a daughter off at college, I had no use for a house this big, nor could I afford her. Bailey, who was on a full-ride scholarship at Notre Dame, barely made it home except for Christmas and spring break, so staying in this house with all its memories hurt too much. The upkeep and payment with only one income made staying there a monthly struggle, so selling and moving on was my only option. Time to move forward, downsize and figure out my life as a single woman with a grown daughter.

Doug had been my high school boyfriend; we married at eighteen because we had a baby on the way. It wasn't something I'd planned, but you roll with what life hands you, and Bailey was a blessing I would never regret. Doug had been an easy husband: laidback, friendly, and a great father. Would I have married him at eighteen if not for Bailey? Probably not, but I loved him when I married him, and I loved him when he died. Was it a passionate love? No. But love comes in many forms, and comfortable and secure was one of them.

I'd missed a lot having a baby so young, and with Doug gone now, it was time for me to figure out who I was. I'd studied journalism once I gave birth to Bailey, worked my way through college, and when she started school, I took a job at a small paper in our hometown of Topeka. As a journalist, I could work anywhere, and since my childhood dream was to live high in the mountains of Colorado with deer and bears for my neighbors, I looked west. I looked for any job in journalism that would get me close to those mountains. I didn't care where, because the job wasn't as important as the location; I just needed the mountains of Colorado. So, with my Jeep loaded and my destination of Crested Butte, Colorado, in my GPS, I looked back one last time at my former life and closed my eyes to the memories to hold them close. It was time to move forward. I crawled inside my Jeep, took a deep breath and headed for the interstate.

Heading west towards my new life and new adventures as an entertainment reporter for the Gunnison Times, I wondered, not for the first time, if Doug would be proud of me for taking this step. As I entered the on-ramp, the sun broke and shined down, lighting my path. I'd like to think that was Doug sending me his blessing and wishing me luck on my new adventure, but either way, I'd take that as a sign that brighter days were yet to come.

One

Those Fucking Eyes

Four months later...

She came. I knew she couldn't stay away. My first kill hadn't given me results. My beautiful Jennifer hadn't come. So I adjusted, and now she was here. I knew the pull of the story would bring her. It's why I'd killed. It's why I dumped the body off this road she traveled from the mountains. She'd see and then she'd come. She wanted to investigate, write stories that mattered. It was her dream. With her husband dead and her daughter gone, she was rebuilding her life, starting over. My brave, beautiful girl. I'd make that happen for her. I'd kill to make her dream come true. I'll prove my love, and then she'll know we belong together.

"Sheriff?"

Looking up at my Deputy as he ducked under the crime tape, I wondered, not for the first time, why in the hell he'd become a cop. He didn't have the stomach for the job; evidence to this was now on the top of his boots. He'd taken one look at the bloated body of an unknown white female and made it three feet before he lost his

3

breakfast. Dead bodies are part of this job—the ugly part—but after five years on the force, you'd have thought he would have adjusted. Barry looked almost scared to come closer. So out of deference to his granddaddy, the former Sheriff of Gunnison County, I moved towards him.

"Barry, you got something for me?"

"Sheriff, that new reporter from the Gunnison Times is here. She was driving past and saw the squad cars and coroner. She wants to know what's what. Do you want me to send her away or give a statement?"

Christ, that's all I need. The second body in two months, and if the press got a hold of this, I'd lose control of the situation fast. Glancing over Barry's shoulder at the leggy brunette, something told me to talk to her myself.

"I got this, Barry." Moving towards her, I couldn't stop my eyes from taking her in: long brown hair with those reddish highlights women liked, coffee-brown eyes that made you think of a baby doe, and full pouty lips that begged to be kissed. Looking at her left hand for indication of marital status, I noted no ring. Too bad she's a damn reporter; I hadn't met one I liked yet, no matter what the package.

"Ma'am."

"Sheriff, I'm Jennifer Stewart with the Gunnison Times. I was driving past and caught sight of the Coroner. I'm assuming you've found another body?"

"Ms. Stewart, I'm not at liberty to discuss what's happening here."

"I'm aware of that, Sheriff, but since I've come across this scene, you must know I'll be phoning this to my

4

editor, and you can either give me something or I'll have to draw my own conclusions. This is the second body you've found recently, correct?"

"Again, Ma'am, I'm not at liberty to discuss an ongoing investigation. But I will say this: if you print that we have a second body, when you have no idea what we have, I'll be phoning your editor and advising him of staff reporters who don't substantiate facts before going to print."

Narrowing her eyes over my shoulder, she smiled and then shrugged her shoulders.

"Guess it's a good thing your Deputy already told me you have an unknown white female that seems to have been strangled just like the last victim you found two months ago."

"No comment, and Ms. Stewart..." I paused before lowering my head, getting right in her face. Then I warned, "Don't try to play hardball with me. I don't easily fall for the charms of pouty lips and big, brown eyes. Stay away from my crime scene and wait for a press release like the rest of the scavengers." I heard her draw in a breath as I turned and walked back to the victim.

"Barry," I barked as I made my way around the Coroner's van, my Deputy's eyes on me as I approached. "When I tell you to not talk to the press, I fucking mean it," I hissed.

"Christ, Jack, she had me talking before I knew what hit me. Those fucking eyes of hers—"

"I don't want to hear about her eyes, her tits, or her ass. Think with your head, not with your dick."

"Gotcha, Jack."

I stormed towards the coroner's van and tried to

shake off my encounter with Gunnison's newest reporter. I wanted to kick myself for reacting to her. Jesus, those tits in that tight t-shirt and the smell of honeysuckle and sunshine coming from her hair had my balls drawn up tight. The more she talked, the more I wanted to grab her face and kiss those fucking lips until she couldn't talk.

"Give me something to work with, Drew." Drew Young, the county's coroner and an old friend, was bending over the body examining her neck. At forty-two, Drew was still in great shape. His hair had a touch of gray around the temples; his body was fit from years of mountain climbing and kayaking. Divorced with two kids he saw every other weekend, he screwed anything with two legs because he's still looking for the right one.

I'd stopped looking, resigned to the fact there wasn't the perfect woman out there for me. I'd never been married, never met a woman who didn't try to change me. I was a lawman like my father and his father before him. It started with my grandfather, a distant relative to the namesake of our county, a name all my family had been proud to wear. But years turned into twenty, and at the age of forty, I figured my time to settle down and have a family had passed. My Dad passed away five years ago: heart attack struck him just three months after retiring. My mother always said the job would kill him, although I don't think she meant all the years eating greasy food and sitting behind a desk. Dad had been the sheriff for Ouray County for twenty-two years. Barry's grandfather, the former sheriff of Gunnison County before he retired, and I took over, had been a friend of my dad's on the Gunnison force. When Dad was ready to run for Sheriff, he wouldn't run against the then sitting Sheriff, who was also his friend, so he moved to Ouray County after I graduated high school and ran for Sheriff there instead.

"Cause of death: strangulation, just like the last victim," Drew answered, pulling me out of my thoughts.

"Jesus, Drew, I could see that for myself. Tell me you got something I didn't see."

"Lividity tells me the body was dumped, Jack, so she was killed somewhere else. There are liver marks on her back, in some type of pattern, and my guess is she's been dead four days; age is hard to tell due to the bloating, but my guess is 35-40."

"Get her over to the morgue and get to work. Find me something I can pin on this bastard."

Drew nodded and then went to work covering the victim's hands with plastic bags to preserve them during the transport. Anything she may have touched or scratched right before she died could be under those nails, and we couldn't afford to lose a single piece of evidence. Looking down at this stranger with long brown hair, I prayed I could find out where she came from and who killed her. Somewhere out there was a family that's going to need closure, just like the last female we found.

"Christ, I got a bad feeling about this, Drew." He never looked up from his work, just nodded in agreement.

"Both have brown hair, brown eyes, and the ages are the same. Are you thinking what I'm thinking?" Drew added.

"Fuck, yeah. I do not need this in my county, Drew. Folks come here to have a vacation, not to get

7

strangled."

Drew stood and motioned for his tech to load the body onto the gurney and then turned to me, his eyes drifting behind me, and then they grew bigger.

"Jesus, who's the sex on a stick?"

I looked over my shoulder and saw Ms. Stewart was still standing behind the yellow tape, talking on her phone while writing in a notebook. For some reason, my hackles went up at Drew's attention.

"Get your head in the game and out of her pants."

"Whoa, sorry big guy, didn't mean to step in your territory."

"Christ, she's not my fucking territory, just keep your head in your pants. She's a fucking vulture from the Gunnison Times."

I watched as he glanced one more time in Ms. Stewart's direction; then Drew slapped my back and made his way over to his van. Turning to Barry, who had his back to the crime scene and his eyes on the reporter, I sighed, walked over to my truck and then looked back at Barry.

"Keep this scene secured till the mobile lab can get here and sweep for evidence. And don't fucking talk to anyone from the press, do you hear me?

Barry gave me a chin lift; then I climbed in my truck. As I pulled out, I looked in the rear-view mirror, and watched as Ms. Stewart approached Barry. He put his hands up and shook his head, indicating no comment. Thank fuck for that.

***

"Come on, Bob, give me a chance." I was begging on the phone when Sheriff Gunnison headed to his truck. I lost track of my thoughts watching those massive thighs carry his large muscled body; I'd never had a reaction like this to a man... Before he came over to talk with me, I'd watched him interacting with Barry. Barry was a decent-looking man nearly eight years younger than me. He was taller than my 5' 5", but not by much; he was built lanky, like a runner, with mousy blond hair and green eyes, and I'd met him when I first moved here four months ago. We'd had coffee once, and I think he wanted more, but the attraction wasn't there for me.

I didn't know when I'd be ready to date again, and was thinking celibacy was looking good when that damned man looked up at me, and my breath stilled. Well over six feet tall, with dark brown hair, crystal blue eyes, and a rugged jaw with a two-day growth. And that broad chest and those muscled arms. They made me weak in the knees. As he'd walked to me, I kept telling myself, "Be professional, you can do this." So when he opened his mouth and said 'Ma'am," I launched right into what I thought was a professional sounding introduction. The more he spoke in that rough voice of his, the more determined I was. But the harder I tried, the madder he got. "*I don't easily fall for the charms of pouty lips and big, brown eyes.*" Remembering those words as he walked to his truck, I was pulled from my daydreaming as a voice on the phone talked back to me.

"Jennifer, I didn't hire you to cover crime. Finish up there and get to the paper. We have to go over this month's event calendar."

"But, Bob, I'm already here. I promise I won't let this interfere with my other obligations."

"Jennifer, I'm not having a female reporter for craft fairs running around after a killer. I'll put one of the men on this story when it breaks. Now get moving and I'll see you in thirty minutes."

"Dammit." I threw my phone in my bag as the sheriff drove away. I watched him for a second, and then, making a decision, I approached Barry. He put his hands up in a gesture of "don't come any closer," and shook his head no, but he spoke the opposite:

"Just keep your distance till the sheriff is out of sight. I don't want another ass-chewing."

"I'm so sorry, Barry, I wasn't thinking when I told him what you'd said."

"It's ok, Jennifer, his bark is worse than his bite. But if I tell you anything else and he finds out—"

"I swear I won't say another thing, and I really appreciate your help. I have to head back down now; I'll catch you later, ok?"

"Later, Jennifer. Maybe we can grab coffee again sometime."

"If I can free up some time, Barry. Thanks again."

I headed to my jeep and tried not to think about why Barry was willing to help me. My intuition said Barry was interested in me, and that made me feel like dirt. I didn't want to lead him on; he was just a friend. Surely he knew that friends do things for friends, right?

Nibbling on my lip as I headed down the mountains of Crested Butte to the town of Gunnison, my thoughts kept drifting back to those angry, blue eyes and chiseled jaw.

"He thinks I have pouty lips."

I rolled my eyes and trained my thoughts back on the matter at hand. There's a killer on the loose, and if this last victim was strangled just like the first one, that could only mean one thing: a serial killer. The thought of being on the ground floor of a story like this got my heart pumping. Four months of covering arts festivals and balloon races were starting to bore me. If I investigated this story on the side, I could prove to my editor I was worth taking a chance on and maybe he'd move me from puff pieces into the meatier stories. This was every journalism student's dream when they entered college: hardcore, knuckle-cracking pieces.

Looking ahead for my exit into Gunnison, I saw the flashing lights of the sheriff's truck on the side of the road. As I drove past, he was exiting his vehicle that was pulled behind an abandoned car, and it occurred to me if I did investigate this killer, I might just run into the sheriff again. Damn, that might not be a good thing. Something told me he wouldn't take kindly to a "scavenger" nosing around in his business. Somehow I'd pissed him off and put a huge bulls-eye on my head. So I decided I'd keep my investigation to myself lest I ruffle the sheriff's feathers even more. "Well, Jennifer, you wanted to be an investigative reporter. Time to prove you can do it: it's put up or shut up time."

I took my exit into Gunnison and headed for the paper, deciding there was no time like the present. Taking the turn onto Main Street, I pulled into the parking lot near the Times building and grabbed my stuff. I jumped out and headed for the door that would take me to my desk so I could start my research on this

11

killer. *Forget the sheriff, forget your boss, do this for you. Prove you've got what it takes.* Pep talk in place, I fired up my computer and got down to the business of serial killers.

Two

Just Jack

"Jennifer, did you see the Baptist Church has a bake sale on the 30th?"

Looking up from my computer, I nodded my head in the affirmative and went back to my research of well-known serial killers. I wanted to see what made them tick, what the police had done to catch them, and read the stories of the journalists who'd helped catch them. Searching through the killer's names, I stopped on the BTK killer who'd terrorized my home state of Kansas from 1986-2004.

The killer collected trophies?

Grabbing my spiral and making notes from the article, I felt, rather than saw, a presence behind me.

"Ms. Stewart, didn't we already discuss interfering in my investigation?"

Closing my eyes to the sound of that voice speaking inches from my ear, I dropped my pen and swiveled quickly to the monitor, turning it off. I looked up into those crystal blue eyes and froze. Before I could respond, Bob, my editor, took notice of the sheriff and approached us.

"Sheriff, to what do we owe this pleasure?"

"Just checking to make sure Ms. Stewart understood the gravity of the situation, Bob. I don't need some reporter going off half-cocked printing allegations that haven't been substantiated. But seein' as she was hard at work disobeying my order, looks like I need to restate, again, we do not know what we are dealing with, and any stories leaked by the press will not go unnoticed by my office."

Bob looked at me, exasperation clear in his eyes, and then turned back to the sheriff with his good-ol'-boy smile.

"Sheriff, Mrs. Stewart hasn't been assigned to investigate this story. Any ideas she had were put to rest this morning."

I felt heat hit my face. *God, this is embarrassing.* I took a deep breath and turned away so they couldn't see my face. I was mortified at being reprimanded in front of the sheriff. If I ever hoped to further my career, I would need good standing with his department. I knew I needed to bite my lip and suck up this slight, but having been slapped on the hand like an errant child stoked my temper.

"See to it she keeps her nose out of it in the future."

"I can assure you she *will* keep to her articles about the host of exciting adventures to be had in our fair county."

Standing quickly, I'd had enough about keeping my place. I grabbed my purse, stuffed my bag with my articles and notes in it, and then turned to them both.

"You'll excuse me, gentlemen, but the air of oppression is a little thick right now. I'm sure I have a bake sale I need to see to."

I heard a chuckle from Lorraine two desks over as I stomped towards the front door. As I was pulling the door open, I felt a hand at my elbow stopping me.

"You need to stay out of this, Mrs. Stewart. Two women have died. Think of your husband, your kids, if you have them. You nose around in this, and you could end up hurt or worse."

"I'll take that into consideration, Sheriff. I wouldn't want to worry anyone. Now, again, if you'll excuse me, I'm sure I have a pot roast I need to put in the oven."

Sucking in a breath to ward off the tears his words caused, I pushed through the door and tried to keep from running. Stupid, so stupid, I couldn't remember the last time I made a pot roast...Isn't it funny the things you miss?

***

I watched the little spitfire hurry down the block, then turned to Bob and gave him a chin lift. As I opened the door, Lorraine, who was as old as time and a fixture of the Gunnison Times, stopped me in my tracks.

"I'm guessing you've never met Ms. Stewart before today, boy."

"Nope, haven't had the displeasure 'til today."

"Word of advice, go easy on her. She just moved here four months ago after selling her house. She could no longer afford it due to a drunk driver killing her husband."

Christ.

I closed my eyes then hung my head.

"Jennifer acts tough, but she's got a soft spot and a heart of gold. Got married out of high school to the guy and had a baby not soon after. Baby's all grown up and out of the house."

I turned my head and looked back down the street, then turned back to Lorraine and mumbled, "Shit."

"That about covers it. Now, what'cha gonna do about it, boy?"

I stared at the old woman for a few seconds, then turned on my heels and went out the door in the same direction as Jenn had gone.

***

So, killers collect trophies? I wonder if the police have discovered if the victims were missing anything.

I pulled out my notepad and made a notation: "Ask Barry for the names of the first victims' family." Tapping my pen against the paper, trying to remember the first victim and what I knew about her, I looked around the park I had gone to and saw mothers with strollers had emerged to enjoy the last few weeks of warmer weather.

In the fall, weather changed quickly here. You could have seventy degrees and sunny in the morning, and then, by nightfall, snow could be threatening. Breathing in the fresh air and thinking I'd better get my tires changed to all-weather for the upcoming winter, I felt the bench beside me shift with the weight of someone sitting down. Out of the corner of my eye, I saw the large frame of the sheriff. *Damn.*

"I didn't know." Great, sympathy from this already fascinating man would do me in, so I steeled myself against his pity.

16

"How could you?" I replied, letting him off the hook.

"Lorraine said you moved here on your own." Making a notation never to unload my problems on the clearly "Chatty Cathy," I turned to those blue eyes and shrugged.

"I had a dream when I was a kid to live in the mountains with the bears." He raised his eyebrows and grinned.

"What?"

"Never met a woman who wanted to live with bears."

"Never met a man as bossy as you."

I watched as his grin turned into a smile that could melt butter, and I found myself looking at his lips. I forced my eyes back to the park and watched a mother with her hands held out to her son as he let go of the slide.

"Jack Gunnison."

"Pardon?"

"Let's start over. My name is Jack Gunnison." I studied his face. I could tell he was sincere and nodded.

"Ok, Sheriff, Jennifer Stewart."

"Just Jack."

"Sorry?"

"No Sheriff, just Jack." I smiled at his offer.

"Ok, Just Jack." I didn't think it was possible, but his smile got even bigger. Oh man, that smile was dangerous to women at large.

"Jack?" I turned my head and saw a beautiful woman with blond hair and big, blue eyes. She looked pissed. Scratch that, she *was* pissed.

"I see it didn't take you long to move on, although I wouldn't say you moved on to greener pastures."

"Christ, Naomi," Jack hissed.

"You told me a few weeks ago you didn't want to be tied down, and here you are cozying up to some random woman while I'm sitting at home wondering what I did wrong."

"I'm not doing this here, Naomi. I already said what I had to say."

"You didn't say much of anything. Eight months we saw each other, I thought we were going somewhere, and then you just moved on."

Oh God, I don't want to be here right now! Looking for any excuse to leave, I grabbed my bag and stood.

"I'll just be heading back to work, Jack."

"Jenn, you don't need to leave. This conversation is over."

"Yes, *Jenn*, head on back to work," Naomi snapped, sarcasm dripping from her words. Yikes!

"I, um, Jack, I'll, ah, talk to you later, ok?" Without letting him stop me, I pushed past the blond bitch.

I had been married for nineteen years. Doug was my first everything; I had little experience where matters of the heart were concerned. I had no idea what to do or say in this situation; hell, I'd never been involved in a breakup. So I hightailed it across the park and headed in the direction of my jeep. Looking back once, I saw Jack's eyes on me while Naomi cried into her hands. I was so out of my league with this guy. He should have a warning label on his back saying, "Proceed with caution: smile will dazzle you."

"Jennifer, are you talking to yourself now?" Screeching to a halt at hearing my name, I turned to see Barry standing at his truck parked next to mine. In fact, that's how I'd met Barry the first time; he'd parked next to me.

"Ha, no," I stumbled, trying to come up with a valid reason. "I was just, ah, just reciting a song." He didn't buy it. Damn. I watched Barry look back across the park, watching Jack talk to Naomi. I cringed; he must have seen me scurrying away like a coward.

"Word of advice, Jack isn't the type of guy to settle down. He's been on his own for twenty years, and he's had women, but they never last. Every time he spends time with one, they think they'll be the one to tame him, but it never happens."

"Good to know. Not that I have any intention of getting involved with him." Barry stared at me, searching for something, so I smiled and pulled my door open. "Later, Barry." He nodded and gave me a two-finger salute, then climbed in his truck. I watched him drive off, then looked back to see Naomi and Jack in an embrace. *Looks like this one might last.*

***

Entering a small cafe in Crested Butte, where locals like to gather, I noted the time. McGill's was open from 6:00 A.M. to 2:30 P.M. daily. It was pushing two o'clock, so I only had enough time to order takeout. Rosie, one of the waitresses who'd been there for close to twenty years, took my order, so I sat at the bar to wait.

McGill's was located on Elk street, in the heart of what was considered Main Street. Only mom and pop stores were allowed there, maintaining the quaint feeling of yesterdays gone by. Ben, a longtime local, was sitting at a table drinking coffee with Gerald. Both men were in their sixties and they'd moved up to Crested Butte years ago. Ben had a B&B on the outskirts of town, though I didn't think he actively looked for bookings; he was always here when I came in. But I was still shocked when I learned this big bear of a man catered to people year-round. Just under six foot, with longish, gray hair, he was big, but in good shape for a man his age, and lived life every day like it was his last. I knew he was a throwback from the Hippie generation, because Ben still looked and dressed like one.

Gerald ran one of the ski lifts on the mountain during ski season, and in the summer, he took tourists on rafting tours down the Gunnison and Taylor Rivers. He was a tall, lean man with piercing blue eyes and an easy smile. He could be shy sometimes, but he seemed to have a heart of gold. Both were some of my favorite locals.

"You just gonna sit there, Jenny, or get your cute butt over here and say hello?"

"Ben, stop calling me Jenny and quit looking at my butt."

"Can't. You remind me of my first girl back in high school and we called her Jenny. As for your butt, it is cute; shapely too. It looks like an upside-down heart."

"Oh, my God, you're a dirty, old man," I shouted.

Gerald, or Gerry, hooted out a laugh and Ben joined him. I felt my face get warm with a blush and looked back at Rosie, who was smiling at the two old farts. Grabbing my bag, I pulled out my notes and tried to ignore them.

"What the hell are you reading?" Rosie asked, leaning

across the bar and looking at my notes.

"Time frame I put together of the two bodies found dumped outside of town."

"Two bodies? They found another one?" Before I could answer her, I watched from the mirror over the bar as Ben and Gerry looked up at her shouted replay and stood from their seats. Obviously deciding they wanted in on the conversation and bringing their coffee with them, they walked over and each sat to one of my sides. Without a care in the world if it were nosey or not, both looked over my notes, talking to each other while I sat there, dumbfounded.

"Both women, late thirties, not local, huh. Bet the sheriff knows what's goin on; maybe we should call a town meeting. What do you think, Gerry?"

"Sounds reasonable. Can't be too careful these days. Can we have it here at McGill's, Rosie? You could serve some finger food and coffee."

"Sure, we can have it at four tomorrow. It gives me time to clean up before everyone gets here."

"I'll call Jack and have him meet us here at three so we can talk beforehand," Ben insisted.

And before I could even open my mouth to object to anything they'd just said, and most definitely object to them calling Jack since he'd just told me to keep my nose out of his business, Ben was on the phone barking out, "Jack, Ben here." *Oh, please, someone shoot me.*

"We need to meet tomorrow at three to discuss these killings. Gonna have the locals here at four tomorrow so you can catch us up to speed."

I was contemplating moving to Breckenridge the minute I heard what he said to Jack. Surely they needed

21

a friendly journalist to write their event calendar.

"Jenny told us."

I wondered how long it took to pack up a one-room cabin. I could be on the road by nightfall, maybe seven.

"Jenny, Jennifer Stewart. Pretty thing with a cute butt, surely you've met her."

I heard Jack's voice grow louder the longer he was on the phone. Now I was determined more than ever to give notice at the paper on my way out of town. So I picked up my notes and started stuffing them in my bag when a phone was shoved into my face.

"Jack wants to talk with you," Ben chuckled.

"Umm, I'm pretty sure he does, but I'm also pretty sure I don't want to talk to him, so I'll just be going now. Night, all."

It was moments like this I was not ashamed to admit... I was a chicken. As I turned to run out the door, forgetting I'd ordered a meal to go, I was quite sure I heard Jack laugh on the other end of the phone. *Maybe I'll forget packing and leave from here!!!*

Three

Ball Breaker

"Jack."

"Christ, you're wet."

"Jack."

My eyes flew wide open. Images of long legs and brown, coffee-colored eyes flashed across my memory. "Shit." The images seemed real, the memories like they'd just happened. I lay there a moment, trying to slow my breathing. "Jesus," I muttered. Sitting up and glancing at the clock, I noted the time: 3:15 A.M. My thoughts turned to those brown eyes, and I wondered if she was sleeping or working on that damn article. Long legs that wrapped around my back, while those eyes closed as she moaned my name, passed through my mind's eye. *Shit.* I rubbed my eyes to get rid of the image and mumbled, "Jesus, I need a vacation." Reaching down and swiping my jeans off the floor, I pulled a shirt from my drawer, grabbed my boots, and headed to the kitchen to start a pot of coffee. While I waited for it to brew, I thought about this piece of shit killing women. *He's dumping them where we can find them; he's not burying them; he wants us to find them...but why?* "I wonder if he returns to his dumpsites." Thinking on that,

I decided to check out the possibility; it was better than sitting here stewing before heading into the office.

***

She's curled up like a kitten, the light of the moon shining on her brown curls. She's so brave moving here alone. I leaned down and whispered, "I'll keep you safe. Sleep well, little one."

You know when you're sleeping but not quite asleep, and you're not sure if you're dreaming? I was lying in my bed curled around my pillow, and I swear I heard a whisper. Too afraid to open my eyes and too sluggish with sleep to actually believe I felt a warm breath on my neck, I continued to doze. Then I heard a floorboard creak. I held my breath, listening, and then heard my front door open and then close. Now I was sure I wasn't dreaming. Heart pounding, but afraid to move, I listened again for movement. Slowly, I rolled over and opened my eyes. I turned my head to the window and screamed when I saw a dark figure staring back at me. Scared shitless, I rolled to my phone on the nightstand, grabbed it, and dialed 911 as I fell to the floor.

"Gunnison County Sheriff's Department."

"Someone is outside my window; I think they were in my cabin." I was crouching on the floor, looking back at the window, but seeing no one there now.

"Ma'am, I need you to remain calm and give me your name and address."

"Jennifer Stewart, is the sheriff there?" I asked.

"Ma'am, I need your address."

"204 Old Saw Mill Road, first cabin on the left. Is the

sheriff there?"

"Ma'am, I'm sending a deputy to you now. Are your doors and windows locked?" I looked at my front door, afraid to move toward it.

"I don't know...I...Can you call Jack?"

"Ma'am, the sheriff is off duty for the night, a deputy will be there shortly. I need you to check your doors and windows and make sure they are secure." Shaking my head at the woman's voice, not wanting to move, but afraid not to, I stood and started heading toward the door.

"Ok, doors and windows. I can do that." Suddenly, a loud noise came from the front porch, and I screamed, ran to the bathroom, and locked myself in, sliding down the door to the floor.

"Ma'am, are you still with me?"

"He's outside," I whispered. "Please call Jack, please, please, please."

***

"Gunnison."

"Sheriff, we've got a woman on the emergency line with an unknown intruder still on the premises, at 204 Old Saw Mill Road."

"Did you send a deputy to investigate?"

"Got Grady heading over, Jack, but she keeps asking for you."

"What's this woman's name?"

"Stewart, Jennifer Stewart. Hold one second, Jack. Amy, is Ms. Stewart secure?"

Before I could ask why she was asking for me, my

blood ran cold when I heard Jenn scream, then plead over the dispatch speaker, *"He's outside, please call Jack, please, please, please."* I didn't hesitate when I heard her scared voice. "Phil, call Grady, tell him I'm in route and ten minutes out from her location."

"Will do, Jack," he replied and hung up.

I whipped my truck around and hit the gas, taking turns on the winding road up the mountain faster than was safe. Within seven minutes, I was bearing down on Old Saw Mill and saw headlights from a truck heading towards me. As I passed, I made a note of the color: light tan, silver or gray. Then I pulled a right onto Saw Mill and hit the gas. As I came up to the small cabin, I saw no lights, and no one lurking around. I threw the truck into park and then ran up the steps to the door and pounded.

"Jenn, it's Jack, open up." Trying the doorknob and finding it locked, I pounded again then heard a noise inside.

"Jack, oh, God, hold on."

I heard the lock turn, and the door flew open. Jenn didn't think twice: she threw herself at me, wrapped her arms around my neck, and then she started to cry. I took a step back as her head buried in my neck, and I'll be damned if that didn't wash right over me and settle warm in my gut, as the word *"Mine"* rang in my head. I didn't hesitate; I wrapped my arms around her and buried my face to her ear and whispered:

"I got you, baby."

"Jack, he was in the cabin. He whispered in my ear."

As natural as if I'd been doing it all my life, I picked Jenn up in my arms, walked into the cabin, and slammed the door with my boot. I moved to her couch and sat down, Jenn never breaking her hold on me.

"Talk to me, Jenn." She pulled back and dried her eyes with the cuff of her shirt, then breathed in and let it out. In the low light, with messed up hair, red eyes and nose from crying, I realized I'd never seen anyone more beautiful, and I instantly wanted to find this asshole who'd scared her to tears.

"I was sleeping, or I think I was sleeping; anyway, I felt a warm breath on my neck which is what woke me, or not, I'm still not clear on the whole sleeping thing. Then I thought I heard someone whisper, but I'm not sure what he said. So I lay there for a moment, listening, and I heard a floorboard creak. I lay there some more, and I heard my front door open and close, *then* of course I lay there a little longer, listening again, and heard nothing. I waited a bit longer, listening for more noise, and then rolled to the window. He was there, looking down at me, and that's when I called the station; then something loud hit the wall on the outside and then you came." If the situation hadn't been so serious, I would have laughed at that explanation. I'm not entirely sure she took a breath during that whole speech. Holding my smile back, I questioned her some more.

"Did you get a good look at this person?"

"It was a man."

"Then you got a look at him."

"No."

"Then how do you know it was a man?"

"It looked like a man"

"How do you know, if you didn't get a look at him?"

"It just looked like a man. He was tall, bulky; head hit the top of the window. He was dressed in a dark jacket and jeans, a man." I looked to the ceiling, wondering what she considered a good look. She saw everything but the face.

"Ok, Jenn, I'm gonna go outside and look around, you lock the door behind me."

Jenn moved from my lap and followed me to the door. I heard the lock engage and pulled out my flashlight. The ground was too hard for footprints, but when I moved to the window, I found a plant in a ceramic pot, smashed on the porch. It looked like it had been thrown, not tipped over. Something slithered down my spine. If this were a random break-in, why throw something in anger? I looked around the porch and noticed hanging pots from the roof trusses. It was possible, when she caught them peeking at her, they knocked it off in their haste to get away, and it shattered. A sexy woman alone might attract a Peeping Tom. As for the whispering in her ear? She could have dreamt that. The intruder could have entered the cabin looking for something to steal; when she stirred they left the cabin, and then looked through the window to see if she woke up. When she saw them, they turned and ran, knocking the pot off, causing the loud noise. This seemed the likeliest scenario, but I'd make a note for the boys to keep an eye on this area.

***

Pacing the floor while I waited for Jack to return, I thought about the man at my window. Did I know him? Was there anything familiar about him? I heard Jack knock and opened the door. Watching Jack enter, I noticed what a large man he was, how he filled the room with his presence. Tall and bulky instead of lanky, with large muscled arms and a broad chest, he just exuded strength. No wonder Naomi didn't want to let him go; all that and brains to boot!

He broke me from my daydreaming when he started talking. "Found a broken flower pot on the porch. The intruder probably knocked it off after you caught him looking in the window."

"Ok, that makes sense."

"I think he entered the cabin to steal something, and when you stirred, he left out the front door and then peeked in the window to double check you were still asleep."

"How did he get in?"

"You sure you locked your door before bed?"

"Yes, no...I'm not sure of anything. I was tired and trying to decide whether to pack and move to Breckenridge when I went to bed."

"Move to Breckenridge?"

"Um, yeah, I was sure you were going to lynch me after that phone call from Ben." Jack's face broke into a smile, and he chuckled. He was a rugged, sexy man, but when he smiled, he was dazzling.

"I'm glad to see you're taking me seriously about investigating this killer."

"Oh, I know how much you don't want me to investigate, Jack, believe me; I got that message loud and clear. I'm just poking around, getting facts, so when this guy is caught I'm already ahead of the game. I'm not stupid; I don't want to get in the crosshairs of a killer." Jack studied me for a moment, and something settled in his eyes, something like acceptance.

"Ok, Jenn, you do your research, but no going to press with anything unless I give the OK."

"I can do that, I promise; I can dig for information, and write my story as it unfolds, then turn it in to Bob once you've caught this guy."

"I can live with that as long as you stay out of my way *and* don't put yourself in danger. You hear what I'm saying? Research only, Jenn."

"Got it, Sheriff."

"Just Jack, remember?" I smiled at that; he'd remembered this afternoon.

"So how'd it go with Naomi? You guys back on again?" He grinned slowly, and then shook his head.

"No, Jenn, we aren't back together. I don't like women who try to change who I am. I'm not nine-to-five suit material. I wear jeans, I hunt bad guys, and I rescue damsels in distress."

"Well, this damsel is mighty glad you came so quickly, just so you know." *Oh, my God, I'm flirting. Where in the hell did that come from?* I looked away, embarrassed, and heard Jack chuckle.

"Duly noted. Glad I could be of service."

"Me too, Jack, and I promise, not to call in the middle of the night again if I can help it." Jack grinned a sexy grin, and I felt my knees go weak.

"You know, for a reporter, you're kinda sweet. Not at all what I expected after this morning. Gotta say, babe, it's nice to see." *Wait, I'm not sure that was a compliment.* I wanted to be seen as a serious reporter, not sweet.

"I can be a bitch. I can eat up balls, spit them out, and then trample them with my boots." Jack's eyebrows shot to his forehead.

"Eat up balls and spit them out. Jesus, I'm going to have to keep a close eye on you. Men will be falling all over themselves to get to your brand of ball-breaking."

"Keep an eye on me? Why would you have to keep an eye on me?"

Jack's hand came up and tucked a piece of hair behind my ear. Watching his hand as he did this, he then curled it behind my neck and slowly drew me to him. I watched his eye come to mine, and on a deep breath, he kissed me. Sweet and slow, with liberal amounts of tongue, it was a tentative first kiss, meant to test the waters, but inform you of his intentions, and it definitely left me wanting more.

"That's what that means," he breathed against my mouth. *Wow, good to know.*

"Now, lock up behind me as soon as I leave and if you need me again, don't hesitate to call." I was still in a trance from his kiss and just nodded my head as he walked to my door. Jack opened it, then turned back grinning at me.

"See ya, Ball Breaker."

"See ya, Just Jack," I replied as he walked out the door and down my steps to his truck. I got a chin lift as he climbed in, then he waited for me to close my door. I turned the lock and watched from my front window as he turned out of my drive and headed back down the mountain. It was after he was gone and I was thinking about his strong hands and soft lips on mine when I realized I'd forgotten I'd been broken into. Shit, I'd been dazzled...That man was lethal to more than one part of my body.

Moving toward my bed, I saw a business card lying on my table. I picked it up and read the fine print. Jack Gunnison, Sheriff, Gunnison County. *I bet there's a fascinating story behind that name.* I grabbed my phone where I'd left it on the table and punched in the number of his cell. When the cursor flashed for the name, I started to type in "Jack" but stopped, smiling. Then I typed in "Bossy" instead. For some reason, that just fit him, since the moment I'd met him, he'd been bossing me around.

I decided to send him a text so he'd have my number, but why? I had no idea; I needed to keep my distance. Anyone who could kiss me dizzy could not be good for my state of mind. And after Barry told me women don't last with Jack, I didn't need to be added to the long list of women he'd dumped. But good manners pushed me to do it, so I hit the fabulous little microphone on my message screen, and spoke into it.

Thanks for rescuing me. In case you rescue more than one damsel in a night, this is Jennifer.

I put my phone down and headed to the bathroom, not expecting a text back or at all since he was busy, so I was surprised when he texted back quickly.

Jack: You lock your doors?
Me: Of course.
Jack: Windows?
Me: Yes, Jack.
Jack: Then get to sleep, babe. No thanks necessary. The pleasure was all mine.
Me: Anyone ever tell you that you're bossy?

Jack: Nope.
Me: Interesting.
Jack: Sleep.
Me: Fine.

No more texts came, so I went to the bathroom and then climbed in bed and curled around my pillow. I thought about the last two hours and decided Jack might be a good guy, but he was very, very dangerous to my heart.

Four

It Takes A Village To Solve A Crime

"Jenny, get your ass over here, girl!" I heard Ben shout as I entered McGill's. I was getting a to-go order. Their pancakes were the bomb, and after the night I'd had, I needed some stick-to-your-ribs comfort food. Ben and Gerry were sitting at their regular table as I walked in, so I walked over to them and smiled.

"Morning, gentlemen. You doing ok this morning?"

"What's this we hear about an intruder up at your cabin last night?" Gerry shouted.

"How on earth did you hear about that so soon? Jack just left four hours ago."

"Nothin' gets past this town, you know that, girl. Now answer the question: did you have someone break into your cabin?" Gerry asked again.

"Unfortunately, yes, but they didn't take anything, except my pride. Jack thinks they were looking for something to steal, and I scared them off when I woke up."

"Jack, you say, made the call on his night off?" Ben asked surprised.

"He was up already, so he was close when I called the station."

34

"He isn't concerned it was the killer at your place last night?"

"Uh, I don't think so. Why would the killer be after me?"

"You fit the profile," Ben explained.

"Profile? What profile?"

"The one Gerry and I put together after you left last night." *Oh, good lord, why did I open my notes in front of these men?*

"Gerry and I worked on it last night and figured out these women were all 35-40, had brown hair, brown eyes, and they were also single. That's what serial killers do: they find a type and go after them." Impressed they'd come up with that, I told them, "Ok, guys, good catch. I'll pass that along to Jack if I talk to him."

"If you're gonna be investigating this for a story, Ben and me think we should help you out. We know everyone within five counties; we'd know a killer if we saw one."

I raised my eyes to the ceiling, looking for strength. These men were like crazy uncles, and I loved them dearly. I'd rented my cabin from Ben, and he'd left his cool log furniture so I wouldn't have to buy new. But I'd promised Jack no interference, and something told me Ben and Gerry putting their two cents worth in might piss Jack off. I'd seen him bossy, and I didn't want to see him pissed.

"Guys, I don't know what to say. You—"

"Nothin' *to* say, Jenny. We're gonna help you on this and that's that. Now, we'll meet here every day after Rosie shuts down. She's got the inside scoop on the women around here, and maybe we can figure out who the next target is. Then Jack can just be waiting to grab this guy when he strikes," Ben finished, and I stopped right before I could argue against his idea. Opening, then closing my mouth, it occurred to me that *that* wasn't a half-bad idea. If this guy had a type, then we could figure out who in the county matched it and feed the info to Jack.

"Aren't the women they found strangers?" I inquired.

"First victim, Jamie Smith, was from over in Ouray, and the one found yesterday was identified as Cindy Baker from Lake City."

"Ben, how do you know this?"

"I got ears, Jenny. I use them."

Right, these men knew everything that went on in this town. How could I forget? I pondered this information for a moment and then figured that it couldn't hurt to go along with their plan. Sitting in a diner with Ben, Gerry, and Rosie, talking the story through, could only help clear up ideas.

"Ok, guys, you've got a deal. I'll meet you back here at three if that works for you?"

"That it does, Jennifer," Gerry called out with a smile on his face.

"Orders up, Jennifer," Rosie shouted, so I headed to the bar, paid my ticket, and waved at the boys as I headed to my car. For the first time since I got to Colorado, I felt excited about my job, but then I stopped and turned my thoughts to the women who had died and felt like the scavenger Jack said I was. I needed to find a way to help, not just sensationalize the story. There were enough bottom feeders in the press. I didn't need to become one of them.

***

"That's right, Agent Rowe: two murders in two months, both victims had brown hair, brown eyes, and they were in their mid to late thirties."

Scribbling on my notepad, I waited while Agent Rowe with the FBI searched the national database for any killings that matched ours. Forensics had come back on the latest victim. Cindy Baker from Lake City, was a single woman who worked at the Java Hut in the tourist town. She was divorced with no children and had moved up to Lake City in the last year from Pagosa Springs. The first victim, Jamie Smith from Ouray, was also a transplant from Denver. This explained why no one had known either woman.

"Sheriff, we don't have any known murders matching your victims. If you have another body turn up with the same M.O., give me a call back, and I will present the info to my superior and we can start a profile."

"Agent Rowe, I'm trying to avoid another victim, you're supposed to be the experts on serial killers, and I'm inviting you to come to my county to assist."

"Sheriff Gunnison, I appreciate the position you're in, but we have thousands of murders we're investigating at this time, and until it's clear we have a serial on our hands, *my* hands are tied."

"I'll be sure to pass that along to the next family I notify when another one of my residents turns up dead," I bit out. Slamming the phone down, I raked my hand through my hair, muttering, "Fucking Feds." Most small town sheriffs didn't like the Feds pissing all over their jurisdiction, but I couldn't give a shit if it meant one of my own was safe from this asshole. I needed to find this guy and find him fast. Yanking up the phone, I dialed Drew.

"Drew, you got time to meet with me?"

"Up to my elbows in guts, Jack, but what can I do for you?"

"I want to take a look at the lividity marks on the back of Cindy Baker."

"Ok, I've got another two hours' work in front of me, however. Meet me at the morgue in two and a half? Does that work for you?"

"I'll make it work. See you then," I said as my only goodbye.

"Grady," I shouted down the hall to my deputy. Grady Hall, who had two years on the force and was a competent cop, was also the mayor's son. Though only twenty-three, he worked hard and had a sharp mind. I saw a future sheriff in him and tried to include him in all investigations to groom him for this job.

"You bellowed, Jack?"

"Get me the phone records of both murder victims and a timeline for their last-known whereabouts."

"You got it, Jack."

"Where's Barry?"

"He called in, said he was checking on the Stewart woman, making sure she didn't have any more trouble last night. He should be back in about an hour."

"Who told him to do that?"

"I figured you did."

"Christ."

Barry was checking on Jenn...Since when did he do a callback when he didn't even take the callout? I felt anger crawl up my gut and tried to press it down. *Did*

Barry know Jenn before yesterday? Was that why he'd leaked information about the second victim? "Her fucking eyes, my ass." I felt my jaw tighten and my anger spike. "Christ." I grabbed my phone, found Barry's cell number and hit send.

"Todd."

"Barry, you wanna tell me why you're on a callback with Ms. Stewart?"

"Uh, just checking in with her, making sure she's ok. Why?"

"I was the lead on her break-in, so why are *you* on *my* callback?"

"Jesus... she's a friend, ok...? I just wanted to make sure she was all right."

"What kind of friend, Barry?" He paused before answering and I felt my anger spike.

"That's none of your business, Jack. You wanna bust my balls about being on your callback, fine, but I don't have to answer to you about my relationship with Jennifer."

"Fair enough. Now get your ass back to the station." I disconnected and immediately dialed Jenn's cell.

"Hello."

"You at home?"

"Jack?"

"Babe, are you at home?"

"No, I'm on my way into the paper, why?"

"Good. Lunch. Mike's Burgers. Noon."

"You sound pissed. Has there been another murder?" Taking a deep breath to tap down my anger, I tried again.

"Bad morning. Can you make lunch at noon?"

"Um, yeah, but why are we having lunch?"

"Jenn, you gotta eat, I gotta eat, so we're eating together."

"Right.... um, Jack?"

"Yeah?"

"Is this you keeping an eye on me?" she asked, sounding sweet and confused.

And there it was, the reason why she intrigued me... No games to get my attention, no acting coy or disinterested, just sweet and honest.

"Yeah, babe, this is me keeping an eye on you."

"Ok," she whispered. And for the first time this morning, I smiled.

***

"You want menthol for your nose?" Drew asked as he shoved a jar in my face.

"I'll survive; I hate having to smell it the rest of the day."

Standing in the morgue with the body of Cindy Baker, I thought, again, that I needed a vacation. Two women dead and no clue to the killer, and once the residents found out what was happening there would be panic. Every man or woman who'd ever had an odd encounter would call in, and we'd be so overwhelmed with calls, it would be hard to separate fact from fiction.

"She's on her stomach so we can look at the lividity marks. I also took thermal pictures to see if I could raise the image." Drew pointed to an x-ray hanging on the light board, and I could see two-inch lines running down her back.

"Ok. Show me the body."

Drew threw back the sheet and the bloated body of what was once a beautiful woman lay face down in death. I ignored the smell and concentrated on the marks: four distinct straight lines, two inches wide and two inches apart, covered her from ankle to shoulder. Studying the marks, it hit me.

"Those look like they came from the bed liner of a truck?" Drew studied the marks, then looked up at the x-ray picture and nodded.

"I would agree that those look consistent with a bed liner."

"Did you find any fibers on the body or clothes?"

"Dirt consistent with the dump site, some fibers that we're running through mass spec. I'll call you when the results are in."

"You get anything from under the fingernails or teeth?"

"Nothing in her teeth; stomach content shows she ate three hours before death, and that her last meal was pizza. Fingernails showed nylon fibers, and again, they're currently running that through mass spec."

"Ok, keep me updated. I need to find this sonofabitch and fast."

"You'll be the first to know when the results are in."

I slapped Drew on the back and made my way out of the morgue. I looked at my watch and noted the time. I needed to get to my truck and head over to Mike's for lunch with Jenn. I didn't have time to start something with this woman, but I'd be damned if that was going to stop me. You made the time for a woman like Jenn, because if you didn't, someone else would.

***

"You're having lunch with a man?"

"Bailey, it's just lunch. He asked me and I agreed."

"Mom, I think that rocks."

"You do?"

"Well, yeah. Dad's been gone over a year, and you're young and beautiful. Why not find some guy to rock your socks off?"

"Bailey, I'm having lunch, not sex," I told her drily.

"So have sex for dessert."

"This is what I get for having a kid when I was so young: you think I'm your best friend instead of your mother. I'm not discussing sex with you."

"Who aren't you discussing sex with?" said a deep voice behind me.

I was waiting for Jack outside Mike's Burgers, talking with my know-it-all daughter, when I heard Barry's voice in my ear. I turned and laughed, "No one, Barry, just talking with my daughter."

"Ah, gotcha." Raising my finger, indicating I needed a minute to finish my call, I turned my back to him.

"Bailey, I have to go, but I'll call you tonight. Everything going ok? You need anything before I go?"

"School rocks, Mom. Don't worry about me. You're finally in Colorado; go have fun." Smiling at her response, I looked up and saw Jack coming down the sidewalk. I felt my heartbeat pick up just from watching him walk. One thing was for sure: with Jack around I wouldn't need to worry about aerobic exercise.

I heard Bailey talking in my ear, and I tuned in long enough to hear her say she needed to go, so I took my eyes off Jack and responded:

"Ok, Bailey, talk to you later. I love you."

"Love you too, Mom. Bye."

Jack approached with a scowl on his face, looking past me. I turned and remembered Barry was there, still standing behind me. As Jack walked closer, he looked at me before he turned to Barry.

"Barry, you on lunch?"

"No, I was just checking with Jenkins next door about the vandalism he had last week and saw Jennifer standing here."

Both men seemed angry. I wasn't sure what was going on and, to be honest, I figured I didn't want to know. Jack looked down at me and smiled, dazzling me again.

"You ready to eat, Jenn?" I nodded since I wasn't sure I could find my voice.

"You two are having lunch together." Barry's statement came out like an accusation, and it startled me. Jack reached up and put his hand to my neck and gave me a light squeeze.

"You have a problem with Jenn and I having lunch?"

Barry looked at Jack's hand on my neck and narrowed his eyes. I could then see my mistake with Barry. Having coffee and being friendly was coming back to bite me in the ass. My husband used to say men couldn't just be friends with women. Men either wanted to have sex with you or they didn't; and if they didn't, they wouldn't spend any real time with you. I didn't agree with that, though. I thought men and women could be friends without having any sexual tension, but clearly, Barry was not one who fell into that category.

43

"No, Jack. I guess callbacks can be done on lunch hours," he replied snidely.

"Not a callback, Barry. There a reason you got a problem with me having lunch with Jenn?" I looked down at my feet; I was too embarrassed by this pissing match and wished I'd waited inside.

"No, by all means, enjoy your lunch. Jennifer, as always, a pleasure to see you." And with that he gave me a two-finger salute and walked back the way he came.

"You and Barry got something going on I need to know about?" I looked up at Jack and watched his jaw go tight as he watched Barry walk away.

"Um, no, we're just friends. He took me for coffee once when I first moved here, and we bump into each other from time to time."

"Good, keep it that way; I don't like to share."

"Share? I'm not sure I'm ready for any type of relationship, Jack."

"Babe, you may not be ready, but that's not going to stop me from trying to change your mind," he replied, smiling, his rough voice washing over me. *Damn.* My traitorous heart liked hearing that and started racing. My head told me to run, but I stupidly listened to my heart and smiled back at him. *I know, I know, it's that damn smile.*

"Ok, Jack," I whispered in reply. Jack's smile turned to a sexy grin and his eyes dropped to my lips. I sucked in a breath as his head lowered, his lips gently brushing mine. A warm tingle coursed through my body as he wrapped both arms around me and crushed me to his chest. We were in public, but I didn't care. Jack deepened the kiss, his hand coming up my back and into my hair, securing me deeper into him. Slowly, the kiss ended, and he let me go. I took a wobbly step back and looked up at him. Jack's brows moved together in reflection, like he was working something out in his head. Then he smiled and my knees got weak.

"Now that's more like it, boy." I turned my head to see Lorraine grinning from ear to ear. My face flushed in embarrassment, but Jack just grunted and grabbed my hand before he pulled me towards the door, mumbling, "You got that right."

Five

You Scare Me

The way her hair tumbles down her back in curls, she looks so much like Jennifer. She senses me, looking over her shoulder, aware that death is stalking her. I'm sorry I have to do this; I'll do anything for Jennifer to make her happy, make her mine. My pulse increases, the time is coming. I can feel it. Like a cat, I strike, wrapping the rope around her neck, feeling her life drain away. "Shh, die knowing you're a gift for an angel."

Sitting in a booth at Mike's Burgers, not having visited this burger joint yet, I told Jack to order for me. Two burgers with rings and two root beers were served, the food piled high and delicious. The décor was inspired by the old west with red-checkered tablecloths, knotty pine walls, and pictures of chuck wagons with burgers grilling over an open flame. It was early October and the lunch crowd consisted of locals. The winter tourism for the area hadn't started, making the streets and restaurants of Gunnison easier to navigate. Jack fielded questions from business owners in the area and the constant flirting from several of the waitresses. Learning long ago that women liked to flirt and not to take offense, I was still shocked at how much they did it. Even though he was eating with me, it didn't stop these women from trying to get his attention. I was grinning at Jack while Trixie, a fake-boobed waitress who looked like she'd spent one too many nights drinking, was trying to get him to agree to a movie Saturday night. Jack caught my smile and rolled his eyes. "Trixie, babe, I'm busy Saturday. I appreciate your asking, but I'll have to pass. You might give J.D. a call; I know he and Judy broke up, and he might be feeling lonely right about now." *Diplomatic, cares about her feelings, nice guy and hot...I'm in trouble with a capital T.*

"How's your burger?" Jack inquired once she had left. I jolted out of my thoughts and tried to cover the fact I'd been staring. Jack pointed at my food and smiled, then his smile got bigger as he watched me recover. I'd totally been caught daydreaming.

"Great. The rings are in a food group all of their own and will end up on my hips, but that's not gonna stop me from eating them," I laughed while stuffing my mouth with the heavenly rings. I was grabbing my root beer to wash them down when Jack floored me.

"I won't complain if they do. Women *should* be curvy." Trying to hold the root beer in my mouth, I swallowed and gave him a disbelieving look, catching his own smirk at my reaction. *Nope, not going near that comment.* I shook my head to avoid answering when Gerry walked up to the table, saving me from embarrassment.

"Jennifer, don't be late for our meeting at three," Gerry ordered.

"I won't miss it, Gerry. What are you doing off the

mountain? Are you meeting clients for rafting?"

"Just needed to order some more life vests from Jenkins' and picked up a dry erase board so we can keep track of our suspect and victim's list."

"That's a great idea, thanks." Smiling, I turned back to Jack and caught the scowl on his face.

"What?"

"What the hell are you two up to?"

"Just research, Jack. Since Ben and Gerry know everyone, we're gonna put together a suspect list for you." Jack leaned back and chewed on that information, looking between Gerry and me, before he threw his napkin on the table and began his lecture:

"Jenn, what'd I say about getting involved with this investigation? Let's say the killer is one of our own, and he hears about you and the boys making a suspect list...You think he isn't gonna take aim on any of the three of you for doing it?" I looked back at Gerry, thinking that it actually made sense.

"I, uh...Gerry, maybe we shouldn't advertise what we're doing. Should we meet at my cabin instead?" Gerry looked like he was pondering this when Jack broke in again.

"Jenn, research on serial killers doesn't mean making a suspect list. That kind of shit will get out. You and the boys back off and let me do the investigating, do you hear me?"

I narrowed my eyes and gave Jack my best "excuse me" look, but of course, he didn't even flinch. I appreciated his concern, but he couldn't dictate what I could and couldn't do. Jack watched my reaction, and his face got hard as well. We were locked in a staring match when Gerry chuckled and broke my concentration, saving Jack from the daggers I was spearing him with. I looked at Gerry and bugged my eyes at him; he just patted me on the shoulder and turned to Jack.

"Sheriff, we're helping her with the research *to* keep an eye on her. You don't need to worry; we've got her back."

"Jesus, I've got Nancy Drew and the Hardy Boys on my hands." *Seriously?*

Ignoring his obviously funny comment, but not about to react to it, I wiped my mouth, pulled out my wallet, threw money on the table, and then stood. Jack's face turned hard again as he looked at the money.

"I ask a woman out, I pay. End of discussion. Put your money away, Jenn."

"I'd feel better paying, Jack. I don't need anyone telling me what to do. I've spent the last thirty-nine years doing what everyone else needed me to do. Now I'm gonna do what I want, and I want to pay for my own damn lunch," I hissed, then nodded at Gerry, "See you at three," before I turned on my heels and left.

Insufferable man thought he could order me around? Who did he think he was? Ok, maybe he's the sheriff, but still, I didn't need him barking orders at me. No wonder he's still single. Who'd put up with *that?* I'd just give him a wide berth and do my own investigation, and he could kiss my curvy, onion-ring-padded ass.

***

"She's got attitude. You've got your hands full there,

Jack." Gerry was not wrong. Jenn hurried her cute ass out of Mike's before I could even stand. Christ, if that little display didn't turn me on even more than I already was. I decided to let her go instead of following her. Something told me I wouldn't get anywhere if I tried. "Gerry, what in Christ's name are you thinking, helping her look for this guy?"

"Jack, it was clear she wasn't gonna stop. She's got a fire in her belly. It's better she does it with Ben and me looking out for her than her running around half-cocked on her own." I sighed, threw money on the table, and then put out my hand to shake Gerry's.

"Keep her out of this as much as you can. I don't want her to pique this guy's interest."

"I'd say she's already got enough interest between you and Barry Todd sniffing around her."

"Noticed that, did you?"

"Hard to miss Todd. He's got these damn puppy dog eyes whenever she's around...She's not exactly your type though, Jack. I don't want you to break her heart; she's been through enough," Gerry warned me, and my hackles rose.

"Old man, I'm not setting out to hurt anyone, so back off."

"Jack, you're not exactly known for longevity; not sure you have it in you."

"Jesus, first of all, we've only had lunch, and secondly, did it ever occur to you that maybe the reason no one has ever lasted was because they tried to change me? Tried to tame me? I'm not opposed to settling down, but what I *am* opposed to is feeling the need to change who I am in order to do it. I'm a lawman who does whatever it takes to get the job done, and that means working all hours and missing shit or being late. Haven't met a woman yet who didn't want me home by five."

"All right, Jack, all right, you've made your point. I just hope you figure out if Jennifer is one or the other before she gets her heart broken. She's special to Ben and me. We'd take it personally if you hurt her. I know she's a grown woman, but she's alone and vulnerable right now."

"Point made, and I'll bear that in mind. Now, are you done warning me off Jenn? 'Cause honest to God, Gerry, you don't know me, how I think or what I feel, so I'd appreciate you backing the fuck off."

We stared each other down for a moment until that sonofabitch smiled at me, then laughed before he slapped his leg and blurted out, "Never thought I'd see the day. Jack Gunnison is hung up on a woman, and not just any woman, no. He's hung up on a woman who has no problem telling him off and doing whatever the hell she wants to do."

"Gerry—"

"You can deny it all you want, Jack, but you've never cared about what someone thought of you or how you handled women. No, this is different even if you haven't figured it out yet. Yup, gonna enjoy watching Jenn turn you inside out."

I stared at Gerry as he walked out of Mike's, laughing his ass off, and damn if I wasn't a little scared he was right. There was something about Jenn that was different from the other women I'd dated. She was driven like me. in the past, I'd always gone for women who needed a man to complete them, and it had gotten me in trouble more than once. I couldn't count how many times I'd been hung up on or cussed at for missing dinner because I was called out on an emergency. Thinking about what Gerry said, and not giving a damn if Jenn had cooled her heels or not, I pulled out my phone and called her.

"I'm not speaking to you right now," she shouted into the phone.

"Jesus, you're stubborn."

"I'd respond to that, except I'm not speaking to you right now."

"Babe, cut the crap. I'm not going to apologize for worrying about you."

"Jack, I could understand if it was just that, but you're telling me what to do. I promised not to interfere, and I'm not. I don't need *or* want someone telling me what to do. I got married out of high school, delayed college for my daughter, married Doug before I was ready, and spent all those years taking care of them. I'm devastated he's dead, but at the same time I'm finally living my life on my terms. I'm sorry, Jack, but this can't go anywhere—"

"Bullshit."

"Excuse me?"

"I call bullshit, Jenn."

"About what?"

"I wasn't telling you what to do. I'm the sheriff of this county. I was telling you to back off so I could do my job, which, incidentally, is keeping the residents, meaning you, safe. I'd tell anyone who was acting recklessly and putting his or her safety at risk to stop. You're using that as an excuse to end things that haven't even begun. I'm telling you right now: I'm not backing off. You intrigue the hell out of me with your smart mouth and sweetness all at the same time. I haven't met a woman in twenty years who's piqued my interest like you have, and I'll be damned if I'm going to let you run from me because you're stubborn." That shut her up, and I heard her breathe hard on the other end of the phone. I waited for her to reply but got dead air.

"Jenn. Swear to Christ, you're the stubbornest woman I've ever—"

"You scare me," she whispered.

"Yeah? Well, join the club, 'cause you sure as shit scare the fuck out of me."

"Sorry."

"For what?"

"For yelling at you."

"Jesus, you're somethin' else."

"I said I was sorry. Jeez."

"Jenn, swear to God, it's a good thing you're on the phone or I'd spank your ass, then kiss you till you couldn't see straight. I'm heading back to the station to try and find this sonofabitch or I'd drive to you right now." Jenn gasped; then she giggled. *Is this woman real?* She giggled like a schoolgirl, and that went right through me, too. Christ.

"Ok, Jack, I'll talk to you later."

"You still planning on meeting Ben and Gerry?"

"Yes." Reigning in my temper, I decided I'd fight that battle later.

"Ok, Sweetness, be careful and don't talk about this with anyone but them."

"Wasn't planning on it, Jack, but thanks for worrying."

"Talk to you soon, babe."

53

"Bye, Jack."

Fighting my need to go find her and make her listen, I headed to my truck. While I was walking, I got the feeling that I was being watched. Looking around but not seeing anyone, I climbed into my truck and pointed it in the direction of the station. Thinking about Jenn and her sass, I smiled when I thought about sparring with her again. That woman had no problem going head-to-head with me, a feat most would not try to do, but hell if that didn't turn me on even more. She was a spitfire tied up in a sweet little package. Now, all I had to do was get her to follow an order.

I was almost back to the station when I saw Barry sitting in his patrol car just off Main. Deciding that a conversation was needed and not wanting to do it at the office, I pulled over and got out of my truck, walked across the street, pulled open the passenger door, and then bent my body into the unit. Barry looked at me and said nothing for a moment, then laid it out for me.

"You fuck her over, I'll be waiting in the wings."

"Christ, twice in one day I get shit about breaking hearts."

"You're not known for sticking it out."

"I'm not known for putting up with bullshit either, but it happens."

"So you're saying it's different this time?"

"I'm saying it's already different. She's not like the others 'cause she pisses me off." Barry's head snapped back when I said that, the confusion clear. *Join the club.* So I tried to explain.

"Women don't piss me off; they annoy me first." He still looked confused.

"Jesus, I've never been with a woman who pisses me off because she won't listen."

"How the hell does that make Jennifer different than all the other women whose hearts you've broken?"

"How the hell do I know? I've never been pissed at one! Jenn pisses me off enough to arrest her ass just to keep her safe. Does that tell you something? 'Cause if it does, enlighten me. I'd *really* like to know why a woman who pisses me off turns me on."

"Jesus, Jack, I'm not gonna interpret this shit for you. You like to fight with women, fine. Just don't fucking string her along while you're having fun."

This was getting us nowhere. Barry wanted Jenn, and I wasn't about to let him near her. Where the hell these possessive feelings for a woman I only met yesterday were coming from beat the hell out of me, but I learned a long time ago to trust my gut; it'd never let me down. I opened the door to get out and then turned back to Barry, who was still pissed off. "I'm not backing off. You got a problem with that, fine. I can respect that. But in the future, you keep your shit together and don't bring your feelings for Jenn and me to the office." I didn't give him a chance to respond. I got out and headed to my truck. I had a killer to find, and I needed to focus on that.

Six

A Gift

"Ok, guys, I spent last night going over profiles of serial killers. The FBI said that serial killers usually aren't loners, are gainfully employed, have families in many instances, and almost never come across as creepy."

Sitting in the back of McGill's with Rosie, Ben, and Gerry as my audience, I laid out what I'd researched about serial killers. To say I was creeped out was an understatement, but you couldn't choose your subject matter in journalism; it picked you. The amount of information that could be obtained on the Internet about these monsters was staggering.

"I was under the impression that serial killers are almost always white males, but my research cleared up that point, and I also found out that they span all racial groups. The motivation behind serial killings is not always, or for the most part, even sexual in nature. Financial gain, attention seeking, or just for the thrill of the kill, just to name a few, are more likely. They operate within a comfort zone, have anchor points close to home. They very rarely travel the interstate unless they are so comfortable with their expertise they do it to avoid detection. Their IQ ranges from borderline to extremely smart. Most don't consider themselves invincible, but as they get comfortable with killing, they become braver and braver. This usually makes their kills sloppy and helps lead to their detection. Some stop, replacing other activities for the thrill they receive from killing, i.e. auto erotica, masturbation, and cross-dressing. But, ultimately, they all have one thing in common: they are psychopaths. Psychopaths are persons with antisocial personality disorder, which manifests in aggression, perversion, and sometimes criminal and amoral behavior without empathy or remorse."

"Jesus, Jenny. Are you sure you want to investigate this guy?"

"Oh, come on, Ben. This is fascinating although creepy stuff," I defended.

"I'm with Ben, sugar. I'm not sure I'll be able to sleep at night knowing all this." Looking at Rosie's wide eyes, then back at Ben and Gerry, I sat down hard on my chair.

"Guys, it was your idea to help me and now you want to throw in the towel?"

"I can't think of anyone in our county that matches that description," Gerry spit out.

"That's what makes them so hard to catch. They blend in; they could be the loving father living next door."

"Well, if that's the case, we won't be able to come up with any suspects. Not unless we put all of the men who live in the county on it," Rosie countered.

"We can eliminate those over the age of fifty-five, and those under the age of twenty, for starters. The same goes for disabled."

"Good to know we aren't suspects," Ben laughed.

"Ben, you've got arthritis in your hands. I doubt you'd

have the hand strength to strangle a woman."

"Why aren't we putting women on the list?" Rosie asked, almost offended that I left our sex off the table.

"Because women tend to kill men, and these murders take place at close range. Muscle is needed to detain these women in order to strangle them."

"Have you seen Janice Rutherford? Woman has arms like a man. Bet she could arm wrestle and win against most, except Jack." I didn't need to be thinking about how big Jack's arms were right now, but that didn't stop me from noticing the dreamy look Rosie had when she mentioned him. Ignoring this, I moved forward with our discussion.

"All right, Rosie, I'll put Janice on the list. Happy?"

"How about we *all* make a list of the men we know in the county that fit the age range and physical strength? Then we can compare and come up with a master list," Gerry suggested.

"I like that. And what about women who fit the victim profile? We need a list of all women with brown hair who live in the county as well," Rosie threw in.

I looked at the three of them; then Ben stood up, walked over to the board, and picked up a marker, writing my name. *Shit.* Looking at my name, then not wanting to look at it, I grabbed my hair, and pulled it into a ponytail, trying to act like that didn't freak me the hell out. The three of them stared at me for a moment, and, feeling self-conscious, I snapped my fingers and pointed to their papers. "Guys, names, please. I need to leave by four."

***

Phones were ringing off the hook when I entered the station at 4:30. I grabbed the phone, punching line one, and wondered where the hell Debbie, our receptionist, was.

"Sheriff Gunnison."

"Ah, good, just the man I wanted to talk to." Sighing for patience at the sound of the Mayor of Gunnison's voice, I steeled myself for what was next.

"Mayor Hall, what can I do for you?"

"Sheriff, we need to call a meeting to discuss the recent deaths in our county to ascertain that all is being done to catch this killer." The sarcasm in his voice wasn't lost on me. Mayor Hall's son, Grady, worked as my Deputy, and it was known by all that he had high hopes for his son. He wanted Grady to be Sheriff, and the only problem with that was me, plus the fact that Grady was too young. But that didn't stop him from pushing his agenda every chance he got. He needed me gone to accomplish that, and a serial killer avoiding police capture would be a perfect excuse for him.

"I can assure you all is being done to apprehend this killer, Mayor."

"I'm not sure that's true, Sheriff. I'm thinking your mind is elsewhere at a time when you should be giving this killer your full attention."

"And where do you think my attention is, Mayor?"

"Well, if my eyes weren't deceiving me, your attention was on Jennifer Stewart's lips, instead of on a killer. Or was that not you I saw practically mauling the poor woman at lunch?"

My ire spiked. Mayor Hall had been five years ahead of me in school, class president and all-round prick. His wife of twenty years left him for another man five years ago, and he was always searching for the next first lady of Gunnison. The fact he knew Jennifer by name, when she'd only been here four months, caught my attention.

"I wasn't aware the mayor or the council had jurisdiction over my lunch hour or my personal life, John."

"No, that's true, Jack, but if you're too busy pursuing the new reporter to make time for this killer, I'm sure that we can find someone who will take the job more seriously." I counted to ten to rein in my temper, but it didn't work.

"John, let's cut the crap. My department has handled this case by the book from the beginning. With a second murder, it's clear to my staff and me that we have a serial or a copycat on our hands, whether the FBI can classify this or not. No one in my department is taking this lightly, and we are all putting in overtime on this case. So unless you and the council have information in regards to this killer, I don't have time to waste being in a meeting when I should be spending it tracking down this asshole. As for the matter of my lunch hour and whom I spend it with? Don't hold your breath waiting for that person to change anytime soon."

"As always, it's a pleasure to talk to you, Sheriff. I'll be advising the council of our conversation, as well as letting them know you have more important pursuits at the moment."

"You do that, John." Slamming the phone down, I looked around for Debbie. Seeing Grady come from the interrogation room, I shouted at him:

"Grady, where the hell is Debbie?" His eyebrows rose

at my tone; he looked at her desk, then back to me again.

"She had a doctor's appointment at five, Jack. She can't miss them with the baby due next month."

"Christ, I forgot. Ignore me, Grady. Your Dad just phoned and I made the mistake of answering the phone."

Grady, more his mother's son than his father's, worked hard and didn't want a leg up because of his father, especially not since he couldn't stand him any more than I did. The fact his dad had screwed everything with two legs before, during, and after his mother walked out on him, might have had something to do with his feelings. How a man like John Hall had produced a man like Grady *proved* you could overcome your environment.

I started to move towards my office when the phone started ringing again, so I grabbed it and answered.

"Sheriff's department, Sheriff Gunnison speaking."

"There's a body of a woman off the jogging trail near 135 and the Gunnison River," someone whispered on the phone. Feeling the hair on the back of my neck stand up, my gut told me I was talking to the killer.

"You put her there."

"Perceptive, Sheriff."

"Why don't you stay with the body and I'll come to you? You can give yourself up, and we'll get you some help."

"Sure, Sheriff, come on down. I'm feeling repentant right now. Come get me and help me stop." The sarcasm was dripping from his words. I snapped my fingers at Grady and indicated I needed a pen and

61

paper. He quickly handed them to me, and I wrote, *Killer on the phone, body at 135 and Gunnison River crossing, find who is closest and get them there now. I'll keep him on the line.*

Handing the note back to Grady, he read it, nodded, and then headed to the dispatch office.

"Tell me why you're doing this," I barked.

"It's a gift."

"For who?"

"An angel with brown eyes."

"You need to turn yourself in before any more mothers, daughters, or wives are gone, destroying more families." I lowered my voice, hoping to humanize these women he hunted, putting a face to the bodies. I continued this tactic, trying to keep him on the line.

"Jamie Smith's sister Julie collapsed at her funeral. They were so close she was inconsolable at the loss. Cindy Baker was one of seven children, the oldest of the girls, and the one they all turned to since their parents died. Her brothers and sister are destroyed by her death. You need to turn yourself in so we can help you stop."

"Shut up, I know who they were. They were gifts. She'll understand they were gifts." His voice still in a whisper faltered, and an anguished cry rang out. Whoever this killer was, it bothered him, but not enough to stop.

"Whoever she is, she won't want blood on her hands. You need to stop." The line went dead with no warning. "Shit," I mumbled and ran to the dispatch office.

"Phil is three miles away, he should be there any minute," Grady relayed as I entered. Grabbing the handheld, I patched into Phil.

"Phil."

"Wood here."

"He just hung up. He could be close, so stay sharp."

"Roger that, Jack."

While we waited for Phil to call back, I looked over and saw Barry walk in, his face blank as he held my eyes. I gave him a chin lift, and he did the same, then I turned back to the radio and waited.

"Base, Jesus, base, Wood here. A female victim at Gunnison crossing. Jack, it's Shannon Davis." My eyes closed for a moment, then I grabbed the radio.

"Do you see that sonofabitch? Wood, secure the area, check and see if that sonofabitch is still there."

"Roger that, Jack, weapon drawn and searching perimeter."

"Sonofabitch," I roared, throwing the handheld on the desk. I pushed my hands through my hair and paced while waiting to hear back from Phil. Everyone was watching me, waiting for my lead, so I took a deep breath and moved past the knot in my gut.

"Grady, call the Coroner. Barry, head out to the scene and help secure it. I'm gonna head over to the school and see if Kyle is still there or got a ride home with friends."

Grady left the office to call Drew, Barry headed out, and I waited to get confirmation that the scene was clear, and that my deputy was safe.

"Wood to base, scene is secure. No sign of unsub."

"Barry's on his way and so is the coroner. Hold tight. I'll be there once I've contacted Shannon's family and know Kyle is safe."

"Roger that, Jack."

Holding on to what little thread of patience I had left,

a reason to breathe

I went to my office and closed the door. Shannon Davis and I had dated three years ago. She was newly divorced and had a cute kid. She needed a man who was there regular hours, and I didn't fit that. We tried for a while, but we fought constantly about how much time my job required. So we ended things amicably, and she moved on to someone else. But I was fond of her and her kid, and always made a point of saying hello if I saw them out. *Christ.* Reaching for my keys, I thought about little Kyle Davis, and wished like hell I didn't have to shatter his world.

Seven

Smartass

Traveling down the mountain into Gunnison, I figured getting this list to Jack was important, even if it meant being in the same room with him a second time in one day. I'd gone home after playing "Name The Killer" with Ben and Gerry and worked on my story. But women were dying and the longer I sat there, going over the information, I knew I had to get it to Jack, sooner rather than later.

But I couldn't stop thinking about lunch and what he'd said, and I'll admit I was nervous about seeing him again. Was I even ready for a relationship? And let's not forget Jack couldn't seem to commit anyway! Seriously, I'd have to be all kinds of crazy to start something with this man. But even so, I'd admit I'd never felt this way before. I felt out of control, as if I couldn't trust myself around him. Knowing this, I had to learn to stand firm and not let him back me into the proverbial corner with his charm and web of seduction.

So tonight, I was going to try a new tactic. I was going to walk in there and approach him like a reporter, just hand over the list and keep it professional. I just had to remember that he was the sheriff and I was a reporter working on a story. Simple... So simple I wasn't holding out hope this would work.

Pulling up to the two-story, red brick building that housed the sheriff's department, I took several deep breaths to steady my nerves before exiting my Jeep. *You can do this. Be professional, get in and get out. No muss, no fuss.*

Checking my watch and noting it was already 8 pm, I got out, grabbed my stuff, and headed to the entrance of the building. Inside the reception area, I was surprised to see someone still on duty at this time of night.

"Hi, can I help you?" asked a young woman in uniform.

"Hi, yeah, I'm Jennifer Stewart. I need to speak with the sheriff if he's still in?"

"Is the sheriff expecting you?"

"No, I didn't know I was coming, or I would have made an appointment. Is that a problem?"

"Oh, no. He's usually gone this time of night, but we had a busy evening, and he just got back. I'll buzz back and see if he has time."

Smiling at the friendly woman, I turned back to look at the pictures of previous sheriffs. I eyed Jack's grandfather immediately. For an older man he was seriously hot; the genes in Jack's family were definitely testosterone driven. You could tell just by looking at the man he took no shit and commanded respect. Glancing at the picture next to his, I noticed Barry's grandfather as well. The former sheriff had a more laidback look to him, but his eyes held something that told you he was sharp. I looked between the two former sheriffs and wasn't surprised that, just like their grandsons, one was more powerful and handsome, and one looked like he could be your friend.

After standing in the lobby a few minutes, I started wondering if Jack had time to meet with me. With an investigation to run, he might be busy, and I was thinking about leaving the file with the receptionist when I felt a presence behind me.

"That's my grandfather, John," I heard softly in my ear. Jumping, then turning to see the current sheriff grinning down at me, I froze and stared into those amazing eyes. Oh, yeah, I was caught in his web; I was a fly to his spider, and If I wasn't careful he was going to devour me. *Focus, you can do this...be professional!*

"Sheriff, sorry to drop in on you like this, but I wanted to give you our list of suspects." Jack grinned like something was funny and then grabbed my hand, dragging me down the hall and into what looked to be his office. He pulled out a chair and motioned for me to sit, then backed against the front of his desk, leaned forward, and looked down on me. His large frame was so close it made me nervous, so I shoved my file between us, trying to break the mood. He looked at the file, then back at me and smiled even bigger. Something about his face told me he knew my game and thought it was cute, so I cleared my throat to get us back on track and explained the lists.

"Here are the names of men who live within five counties of where the bodies were found. We eliminated anyone over the age of fifty-five and anyone under the age of twenty. We concentrated on men, but Rosie thinks Janice Rutherford has the arm strength to strangle and detain a woman, and there are no people with obvious physical limitations or disabilities on the list." Jack stared at the file with a humorous look, then took it and began reading. I tried to keep my face and body as casual as possible, indicating I was not the least bit intimidated by him, and was thinking I felt more in control than a few minutes before when Jack's eyebrows hit his hairline, and his eyes shot to mine.

"I'm on this list," he growled.

"Well, yeah, you fit the age range," I tried to explain.

"My whole staff is on this list," he growled again.

"I know, Jack," I replied, starting to get nervous.

"Christ," Jack hissed, and I jumped to our defense.

"Jack, we had to be fair. We couldn't eliminate you just because you wear a badge. My research found army pilots and professionals, all serial killers and all respected members of society." Jack held my eyes for a moment, and then read through the list again. Shaking his head, he moved around the back of his desk and took a seat, all business now.

"Ok, Jenn, I'm reminding you that anything I say is off the record. Are we clear on that point?"

"Right, off the record until you give me the go-ahead."

"There was another killing this afternoon, a local woman this time, and my staff, with the exception of Phil who was out in the field, were all here when the killer called, and *I* answered the phone."

"Oh, my God, another woman."

"Yeah, babe, another woman. Sick fuck grabbed her while she was out jogging this morning. She'd been dead hours when we found her."

"Wait, you spoke to the killer?"

"Yeah."

"What did he say?"

"Sorry, Jenn, I can't release that information to the press, not even to you." Nodding and thinking about the poor woman who died while Jack went back to our notes, I couldn't help wondering what he said. That must have been so weird, talking to an unknown person, knowing they had killed someone. I felt chills run up my arms, and I rubbed my hands up and down to warm up. Jack was still going over our notes when his head shot up and he mumbled, "Christ," again.

"What?"

"You have a victim's list." *Oh, boy.*

"Yeah, we figured since this guy has a type, we would list everyone in the county who fit that description."

"Jesus, Jenn, you're on this list."

"Yeah, not a list I want to be on, either."

"Yeah, babe, this also puts your intruder last night into a whole new light."

"But you said it was just someone looking for something to steal."

"And that may still be the case, but considering you're on this list, I'm not taking any chances."

"Ok, what do you suggest I do to keep safe? Take a self-defense class?"

"First of all, you can stop researching this guy, and second, I'm coming over after I've finished here to check your locks and windows."

Knowing arguing with him about my research would only start a fight, I decided to ignore that order and nodded. Jack, being a smart man, saw right through how quickly I agreed, and bossy Jack took over.

"I mean it, Jenn. No more investigating or research.

We have no idea who this guy is, and your list proves he could be anyone."

"Jack, I'll keep my research to my home and office, but I'm not going to stop. Whoever this is doesn't care if I write a story about him killing women. He would probably love the attention."

"Why are you so stubborn?"

"Why are you so bossy?" I countered.

"It's my job," he shouted.

"Well, it's my job to be stubborn."

"What?" Jack snapped in exasperation and just a hint of disbelief. Grabbing my purse from the floor and standing, I threw my bag over my shoulder and then leaned across Jack's desk.

"A good reporter is tenacious and doesn't back down, *ever*, so that makes us stubborn, *hence* it makes it our job to be that way." Then I turned toward his door but didn't make it. No way in hell was Jack going to let me have the last word.

Jack stood from his chair and grabbed me by the elbow as I tried to leave and swung me around. His jaw was tight, and he looked pissed. He didn't speak, though; his eyes were focused, like he was working something through, then, without warning, he grabbed my face and kissed me. Sucking in my breath as his mouth connected with mine, I breathed in his scent of mint and coffee. I resisted at first. Something about the kiss felt as if he was trying to kiss me into submission. However, there was only so much my body and mind could take of this man, so I melted after a moment and Jack felt it and responded. He shoved one hand in my hair and jerked my head to the side so the angle of the kiss got deeper. His other hand slid down my back and grabbed my ass, squeezing once, and then pulled me into his hips. I gasped as my front met the evidence of his attraction, and damn if I didn't, without even thinking about it, rub up and down that man slightly. As my hips met his, he moaned in my mouth and deepened the kiss. Even his tongue battled for dominance, and I found I was inclined to let him win. Slowly, the kiss ended, and Jack moved from my lips to my neck, nipping and kissing his way to my ear.

"Jesus, what are you doing to me?" he whispered.

"Nothing," I gasped when his tongue circled my ear.

"Baby, if that's nothing, you're gonna kill me when it means something."

Moving his lips back down and nipping the spot where my neck met the shoulder, the moment was suddenly broken when we heard a knock on the door. Before they waited for a reply, the door opened, and in walked Mayor Hall. I tried to pull back from Jack, but he held me in place. I looked down at the floor, too embarrassed to meet the mayor's face. Jack had no problem looking at or confronting this man, nor any problem with holding me close, almost possessively. I needed to break free so I could get the hell out of there and escape not only the embarrassment of getting caught by a man I was supposed to have lunch with this week—*don't ask*—but also to escape the man holding me close. I should have faxed the damn lists. Why did I come here? To see Jack, I realized with clarity...*I'm such an idiot.*

"You mind waiting for a reply before you walk into my office unannounced, John?"

"My apologies, Sheriff, I was under the impression you were at work, not on a date."

"It's after five, John. If I'm putting in overtime on my own dime, and my woman wants to pop in for a visit, she'll fucking pop in for a visit. Now excuse me while I walk her safely to her car since there's a killer on the loose. Take a seat, and I'll be right with you." Jack grabbed my hand and led me out the door and back down the hall to the front. He didn't stop until he had pulled the doors to the station open and walked me to my Jeep.

"Jack, I'm sorry if I got you in trouble with the mayor," I hurried to say, trying to break the silence and the more than uncomfortable situation.

"Sweetness, I don't give a shit if he's pissed or inconvenienced, you kiss me like that again, and I'll make the whole fucking town wait." Grinning at him— 'cause how could I not after that statement—I giggled like the adolescent schoolgirl he'd turned me into, and, for some odd reason, that made him grin.

"Ok, baby, get your ass home and lock the doors and windows when you get there. Be aware of your surroundings before you exit your car, and call me to let me know you got there safely."

"Yes, sir, Sheriff," I laughed as I saluted him.

"Smartass," Jack answered before he kissed me sweetly, then smacked my ass, opened my door, and deposited me on my seat before he slammed it shut. Jack stepped back on the curb as I started my Jeep, and I gave him a smile and wave as I pulled out and headed toward the interstate.

How the hell did I lose control again? I was supposed

to walk in, hand over the lists, answer any questions he had, and then leave. Simple. So not simple. *Well done, Jennifer.* Jesus, that man was overpowering. I became a mindless idiot when he touched me. I needed to regroup and think this through. No, I needed to pack up and leave like I should have last night. Before I made any rash decisions, though, I needed more energy to think clearly, and coffee seemed to be in order. So I made a U-turn and headed back toward Gunnison and The Bean.

Eight

Game On

"All right, Mayor, what can I do for you?"

Mayor Hall was standing at my window, looking at the street when I came back to my office. He didn't turn around to face me, though. He just kept facing the window, looking outside.

"She's a very attractive woman, isn't she?" he observed.

Crossing my arms over my chest, not surprised by his comment, I knew when we spoke on the phone this afternoon he was interested in Jenn. I didn't bother answering his stupid question. Jenn was beautiful and soft in all the right places. A face that made you think of an innocent girl with those big brown eyes, so yeah, she was attractive, but what really stood out was the light that lit her face when she smiled. That smile could make you do just about anything.

"You're not here to talk about Ms. Stewart, Mayor, so let's cut to the chase."

"Indeed, Jack, I'm here to find out how the investigation is going." I moved to my desk and sat down, then laid it out for him.

"Still waiting for Drew at the morgue to get back to us.

Shannon Davis was caught off guard; we're hoping to find something on her body. There were tracks in the mud near the river, but we have no way of knowing if the killer made them. Plaster casts of the prints were collected, and we have them in evidence. Grady is searching phone records; Phil is looking through files of shoe treads, trying to find a match, and Barry is out canvassing the area looking for any witnesses. The FBI has been notified, and all of our evidence and notes have been copied and transferred to them for a profile, and last-known whereabouts are being worked up."

"Impressive. You seem to be on top of the matter."

"As I said on the phone, John, we're all putting in overtime." The asshole was still standing at the window with his back to me. So I waited for his next move. I didn't have to wait long.

"Jack, I'm counting on you to bring this guy in, but if your priorities are elsewhere, I'll know, and I will bring it up with the City Council. Next year is an election year for both of us; I'd hate to see your chances of re-election hindered by an untimely "sowing of your oats," as they say. My advice to you is to move on from the reporter and keep your head in the game."

And there it was: the threat to lose my job if I didn't back off Jenn. Stupid sonofabitch thought he could control me with that threat? I'd been Sheriff for seven years and had run this office with a firm but fair hand. My arrest rate was one of the best in Colorado, and my office had a great reputation with the people, the same people who voted. How this asshole thought he could threaten me with my job when it was the people who voted me in or not, was beyond me. Short of a complete breakdown of the office or some sort of scandal, the City Council had no authority to fire me. Only the people could by casting a ballot.

With his back still turned to me, as if I were insignificant, I answered that sonofabitch.

"John, appreciate the heads up, but if you'll excuse me? I have work to do before I head out."

"I see you're going to ignore my advice."

"Yup, my record speaks for itself, but if the good people of this county want to vote me out, that's their prerogative." The mayor finally turned and stared at me for a long moment, then he finally moved away from the window and put out his hand to shake mine, so I grasped it in a firm grip.

"Give my regards to Jennifer when you see her, and remind her of our lunch date on Thursday." I felt my hand tighten on those words; even though I staked a claim with the "my woman" comment, his grin told me he wasn't going to back down. So I smiled at him and tightened my grip even more.

"I'll be sure to pass on your message."

"You do that, Jack," John answered then turned and walked out of my office.

"Christ." I did not need this complication with everything that was happening. I picked up Jenn's folder but quickly slammed it back down. Looking out the window, I saw the mayor walk to his truck. He looked up and saw me staring. Then the asshole put his finger to his forehead and saluted me with a grin before he climbed into his truck and drove away.

"All right, asshole, game on," I mumbled as I grabbed Jenn's file and headed down the hall to find Grady.

***

Running on empty and needing a boost, I stopped at The Bean on Main Street to grab a coffee to go before hitting the interstate to drive back home. Mandy, one of the baristas I'd met when I first moved here and had instantly hit it off with, was younger than me by nine years, single, and cute as a button. With short, dark hair, brown eyes, and a pixie face, I had no doubt she was beating off men with a stick. We'd hung out a few times - gone to see a movie, get dinner, and once we went to a crafts fair in Ouray. I was hoping she was on duty and had time for a break, but when I pulled open the door, I saw Barry at the counter. My immediate reaction was to turn tail and run. I'd never been good with confrontation, and today's incident at lunch made me uncomfortable. But needing to get some of the headaches out of my life so I could concentrate on my story and what to do about a certain bossy sheriff, I figured there was no time like the present and headed to the counter.

"Hey, Mandy, Barry. You two doing ok this evening?" Barry turned his head to me but didn't offer up a smile. Mandy being Mandy jumped right in.

"Hey, Jennifer, you finished for the day?"

"Yeah, just getting coffee to go, then heading home."

"What's your poison?"

"I'm not picky, but something with chocolate in it." Mandy moved to make the coffee, so I turned to Barry and smiled. Barry took a drink of his coffee, studying me, so I searched for something to say.

"I heard there was another murder."

"Not at liberty to talk about the case, Jennifer." I

nodded in return, understanding more than what was spoken. Damn.

"Sorry. Of course. Are you working tonight?"

"Yup, just getting coffee for the road," he replied while picking up his cup and keys and then moved to leave.

"Well, stay safe," I mumbled as he walked away from me.

Barry stopped, looked back at me, saluted, and then kept moving toward the door. When he reached it, he turned back and warned me once again about Jack.

"Jennifer, remember what I said... Jack isn't the type to settle down. Just be careful." I had no response to that. He was probably right, and I probably did need to keep my distance. Someone just needed to inform Jack of that.

I watched Barry walk out the door and then turned around to find Mandy with a cup of coffee in her hand, a smile on her face.

"You're like the shiny new toy."

"What's like a shiny new toy?"

"You are... All the men want you; all the women want to be friends with you and all the old men want to protect you."

"Great, so what you're saying is once the shine has worn off I'm screwed."

"Ha, yeah, probably. Just like the rest of us. You'll be a mere mortal once again and totally screwed over by men."

"Bitter much, Mandy?"

"Hell yeah, men have been nothing but trouble for me."

"I'm so out of my league with these men asking me

out. My only experience with dating was my husband twenty years ago."

"Heard the sheriff curled your toes today outside of Mike's," she laughed and then wiggled her eyebrows.

"Pfft, he curled my toes, my hair, and left me in a puddle."

"That good, huh?"

"Unfortunately, yes. That man throws me off balance. I wasn't looking for a relationship, and he just keeps moving forward no matter how hard I dig in. The minute he touches me I lose control. I only met him yesterday, and he's kissed me *three* times. Off the chart hot kisses mind you, but still, who moves that fast?"

"I don't know, Jennifer, there're a lot of women in this town who would like to have your problem. If Jack Gunnison were pursuing me, I'd walk slowly."

"Mandy, if I can't think straight around him, then he holds all the cards. I don't remember it being like this with my husband; this can't be normal behavior. The attraction is off the charts incredible, sure, but it would be with someone like Jack, wouldn't it? It's just...he's so damn bossy; he orders me around like he expects me to obey."

"Jack's used to being in charge, he's an alpha male or more like *the* alpha male. You'll just have to put your foot down," she advised as if the answer to my problem was that simple. But somehow I didn't think putting my foot down would even register on his alpha index. Deciding I needed to focus on something other than that bullheaded man, or I'd be stewing over him all night, I moved to the other topic I wanted to discuss.

"Hey Mandy, you've heard about these killings, right?"

a reason to breathe

"Yeah, heard he got a local woman today. I didn't know her, but I'm starting to freak out over this. I've even got my brother coming to pick me up after work."

"Well, I'm working on the story with the help of Ben and Gerry and we made up a list today of possible suspects. You seem to know everyone around here. Could you take a look at the list and see if anything springs to mind?"

"Sure, I know every creep in this county. In fact, I'm pretty sure I've dated them all. I'm due a break, so grab your coffee and I'll meet you out front on the deck."

Moving outside as Mandy asked, I grabbed a table off to the side and away from other customers. Mandy joined me a few minutes later, and I handed her the list when she sat down. As she started reading the list, she laughed.

"Ha, you have the sheriff and his deputies on it?" She continued reading and then stopped. "Jesus, you have put my brother down, too. What the hell, Jennifer, is there any man who isn't on here?"

"That's the problem. The list is too long, and we need to narrow it down. The age ranger for serial killers is so wide; we had to list practically every man who wasn't in diapers or using a walker."

"Well, I can tell you, based on today's murder, these two are innocent. They work with me and were on duty. Father Jenson is off the hook, too. He was busy at the church with the women's auxiliary, and my mother was there. Give me a pen, I'll circle the ones I saw today; I was out running errands and went to several businesses."

Mandy made my long list shorter by twelve men, but

the list was still lengthy. Since the bodies kept showing up in Gunnison or Crested Butte, something told me the killer was local, so I asked her to circle the men who lived the closest to Gunnison. Mandy was still looking over the list when she tapped the paper with her pen.

"Hey, this guy, he's always given me the chills when he comes in because he stares at my boobs constantly." Thinking her boobs were one of her best features and probably the first thing men noticed about her, I didn't think that was proof but I'd never met this Chad Brown, so what did I know?

"He also lives in a cabin off route 135, maybe two miles from where they found the last woman." That got my attention. I put a star next to his name and wondered if I should call Jack and tell him when Mandy's boss stepped outside.

"Mandy, it's slow tonight, why don't you head home?"

"Killer," Mandy replied and then turned to me. "Give me one second, Jennifer, I'm gonna call my brother to come get me."

"I can give you a ride. It's not out of my way,"

"That would be great, thanks. Are you ready to leave now? I can call my brother from the road if you are."

"Whenever you are is fine by me."

Mandy stood, so I followed suit and after she retrieved her jacket and purse, we jumped in my jeep and headed out 135 toward her home. We'd been shooting the breeze, making plans to see the new movie that was coming out, when she shouted and pointed.

"Hey, that's Chad's place up ahead. You wanna drive past and look around, see if he has any dead bodies buried in his backyard?" Thinking that sounded like a terrible idea and also thinking that it sounded like an awesome idea, I battled with myself for an answer.

"Shit, I don't know. What if he catches us?"

"There are two of us, he can't get us both." I glanced at her and wondered if she might just be a little crazy. For someone who was scared of this killer, she didn't seem to mind jumping into a possibly dangerous situation. Didn't she realize that if he had a gun, he could shoot both of us and then bury us in his backyard, and no one would be the wiser? Then again, I was a little crazy too, so why not?

"I can't believe I'm agreeing to this, but ok, let's do it."

"It will be fine; he'll never know we were there."

The phrase *"Famous Last Words"* ran through my head as I pulled off the road and turned off my lights. There were no lights on in his small A-frame. No cars or trucks in the drive, either. It appeared he was out, and I didn't know if that made me feel better or not. Pulling past his cabin and parking up the hill, we got out of my jeep and crept down the road, heading to the side of the cabin. There were two windows and the lights were off. I didn't know what we thought we could see, but I cupped my hands around my eyes and tried to look inside. Light shined in the room, and thinking the light inside came on, I jumped back and looked at Mandy. She had a flashlight in her hand.

"Do you always carry a flashlight?"

"A girl can never be too prepared. I've got everything in this bag: flashlight, tools, extra batteries, even some rope." *Rope?*

"You scare me a little, just so you know."

"I get that a lot."

"You look like a pixie, but you're really more like a gremlin."

Mandy smiled and winked at me, then pointed the flashlight in the room as we tried to look around. It was a bedroom; the bed was unmade, there were clothes all over the floor and dishes stacked on the nightstand and dresser.

"The guy is a pig, no wonder he isn't married," Mandy mumbled. I moved to the next window and tugged her arm as I passed so she'd bring the flashlight. It was the living room, and it was just as messy as the bedroom. I was just about to tell her we were wasting our time when an SUV pulled down the road from the highway and then pulled into the driveway. *Shit.* We moved back down the side of the cabin and plastered ourselves to the side. My heart was racing as we heard the door to the SUV slam shut, and then heard stomping on the steps heading to the front door. Holding my breath, afraid he would hear me panting, we heard the door open, and I was just about to let out my breath when my cell phone rang out loud with my stupid, stupid ring tone. John Denver's "Rocky Mountain High" set on loud broke the quiet of the night, and I scrambled to pull it from my pocket.... *Shit, shit, shit. Please God, let him be deaf.* I hit reject on my phone and looked at Mandy, whose eyes were huge. I was so busy messing with my phone, I never heard if the front door closed. Using my eyes to indicate we should get the hell out of there, Mandy nodded in agreement, so I held up my hand and counted down: one...two...three, and we took off running...only to be stopped by the sound of a shotgun firing.

"Stay right where you are, put your hands up, and walk back towards me," said a very pissed off man. We both put our hands in the air as my phone started ringing. John's golden voice mocked me in the night again.

"Keep moving, get your asses up here, and sit down while I call the sheriff."

"I'd rather you shoot me now than deal with the sheriff," came from my mouth for some reason. I might not know Jack well, but I was pretty sure the lecture I was going to get, on top of being arrested, would be worse than when I told my parents I was pregnant at eighteen. Mandy chuckled, so I shoved my shoulder into hers as we walked toward the cabin.

"What the fuck?" said the man when we made our way up the steps.

"Hey, Chad," Mandy replied, and he narrowed his eyes at her.

My phone started ringing for the third time, so without thinking or looking to see who was calling, I answered it.

"Hello."

"Jenn, where the hell are you? You were supposed to call when you made it home," yelled a pissed off Jack. *Oh, dear lord.*

"Get your hands in the air," barked Chad. Of course I listened to the man with a gun and threw my hands up. Without. Hanging. Up. I could hear shouting from the phone when Mandy stepped up and said:

"Chad, we can explain.... where were *you* today around three?"

"I was in Denver on business. My grandmother died,

and I met with her attorney, why?" he replied sarcastically. Mandy's hands were on her hips, giving him attitude as if he weren't standing there with a loaded gun.

"There was a murder today and if you *were* there, then there's no harm, no foul."

I looked back and forth between them, wondering, not for the first time, why me? Arms raised, I could still hear Jack shouting comments. Pretty sure there was a *"Christ." "Fuck." "Sonofabitch."* And *my* personal favorite... *"Pain in my fucking ass."* Needless to say, even if Mandy talked us out of this, I was screwed.

"Whoa, wait, you're here 'cause you think I killed someone?"

"Well, you're on our list, and we have a lot of people to check out." That comment got a *"Jesus fucking Christ"* response from the phone, and Chad turned to me.

"Who are you?"

"I'm Jennifer. Nice to meet you, and sorry for thinking you could be a killer. We don't really think you did it; we're just checking out everyone in the age 20-55."

"I don't give a fuck, so sit your ass down while I call the sheriff." I heard a barked laugh on the phone and decided I might as well end this torture. I handed over my phone to Chad and said.

"Here, you talk to him. Tell him I'm *not* a pain in the ass, I'm *stubborn*, and not to bother coming by tonight 'cause I'll be busy packing for Breckenridge." Chad took the phone from me with a confused look, put it to his ear, said "Hello," and then winced.

"Sheriff...yes, sir...yes, sir...no, sir...uh, yeah, I'll tell her." Then Chad hung up.

"Well, what'd he say?" I asked. Not that I really wanted to know. I was pretty sure I could guess, but curiosity killed the cat and all.

"He said to get Mandy's ass home, get your ass home, and if you went anywhere near Breckenridge he'd have you hauled in for whatever charges he could think of."

I looked at Mandy, grabbed my phone from Chad, and without another word headed to my Jeep. *I swear Kansas looks better and better every day!!!*

Nine

I'm Mocking You

That sonofabitch, he's waiting for her. The anger rose up my throat and almost choked me. I knew he couldn't see me, but he turned his head and looked right at me as if he sensed me. I watched that smug bastard as his eyes scanned around, searching for what he couldn't see... That's right, Sheriff, I'm here, I can see you. I'm watching you...can you feel me? Not tonight, but soon, very soon, one way or another you will die...then MY Jennifer will be free of you."

Denver, I bet I could find a job in Denver.

I'd decided Breckenridge wasn't big enough to hide in; I needed a big city to avoid the long arm of the law, or, in this case, one lawman in particular. I could buy a cabin closer in and drive to work like all the other mountain dwellers. I turned onto Old Saw Mill Road and as the lights of my cabin came into view, so did the truck of the Gunnison County Sheriff. *Dammit, caught before my escape.* I pulled in next to his truck. Jack leaned against it with his arms crossed over his chest, glaring at me. I smiled weakly at him, and he just shook his head slowly at me. I knew I should be contrite, but I felt my survival instincts kick in, and I squared my shoulders for the confrontation that was coming. Jack shoved off his truck and headed to my door to open it, so I grabbed my bag and turned as he pulled it open.

"I should tan your hide," was the first thing out of his mouth, and, being the idiot I was, evidence to this fact after agreeing to look for dead bodies in the first damn place, my temper flared.

"Oh, yeah? Well, you can try, but I'll warn you now, I took self-defense classes back home and my instructor said I had a mean aim.... between the legs." Jack didn't even react to my threat, just leaned closer and barked out his reply:

"Woman, you had a gun pointed at you tonight, you were trespassing, and let's not forget conducting an investigation into a killer, which, I might add, you're on the victims list of. You were reckless, you disobeyed me, *and* you put Mandy in danger."

"I am not reckless; we wouldn't even have been caught if *you* hadn't called me." Jack's head snapped back, and he looked at me like I had grown two heads. I took this opportunity to move past him and ran up the steps, unlocked my front door, pushed it open, and flipped on the living room lights. Jack slammed the door behind me.

"I'm not done talking about this, Jenn."

"Fine, tell me how stupid I was, tell me how you're gonna arrest me if I leave the county, threaten me with interfering in an investigation, and then leave. I've had a weird twenty-four hours, Jack, and I just want something to eat and go to bed."

"How come I get the feeling anything I say is gonna

go in one ear and out the other?"

"Perceptive man," I shouted.

"Christ, you're a pain in my ass," he shouted back.

"Well, there's the door, Jack, don't let me keep you." I turned towards the kitchen and grabbed the kettle, filling it with water. I heard the door behind me open and then slam, and just like that I deflated. *Shit.* Lowering my head and taking a deep breath, I knew it was for the best, that the man would chew me up. I had no business starting something with him. He was too bossy, full of himself, beautiful, interesting, and altogether out of my league. But that didn't stop me from wishing it could be different. With all my mouthing off about not wanting him to pursue me, saying he was moving too fast, the truth hit me hard...I may not like it, but I clearly wanted it.

"Shit." Sighing, I turned to the stove and gasped when I looked up and saw Jack leaning one shoulder against the front door, silently watching me.

"You got a temper on you, babe." I could feel the blood rise on my face, so I ducked my head and continued on to the stove.

"You gonna tell me why you put yourself and Mandy at risk?"

"It just sort of happened, Jack. Mandy was going over my suspects list and when I gave her a ride home we were passing Chad's cabin and it just, ya know, happened."

Jack shook his head again and stared at me for a moment, then he looked back at my windows and moved toward them. He checked the latches on each window and then moved to the bathroom. I stayed in the kitchen, got a mug down and a packet of hot cocoa mix, trying to stay busy and not watch Jack move around my house. Having him in the cabin, taking care of me, I realized how long it had been since I'd had anyone in my life on a daily basis. With Bailey at school and Doug gone, I went to work and came home. Other than Ben, who stopped by frequently to check in on me, I hadn't had anyone in my house since I got here. And all those plans I had for hiking and riding the river with Gerry had never happened, either. I may have moved to my dream, but it occurred to me I wasn't exactly living that dream. Jack being here reminded me of what it was like to come home from work and have someone waiting for me, and it was painful to remember.

"Windows are secure; the locks are solid. Noticed your front door has double locks and a barrel bolt, so use them all." That caught my attention, and I looked to the door. When I left this evening, I had a single lock and no barrel bolt. Looking around, I saw an envelope with my name, *"Jenny"*, written on it in Ben's hen scratching lying on the table by the front door. I walked over and opened it and saw a short note with keys. "*Jenny, keep them locked, Ben."* I smiled. Having a father figure looking out for me this far from home warmed my heart, but it just intensified the feelings I was already having. I felt a tear fall down my cheek and wiped it away, but there were more replacing it. I didn't even know why I was crying. Loneliness maybe, or knowing someone cared and was looking out for me? I was about to turn around and move back to the kitchen when I heard Jack move in my direction.

"Sweetness?" I heard from behind me, and then Jack wrapped both his arms around my waist and pulled me into his chest. I closed my eyes at the feeling of arms around me again. What was wrong with me tonight?

"Hey, Jenn, talk to me. Why the tears?"

"Sorry, it's just been a while since I felt cared about, and Ben reminds me of my dad." I pulled away from him and wiped my face with my hands, then picked up my key chain to attach the new keys.

"Must have been hard moving here on your own?"

"Actually, it's one of the easiest things I've ever done." I looked back at Jack and smiled, then moved back to the kitchen.

"You want some hot cocoa?"

"I'll pass, thanks, but tell me: why was it easy?"

"It's been my dream since I was little. When Doug died and Bailey left for school, I thought about what I wanted in my life, and the mountains were the first and only thing that came to mind."

"That's still a big step to take, moving away from your family."

"My brother moved to California ten years ago, and my mother and father retired to Florida three years ago, so I wasn't leaving anyone behind except for a few friends."

"So here you are, ready to take on the whole of Colorado and a killer at the same time." Rolling my eyes since he managed to get us back to the subject of my disobeying him, I decided not to fight again.

"You made your point earlier, Jack, and you're right. It was stupid what we did and I don't plan on making the same mistake."

"Babe, I've known you about thirty-six hours, and in that time I've learned pretty damn quick that you're going to do whatever the hell you feel like doing. That being said, I'm gonna do my damnedest to try and keep up with you so I can catch you when you fall. But honest to God, right about now, locking you in a cell sounds pretty damned good to me; at least I know you're safe there." I rolled my eyes, but then it hit me what he said.

"Has it only been thirty-six hours? It feels longer."

"Longest fucking thirty-six hours of my life."

"I know what you mean."

And I did. Two bodies, one break-in, three toe-curling kisses, a gun pointed at me, three men either asking me out or giving me puppy dog eyes, and let's not forget Ben and Gerry. Mandy was right: I *was* the shiny new toy, and, just like with all toys, they would get tired of playing with me. *Was I hoping for or dreading that day?*

"Jesus, you're somethin' else, you know that?"

"What'd I do now?"

"If I didn't know any better, I'd say you're fearless."

"Ha! I'm scared to death most days, Jack. I just hide it well."

Jack had been slowly moving toward me during our conversation and by the time I finished my statement, he was looking down at me. Without warning, he picked me up and deposited me on the countertop so I was even with his face. He pushed in, forcing me to open my legs, then grabbed my ass and pulled me against his hips, making me suck in a breath at having his crotch up against my heat.

"You scared of me?" he whispered, looking into my eyes.

"Yes," barely came out, but I nodded with the word.

"Let's see if we can change that?"

92

And just like the last three times he kissed me, I didn't stand a chance. He went slower this time, keeping his eyes locked on mine as he lowered his head infinitesimally, and my heartbeat picked up. Right before his lips touched mine, he smiled, and then his eyes lowered to my lips and he closed in, nipping my bottom lip. I moaned as the shock of it went straight through me like an electrical current. Jack's eyes darkened at my reaction, and he whispered, "Jesus." I didn't need any more prompting. I threw my hands in his hair, wrapped my legs around his waist and went straight for his mouth. His hand grabbed my hair, and he pulled, holding me back. He looked down at me with a face full of need, and I felt that run through me and up the amps of electrical current coursing through my body. Jack moved to my exposed neck and kissed his was up to my ear and then nipped my lobe. I shuddered, and he growled in my ear, "You like my teeth?"

"Please," came from my mouth. Even though I'd never been bitten, the evidence pulsing between my legs suggested that I did, in fact, like his teeth. He nipped and bit his way down my neck. I was a trembling mess when he came back to my mouth. "Jack—" was all I got out when he slammed his mouth over mine.

He leaned into me, and I found myself flat on the countertop, my hips arched up to feel the pressure of his body on mine. Jack's free hand moved down my side and lifted the hem of my shirt. Then, with light fingers, he caressed my side from my ribs to my hip, causing a shiver. Jack ripped his mouth from me and put his forehead to mine.

"If I don't stop now, I'll be buried deep in you till

morning."

"Right now I can't think of a reason to stop you."

"Baby, do not tempt me. I'm trying to be honorable here."

"Jack, I haven't had sex in sixteen months," I whimpered. God, I sounded pathetic, begging him when I knew I shouldn't be jumping into bed with this man.

"Jesus," Jack replied, conflicted.

His mouth said no, but his body rubbed against mine, and I felt a building in my core. I groaned and bucked my hips, and he rubbed again.

"Jack, more," I begged, and his face grew darker, hungrier. His hand moved up to my breast; his thumb and finger found my nipple, and then he pinched and pulled as I whispered, "Yes." He ripped my shirt up, and pulled my bra down, attaching his mouth to my breast. He sucked my nipple deep and then used his teeth; the resulting friction and his mouth pushed me further toward orgasm.

"Jack, please." I couldn't wait any longer; I needed this. Then, with more pressure and a hard pinch on my nipple, Jack threw me over the plateau and into bliss saying, "Let go, baby, I got you. You're safe with me." I tensed when it hit me, holding my breath as the warmth ran over my body, and then relaxed as it swept through me like no drug could. Jerking with the aftershocks, I saw Jack's eyes watching as I fell over into sexual heaven. "Jesus," he groaned and lowered his head to my ear. "Gotta tell you, Sweetness, you're every man's wet dream. I can't wait to watch your face when I'm deep inside you."

I was too relaxed to care. I nuzzled his neck, nipping and licking. My sex-starved body decided being a slut worked for her, and after hearing Jack talking dirty, I was ready to test his theory. Jack inhaled deeply as I worked his throat, moaning.

"Jenn, baby, only so much a man can take."

"Let go, Jack, your heart's safe with me," I whispered in his ear, and he froze, turned his head to look at me, his face going soft. *Do not ask me why I said that, I plead the fifth.* Jack smiled at me, then kissed my lips gently and on a whisper said, "Good to know, Jenn."

I was about to come up with some flippant excuse for talking about hearts and flowers thirty-six hours after meeting this man, but something crashed through my window, shattering the calm.

Jack jerked up, bringing me with him, then shoved me down into a squat on the kitchen floor and ordered, "Do not fucking move, do you hear me?" Nodding my full agreement, 'cause after the last two days I wasn't arguing, I watched Jack draw his weapon from his holster. He moved to the window, looked outside, and then moved to the door, unlocking it. He brought his gun up in front of his chest then moved through the door, swinging his outstretched arms back and forth, scanning with his gun. After what seemed like an hour, but was more like five minutes, he came back inside and shut the door before locking it. I stood and watched him move toward whatever broke my window, then he bent over and picked up something dark, and I gasped when I saw it was a bird.

"It's too dark for birds to be out flying, isn't it?"

"It's a mockingbird; they like to come out at night, and

they'll drive you nuts with their mocking calls."

"Is he dead?"

"Yeah, baby, a bird flies through a window, it usually kills them." Nodding as Jack went to my kitchen and got a plastic bag to put the bird in, I got a broom and dustpan to sweep up the mess. Jack came back after digging in my odds and ends closet with duct tape and heavy cardboard he'd found in my craft box. Purple sparkled cardboard, a leftover from a graduation party I'd made invitations two years earlier for, now graced my window.

As we cleaned up the mess, Jack got a call from the station and had to leave to take it, so I walked him to my door. With everything that had happened with the bird, I hadn't had time to think about what had occurred in the kitchen, but that didn't stop Jack from reminding me.

"You ok with my taking off after what happened?"

"Jack, I...oh, man, this is embarrassing." Jack put his hand to the side of my face and rubbed his thumbs across my cheeks, then dipped in close and, with a gentle voice, eased my nerves.

"Jenn... look at me." I looked up into his crystal blue eyes and saw them gentle and warm, looking back at me. "You're amazing and sexy as hell. Do not be embarrassed. I'm only sorry I have to go."

"You've got a job to do, Jack. I know that, I'm not mad you're leaving." Jack seemed surprised by my answer and studied me for a moment like he was looking for the truth of my statement.

"Christ, you get me, don't you?"

"Get you?"

"Get that my badge means more than a paycheck."

cp smith

"Of course. Isn't that why you do what you do, 'cause it means something to you and the people you protect?" His face got even warmer, and he whispered, "Jesus, you're something." So I smiled at his compliment. He watched my smile, then he leaned in and kissed me softly before he pulled back and winked.

He barked out, "Lock up, I want to hear it click before I leave." I nodded my agreement and opened the door for him to leave. He walked out onto the porch, then turned back and smiled.

"Night, Sweetness."

"Night, Jack." Then he moved down the steps, turned back and waited for me to close the door and lock it. So I did as he said and locked my doors, then watched as he pulled out of my drive. Looking back around my cabin, I noticed the silence was deafening...A killer, men with guns, and a gorgeous sheriff with a magical mouth...

Welcome to Colorado, Jennifer. You asked for it, you got it. Now what are you going to do with it?

Ten

Better And Better

I woke slowly as my alarm played the soulful sounds of Lifehouse singing *"From Where You Are."* The words spoke of wasted years, wishing someone wasn't gone, and I felt a lump form in my throat. It was times like these, first thing in the morning, when I was lying in bed and listening to the quiet, that I got scared and lonely. And that song wasn't helping. *Pity party, Jennifer, really? Bailey is beginning her life and doesn't have time for her mother, but that's normal. And you've met a few people here and made friends, even if you did keep to yourself the first few months.* Boy did that change this past week, though. Invitations to lunch from two men, Mandy inviting me to hang out again, and then Ben and Gerry offering to help with my investigation.

And then there was Jack.

How in the hell did I go from not knowing the man one day to what had happened last night? And since we're speaking of the sheriff, I wondered what he was thinking this morning. He seemed interested, acted like I was different, but could I trust that? Or was I just another woman to try on for size? Would he add me to his growing list of women who didn't make the cut?

"Naomi is beautiful and sexy, and she only lasted eight months," I stated. Was Barry right? Was Jack's problem with women that he just couldn't commit? It made perfect sense: if he hasn't been married by now, the question was if I wanted to take that chance with him? Get in deeper than I already was and risk my heart? Staring at the ceiling and weighing the pros and cons of a relationship with Jack, I realized I was taking all the risk, not him, and I just couldn't do it. Nope, there were just too many questions and not enough answers to chance my heart, and that sucked, 'cause, bossy or not, he intrigued me like no other had before.

I sat up, moved to my bag, and pulled out my calendar. I needed to look over my schedule and see what was on the table for the day. Put my focus back on my responsibilities for the paper and work the killings on my own time, and, more importantly, keep out of Jack's way. Simple. Yesterday and all the craziness needed to be filed under *"Exciting, but scary"*, and I needed to move on to boring, predictable bake sales, even if I gained twenty pounds. This felt good. I felt focused. I'd keep my eyes on the prize, keep out of Jack's way, and all would remain as it was. Boring, but safe.

***

My phone rang as I was driving into Gunnison. I looked at the caller ID and saw it was Bossy. Should I answer or ignore him and hope he'd get the message? Then it occurred to me that Jack was bossy, stubborn, and tenacious, and he probably wouldn't stop calling if I ignored him. Deciding to take the bull by the horn and get this over with, steeling myself against the sound of his voice, I answered, "Hello."

"Babe, just checking to make sure you didn't have any more bird attacks." *Ha, funny man!*

"Nope, I didn't become a heroine in an Alfred Hitchcock movie," I answered, but wanted to kick myself for being flirty. *Focus, Jennifer.*

"Good to hear, baby," Jack replied and hearing him call me baby weakened my resolve. Thinking indifference might work with Jack, I took a breath and went for the big brush-off.

"Well, thanks for calling and checking, Jack, but I gotta run. Bake sales to cover and cookies to buy." That sounded friendly but got the message across, right? I waited for his reply but got dead air.

"Jack?"

"There a reason you just went from sweet to indifferent in the blink of an eye?"

"Sorry?"

"Jenn, is there a reason you're dismissing me like a stranger?"

"Um, I, wow, you're not making this easy, are you?"

"Seems where you're concerned, nothing is easy, so no, I'm not making this easy when everything about you makes me hard." I sucked air in sharply at that blatant sexual reference and swore I felt my nipples get hard.

"Jack, I—"

"Do not pull back, Jenn. I told you last night you have nothing to be embarrassed about."

"You can't just let this go and chalk it up to extenuating circumstances?"

"Hell no," he growled, and that felt good, too. *Damn.*

"Ok, Jack, here it is. I like you, you're hot, funny, really smart, but you've never been tied down, and why would you when you can have any woman in town, right? I mean, I get that, you look like you do and wear a badge, why limit yourself to one woman? I get it, really I do, but I'm not the type to be someone's flavor of the month. So if it's all the same to you, can we just be friends?" I held my breath waiting for his explosion, but it didn't come.

"Christ, I pegged you completely wrong when we first met." *What?* "Thought you were a typical nosey in-your-face reporter, but then you showed me a different side and I liked what I saw. But, babe, gotta tell ya, this innocent side, the one where you have no clue of the fact that *you* could have any man in this town and still you'd be settling? Total fucking turn-on; and you think I'm gonna settle for friends? Hell no."

I had nothing to say to that; I mean what *do* you say to that? This man was good, real good, how could you walk away from that? *Shit. I'm so screwed!*

"Jack—"

"And now on top of sweet, I get innocent, too? No way, Jenn, no fucking way."

"Ok, Jack." I couldn't argue with this man, damn him; he just reeled me in. I should have never answered the phone.

"Damn right."

"I said ok, you don't have to be bossy."

"Oh, I'm gonna be bossy. In fact, I'm gonna be bossy right fucking now. I don't share, so lunch with the mayor better be a one-time only thing, understand?"

"How did you know about that?"

"Mayor Hall enlightened me last night. Now, did you

get what I said?"

"Yeah, I get you Jack, but I don't respond well to being bossed around, so do *you* get *me*?"

"Deal with it," he barked out.

"Whatever," I snipped and he chuckled. *I am so screwed.*

"All right, Sweetness, now that we have that out of the way, I have work to do. You stay safe and don't go looking for any more dead bodies." I rolled my eyes at him.

"Yes, sir, Sheriff, sir."

"Smartass."

"Bossy."

"Later, baby."

"Later, Jack."

***

Shaking my head at Jenn as I hung up— 'cause honest to God, the woman could drive me to drink—I gave her a couple of moments more thought, grinning at how damn cute she was, and then I moved to concentrate on this killer.

We knew he targeted women with brown hair and brown eyes. Based on the history of serial killers, we could assume he'd had a bad childhood and a mother with those characteristics, or got scorned by a woman who looked similar. Phone records showed no connection between all three women. They'd never lived in the same place; their families didn't know each other, so the only things they had in common were their looks and their age. Toxicology showed no drugs or alcohol; last meals were different, so they hadn't all gone to the same restaurant and been singled out there.

Basically, we had shit to go on, except all three had nylon fiber under their nails, indicating that the rope used to strangle them was nylon. I'd sent Grady to Jenkins to get a sample of all nylon ropes, hoping there might be a match we could cross-reference to sales and to this killer. I had placed a call to the FBI to see if they had a profile ready for me, and other than hundreds of calls from concerned citizens reporting their neighbors as the killer, all we could do was wait and pray this asshole slipped up.

***

After hours of combing through reports, I needed a fresh coffee and an aspirin the size of Texas. What evidence we had hit a dead end. Nothing linked these women except their physical appearance.

Rubbing my hands over my face, thinking I needed a damn vacation for the hundredth time that day, I pushed up from my desk and headed down the hall to get another coffee. Grady was coming through the front doors when I rounded the corner, so I stopped and waited for him to approach.

"Jack, got those samples from Jenkins and took them over to Drew to compare with the fibers under the victims' nails. Daryl Jenkins has software that keeps track by phone number what people buy, and he copied a list of everyone who bought any of the nylon rope in his store in the past year."

"Good job, Grady. Put the list on my desk and then call

Drew and tell him I need the analysis of the ropes compared to the fibers ASAP."

"Will do, Jack."

Turning to fill my cup in the kitchen, I looked up and saw Naomi walk into the station. Jesus, I did not need another confrontation with this woman. No matter how hard I tried, she couldn't seem to accept that we were done. It had been over for months on my end, but I kept going back thinking maybe I was wrong. I wasn't, and this side I was seeing only confirmed it. Deciding to head this off, not wanting to drag out another conversation with this woman, I crossed my arms and waited for her, but I let the expression on my face speak for me.

"Jack, can I talk to you?"

"Naomi, got work to do,"

"You had time to kiss another woman on the sidewalk yesterday, but you can't make time for the woman you were screwing for eight months?" she hissed. I grabbed her by the arm and pulled her into the kitchen, away from listening ears.

"You've got three minutes, then I'm going back to work." She gave me sad eyes and then the tears came. Taking a deep breath and wishing I'd stayed in my office, but also not wanting to be a jerk, I pulled out my handkerchief and handed it to her.

"Jack, why...? I don't understand. Please, can't you give us another chance?" Closing my eyes to the pain in her voice, I didn't know what else I could say to this woman without hurting her more.

"Babe, it's just not going to work. You're right for someone; it's just not me."

"And I suppose that Stewart woman is?"

"Jesus, Naomi, let's not get into this shit. You need to move on. I'm sorry you're hurting, but it's over, and you need to accept it."

"Accept that for eight months we were building something and then you just kicked me to the curb?"

"Dammit, woman, I tried to make it work, but you wanted me to be someone I'm not. You wanted something I couldn't give you, and you didn't listen when I explained I wouldn't change, so I was done." She nodded her head, agreeing with me, and I knew what was coming.

"You're right, Jack. I did. I tried to change you, but I've learned my lesson, honey. I have, I promise. I just wanted you around more. Dinner at night, a movie or even a weekend trip, was that too much to ask? But I'd rather have a little of your time than none at all. I'll be less demanding of your time, I promise, Jack. I will, I get it now, you'll see."

"Naomi, *you* shouldn't have to change for me any more than *I* should have to change for you. I'm not the man you need, babe, and you *need* to get that." Her face drew up in a scowl and turned bright red as her anger kicked in, then that anger turned to desperation, and she started sobbing and breaking her words.

"P... Please, Ja... Jack, I love you."

"I know you do, and I'm sorrier than you know that I've hurt you, but babe, hear me, please, for your own sake and mine: it's over."

Naomi stared for a moment through tear-soaked eyes, and, then out of nowhere, she slapped my face. I didn't move, and I didn't stop her. I stood there as she pounded on my chest with both fists, then buried her head in my chest and sobbed. Her behavior had been escalating to this, and now that she'd had this breakdown, hopefully she'd accept it and move on.

I put my arms around her and held her loosely, feeling like shit, but praying to God she finally got it. In timing that could only be described as fucked up, I heard a gasp and looked to the door, finding Jenn standing there. I didn't want her to get the wrong idea, so I raised my hand and gave her a finger indicating I needed a minute. She looked at me, then at the crying woman, and then sadness and empathy crossed her face. I was trying to indicate with my eyes she should head to my office when Naomi chose that moment to look up at me, saw my eyes over her shoulder, and turned and saw Jenn standing there.

Naomi wasted no time. Before I could react, she turned and shrieked.

"You fucking whore! You fucking, fucking whore! He's my man."

"Christ, woman," I barked as I grabbed her arm to keep her from attacking. Jenn seemed stunned by the outburst, so I got her attention before this escalated.

"Baby, go to my office, I'll be there in a minute." Jenn looked at me with huge, brown eyes, then nodded and headed down the hall.

"BABY, did you call her baby? You've never called me anything but babe," Naomi shouted, trying to pull her arm from mine as I walked her to the front of the station.

"Naomi, swear to Christ, stop struggling and keep your voice down."

"FUCK YOU, AND FUCK HER!" she screamed. I made

it to the doors and escorted her out to her car. She yanked her arm away and then spat in my face. Jesus, I should have ended it with her sooner. That was on me, but I was done, and I let her know it in no uncertain terms.

"Get in your car and leave right now. This is done, I am done, *we* are done. Do. You. Understand. Me.?"

I didn't wait for an answer but yanked her door open and watched as she settled behind the wheel before I slammed the door and started to head back toward the station, wiping my face with the sleeve of my shirt. I heard her start her car and then her tires squeal as I opened the door to the station. When I entered, I saw heads look up and then back down, but no one made eye contact. I walked to the men's room, washed my face, and then headed to my office.

When I got there, Jenn was standing next to my desk looking at the report from Jenkins. The minute I saw her, I calmed down. I watched her try to read the list that Grady left on my desk and smiled.

"If I didn't know better, I'd think you were just stringing me along for your story." Jenn jumped and had the decency to look guilty and shrugged.

"Sorry, Jack, I went to put the cookies on the desk and saw the list of names. Is that your suspect list?" Amazed that she didn't look the least bit upset by Naomi's behavior, I shook my head and walked towards her.

"Jesus, a woman screams at you, calls you a whore, and you act like it's no big deal and then move on to snooping?"

"Uh, well, I might have been worried when I first got here, but after she acted that way, I figured if you wanted her, then you weren't worth my time. So yeah, I'm over it. 'Cause, Jack, in case you missed it, she's a bitch." I tipped my head back and laughed. Christ, this woman was like no one I'd met before.

"Baby, you just keep getting better and better."

"Is that good or bad?"

I grabbed her around the waist and hauled her up to my chest.

"It's fucking great." Then I nipped her lip, and she gasped, so I kissed her hard and lost myself in her sweet scent and soft lips. A part of me wondered how the hell someone like her fell into my lap, but I wasn't gonna question it, and I sure as hell was gonna do everything I could to keep her right where she was.

Eleven

Fade To Black

After dropping off the cookies with Jack, I headed to my office to write my story on the bake sale. Lorraine saw me coming through the door and waved me over to her desk. I had a feeling I knew what this was about, but was surprised when she opened her mouth.

"Heard through the grapevine you're pursuing a story on this killer."

"I, well—"

"I'm in," she whispered, looking around to see who was listening. Taking my cue from her, I looked around as well and in a hushed voice asked what the hell she was talking about.

"What do you mean, you're in?"

"I want in on the story. We can work it together like Bernstein and Woodward."

"Lorraine, I don't have permission from Bob to do this story. I'm only working on this in my off time."

"Even better. Bob can't stand over our shoulders barking out how to investigate this." Thinking that someone with her experience in journalism would be a benefit to me, I looked around one more time and then leaned in.

"Ok, Lorraine, how do you want to split this up?"

"How far have you gotten?"

"Ben and Gerry helped me put together a suspects and victims list yesterday. I've showed it to Jack, and Mandy's had a look at it as well. She helped whittle down the list. She was out yesterday afternoon running errands and spoke with several of the suspects during the time of the killing." Lorraine was writing in her notebook while I spoke, nodding her head as I relayed this information. When I finished, she looked around again, and I realized this was starting to feel very Bernstein and Woodward. "You got a copy of the suspect list I can have?" she whispered conspiratorially.

"Yeah, hold on. I'll go run a copy for you."

I moved to the copier and ran additional copies, all the while keeping an eye on Bob. I was looking over the list when it hit me the last name of one of the men was the same as Lorraine's: Tom Beckett. I'd met her son once or twice when he came into the paper to visit his mother. Oh, man, I hoped this didn't piss her off. But surely she'd understand, the list was long, and so many people were on it. I looked around one more time before heading back to her desk.

"Here ya go, Lorraine, but I need to warn you: every man within the age range for serial killers is on this list, so your son Tom is on also it. I hope you don't take offense."

"Please, I may be old, but I'm not stupid. That doesn't matter if he's innocent, which he is: he was out of town yesterday, up in Denver, so he's got an alibi."

"Good, we can mark him off our list then."

"You said you met with Ben and Gerald?"

"Yeah, they heard me talking about the killer and saw my notes, so they figured, since they know every one in five counties, that they could help."

"Smart, Jennifer, use the public and their knowledge when you're investigating. You never know what someone knows that can break a story wide open." Smiling at the compliment, I grabbed a chair and sat down next to her.

"Jack has another list. I tried to look at it but he caught me, so I didn't see it. He knows I'm writing the story and said he would help me, but I can't put it to print until he says so. I'm hoping he'll share information."

"Take him to bed. I bet he'll share it then."

"Oh, my God, you didn't just tell me to sleep with Jack for information."

"Whatever gets the story, I always say, but in this case, with a man looking the way he does? I may be old, but I'm not blind. You'd be winning on both accounts."

"Lorraine, I'm not sleeping with Jack to further my career."

"Suit yourself, but after that kiss I saw yesterday, I don't think he'd mind." The gleam in her eyes told me she was joking, so I laughed and then stood to go to my desk. As I was turning, Lorraine grabbed my hand, so I moved back to her.

"Jack's a good man, he just hasn't found the right woman yet." I looked at her for a moment and then nodded my head. It was nice to hear something positive about Jack and his serial dating.

"Call Ben and Gerry, tell them I'm in, and that we need to meet. I want to pick their brains on this list."

"Ok, I'll call them as soon as I finish my piece. You

want to meet at my cabin or have them come down the mountain?"

"Tell them to meet us at The Trough at seven. I'm in the mood for steak and a healthy dose of spirits."

Nodding, I moved to my desk and pulled out my notes. I hadn't been to The Trough since moving here, but I'd heard their steak and seafood were the best. Opening my Word software, I began typing my article for the bake sale and then thought better of waiting to call Ben and Gerry. Thinking they might need more notice than a few hours, I grabbed my phone and hit send on Ben's number. While it was ringing, I heard Lorraine talking to someone and turned to see her son standing next to her desk.

"You got Ben."

"Ben, this is Jennifer."

"Jenny, what can I do for you?"

"Lorraine Beckett is offering to work on the serial killer story with me and wants to meet with you and Gerry. Are you free tonight at seven to meet us at The Trough?"

"I'm good to go. I'll call Gerry and see if he's free. Either way, I'll meet you there at seven, ok, darlin'?"

"Thanks, Ben. You know I kinda love you, right?"

"Ha, been a long time since a pretty young thing said that to me."

"Well, get used to it, old man, 'cause you're the bomb."

"Ok, darlin', if you say so. I'll see you in a few hours."

"See you at seven, Ben."

"Later, darlin'."

***

The Trough was crowded when we entered; Lorraine had invited her son to join us, and since she was helping me with the story and her son had an alibi, I figured she would remind him not to talk. Ben had reached Gerry, and they were both waiting for us when we arrived. Tom was forty-five, divorced, but not dating anyone. Though I wasn't sure why he wasn't dating, because he was a good-looking man: he had medium-blond hair and green eyes that would turn the eye of any woman. Even mine if I hadn't already seen Jack. But then again, there weren't many men who could outshine the sheriff.

Once inside, we got a large booth that could seat six people. Ben and Gerry took one side, Lorraine sat on the curve, and Tom and I sat next to each other on the opposite side. It wasn't a tight fit, but Ben had considerable size and needed the extra room, and, not wanting to squish Lorraine, I sat closer to Tom than I was comfortable with.

The waitress took our drink orders: the men ordered beer and the women red wine to go with our meal. Once the waitress was gone, Ben turned to Lorraine.

"Ok, what did you wanna to talk to us about?"

"We need to narrow down the suspects list, and you gentlemen are the only ones who can help." Gerry nodded at Lorraine's request and took the list she brought with her.

"Ben and I have been going over the list again since there was another killing, and a lot of names can be crossed off since most were at work."

"I agree. Last night, Mandy shortened the list by twelve and Tom here has an alibi for yesterday, so we can mark him off the list as well."

"I'm sorry, did you just say I was on the suspects list?" Tom asked.

"Yeah, sorry about that, but all men within a certain age range and no physical limitations were put on the list. So don't be offended, even the sheriff made the list."

"I should think so considering he dates and dumps women like a sixteen-year-old football player." I turned to Tom and noted the anger on his face. Wondering if he had a history with Jack, I asked him, "You sound like someone who has issues with the good sheriff."

"He dated a woman I'm quite fond of, and she was devastated when he broke things off with her."

Great, another woman whose heart was broken by the town's resident heartbreaker, and I just agreed to see him. Well, I'd just pace myself with Jack, slow him down, make sure we didn't move too fast. Then I remembered last night and snorted. If Jack and I moved any faster, we'd be married by the end of the week. *Yikes!*

"You think it's funny he hurt my friend?"

"Oh, God no, I was just thinking about something else and...You know what, never mind, I'm sorry; I didn't mean to be unkind." Tom's face softened, and he raised his hand to me.

"Apology accepted." I looked to his hand and put mine in his and shook it. "Thank you."

"Ok, let's get back to the matter at hand. While we're eating, Ben and me, and you, too, Lorraine, will go over this list and mark off people. Sound good?"

I watched as the three of them confirmed and argued about who they saw yesterday and who was out of town. Our food came and just as the reviews suggested, it was outstanding. We'd all chosen steak—big surprise—and it was thick and delicious. Tom and I chatted about nothing important, just about me liking Colorado and working at the paper. Ben, Gerry, and Lorraine worked while they ate and the list was shorter in no time.

With the checks paid, Lorraine and I made plans to meet in the morning and then moved to exit the table. Tom got up and was helping me to my feet when, suddenly, Naomi came charging at me. She shoved me sideways and started slapping me, screaming about me *"stealing her man."* I'd never been hit in my life, so without thinking, I reacted. *Father forgive me, for I know not what I do.*

I punched her hard in the nose. I know....it shocked the hell out of me too. But to be honest, it felt good after this afternoon. Tom pulled me back, and Gerry jumped up and took hold of Naomi. Then Ben pulled out his phone, and, before I could say boo, he was on the phone with Jack.

The restaurant had gone quiet; all eyes were on us because Naomi hadn't stopped her tirade. She was clearly drunk. The manager rushed over to intervene, and that just made it worse. Naomi struggled against Gerry, spitting and hissing like a damn cat, telling the manager, Lloyd Pinkerton, she was going to sue him for *"unlawful concentration"*—her words, not mine—and I'd have corrected her if I wasn't concerned she would jump me and beat the shit out of me.

Fortunately, not soon after, Jack and a deputy I knew as Phil walked in. Jack took one look at the situation and his face got hard, his jaw ticked with anger. I shrunk back, not wanting to be close when he let loose.

He walked up to Naomi and looked at her nose, then turned to me and scanned my face.

"Cuff her." *Oh, shit*

"Come on, Jack, I didn't mean to hit her, she was slapping me. Please don't arrest me." Jack looked at me like I was nuts.

"Jesus, Jenn, I wasn't talking about you." *Oh, well then, carry on.* I nodded ok and went to sit down. Tom had a hold of my arm and joined me in the booth.

Jack watched this.

He looked at me, looked at Tom, then his jaw started ticking again. *He's such a man!*

I scooted over, putting some distance between Tom and me, and this seemed to appease Jack. He turned back to Naomi.

"You have the right to remain silent—"

"You can't arrest me! Your whore punched me in the face," she argued.

"Anything you say can and will be used against you in a court of law—"

"Phil, don't you dare put those cuffs on me," Naomi shouted, struggling to pull away from him.

"You have the right to an attorney. If you cannot afford an attorney, one will be provided for you—"

"Jack!" Naomi screamed as the cuffs were snapped closed around her wrists.

I couldn't watch anymore. This woman was drunk because she was heartbroken. Bitch or not, I was pretty sure she wouldn't have struck me sober.

"Jack, stop," I called out. He turned back to me, and I shook my head. "I'm not pressing charges. Please, just let her go and help her home so she can sleep it off."

Jack watched me for a moment and his eyes grew soft. Then he turned back to Phil and motioned for him to turn her around. Jack pulled out a key and uncuffed her, then walked her toward the door with his hand at her arm. She struggled against him the whole way before he stopped and whispered in her ear. Whatever he said stilled her, and she walked quietly with him out the door.

"Holy cow, that was more excitement than I've had in years. Jennifer, we must go out more often," Lorraine laughed, and I looked at her like she'd lost her ever-loving mind.

"I hit a woman! I've never hit anyone in my life."

"Honey, you gotta learn to live a little," Lorraine replied. Ben and Gerry started laughing, and Tom helped me out of the booth while he chuckled.

Mr. Pinkerton, the manager, apologized for the disruption, but we all waved him off. It wasn't his fault Naomi lost her head.

As we left the restaurant, I was wondering if Jack or Phil took Naomi home when I saw the man himself, leaning against my Jeep. I smiled and headed towards him, but for some reason, Tom decided I needed to be walked to my car. I tried to tell him I was fine and could make my way safely to it, but he didn't listen. As we walked up to Jack, he raised a questioning eyebrow, looking between Tom and me.

"Sheriff, you didn't have to wait around to make sure Ms. Stewart got to her car safely. I can handle it." *Oh, boy!*

"I have no doubt you can handle it, Tom. Problem is, I

have an issue with you handling any part of Jenn," Jack replied as he pushed away from my jeep and stood tall. A good four inches over Tom, I might add.

Jack reached out and grabbed my hand, drawing me to him, and continued, "So if you'll excuse us, I'd like to speak with my woman...in private."

"Your woman?" Tom turned to me and raised an eyebrow. I didn't know this man, but his attitude was starting to piss me off. So I moved into Jack, his arm wrapped around me as mine wrapped around him, a united front against...well, I really wasn't sure, but it felt like an attack. Tom studied us for a moment then gave a slight bow and continued speaking.

"My apologies. Had I known, I would have left you to the more capable hands of the sheriff, of course." Now he was just being sarcastic, and he leered at Jack. *Arrogant asshole*. Jack drew me closer into his body, and Tom turned without saying another word and headed back to his mother.

"Like I said earlier, Sweetness, any man in town..."

"I remember, Jack, but you should know that one hasn't got a chance in hell. I mean, what kind of man bows?"

Jack chuckled, then brought his hand up to my face and rubbed his thumb across what I'm sure was a handprint on my cheek.

"Can't believe that bitch slapped you."

"That makes two of us."

"You wanna tell me why you're having dinner with Lorraine, her son, and the Hardy boys?"

"Just going over the suspect list and eliminating those who had alibis for yesterday."

"At least you weren't peeking into windows. Where's Mandy tonight?" I rolled my eyes, and he chuckled again.

"Ok, baby, time for you to head up the mountain. Do you need me to follow you? I'm on duty and can't stay, but I'll follow if you need me."

"Ben and Gerry are going to follow me, so no, but thanks, Sheriff. All this special attention you're giving me will go to my head."

"Jenn, you want special attention, you only have to ask." Sucking in my breath, thinking about what that special attention might be, I responded without thinking.

"Pretty sure I asked last night and you said no." Jack looked shocked but recovered.

"Pretty fucking sure if that bird hadn't broken your window, I would have said yes."

"Then stop by after your shift and make it up to me." *Where had that come from?*

"Try and stop me," he growled, and just like that I was putty in his hands, and Jack kissed me.

I rose up on my toes and threw my arms around his neck as his hands cupped my ass and forced me into his growing erection. I whimpered, and he kissed me deeper. A cough from behind us broke the spell. Jack pulled back an inch, but just kept staring at me. "Fuck me," he whispered and I replied without thinking, "No, fuck me." Jack closed his eyes, sucked in a breath, then hissed, "Truck, now."

Without another word he turned to Ben and announced, "I've got her. She needs to swear out a statement, and then I'll see she gets home."

Without waiting for a reply, Jack grabbed my hand

119

and walked me to his truck, opened the door, picked me up and threw me in. I was breathing hard, 'cause I knew where this was headed, and I was freaked out, yet ready at the same time. Jack climbed in, turned to me, grabbed my neck, and pulled me to him. Then he slammed his mouth on mine, our tongues battling.

He ripped his mouth away and growled, "You with me baby? 'Cause there's no turning back after this, no way. Once I slip into that sweet heat of yours, you're mine, do you hear me? You. Are. Fucking. Mine."

Dazzled like always, I swallowed and nodded, "I'm with you, Jack." His face got darker, and he kissed me once more, then started the truck and took off heading out of town. Panting and my nerves raw, I looked over at Jack's rugged face and just knew I was making the right choice. We didn't speak; Jack held my leg, rubbing his fingers over and over the inside of my thigh, keeping my thoughts on what he would do with those hands.

Halfway to my cabin, the calm of the night was broken when a tire exploded. Jack held tight to the wheel to keep us on the road, pumping the brakes, trying to slow the truck, but it veered. I braced for impact as the truck pulled to the right, jerking us onto the shoulder and heading toward a fallen boulder directly in front of us. Jack threw on the brakes, hoping to stop us, but it was too late.

Right as the airbags exploded, I screamed, "Jack!", and everything went black.

Twelve

My Spidey Senses Are Tingling

"You hear me—Jenn, baby, are you with me? Jenn— Sonofabitch." There was a ringing in my ears and my chest felt like I'd been hit with a sledgehammer. I could hear Jack yelling, so I blinked my eyes open and tried to focus on his face. Jack had a cut on his forehead, causing blood to run down his face. I couldn't form words yet, but moved my hands and feet to make sure they still worked. Thank God for seatbelts. I saw Jack exhale, like he'd been holding his breath, and he whispered, "Thank Christ."

"Jack, we hit a really big rock." Jack scowled a little, then shook his head.

"Yeah, baby, and *you* hit your head." Nodding gently in agreement, I tried to sit up, but Jack kept his hand on my chest to keep me still.

"Lie still, baby. I called an ambulance. We need to get you checked out."

"Jack."

"Yeah?"

"First the bird and now this? I think someone is trying to tell us something." Jack's head jerked a bit, and then his eyes lost focus as he stared in the distance, lost in thought.

"Jack."

"Huh, yeah?"

"I lost you there for a second." His mouth turned into a sexy grin, and he leaned down and kissed me gently, then spoke softly against my lips. "I was just thinking about all the things I didn't get to do to you... and, baby, it would have been extremely fucking thorough." I inhaled quickly, my imagination in overdrive. Jack nipped my lip and then smiled at me. Hearing an engine behind us, his head turned, and he pushed up when he heard the siren from the ambulance. He moved his hand and waved, saying, "Looks like the Hardy boys are here, too."

Jack opened his door. It made a loud groaning noise and wouldn't open fully. He slipped through the opening, and I could hear him talking to someone. Still lying on my back, I pushed up and released the seatbelt, rubbing my chest where it snapped tight, holding me safe during the impact. Other than a pounding head and bruised chest, I felt fine, so I tried to open my door, but it wouldn't budge.

I heard Jack say, "We need to get her out and away from the truck in case it catches fire," which made me turn to look at the crushed hood. I saw the steam from the radiator hissing into the air and decided it was time to move. Jack may be worried I had injuries and that I should lie still, but I wasn't staying in the cab a second longer. I scooted across the seat, stuck my legs out the door and put my feet on the ground, and then passed through the opening of the driver's door.

"I'm out, I don't like fire."

Jack turned, said, "Shit," and moved to me, and before I could say *stop*, he picked me up and carried me towards the arriving ambulance.

"I told you not to move, what if you have a spinal injury?"

"Uh, *"truck may catch fire"* trumps *"spinal injury".* Besides, I feel fine other than a killer headache."

"Jesus, you're stubborn," he grumbled.

"Pfft, and you're bossy as hell."

"Get used to it."

"Same goes for you, Bucko."

I heard Ben chuckle behind us, so I looked over at him and smiled. He winked at me, then nudged Gerry, who was watching the interaction.

"Got your hands full there, Jack," Ben laughed.

"Don't I fucking know it," Jack growled.

"Hey, I could say the same thing."

Three men chuckled, and I rolled my eyes as Jack continued to carry me. Just as we made it to the arriving ambulance, we heard a whoosh, and Jack, Ben, Gerry, and me in Jack's arms turned and saw a small fire coming out from under the hood of the truck.

"Fuck," Jack said, and I couldn't agree more: my purse and my satchel that held all of my work and notes were in the truck.

"Dammit, my notes, my purse." Jack turned to Ben and started to hand me over to him, so I resisted.

"What are you doing?"

"Getting your bags."

"Jack, no, the truck is on fire, it might explode."

"Won't take a second, baby, hold tight," Jack explained, exasperated, as he handed me off to Ben as

I continued to protest:

"Won't take a second? Jack, don't you dare," fell from my lips as he walked right up to the back of the truck, kicked in the rear window with his boot, then leaned in and grabbed my stuff. He then turned and walked right back out from the truck bed and up to Ben and me. He handed me my bags, then took me back from Ben and walked over to the waiting medical team, who were watching the truck engulf in flames.

"You're kinda crazy, you know that, right?"

"Yup."

"You could have been killed."

"I wasn't," Jack simply said as he handed me off to the EMT's.

"Who does that? What if the truck exploded?" I yelled while the tech tried to wrap a blood pressure cuff around my flailing arms. The second EMT, a woman, was dabbing at Jack's cut as I yelled at him.

"Babe, hold still. Jesus, you're always fighting something."

I narrowed my eyes at him and hissed, "Fine." I shoved out my arm and held it level with my chest so Mr. EMT could get my pressure, then I turned my eyes to Jack and glared. Jack, being Jack, just grinned. *I'm adding cocky and arrogant to bossy.*

"You're cute when you're angry," Jack laughed. *Seriously? He thinks he can win me over with that...*

"I'm not speaking to you right now." And I meant it.

"Obliged...all that yelling was giving me a headache." *Grrr.*

"I should tan *your* hide, Sheriff." That got me a wide grin, and knowing I wouldn't get through to him, I shut my mouth and looked away, mumbling, "Bullheaded, bossy, reckless and now arrogant and cocky...I should have my head examined."

Mr. EMT chuckled at me, and I looked up at him and grinned. Wondering where Ben had run off to, I looked around and found him talking with Barry, who had driven up a few moments before. The Gunnison Fire Department showed and was putting out the fire. Thankfully, the engine never exploded, but the truck did catch fire, and my belongings would have been destroyed if not for Jack. Not that I was going to mention that.

After cute EMT girl was finished putting a butterfly bandage on Jack's head, he walked up to me, looked me over, and then kissed my forehead. I tried to ignore him, but I couldn't, so I smiled at him. Jack shook his head at me, making it clear he thought I was a nut— *whatever*—and then he moved to the fire department and spoke with the Captain. I saw him point to the tire that exploded, and the Captain nodded his head. He then spoke to another fireman at his side. That man moved to the back of the hose truck and pulled out a tire iron, then moved to the now flameless truck and started to remove the damaged tire. I found this curious. Why did Jack need the tire? Tires exploded all the time, didn't they? My need to know everything, a good trait to have if you're a reporter, kicked in, and I spoke out loud to no one in particular.

"Now why does he need that tire?" Not expecting anyone to reply, I jumped when EMT guy, or Jake Jarred, as I now knew, spoke up.

"Probably because all the department vehicles got

new tires last month," Jake replied. Then he continued, "I bet there was a defect in the tire."

"So if a new tire explodes, it would have to be from a defect?"

"I'd think so, or someone shot it out while you were driving, but that would take a really good shot, or luck, I suppose."

"I don't remember hearing a gunshot."

"A long-range rifle would be silent from a distance."

"Who knows how to use that type of weapon?"

"Here in Colorado, in the mountains? Everyone old enough to shoot, including the women."

Well, that narrowed it down by the number of children in the area. Tapping my finger on my arm and wondering why someone would shoot out the sheriff's tire, it occurred to me that I might be jumping to conclusions. As Jake said, it was probably a defect in the tire, but it bugged me, and I couldn't let it go until I'd talked to someone. I looked around for Ben and found him with Gerry. Deciding I would pick Ben's brain, I thanked Jake for helping me and put out my hand to shake his. Jake smiled and took it, but as he shook it he looked over my shoulder and his smile fell. I looked behind me and saw Jack scowling at our friendly handshake and rolled my eyes. That man had a serious caveman complex!

Saying goodbye to Jake, I jumped down and walked over to Ben. Ben gave me a hug when I arrived, and we stood there and watched the fire department finish with Jack's truck. Needing to sort out the questions in my head, I turned to Ben and didn't beat around the bush.

"So, Ben, what causes a brand new tire to explode at

a high rate of speed?" Ben looked surprised by my question and thought for a moment.

"Only thing I can think of, darlin', is he ran over something, or it could be a defect in the tire."

"Could someone have shot it out with a rifle?" Ben narrowed his eyes at me and then nodded.

"Yeah, I could see that, but they'd have to be a good shooter."

"Better than most of the folks who live up in the high country all year?"

"I'd think so. Probably the only one around here who could make that kinda shot is Jack, though." That didn't surprise me; I was beginning to figure out that Jack was good at everything and didn't lose often, either. That would definitely make you cocky and self-assured. So, if Jack were the only one who could make that shot, maybe it *was* just something we ran over.

"What's running through your mind, Jenny?" Ben asked.

"Honestly, I wouldn't have thought anything of it, but Jack took an interest in the tire and had the fire department remove it from the truck, so I asked myself why."

"Good question to ask. Maybe we should be asking ourselves if this is connected to the killer. You being in the truck and doing an investigation? Could be it was you he was after."

"Ben, until right before I got in his truck, *I* didn't know I would be there, so how could the killer know?"

"Good point, so let's assume the sheriff is on to the killer, but he doesn't know it yet, and the killer doesn't want him to figure it out."

"I don't think Jack has found anything yet. He said there's no evidence pointing to anyone."

"Then it's probably just a fluke accident and us standing here speculating is just that: speculation."

"Okay, Ben, you're right. I must have hit my head harder than I thought." Ben ruffled my hair and smiled at me. Then he put his arm around me and pulled me into his side.

"Glad you're ok, Jenny. Would be a dull place again if something had happened to you." I nudged his shoulder, 'cause that sweet old man had no idea his words made me happy. Building something for myself here in Colorado, even if it was just a family of friends, was what I needed, and I'd adopted him as my father figure pretty much from the start. Lorraine taking me under her wing and giving me advice was putting her in the lead as my mother figure. Mandy definitely won the younger, crazier sister role, but where would Jack fall? Boyfriend? Lover? He said that after we slept together there was no going back, that I would be his, so I was thinking *"significant other."* Maybe I should get clarification of this before we slept together. If *I* was not supposed to date around, that sure as hell went double for Mr. *"I've-never-been-married-and-dated-half-the-population-of-Gunnison-County."* Watching Jack while thinking a talk was in order before we moved forward any more than we already had, Jack turned to our group and started moving toward us.

Looking around, he spotted Barry and called out to him to grab a lift to the station. Jack then made it to Ben and me and put his hands on my shoulders and squeezed.

128

"I gotta head to the station, Jenn. Can you catch a ride with Ben?"

"I'll take her straight home and put her to bed myself Jack, don't you worry."

Jack gave Ben a chin lift, then said, "Walk with me." He took my hand and walked me a distance away where no one could hear.

"Seems we've been interrupted again," Jack said grinning down at me.

"Seems we have, but maybe that's a good thing. I think we need to talk more."

"Talk about what?" he questioned.

"About what we're doing, Jack. I think we're rushing this thing between us."

"Jesus, leave you alone for thirty minutes and you start over-thinking things."

"I'm not over-thinking things. I just want to make sure we're on the same page, Jack." He stared at me a moment and then nodded.

"Ok, I get that. I'd take you home myself so we could talk, but as you can see, I've no vehicle *and* I need to file a report."

"Don't worry about it. Go do your job. This can wait until another time. I'm not going anywhere." I meant that too. Something clicked when I was riding in the truck with Jack, and I knew I would stop running from him; but I wasn't moving forward until we had some ground rules in place.

"Better and better," he whispered on a grin.

"What?"

"You, babe, keep getting better and better. You're not busting my balls 'cause I have to head to the station or pissed off that I'm leaving you in someone else's care instead of taking you home so we can talk. You understand I have a job to do, and you don't hesitate or have to think about your answer when I tell you I have to leave. It means you're not playing games and saying what I want to hear, so *you* keep getting better and better." Wow, that was direct and to the point and almost on the verge of insulting. Why would I have a problem with him doing his job? Yet, insulting or not, it was charming my pants off for some damn reason.

"Jack, it's already a given. You don't have to try and charm my pants off." His grin changed to a full-fledged knock-your-pants-and-panties-off smile, and then he pulled me close and buried his head in my neck.

"I intend to charm your top, bra, pants, and panties off you, and, depending on my mood, it may involve ripping, definitely biting... and a whole lot of sucking too," he whispered. I had no words for that. Nothing. I was completely void of speech. I shivered, and he moved to my neck, nipping and kissing, then he moved to my mouth, putting both his hands to my face, and kissed me deeply. I was a puddle of goo when he was done with the kiss, so he wrapped an arm around me and walked me, on shaky legs, back to Ben.

"Take care of her, old man," Jack instructed.

"Like I would my own daughter." Jack smiled at Ben then turned to me, cupped my face again and gave me a quick kiss.

"Later, Sweetness," he whispered against my mouth.

"Later, Jack," I whispered back and watched his eyes go soft before he pulled back and kissed my forehead, too, and walked away heading to Barry's truck.

I turned and watched him climb into the truck with Barry, then I looked at Barry and gave him a small smile and a wave. Barry raised his chin, but no smile. Sighing, because it seemed I'd lost a friend, I looked back at Jack, and he winked at me. So I smiled bright and winked back. *In for a penny, in for a pound, my mother always said... I couldn't agree more!*

Thirteen

Scream My Name

He's close; I can hear him behind me. I can't see him, but I can hear his breathing. He's laughing over and over again. I need to hide, but my legs feel like I'm running in quicksand. I hear a sound and turn to see Jack standing in front of me. His hand reaches out to me, and I reach for him. He'll save me; Jack will keep me safe from this unknown monster. My fingertips brush his, and he whispers, "I've got you, Jenn." A shot rings out and Jack stumbles back, blood spreading across his chest in crimson red, creating an abstract pattern of death. Jaaaaaack!

I woke with a start, my heart pounding as my dream slowly faded and reality hit. "It's just a dream."

I shuddered, thinking about the unknown killer stalking my dreams, chasing me. A vision of blood bleeding red across a white shirt as a pale Jack stumbled back reaching for me, as if I could save him...

"Oh, my God, that was so real." Turning on my side and looking out my window, I saw the moon rays shine down and create a lighted path across my yard. Searching into the darkness, a feeling of being watched rolled through me, and I closed my eyes.

"Stop it, Jennifer, you're safe." Glancing at the clock and seeing it was 12:45, I was surprised I'd fallen asleep so quickly. The adrenalin shot my system took after the crash had worn off, and I was bone tired when my head hit the pillow. I closed my eyes again, trying to settle into sleep, but then lights moved across my eyes, and I opened them to see a truck pulling up my drive. *Jack.*

Bounding from my bed, I headed to my front door. I could hear the sound of boots coming up my front steps, echoing in my cabin. I unlocked the door and threw it open, and Jack's face appeared in front of me, his arm raised, ready to knock. Without even thinking, I threw myself at him. He wrapped his arms around me and buried his head in my neck. His hands moved to grab my ass and picked me up. I didn't hesitate: I wrapped my legs around his waist, and he walked into my cabin, slamming the door with his foot. His mouth found mine and our tongues started a dance of seduction. I cupped his face and changed angles as he carried me to my bed. My tongue battled him for possession, wanting to take the lead, but Jack stopped me cold when he grabbed my hair and yanked my head back.

Both of us breathing fast, Jack looked into my eyes as his jaw grew tight, checking to see if I wanted this as much as him. I did. He saw it and dove back in for more. He controlled the pace; like everything about him, even his seduction of my body was bossy and possessive. He put a knee to my bed and lowered me to it without breaking the kiss. His lips moved from my mouth to my neck, licking and sucking his way to my ear.

"I can't get you out of my mind," he growled.

"Jack."

"I'm dreaming about you, your legs wrapped around my back while I pound into you."

"Oh, God."

"You're wet in my dreams, dripping for me. I need to feel that slick heat suck me in and clamp tight around my cock," he hissed, and I was done waiting. Screw talking, I needed him now.

"Please, Jack, fuck me," I begged.

"I'm not gonna fuck you, I'm gonna devour you till you scream my name."

With that, Jack was done, our mouths met again, and he began his possession of my body. Hands to my tee weren't slow and gentle, but forceful and sure. He grabbed the hem and pulled it over my head, throwing it to the floor. Sucking in his breath, my bare breasts exposed for the first time, his eyes scanned, heat and need on his face. Without a second thought, I sat up and pulled his shirt from his jeans, my mouth at his throat, showing him how he made me feel. His shirt off, I got my first sight of his broad chest, well-defined pecs, rippled stomach, and his bulging arm muscles, surrounded by tribal tattoos. I reached forward and ran my hand down his chest, down his stomach and back up, feeling his power and strength. I leaned forward, tongue to his nipple, and circled one then the other, and that was his undoing.

"Fuck," escaped his mouth and he yanked my head back by my hair. "I'm going to possess you, every fucking inch."

Breathing fast, I nodded and begged, "Please," then

reached for the buckle on his belt, released it and popping the button on his jeans. Jack looked down and watched as I slid the zipper down and released his cock. Smooth like satin, wide in girth and longer than I'd ever seen. I ran my finger over the crest, smearing his pre-cum, making him hiss.

"Jesus, Jenn."

Jack's mouth came back to mine, biting, sucking, devouring, as he pushed me down to the bed. Starting at my breasts, his tongue tasted and teased, sucking deep and biting, bringing my body from a slow burn to full-blown fire.

"I need to taste you and make you scream," Jack growled in my ear, then moved to my panties and ripped them from my body. My hips lifted, wanting his mouth, and he descended instantly. Tongue to clit, hitting the rhythm I needed as if he'd played my body a million times. His fingers ran through my hot, wet folds, and he moaned, "So fucking wet."

"Oh, God, Jack, what are you doing to me?" I panted.

"Making you burn for me."

And he was. His fingers entered me and found my sweet spot, curling them up, tapping, as his tongue kept at my clit. The combination of his thrusting hand, curled fingers, and his mouth built something in me I'd never felt before. It was overwhelming and scary with how big it felt.

"Ride my hand, baby, feel the burn and scream my fucking name," he ordered in a voice that could only be described as sexual possession.

I felt it burning, climbing, and it hit me with a force like no other, and then I did what he ordered. "Oh, God,

Jack." His fingers and mouth kept at my core as I exploded in a body-melting spasm of pure sexual bliss.

Before I could catch my breath, Jack moved, yanked his jeans past his knees, and pulled a condom from his pocket. I stilled his hand and shook my head, "I'm covered, and I haven't had sex in sixteen months."

His eye tightened, and he looked at the condom. "I've never gone without one." He didn't take but a moment to consider going unsheathed and tossed the packet, grabbed my face in his hands, and kissed me hard and deep, stoking my fire instantly. Kicking off his jeans, he raised himself up over me, scanning my body, his hand running its length, as his eyes followed its trail.

"Christ, you're beautiful," he muttered and then moved between my legs.

He held my eyes as he grabbed his cock and swiped across my folds before he slid in slowly, stretching me until I thought I would split. I gasped in a breath, tightening around him, and his eyes closed at the feel of it.

"You're burning hot." His breath hitched as he held still for a moment to control himself. Then he slid out to the tip and slammed back in.

"Jack."

"Jesus, you're so fucking tight, so damned hot."

Pulling out, then slamming back in, his mouth found mine, but his eyes stayed open as his rhythm became faster and harder, pounding me, stretching me, burning me from the inside out. I wrapped my legs around his back, allowing him to slip in further, and he groaned out, "Christ." I lifted my hips, meeting his pace as my nails scored his back. Jack arched into my nails, and his

136

pounding became more intense. He reached down and pulled me up to his chest, his hands at my hips lifting and slamming me back down. "Ride my cock, take all of me," he hissed.

The angle pushed him further in, and I felt the burn again, building to another peak that would spill over into bliss. I arched my back and Jack latched on to my nipple and bit down. That hit me right in my core, and I fell off the peak he'd built and screamed his name.

"Beautiful," Jack growled and pushed me back on the bed, grabbing my legs and pulling them up to his shoulders. His thrusting became more erratic, and his breathing more of a groan as he thrust into me and then slammed to the root, held it as he pulsated on a moan.

He collapsed onto my chest but held himself up with one arm. His face in my neck, lips kissing and tasting, light nips at my ear as we both recovered from our release.

"Jesus, baby, can't remember when I came that hard."

"I'm not complaining. You've got mad skills, Sheriff." Rising up and looking down at me, he smiled and laughed as he moved from between my legs and then curled me up into his chest. We lay like that for a while as we recovered, then I tipped my head back and asked:

"You wanna stay the night? I'll make pancakes in the morning."

Jack grinned, kissed my lips, and answered, "Considering I'll still be buried deep inside you when the sun comes up, yeah babe, I'll stay for breakfast."

"What?"

"Not finished with you by a long shot, that was just a warm-up."

a reason to breathe

"Wow."

"You got that right," Jack grinned; then his eyes went soft.

"Jesus, you're somethin' else." I liked hearing that.

So I told him, "You're not so bad yourself, Jack."

"I thought I was bossy?"

"You're that as well."

"And bullheaded."

"You heard that?"

"Heard the reckless and arrogant part too." I giggled, and his eyes warmed. I could stare at his warm, rugged face all night, but decided I'd rather kiss him, so I did, and he rewarded me for my forward thinking with his body on me, in me, and behind me for the rest of the night.

***

My phone ringing from the bedside table woke me from what little sleep I got last night. Turning to the clock and seeing it was 6:45 and I wasn't due in the station until nine, I knew this couldn't be good. Jenn was lying on me, so I reached across her, nabbed the phone, and I hit answer.

"Gunnison."

"Sheriff, it's Barry. We've got another body."

"Jesus, same M.O.?"

"Same M.O., but the victim wasn't brunette, Jack. It was Naomi."

"Say that again," I growled.

"It was Naomi. She was found on the same road as Cindy Baker."

"Christ, I'll meet you there in twenty. How far apart were the dumpsites?" He ignored my question and asked one of his own.

"You gonna drive like the devil to get there in twenty?"

"I'm not at home."

"You in Crested?" He was fishing, and I knew it, so I didn't make him wait for the answer he knew he would get.

"At Jenn's."

"Right," he replied, but his tone was angry.

"Barry, I don't have time for a pissing match. What's the location of the dumpsite?" Jenn had woken up during this discussion and was staring wide-eyed at me. I rubbed her back, trying to indicate all would be fine as I waited for Barry's answer.

"New dump site is right on top of the old one, Jack. You know exactly where to go." I didn't miss the double meaning of his words. It was obvious that his attraction to Jenn was more serious than I knew, so I'd give him that play, once, but another conversation needed to be had.

"Right, see you in twenty." I hung up before he responded, then rolled to Jenn.

"Did you say there was another body?"

"Yeah, babe."

"Anyone I know?" she asked with fear in her eyes.

I pulled her closer then kissed her temple and whispered, "Baby, it was Naomi." She reacted the way I thought she would, by jerking back with a gasp. What I did not expect was for her to tear up and ask,

"You ok, Jack? I'm so sorry."

"Babe, it sucks like hell that she lost her life like that,

but don't worry about me. I'm fine." She nodded her head, and I pulled her back in. She wrapped me in a hug, and I took it for a moment. I needed to leave, though, so I kissed her head, and then squeezed her so I could get up.

"I'll make you some coffee for the road."

"Appreciate that. Sorry I can't stay for pancakes. You wanna have lunch if I can break free later?" I was putting on my pants when she stopped on the way to the kitchen, then turned to me and bit her lip.

"Um, can't do lunch today, Jack. I have a lunch date with the mayor." Christ, I'd forgotten about that dick.

"Jenn, had my cock buried deep inside you more than once in the past six hours, and believe me when I say this: I. Don't. Share. I'll give you this lunch since it was made before we started, but after today, I'm gonna be pissed as hell if you make any more."

She studied me for a moment then smiled and turned to walk back to the kitchen, demanding as she went, "Goes both ways, Jack. If I'm not sampling the single men in this town, neither are you." Raising my brows at what she said, she caught it and laughed, then corrected herself. "No single ladies for you, no single men for me."

"Looks like we have an agreement then," I replied as I made my way to her. I grabbed her waist and pulled her close. "Far as I can tell, there isn't anyone who pisses me off or turns me on as much as you, and that means I've got no reason to look around." That got me a grin, so I decided to kiss it off her face. After I finished devouring her, I left her standing in the kitchen leaning against the counter, face flushed and eyes bright with the recent reminder of why she was now mine. And considering how much I'd enjoyed it, I intended to keep reminding her for a good long while.

Fourteen

You Done Poked A Viper

Jack left me in a state of, well, unfulfilled sexual need, so much so I considered getting my still-packed-in-a-box vibrator out of storage. I made coffee and picked up my clothes from last night, thinking about Jack the whole time. I can't remember when I'd felt so alive around someone and realized that included Doug. I knew it wasn't fair to compare them; Doug took good care of Bailey and me. Our need to get married out of respect for our situation and our parents wasn't basis for marriage, and even though it was a happy relationship, it wasn't passionate, not at all like I was feeling with Jack, and that scared the shit out of me. *Is this how it's supposed to feel?* I looked at my watch, saw it was 7:30 my time, which meant 8:30 Indiana time, so I picked up my phone and called my daughter, needing an escape from my own thoughts.

"Hola, Mamacita, how was lunch the other day with the sheriff?"

"Good morning to you, too. You don't waste any time getting down to business."

"Got class in twenty, need to make this quick, so: did you like him, will you see him again, have you seen him again, and if so was the sex any good?"

"Jesus, the thought of discussing sex with my twenty-year-old daughter seems wrong on so many levels."

"Get with the times, Jennifer. We women love sex, need sex, and talk about sex, just like the men."

"Bailey, women also need to be careful when engaging in sex, as in taking precautions, so you don't end up like your mother, barefoot and pregnant instead of at school having fun." Realizing what I'd said, I added, "Not that I would trade you for a college experience, not ever, but you know what I mean, right?"

"Got ya, Mom, I know that and I'm careful. What about you? Are you being careful?" I stood there for a second, feeling like I was in the twilight zone. Bailey had always done her own thing, said whatever was on her mind and didn't care what others thought of her. So her asking about my sex life wasn't a topic she figured was out of bounds. Clearly, I needed to adjust to this new stage of our relationship...A baby raising a baby was what we'd always been, and we were so close, like sisters or best friends. She always talked to me and was never afraid to say anything, not like the other kids felt with their mothers. But for the first time since I gave birth, I was regretting that...*You made your bed, now lie in it.* She wanted to know, and I couldn't start acting like a "mother" now.

"Um, yeah, I'm being careful, Bailey. I've been on the pill since I delivered you." And I had. I wasn't ready for her, so I sure as hell wasn't ready for another one. But somewhere along the way, not being ready for another baby never transpired into me even wanting another child. My bond with Bailey was so close that I was afraid

I couldn't love another child as much as her and selfishly didn't want to lose that closeness.

"Awesome. Ok, so in twenty words or less, was he any good, do you see it going somewhere, and does he make you laugh?"

"Ok, Bailey, I used to think there was nothing we couldn't talk about, but I'm starting to think I was wrong."

"That good, huh?" Damn, she knew me too well. If something irritated me, I ranted for hours. If I wasn't talking, it was completely different. She knew I really liked Jack. Knowing she wouldn't give up until I answered her, I went with the truth.

"He's amazing, stubborn, bossy, and fearless... and scary as hell." And he was. He also made me feel so many different things it was a wonder I had room for anything else to penetrate.

"Mom," Bailey whispered, and I felt a lump in my throat. Dammit, I should have thought about how that would make her feel.

"Bailey, I didn't mean to imply your father—"

"Don't, Mom. Dad is gone, and I know you loved him, but I also know you married him for me. You had a great relationship, I know that, too. But this? This is not about him, and you need to quit apologizing for moving forward." God, I loved my daughter.

"How did you get to be so smart at such an early age?"

"Grandma."

"Thanks." We both laughed because it was true. Doug's mother was as smart as a whip, and Bailey took after her. Even looked like her.

"Gotta scoot, Mamacita. Don't do anything I wouldn't

do, and tell the sheriff he'd better be good to you or I'll fly in from South Bend and have a word with him." I rolled my eyes, 'cause she wasn't lying: she would do exactly what she said.

"I'll tell him. Make me proud, baby, and I'll see you in a month. I love you, Bailey, so much."

"Love you too, Mom, bye."

***

After much-needed coffee and a much-needed shower that helped with the loss of sleep and noodle limbs from hours of sexual fulfillment, I changed into something appropriate for my lunch with the mayor. I wore a black, long-sleeved turtleneck —no boobs showing for this girl—with a pencil skirt in a warm taupe color. Black boots and silver hoops finished off the look, and I thought I looked good even if I didn't have the enthusiasm for lunch. To say I didn't feel up to going would be accurate. I wasn't even sure why I'd agreed to lunch with John; he wasn't the type of man I would be attracted to. But he'd pursued, and I couldn't seem to decline, so I was stuck eating lunch with the man, knowing my mind would be on Jack throughout it. *I'll just eat a quick bite, thank him, and make an excuse about a story of some sort.*

That settled, I was gathering my bags when I heard a knock at my door. Surprised I would have company this early, I checked out the window and saw Gerry standing on the porch. I moved to the door and opened it to his smiling face.

"Hey, Gerry, what's up?"

"Heard there was another killing last night and wanted to check on you."

"That's so sweet. I'm shocked, but ok."

"That whole situation last night with Naomi was crazy, and now she's dead... that just seems a little coincidental to me."

"How so?"

"Her getting killed after having it out with you."

"She obviously went out again after Phil took her home. What's that have to do with me?"

"Maybe nothing, but Naomi just ended things with Jack, and Shannon Davis and Jack dated a few years back. Just thinking maybe this killer has a problem with Jack, and since you and him seem to be starting something, I figured I better check on you and maybe convince you to stay away from him until this blows over."

That got my attention. Jack hadn't shared the fact he had dated the Davis woman. Could this be connected to Jack? Should we warn the other women he'd dated if this *was* about him?

"Gerry, do me a favor? Make a list of all the women Jack has dated in the past. Maybe we should consider this is about Jack. Maybe warn these women to be careful."

"I agree, and maybe anyone involved with him now should watch their backs as well."

"I'll take that under advisement, Gerry, but it won't stop me from writing this story."

"You're too damn tenacious for your own good, girl. I just hope it doesn't get you into trouble. You want me to call Ben and meet you at McGill's to make up the list?"

"Yeah, let me call Lorraine and run this past her, and then I'll meet you there."

Gerry agreed and then left to go find Ben. I was getting ready to call Lorraine when my phone rang, and I saw it was Jack.

"Jack."

"Hey, baby, I'm gonna be tied up most of the day with this and I've got the late shift again tonight. Just wanted to let you know I'll be out of pocket if you need me for anything."

"Ok, thanks for letting me know. Hey, Jack...?"

"Yeah?"

"Naomi is the second woman you've dated who's been murdered by this guy. You think maybe this about you?"

"Christ, you're in reporter mode right now, aren't you?"

"Well, yeah. Gerry came by and informed me about Shannon Davis, and it hit me: two women in a row had you in common." I let that hang there to see if he'd come to the same conclusion.

"Yeah," was all I got, but it said a lot. He wasn't arguing with me, so I figured he'd come to the same conclusion. Making a mental note to ask Ben and Gerry who was Jack's biggest rival for women's affections, I was broken from my thoughts by Jack.

"Gotta go, baby. Just wanted to touch base and remind you what I said earlier." Confused by that, I asked.

"Remind me of what?"

"That I don't share. Won't be happy if I hear anything about your lunch with the mayor being anything other than business." Smiling at the phone, because really, who wouldn't like hearing a man like Jack sound possessive in a way that made you feel wanted?

"I understand, Jack." I giggled.

"That's my girl," Jack's voice purred down the line. Caught in his spell again, I cleared my throat to say goodbye.

"Talk to you later."

"Later, baby. Be good."

"Later, Jack. Stay safe."

***

Christ, what a clusterfuck.

Naomi's dead, Shannon's dead, Cindy Baker, Jamie Smith, all dead and I had nothing to lead me in the direction of this guy.

Naomi's body was found in the same spot as Cindy Baker's, the killer making it clear who put her there. Liver temperature and rigor put her death around midnight, and Phil last saw her at 9 P.M. I had a team headed to her house to see if she was abducted from there or left on her own accord. Not to mention, this made it the second woman I'd been involved with who ended up dead, and the coincidence wasn't being ignored. No, wasn't ignoring this bastard. Not now, not ever.

Shannon's funeral was tomorrow, and I planned on having eyes on the funeral for anyone who looked more on edge than just a typical griever. FBI was sending their profile this afternoon, and if they could free up someone from their overworked team, they would send them, but until then, I was on my own.

Drew called and wanted to talk to me about what

he'd found on Naomi. The garage that serviced all our vehicles called to say they found something interesting with my tire. It wasn't 10 o'clock yet, and it felt like midnight. Sleep had been short the last few nights, one from investigating this killer, another from working the late shift, but mostly because of a sexy brunette who I couldn't keep my mind or hands off even if I tried. The mayor wasn't far off base when he said I didn't have my head in the game.

Jenn had walked into my life three days ago, opened her mouth, sassed me, ignored my orders, and then showed her innocent side that made the man in me stand up and take notice. Then she showed her stubborn and independent sides that made the man in me stand up and take notice again. I'd had a very loose hold on dragging her off, spanking her, fucking her and marking her as mine since she opened her mouth, and last night I was done. I wasn't waiting another minute. Then the freak accident with the tire, a tire that was brand new, and with Jenn's comment about someone trying to stop us, started me thinking that tire shouldn't have exploded the way it did. So I had the fire department take the tire to the garage and now I'd got the garage telling me I needed to see something.

My instincts kicked in last night and what they came up with pissed me right the hell off. Depending on what the garage said, it would determine the direction I would take this investigation. I didn't believe in coincidences, and if someone *had* tampered with my truck, then I'd go with the assumption that someone out there had a bone to pick with me.

I didn't know the first two victims, and I didn't know

what to make of them in this scenario. Why kill women I didn't know, and then start to kill women I'd slept with if the killer was the same person who messed with my tire? I needed to think this through; something wasn't adding up. I needed to sit with the evidence and go over it with new eyes. If I assumed I was the connection and examined the evidence we had in a new light, maybe something would hit.

Pulling into Gunnison Auto Repair, I saw Grimsby come out of the back and wave. I got out and headed into the office, where he was pulling up a page on his computer.

"What do you have for me, Grim?"

"Your tire was cut on purpose. The cut was along the center tread, more than three inches... Sheriff, no way was that an accident, and based on what I've found during a Google search, asking the question, *"What causes a tire to explode while driving?"* I found this explanation: *"When a tire ages, it causes the tread to separate, which then allows the inner tube to expand out of the wall, eventually causing a blowout."*

Grimsby moved to my tire and pointed to the tread, then continued, "And look here, Sheriff, you can see where someone went to the trouble of sawing back and forth on your tire to avoid puncturing the inner tube."

"You're telling me that you have no doubt, none whatsoever, that my tire was purposely tampered with?"

"That's what I'm saying."

"That internet search tell you how wide a separation was needed for maximum explosion?" Grimsby smiled, looking like the cat that got the cream and said, "Oh, yeah, three to four inches." *Sonofabitch.*

I thanked Grimsby and slapped him on the back, then headed to my truck. My head was pounding with anger, and I knew that if I checked my blood pressure, it would be sky high. This jackass wanted to fuck with me, try and warn me off, or worse, kill me? Game on. I was determined before, but he'd made a miscalculated error: he messed with me while Jenn was with me, which in turn meant he messed with Jenn.

Grimsby watched as the sheriff climbed into his truck. Shaking his head, thinking that whoever this guy was who messed with the sheriff was a stupid fuck. He didn't know it yet, but he poked a viper last night, and vipers were lethal when they're pissed. Yup, he'd enjoy watching this fucker get his comeuppance. If you were stupid enough to challenge a man like Jack Gunnison, then you were just plain stupid.

Fifteen

Manwhore

I watch her leave, and I realize I need to get control back. I'm getting reckless. Naomi wasn't in my plans, but everyone knew she'd hit Jennifer, and it spread through the town like wildfire. It burned my gut the slut laid a hand on my perfect girl. And then the sheriff, that damned knight in shining armor, had whisked her off in his truck. I was her knight... I should have been the one to rescue her. She could have died last night. When I tampered with his tire, I hadn't thought that Jennifer would be in the truck. Stupid, I should have known. Of course he would put her in his truck at some point, he's pursuing her at a rapid pace. I can see now that killing him will have to be up close and personal. I can't risk something that might put her in danger. Time to eliminate this threat. It's past time for the sheriff to die. I can't let him soil my innocent, beautiful girl. She's perfect, just like my Annie. I lost her once; I won't lose her again.

"Hear you and the sheriff got in an accident last night." I looked up from my porch as I made my way to Lorraine's car and saw Mandy standing at the passenger door, smiling at me. Something in her smile told me she knew what happened last night, and I wasn't talking about the car accident, either. So I ignored her question and waved. As I reached the car and crawled in the backseat, Mandy climbed in and then turned around with expectant eyes.

"Hey Mandy, what are you doing here?" I offered as an avoidance tactic.

"Lorraine figured, since I was already involved, I'd want to help out." Nodding and looking at Lorraine, she shrugged, "I was at the coffee house when you called, and Mandy was there; I told her about your accident and she told me about your trespassing and decided we could use all the help we could get."

"Ok, but Mandy, you can't talk to anyone about this, all right? Jack would have my head."

"Gotcha, mum's the word."

"Thanks for picking me up, Lorraine. I forgot my car was still in town."

"Yes, the sheriff did seem eager to get you home last night." She grinned and then pulled out of my drive. I tried to ignore her meaning, but Mandy wasn't about to let it go.

"So, you and the Sheriff did the horizontal tango, huh?"

"Jesus, Mandy, this isn't high school. I'm not talking about what happens with Jack."

"Oh, come on, is he really as good as everyone says he is? I don't trust those other women to tell me the truth." I looked at Lorraine and saw her equally expectant eyes staring back at me from the mirror.

"What have the others said?"

"That his bat is huge, and he knows how to swing it."

"That, ah, would be an accurate description of his baseball talents." I couldn't believe I'd been goaded into this. I watched Mandy and Lorraine hoot and holler, and then give each other a high five. *Good lord, women are worse than men.* Mandy turned around from the front seat, beaming.

"I knew a man that fine would have to be talented in bed."

"Can we move on to something else?" I pleaded.

"Hell no, I want the details, as in every last inch of them." I stared at her for a moment and then figured what the hell? Men talked about women all the time. So I told them the events of last night, and after I'd finished, they were both quiet. Lorraine, unfortunately, was the first to speak.

"God help me, I miss sex," she said into the rear-view as she turned onto Elk Street heading towards McGill's.

"I miss sex and I'm only thirty." I looked at both women who were expecting a reply, so I figured if you couldn't beat them, join them.

"I missed sex after sixteen months."

"Try not having it for twenty years and then we'll talk." Mandy nodded her head then added, "Lorraine, you know they have these things you can use—"

"Got me one of those, girl, not the same as a sweaty man grinding on you." For the second time that day, I felt I'd entered the twilight zone. Lorraine admitting to using a vibrator was now burned into my brain, and let's face it: I loved her, but this was not something I needed to be picturing. She had to be pushing seventy.

"Outstanding, Lorraine, good to know that when I'm

as old as you I'll still be wanting sex."

"You'll want it. Problem is, will you be able to find a man who can provide it? They get limp at my age, you know." *Yep, another image I need to have removed.* Then it hit me Ben was single.

"Lorraine, why don't you ask Ben out for dinner?"

"You saying his parts still work?"

Shaking my head no, wondering why I'd opened my big mouth, I continued, "I don't really have that information. He just, uh, seems like a guy who might, um, you know, still be able to, ah, storm the cotton gin, as they say."

Lorraine was pulling into a parking space out front of McGill's when I finished that statement, hopefully never to be repeated *ever again,* and looked at me from the rear-view mirror.

"I'll ask him." *What?*

"What?"

"I'll ask him. We aren't getting any younger, gotta take the bull by the horns or the man by the dick, or is it cock? Is that what they're calling it these days, cock or dick?"

I sat in complete and utter silence when she finished, but Mandy burst out laughing, and Lorraine just smiled and winked at me, then got out of the car. *Oh, God, she isn't really going to ask him, is she?* I jumped out of the car, wishing I'd never opened my mouth and followed Lorraine, who was making a beeline for our table.

Ben was in his seat waiting, but Gerry hadn't arrived yet. Praying she was joking, I walked over to Rosie and placed a coffee order, then headed toward the table. I heard Lorraine say, "Call me," and tried not to look at Ben to see his reaction, but, God help me, I did, and he was grinning. Shit, now I knew his equipment still worked, beautiful...

Deciding it was time to move on to something else besides everyone's sex lives, I pulled out my notes and handed Ben, Mandy, and Lorraine a piece of paper.

"Since Naomi is the second woman Jack has dated to be killed, Gerry thought the killer might be connected to him in some way, and I tend to agree. So I want you three to write down every woman Jack has had a relationship with." Mandy took the paper, looked at it and then announced, "I'm gonna need more than one sheet of paper."

"That many?" I squeaked.

"Oh, yeah," she replied with wide eyes.

"Oh, my God." I felt the blood run from my face.

"Now, Jennifer, Jack's a man, he's single, and lots of women throw themselves at him. He hasn't had more than, say, six or seven real relationships since he was twenty," Lorraine added.

"Oh, my God, he's a manwhore, isn't he?" I replied, ignoring her.

"Jenny, he's a man, a man's man. He's busy taking care of the county, and that doesn't give him a lot of time for romance, so he gets it when he can," Ben added.

"So I'm just one of the women he "gets it from" when he can?" I asked, getting sicker by the minute. *Shit, what was I thinking, falling into bed with him so quickly?*

"Now darlin', I didn't say that. He acts different with you. In fact, don't think I've ever seen him act this way, now that I think about it." I didn't know whether Ben was telling the truth or trying to ease my growing anxiety, but I tried not to think I might just be another notch on Jack's bedpost.

"Where is Gerry, he was supposed to be here?" I inquired, sounding a little shrill even to my own ears. The others looked at me funny, and I realized I'd just moved on from the subject of Jack and that I did it with very little finesse.

Ben looked at Lorraine and then answered me, "He got a call from some folks wanting to take a ride down the river. Said he'd be back either in the morning or late afternoon."

"Ok, well, get to writing those lists then. If this killer is connected to Jack, we need to warn these women to be careful."

I lowered my head to avoid their stares and started digging through my bag, pretending I was looking for something. *Shit, am I another notch in his bedpost or am I more than that?*

Needing a distraction to take my mind off this until I could think in private, I decided to work on my story. Going over my notes and putting them in chronological order, I noted who was killed first, where they were from, how long they had lived there, hair color, eye color, and whether or not they knew Jack. The first two didn't, and it made me wonder. If the killer had a problem with Jack, why were the first two women strangers to him? And since Naomi was a blonde and the others brunettes, did the hair color even mean anything?

After fifteen minutes of writing, Lorraine, Mandy, and Ben compared their lists and added some more, then argued over some of the names. When they were done, they handed the list to me, and I looked at them before reading the names.

All three of them looked nervous.

I looked at the list and then went cross-eyed. Thirty-seven names were on it... *Thirty-seven. Holy Shit.*

I cleared my throat and then nodded, "Ok, right, well why don't we split up the list, we can each take names and get through them faster?"

Mandy stood and went behind the bar to grab the phone book from Rosie, and we all pulled out our cell phones. Taking my list of twelve names, I looked up the number for an Amber Mooney, dialed it, and prayed to God I could get through this. Unfortunately, not once did it occur to me that these women might know who I was—a stupid, silly, naive girl from Kansas—before I introduced myself.

"Hello."

"May I speak with Amber, please?"

"Speaking."

"Amber, this is Jennifer Stewart with the Gunnison Times—"

"Aren't you that woman Jack is seeing?"

"Pardon?"

"You're that new woman in town that Jack Gunnison is seeing?"

"I, ah, yes."

"Are you calling to ask me if you should run for the hills?"

"I, uh—"

"Run for the hills, sugar. He's nothing but heartbreak waiting to happen. That man will never settle down. Do yourself a favor and listen to me when I say R.U.N."

"Um, ok, I'll take that under advisement. I was calling to...oh, man...I was calling to tell you, that since there was another murder involving a woman that Jack dated, we thought you should be careful. You know, keep a lookout."

"Oh, my God, am I gonna be next?"

"Oh, I, shit, Amber, to be honest, we don't know what's going on, but since there were two women murdered who dated Jack, a group of us just thought we should warn you. You know, give a heads-up; that's all."

"So this isn't an official warning?"

"NO, no, I'm working on the story, and I just felt it was something that I should do, that's all."

"Oh, ok. Well, thanks for the warning. I guess I should say the same thing to you too. Keep your eyes open and be careful of the killer *and* Jack, if you know what I mean."

Nodding my head, 'cause I knew exactly what she meant, I thanked her for her time and hung up. I looked around the table, and all eyes were on me. I picked up my coffee, took a drink, and started looking for the next woman's number.

Not ready for another phone call like the last one, I listened as Ben, then Lorraine, fielded questions from women about how much danger they were in, when Mandy leaned into me.

"Jack's a good guy. Don't let these women make you think otherwise."

I was staring at Mandy, wondering if I'd make the cut or if I should just cut my losses now and run like Amber said, when my phone rang. I looked down at the screen and saw *"Bossy Calling."* Something told me not to answer it, but I didn't listen.

"Hello."

159

"Jesus, Jenn, what the fuck are you doing?"

"Um, warning women to be careful."

"You're starting a riot, that's what you're doing," he bit off. "My phone won't stop ringing; all the calls are from women I haven't talked to in years. I don't need this on top of everything else that is going on," he growled.

"I was just trying to give them a heads-up, Jack. They need to know to be safe."

"Jenn, *I* don't even know if this is connected to me and you've got every woman I've ever said hi to calling me to find out if they're next." Jack seethed, and I could feel my temper start to rise.

"I can see where that *would* be a problem since you've said "hi" to half the population of Gunnison," I snapped back.

"I never said I was a monk," he shouted.

"Well, thank God for that, because if this list of thirty-seven names even scratches the tip of the iceberg of whom you've slept with, then you're more likely to get invited to Hugh Hefner's house than the house of God," I shouted even louder.

"Jesus, I don't have time for this shit," he barked, and I could feel the tears forming in my eyes. I was just trying to keep these women safe, and *maybe* I didn't think it through before I called them, but even so, finding out how many women he'd been with and how unlikely it was that he would ever settle down and more than likely break my heart, I decided I didn't need some quiet reflection, I needed to end this now and save us both the trouble.

"I don't have time for this, either, Jack. In fact, I'll let you off the hook. Thanks for the ride last night, figuratively and literally speaking, but I have a date to get to, so you'll have to excuse me. I need to go."

"Jesus, Jenn—"

I hung up my phone before he finished and heard coughing around the table. Ben's eyes held sadness and Lorraine actually grinned at me.

"That will get his attention. He's never had a woman end things with him."

"What? I'm not trying to get his attention, Lorraine. I knew he was a serial dater and still let him in. I'm so stupid. I refuse to end up another name on that list." *Even though, technically, I'm already on it. Shit!*

"Jennifer, even an alley cat meets its match, and Jack isn't a serial dater. His mom and dad had a beautiful marriage; he's just been trying to find someone who completes him the way they completed each other."

"You're trying to tell me that out of all the women on that list, none of them was marriage material?"

"I'm telling you they all were, but none of them were the right one for Jack. He needs a woman who intrigues him, one who doesn't lie down and let him walk all over her. One who will do what she wants and ignore his macho man ways. He *needs* a woman who knows her own mind and isn't content with sitting at home waiting for him to walk through the door."

"I'm not sure a woman like that exists."

"I think she does. In fact, I think I'm looking at her right now." Stunned to hear that anyone saw me as a woman that independent, I smiled at her, and she winked. My phone started ringing again, and I saw *"Bossy Calling"* scrolled across the screen. I looked at Lorraine, then looked to Mandy, and then Ben said, "Answer him,

Jenny, he's waiting."

Taking a deep breath, I swiped the phone and put it to my ear.

"Hello."

"You over your snit?"

"No, but I'm getting there."

"You still remember what I said about the mayor?" Rolling my eyes because men moved on from fights like women moved on to gossip—quickly, if you're wondering—I answered him.

"Yes, I remember."

"Good, now do me a favor and stop calling these women. I'll save you some time and trouble by giving you some information: Amber is the only one who hates me, and once you called her, she made it her life's mission to call everyone else. She'll get the job done for you and free up your day... And just so we're clear. If you think I'll let you walk away from me that easily, you need to think again. After last night, no fucking way am I letting you go, so deal with it."

"Whatever," I snipped.

"Smartass."

"Bossy," I smiled.

"That's my girl." *Oh, my God, I think I am....*

Smiling and accepting my fate as Jack's woman, I told him goodbye, "I need to go, Jack, I have work to do and so do you."

"All right, Jenn, call me after your lunch with the mayor."

"Later, Jack."

"Later, Jenn."

I hung up the phone, only to meet three smiling

faces. "Never thought I'd see the day that some half pint of a woman could bring Jack Gunnison to his knees. If I hadn't seen it myself, I wouldn't have believed it," Ben laughed, so I rolled my eyes at him and grinned. These people were as close to family as I had here, and if they thought Jack was worth the time, I guess I did too.

I repeated Jack's message about Amber doing our job, and we decided to head into Gunnison to get my jeep. Mandy and I were climbing into Lorraine's car when Ben pulled Lorraine aside and whispered in her ear, then looked at his watch. Lorraine grew a smile and then kissed his cheek, and all I could think at that moment was: *Wait till I tell Bailey that sex doesn't end at fifty or sixty. Hell, sex doesn't even end at seventy.... Oh, God, does that mean my parents still do it?*

Sixteen

This Is Really Good Wine

"Just get in and get out, Jennifer. Be professional, it's just lunch, there's no reason to be nervous." Since my pep talks about Jack didn't seem to work, I wasn't holding out hope this one would, either. "Why did I say yes to lunch?" *Because he's the mayor and you're a reporter with no connections in town.*

Looking through the windows of The Lumberjack Steakhouse, I saw the mayor being escorted to a table, his head held high working the room as he walked. To say I didn't want to get out of the car and deal with this man after a passionate night spent in Jack's arms was an understatement.

Determined to eat quickly, I got out of my car and headed inside the rustic restaurant. It was tastefully decorated in authentic Colorado country charm, with knotty pine walls, carved lumberjacks flanking the outside doors, and it had a welcoming atmosphere. The wait staff was dressed in red-and-black-checked flannel, and they were throwing huge dinner rolls across the room when I entered. I'd heard about this restaurant, but had yet to eat here. I could tell this would be a fun place to eat with friends you actually wanted to be with.

cp smith

Turning in the direction I'd seen the mayor walking, I found John seated in a corner, in what I would describe as the most intimate location on the floor. He smiled brightly when I arrived and then reached out to take my arm and kissed my cheek, then, ever the gentleman he portrayed when in public, he helped me sit.

Trying to figure out how to act around this man when I wasn't attracted to him, I opted for professional.

"Mr. Mayor, how are you today?"

"Call me John, please, and I'm fantastic now. Having a gorgeous woman eat lunch with me always brightens my day."

I smiled even though I could tell he was trying to charm me, or, more to the point, charm the pants off of me.

"All right, then. John it is, and thank you, you look handsome yourself. But, then again, as mayor you do have to keep up appearances."

"Indeed, I'm very careful with my time, appearance, and, of course, the company I keep," he answered as he raised his glass in acknowledgement of me. I checked the eye roll that I wanted to give him and inclined my head at the compliment.

"So tell me, John, as mayor what do you think are your most important roles for this community?"

"Is this an interview, Jennifer, or a date?"

Neither, I wanted to say but bit my tongue.

"Sorry, it's an old habit I fall into."

John leaned forward and grabbed my hands and whispered, "I'm not going to bite, Jennifer. Give me a chance."

Oh, God, now what do I say? This man was clearly

165

used to getting his way; I'd heard stories about him after I agreed to this lunch, but in an attempt to not anger *"The Mayor,"* I decided to come. Then I met Jack and my desire to be here was nonexistent. *How do I get out of this without pissing him off?* I decided to go with honesty.

"Funny, John, of course I don't think you'll bite, although I must admit I am a little afraid of your claws," I answered, hoping he would catch on to the fact that I knew he could be vicious in his pursuits. The fact that he wanted to find a way to get Jack voted out and his son in as sheriff was not lost on anyone, but he didn't seem to notice or change course.

"You afraid I'll scratch you, darlin', make you bleed?" I shook my head, caught off guard by his provocative tone. Looking for a distraction, I noticed a waiter approaching.

"Oh, look, here's our waiter." A man with a nametag that read Frank smiled down at our still linked hands. I instantly pulled mine from John's, embarrassed, then sat back trying to put as much distance between us as I could. Frank introduced himself as the owner of the restaurant and crooned on about how wonderful it was to have the mayor and his beautiful companion at his establishment for lunch. I couldn't help but think that, between the kiss on the cheek and the hand holding, if Jack heard about it, he wasn't going to be happy. Ha! Pissed was more like it. Frank pulled me from my thoughts of Jack and his temper, announcing he would fix the mayor and me our hearts' desires. A to-go box was on the tip of my tongue, but I bit it.

"Anything you want, on or off the menu, Mayor Hall,

and, of course, for your beautiful companion." Wishing again I'd rethought my decision to come here today, I took the menu and opened it to avoid looking at either man. I had no appetite, though, but I needed to eat and then make an excuse to leave. I wasn't that lucky, because while I was scanning the menu, I heard John order two house specials, a bottle of their best wine, and the instructions that we wanted privacy. *Seriously, what if I don't eat red meat, and what is it with the men in this town, pretty much deciding everything for a woman?*

I handed my menu to Frank and smiled tightly, thinking the only thing he ordered that sounded appealing was the wine, but I just kept my mouth shut. More than ready for this lunch date to end, I started figuring out in my head how long it would take me to eat and then make my excuse to leave.

Frank left, saying he'd be right back with our bread and wine, so I searched for something to say to kill the time until I could fill my mouth with food and avoid conversation altogether.

"So, John, tell me about being mayor. Is it as exciting as it seems, or tedious and boring?"

"Exciting is a term I'd use for someone as sexy as you, so no. Tedious and boring covers most days, but there are benefits...long lunches with tantalizing reporters, for example."

Oh, my God, this guy was a slimy player with a capital 'S'. Did women really fall for this guy? Frank rescued me again from answering when he arrived with our wine and bread. After he filled my glass I reached for it immediately, needing the liquid reinforcements for the lunch ahead, and drank down half of it, feeling the effects hit my head and calm my nerves quickly.

"So, Jennifer, you have a daughter at Notre Dame? You must be proud." Perfect, a topic that wouldn't lead him down paths of flattery or sexual undertones.

"Yes, Bailey. She's great. Smart, beautiful, funny—"

"When she comes to town for the holidays, we can introduce her to my son, Grady, make a foursome out of it."

A foursome? I smiled, but made no comment. No way in hell was I introducing my daughter to his son; he's probably just as arrogant as the mayor. Grabbing my wine and finishing off my glass, I wondered how I got into this situation. Oh, yeah, I'd said yes. Clearly not my smartest move. Speaking of not so smart moves...

"More wine, please," I replied to his request to go on a double date with his son. John smiled and filled my glass, so I took another drink, or a gulp, well chugged it, really. I figured a wee bit tipsy might help me get through this lunch.

John watched me drink and then asked, "So, what do you think?"

"I think the wine is delicious, thank you for ordering it," I replied.

John laughed for some reason and topped off my wine again, then smiled sweetly at me. If he smiled like that and didn't act like an ass, he'd be a real catch. Taking another drink, I felt the warm rush of the wine relaxing my limbs. Much better.

"What I meant *was,* what do you think about your daughter and my son?"

"I think Bailey would love to meet someone her own age," I slurred. Wait, that wasn't right. I didn't want her to meet the mayor's son, did I?

John filled my glass again, and I thought to myself that he was so polite and attentive; so I lifted my glass and took another huge swallow of the best wine I'd ever tasted.

"So what are you doing the rest of the day, Jennifer?"

"Well, after this fantastic lunch I was going to go...um go...there was something I was going to do at the office, I think."

"I have my car with me, so, if you'd like, we could go for a drive and I could show you some of the countryside you haven't seen yet. I have a cabin about thirty minutes from here. You'd love the views." Finishing off my second glass—or was it my third?—I thought about the forest and views and wondered if he'd seen bears there.

"Do you have bears there?"

"Bears? I'm sure there are, why?"

"I haven't seen one yet and would love to see a bear...it's why I moved here."

"You moved here for bears?"

"Um, yeah, I mean...when I was a little girl, I wanted to live with the deer and bears here in Colorado, so when it was time to move, I came here to follow my dream."

"Well, I'm sure if we left out some food, the bears would come. Would you like to do that, take some food up and look for bears?"

"Why not? Sounds like fun."

John continued to talk about his cabin and the surrounding mountains near Ouray, and I continued to sip my wine. Noticing my glass was empty, he picked up the bottle to fill it again, but it was empty. John raised his hand and snapped his fingers, then asked Frank to bring us another bottle.

I was just about to say thank you, since it was the best wine I had in my life, when I heard a voice above me say, "Dad." I turned to see a good-looking, much younger man, dressed in a deputy's uniform. Did he just call the mayor *"dad"*?

"Grady, son, good to see you. Are you eating here or...?"

"I'm here to see Frank about some vandalism. Ms. Stewart, how are you today?"

John snapped his fingers at Frank, drawing my attention away from his son, and then he whispered in Frank's ear when he approached. I turned back to Grady at his question, trying to remember what he'd said.

"I'm peachy keen. Would you like to meet my daughter?"

"Ma'am, if your daughter is anything like you, I'd be happy to."

What a nice kid.

"You wanna come with us to your dad's cabin? We're going up to look around and see if I can find my first bear."

Grady frowned, looked at his father, then shook his head no. He studied me for a moment before he answered, "I'll pass, Ms. Stewart."

"Oh, call me Jenn, your boss does," I giggled.

"Yes, Ma'am, Jenn, I'll be sure to remember that. Dad, Jenn, I'll let you get back to your lunch. I just wanted to stop and say hello." His mention of lunch made me look behind him. Since I'd skipped breakfast, I was really hungry, and my head was spinning from the wine, so I needed to eat.

170

"Is our food here?"

"I thought we might enjoy it more at the cabin. I'm having Frank pack it up for the road." Thinking that made sense, but needing to eat to clear my head, I realized I'd lost track of the conversation when cute man-boy Grady, said, "I wouldn't advise that, Dad," then tipped his hat to me as he stepped back and headed quickly outside, his phone to his ear.

After waiting for our food to be packed, John asked if I was ready to go. Needing some air and a bathroom break, I excused myself to freshen up before we left. *Wow, the room's really spinning...maybe I should get some coffee. We could stop at The Bean on the way out of town. Maybe Mandy would like to come on a road trip, or Jack? I wonder if Jack likes taking road trips? We could make a day of it.*

"Oh, sorry, wrong door,"

Wow, Mandy should hang out here...like right here, outside the men's room. It would save you some trouble if you knew ahead of time what their shortcomings were. Ha, shortcomings. Purse, purse, where's my...did I leave it at the table? I was rounding the corner, moving back to the table to look for my purse when I saw Jack walk in, heading straight for our table.

"Where the fuck is she?"

"Sheriff, is there something I can do for you?"

"Cut the crap, John, where's Jenn?"

"She's freshening up. Now, is there a problem?"

"Just saving my woman from your obvious game of *"get'em drunk'n fuck."*

"I didn't force her to do anything."

Jack tensed and started to move towards the mayor,

171

so I walked up to him and put my hand on his arm.

"Jack." He turned to me, gave me a once-over for some reason, then pulled me next to him while he grabbed my purse off the chair.

"Let's go," he growled.

"Is something wrong?"

"Uh, yeah, Jenn, but we'll talk about that later once you've sobered up." Smiling, since I'd rather spend time with Jack, I turned to John and put out my hand.

"Mayor, thanks for lunch and have a safe trip."

John stepped forward, looking angry, and Jack moved between us, muttering, "Don't touch her." Then he took my hand and led me to the front of the restaurant and out the door. I had a hard time keeping up with his long legs, so I tugged on his hand.

"Jack, slow down, I can't walk this fast. My head is spinning." Jack kept walking, and I kept spinning, until we got to his truck, where he swung me around and then pinned me to the door. I gasped and looked up at him. His eyes were narrowed, and pissed wasn't the word I would use to describe his expression: livid was more accurate.

"Jack, what's wrong?"

"I'm too fucking busy to do what I should do, and I don't need the hassle of beating the shit out of the mayor for getting you drunk."

"He got me drunk?"

"Yeah, Jenn, and if Grady hadn't called me, you'd be on your way to his secluded cabin in the woods, where I have no doubt he would have convinced you to sleep with him."

"I thought we were going bear hunting?" Jack looked

at me funny and then shook his head.

"Jesus, you'd trust anyone, wouldn't you?" Jack whispered as he pushed into me. His hard body pressing into mine sent my thoughts in a different direction than the mayor altogether.

"Jack?"

"Yeah, baby."

"I'm drunk, and you're here and very, very hard up against me...I've got an idea." Jack ran his nose down my throat and back up to my ear.

"What's that?" he whispered in my ear, and then nipped my lobe gently.

"How about you take me to lunch at your house and have your wicked way with me?"

"Jesus, are you real?"

"Last time I checked."

"Let's test that theory then." Jack nipped my neck and then opened his truck door and lifted me into the cab. I watched as he pulled out his phone and called the station to say he was at lunch for the next hour; then he climbed in the cab, gave me a sexy grin, started the truck, pulled out, and headed towards his house.

***

"Jesus, you're fucking drenched," Jack hissed as he slid his hand into my panties, swiping a finger through my folds.

I was trying to kick my boots off when Jack slammed me into the closed door of his house, pressing into me. Capturing my mouth, his hands pulled up my skirt and then moved into my panties, slipping two fingers inside.

173

a reason to breathe

While his fingers built a fire inside me, I tried to hold still but the feeling was so intense I started riding his hand.

"Jack," I cried out, trying to find release, when he growled, "Fucking beautiful the way you light up for me." He withdrew his hand and picked me up, carried me to the sofa, and put me down next to the arm. He grabbed my skirt and pulled it up, then slid my panties off. "Turn around," he barked as he undid his jeans.

I wasted no time and turned to the arm. Jack moved in close behind me and ran his hands up both my sides, taking my turtleneck with them, pulling it over my head. With nimble fingers, he unhooked my bra and slipped it off my shoulders, then with a hand to my back, pushed me forward until I was laid out across the arm. "Gonna ride you hard, baby, so hold on," Jack hissed, and I whimpered as he stepped up between my legs and then tapped them.

"Open up, and let me see you." As if I was hypnotized and could do nothing but what he asked, I opened my legs wider for him, giving him the view he wanted. Jack ran his hand down my ass and then entered my core with his fingers, spreading my wetness, and plunging back in again, stoking the fire within me. I swiveled my hips, keeping rhythm with his hand, and when I felt his hard cock against my leg, I pushed back, wanting to feel him enter me.

"You hot for me?" he whispered in my ear as his fingers curled up and hit the spot. Oh, God, the feeling that was building was incredible, consuming. His thumb rubbed my clit, his fingers tapping my core again, and I knew it was going to be huge when I came.

"Jenn, you gonna ignite for me?"

174

"Yes, Jack," I whimpered, my hand digging into the couch, needing something to hold on to and brace myself against. This feeling he was building in me was earth shattering, and I felt like I would fall if I didn't hang on.

"You wanna feel me stretch you tight?"

"Please, Jack." Jack removed his hand, positioned himself at my entrance, and growled, "You got it, baby." Then he slowly, with the patience I didn't have, pushed inside me. I couldn't wait; he'd built me up to a boiling point, and I needed the friction. I slammed back against him and seated him to the root. "Jesus," Jack groaned while I kept pulling out and slamming back into him.

"You want my cock?" He thrust deep. "You want the burn?" He slapped my ass, and that caused my core to contract around him. Jack hissed and pounded me even harder. But it still wasn't hard enough. I was out of control with need for this man, his hands and cock were taking me places I'd never been before, and I needed more of everything.

"Jack, harder."

He started pounding me so hard I thought I'd split in two. His rhythm became a perfect balance of slamming and hip swirls that hit every nerve. I was right there, and then his hand came forward and met my breast, pinching and pulling my tight-budded nipple. My head flew back onto his shoulder, and I screamed his name, silencing the sound of flesh slapping against flesh. Jack grunted, then bit my shoulder, holding me in place, as he slammed his own climax warm into my core.

His thrusting slowed and became more of a caress as I turned my head and found his mouth, starting a battle with his tongue. As the kiss ended, he wrapped his arms around me and held me tight against his chest. I felt his lips at the crown of my head, and what I thought was a whispered, "Christ, fucking perfect." Considering my climax was pretty amazing, I nodded and agreed.

"Drunk sex is pretty perfect."

Jack chuckled and tightened his arms around me, kissing and nipping my neck. We stayed that way for a few moments, nuzzling and kissing, when suddenly Jack bent, picked me up, and headed down his hall.

"Shower and then coffee," Jack ordered.

"No shower, I'm too noodle-legged to stand," I begged.

"I'm not letting you drive until you're sober, so it's either some coffee and shower or you can stay here and sleep it off."

Liking the idea of climbing into his warm bed, I nuzzled his neck and purred.

"Bed it is," he barely said before I was thrown through the air and landed on his bed. Jack landed on top of me, looked at his watch, and grinned.

"Twenty minutes left of my lunch break. I only need five to change, so I think I'll use the rest of that time to help you sleep."

Liking this idea a lot, I replied, "You gonna talk about it or get to work?"

Jack grinned bigger and replied, "Yes, Ma'am," then got to work helping me sleep, and it must be said, I slept like the dead!

Seventeen

Kryptonite

I woke to the moon shining through the window. My head was pounding, and I had to think about where I was. Jack's face filled my mind, and I remembered our lunchtime tryst. Feeling around for the lamp on the bedside table and turning it on, I cursed when the light hit my eyes. What on earth possessed me to drink that much? *Oh, yes, Mayor Hall, douche bag extraordinaire.*

Looking around Jack's bedroom, I saw clothes scattered on the floor. His tastes in décor were rugged...plain, simple, all man. He had a huge knotty pine log bed, black comforter, and black sheets. Instead of pictures, he had some type of Indian art hanging on the walls, which were painted a warm toffee color. His chest and dresser matched the bed, and from the looks of the hand-turned wood, I'd say he bought it locally from the master carpenters you saw around the area.

I sat up, thirsty and needing a drink. I turned to the edge of the bed and saw a large glass of water with two pills lying next to it. Smiling at Jack being so thoughtful, I took the pills and drank down the glass. Putting my feet to the floor to stand, I looked down at my body and saw no clothes.

"Yup, still naked." I needed my clothes, and a shower, but obviously not in that order. I grabbed a t-shirt from the floor, threw it over my head, and headed down the hall to find my clothes and purse.

The rest of Jack's house was decorated the same as his bedroom. Warm, honey-colored pine log furniture graced the living room and dining room. To say Jack embraced his Colorado heritage would not be wrong. Surprisingly, most of the house was tidy and well-kept; the only exceptions were his bedroom with his clothes on the floor and his kitchen, which opened to the living room. He had dishes stacked in the sink, and that didn't surprise me, either; Jack didn't seem like the type of man who cooked, and washing dishes was more than likely a low priority on his list. All in all, the house was very Jack, and I loved everything about it.

Grabbing my clothes and purse, I headed back down the hall to his bedroom. I pulled my phone from my purse and checked any missed calls. I'd missed five: two from Mandy, one from Lorraine, another from the mayor, and one from Jack. I wasn't about to call the mayor back now that my mind was clear. I realized Jack was right; he'd kept filling my glass, aware of my unease and hoping to get past my defenses. Bastard. So instead I hit redial on Jack's number.

"You're awake."

"I am. Hope you don't mind, but I'm taking a shower?" I turned the shower on to warm the water and then turned around to finish the call.

"You're calling me from the shower?"

"Of course not. I'm calling you from the bathroom before I get in the shower." There was a long pause, so

I called his name, wondering if the call had been dropped.

"Jack, you there?"

"You expect me to work knowing you're naked in my shower?" That made me smile. He was such a man.

"I didn't call to bother you; I just called to see when you would be home so I could get my car."

"Based on my speed, I'd say in about ten minutes," he purred down the line, and I felt my heart rate speed up. *What is it about this man that I can go from being a grown woman to acting like a teenager on her first crush?* Not caring at that point and with memories from this afternoon fresh in my mind, I had good reason to be excited.

"Ok, I'll see you when you get here." I tried for alluring, but it came out kinda croaked, though I didn't think he cared when his reply came back with a tight, "Right. See you in ten."

Wanting to be clean by the time he got home, I jumped in the shower and washed my hair. He didn't have conditioner, though. Men were so lucky like that. I focused on soaping up my body. I grabbed his toothbrush and toothpaste and brushed my teeth in the shower. "She-just-woke-up-from-being-drunk" breath was an instant mood killer in my estimation. While I was rinsing, I heard the bathroom door open and turned to see Jack pull his shirt over his head while locking his eyes on mine. His focused gaze moved down my body, then back up, as he kicked off his boots, unzipped his jeans and pulled them off, then opened the shower door, stepping in behind me.

"You missed a spot," he whispered as he grabbed the

soap, rubbing it back and forth between his strong hands. Seeing Jack standing there like that, water rolling down his body, clinging to the ripples of his muscles, I was incapable of speech. My mouth was open, but no words came out.

He twirled his finger, indicating I should turn around, so I did, all the while praying that my ass didn't look as huge as I thought it did. I felt his warm soapy hands come up to my shoulders, and he started massaging. His hands moved down my back, kneading my muscles as he went, until he reached my ass and whispered, "Spread your legs, baby."

Bossy, even while having sex. I decided I loved this most of all about Jack, so I spread my legs without a moment's hesitation and sucked in a breath when his fingers hit my folds and gently massaged in erotic foreplay.

"Put your hands on the wall and don't move," he crooned in my ear. I turned my head and looked up at his rugged face, and needing to feel his mouth on mine, I leaned up to kiss him. His head came down and met mine, our lips meeting and our tongues tangling; he took the kiss deeper, releasing his hunger. Forgetting he wanted me to put my hands on the wall, I turned into the kiss, wrapping my arms around his neck, getting as close as I could. I reached my hand down and grabbed him, running my thumb across his crest, causing Jack to rip his mouth from mine and throw his head back, hissing "Fuck." I was lowering myself to my knees, his hands in my hair and his eyes hooded, watching me, when the lights went out.

I couldn't see Jack in the dark, but I could feel him

tense, and then he reached forward and turned the water off.

He helped me to my feet, kissed me once and said, "Don't move, I'll get you a towel."

In the dark, he somehow opened the door, found us each a towel, and wrapped me up tight in it. "Stay here," was all he said before I heard him exit the room.

There was no light coming under the door, so I figured a fuse had blown. I dried off and found the shirt I'd worn and threw it over my head, then moved to the door, feeling my way around. Turning in the direction of the living room, I kept my hand on the wall for balance and was getting ready to call out to Jack when I heard a loud crash. Startled, I moved quickly in the direction of the sound, calling out "Jack," when I heard struggling in the living room. I could see two figures battling in the dark and ran towards them. The only thing on my mind was to help Jack.

"Jack!" I screamed as I reached the struggling forms.

In the filtering light, I saw an arm raised high and what looked like a knife glinting from the rays of the moon.

"Jenn, get back!" Jack shouted, and I heard a whispered voice say, "You're corrupting her. I have to kill you." A chill ran through me, and I knew this was the killer. I reached around for anything to use as a weapon, but only met dead air. I needed something, a fireplace tool, anything I could hit this man with. Then a thought struck me: Jack was a sheriff, he carried a gun.

"Jack, where's your gun?"

"Jesus, Jenn, get the fuck out!" Jack bellowed. I turned when he shouted and watched as the knife came down and heard someone grunt.

"JACK!" I screamed, then saw an arm swing and connect, forcing someone's head back, and down he went. Frozen in place, not knowing which man had gone down, I started to move back in fear, when the man still standing turned and ran toward me. When he reached me, he stopped briefly, and I felt his hand brush against my arm, running down the length of it in a caress, then he turned and ran out the open door in the kitchen.

I don't know what possessed me, but I ran to the door and looked outside. I heard an engine start and saw taillights of what looked to be a truck speed off down the street.

"Jack!" I shouted, then turned and ran back into the living room, falling to my knees, reaching around the floor searching for him.

"Where are you, Jack?" I started to cry and then mumbled, "Don't die, please don't die." My hand felt a bare leg. I ran my hand up to his stomach and felt it moving up and down. I needed him to wake up so I started to shake him.

"Jack," I sobbed. "Jack, wake up," I begged as a really ugly sob passed my lips. "Please don't die, Jack, please come back to me."

Over a year ago I lost my husband to a drunk driver, and I was there when he died at the hospital. That feeling of helplessness was maddening. It broke my daughter and left me empty, missing my best friend. Now with Jack on the floor, not responding, I was reliving all those emotions and started to panic. I couldn't see what I was doing; I couldn't see how badly he was hurt. So I stood and moved my way back down the hall to the bathroom where I'd left my phone and searched the countertop. Finding it among the towels, my fingers wrapped around the phone and I mashed buttons, so it lit up. Using the light, I ran back down the hall till I found Jack on the floor, a huge slice in his shoulder and blood pooling on the floor. I looked him over for other wounds and couldn't see any, but I couldn't tell with all the blood.

Jack's eyes started fluttering, and then they opened wide and looked around. Relieved, I threw myself on him, unable to stop the tears from coming, and started bawling. Great, huge sobs came from my body. All I could think was I couldn't lose him, too. Burying Doug had been excruciating, and losing Jack the same way would have killed me.

I felt his arm wrap around my shoulders and heard him say in a soft whisper, "Shh, I got you, baby. I'm not going anywhere." I let out a cry and nodded my head in his neck. Then bossy Jack came back.

"When I fucking tell you to stay, you stay." My head snapped back at that, and I narrowed my eyes.

"What?"

"I was too damn busy worrying where you were to concentrate. Jesus, Jenn, when you got too close, I almost let him go so I could get you away." That deflated me because of course he was right, dammit. I hadn't thought about that when I rushed in.

"Sorry," was all I could say.

"What am I gonna do with you?"

"What do you mean?"

"Jesus, you're a walking, talking danger to me." Hurt by his words I tensed and tried to move back. Struggling to stand up, he wrapped me up and buried his head in my neck, then started to laugh.

"What's so funny?" I hissed, but he only kept laughing, and my ego took an even bigger hit. For some reason, instead of being pissed, I got choked up at him thinking I was a walking disaster, and the tears started coming again.

"Le...let me...up," I cried. Jack pulled his head back and even though he couldn't see my face, he could hear the tears in my voice.

"Jesus, Jenn...you've got me turned inside out.... You're a danger to me because the thought of anyone touching you or hurting you brings me to my knees."

"What?" I whispered.

He continued, "Twenty years...not once in twenty years have I ever met a woman who tied my stomach in knots, and you stomped into my life four days ago, and just the thought of you, Christ... you're my kryptonite, Jenn... *You're* a danger to *me*, because when *you're* around, I can't see anything else," he answered hoarsely.

"Jack."

"So please, in the future, don't be Lois Lane, alright? Just be my sweet Jenn and stay."

I stared at his dark face and felt the warmth of his words run through me...*I was his sweet Jenn?*

I answered him the only way I knew how. I threw my mouth to his and kissed him, and then whispered in his ear, "Ok, Jack, I'll stay next time."

"That's my girl," he whispered back. But then he grunted and cursed in pain.

"Baby, I need to call the station and get some clothes

on." I jerked out of my warm fuzzy haze and remembered he'd been stabbed, and then I moved into nurse mode.

"Lie still, I'll get a towel. We need to call an ambulance and have you checked out. He hit you, and you could have a neck injury, so don't move, I'll be right back."

Using my phone for light, I ran back to the bathroom and looked for towels and a first aid kit. While I was digging, I felt a hand wrap around my waist and pull me back. Jack took the phone from my hand, hit 911, and started talking to dispatch about the break-in, the fight, and the knife, all while holding me to his chest.

Then he leaned closer and whispered in my ear, "Babe, clothes. Deputies are on the way." I don't know how he thought I'd find my clothes in the dark, but I reached down on the floor of the bathroom and searched around until I found both his and mine. A little wet from the shower, but better wet than naked, I pulled them on, and Jack managed to get dressed as well with the light from my phone before the sirens in the distance were right outside. Jack grabbed my hand, pulled me up to his still shirtless body, and put his head to my forehead.

"Jenn, did you recognize this guy?"

"No," I shook my head. "It was too dark."

"There was something about him that was familiar, Jenn. I'll figure it out, but until I do, you can't be alone."

"What? Why?"

"Baby, I know the link to these women, why he's killing brunettes." Confused how he figured that out fighting with the killer, I asked him.

"How do you know?"

He paused before answering, taking a deep breath, "Because it's you."

My head spun when I heard that, and the words of the killer came back to me, *"You're corrupting her. I have to kill you."*

Shaking my head, I took a step back, but Jack grabbed me and held me close as denial turned to fear, and I started shaking.

"No, no, no, that's not true!" I shouted, but I knew, I knew he was right. I pushed hard against him, trying to get away, but he didn't budge. Panicking, my breaths started to come out too fast.

"Jenn, stop. Baby, listen to me. I'll find him, I promise you."

"No, it's not true, it's not true."

"Jenn?"

My name on his lips was all I heard before my brain shut him out and then the lights went out...? Not the house lights, no, I passed clean out like some Victorian heroine in a cheesy romance novel. And in the back of my mind, as I slipped into darkness, I wondered if Jack thought I was worth all this trouble or if he was rethinking his stance on kryptonite.

Eighteen

Don't Say You're Sorry

"Jesus, Jenn, get the fuck out."

"You're corrupting her, I have to kill you."

"Jaaaack"

"Baby, I know the link to these women, why he's killing brunettes."

"How do you know?"

"Because it's you."

"No, no, no."

"Nooo, no, no." I shot up, looked around and found myself in Jack's bedroom. The lights were back on, and the door to the room was closed. A feeling of dread ran through my exhausted body. Jack thought the killer knew me; that he's killing women because of me, but why? I'd been here four months. Who had I angered so much they would kill women to punish me? And why not kill only me if he hated me so much?

Needing to move, adrenaline coursing through my body causing my heart rate to increase, I recognized the signs of an anxiety attack. Right after Doug died and my life was uncertain, I would get them at night. With Bailey off at school and Mom, Dad, and my brother, Ted, all living so far away, I just felt alone, unsure and, weirdly, forgotten. *I need to run, burn this off.*

In bare feet and not caring, I ran to the bedroom door, threw it open and hightailed it down the hall. When I hit the living room, Jack was there in a discussion with Barry, Grady, and Phil. Without a word to any of them, I headed straight to the kitchen door, threw it open, and took off. Cold air hit my face, the shock of it clearing my head. I was surprised the temperature had dropped so much, but I didn't really feel it, so I kept right on running. I heard shouting behind me, surprised it was Barry. I couldn't stop; I had to get this adrenaline burnt off or an anxiety attack the likes I'd never had would cripple me. Jack lived on a dead-end street, and I'd headed towards the end; when I reached it, I turned around and headed back the way I came. As I got closer to Jack's house, I could see him standing at the end of his driveway, arms crossed over his chest, just watching me. I looked at him and shook my head. I needed to keep running to get this out, and I needed him not to stop me. Like he understood, he gave me a chin lift and left me to it.

Twenty minutes and two bruised and bleeding feet later, I came to a stop about a hundred feet from Jack's house. Still standing, watching me, the lights from an old-time gas street lamp glowing down on me as his guide, he walked toward me, stopped in front of me, and looked down.

"You get it out?"

"Yeah, I think so." Without another word, he bent at the waist and picked me up, carrying me back to his house. We entered through the front door, and three sets of eyes were on me. All held a look of concern, but a secondary look of, "is she gonna freak out again?" I was too tired to care. Jack placed me on his couch and bent down to look at my feet.

"You need to soak these. I'll run a bath," was all he said before he moved down the hall. I turned back to the guys and smiled weakly, then fell against the couch and closed my eyes. I heard a cough and turned my head to see Barry ready to ask me something. I raised my hand to stop him.

"I'm fine. I needed a moment to sort through what's happened."

"About that...We need to ask you some questions, and since Jack was the victim, he can't be involved in the investigation."

"Fine, ask away. I won't break." At least I didn't think I would, but I'd already passed clean out, and my new independent womanhood had taken a hit to her ego.

"Did you notice anything about the guy that would help in identifying him? His height, hair color, build, a tattoo, anything, even a smell that might be distinct?"

Closing my eyes, the fight clear in my head, I saw the knife, the height of the men struggling, and started listing everything I remembered to Barry while keeping my eyes closed, deep inside the memory.

"He was shorter than Jack, maybe six foot two. He had a knit cap on his head, the kind with the eyes and mouth cut out like bank robbers wear. The knife had lots of those sharp ridges on them like Rambo carried, and if I had to guess his size, I would say a lot leaner than Jack. I didn't get close enough to smell him, except when he touched me as he ran past, but all I smelt was fresh air, as if he'd been standing outside a long time."

"Jenn." My eyes flew open when I heard Jack call my

name; he was crouched down in front of me again, watching me.

"He touched you when he ran past?"

"His hand, his fingers, they ran down my arm when he passed me." Jack turned to Barry and the boys, and something silent passed between them.

"Jack, are you sure...a hundred percent sure this is about me?" I already knew the answer; it made sense once you looked at it rationally. Women who looked like me died, I met Jack, and now women he dated were dying. He'd said, *"You're corrupting her",* to Jack. This man, whoever he was, seemed to think I needed to be protected from Jack, but why was he killing?

"Jenn, it's like puzzles pieces: separately, they make no sense, but together they form a picture, and that picture is you."

I looked away from his face and nodded my understanding. Without looking at any of them, I thought about the loss of life because some lunatic had an obsession with me. Me—simple Jennifer from simple Kansas—who only wanted a simple life in the beautiful mountains and some adventure, was the obsession of a killer. For those women who were dead, I wished I'd never come here. For the women who could die because of me, I knew in my gut I'd have to leave. If I slipped away when no one was watching, I could get out without the killer knowing and save the life of whoever was next. I thought about all of my options, and this was the only one that made sense. Leave and save lives, or stay and endanger everyone? No choice, really. My mind made up, I just needed to get away from Jack.

***

After my bath, Jack gave me clothes to wear: a huge, soft t-shirt that smelled like him, and sweat pants I rolled at the waist to keep up. Luckily, while soaking in the tub, I'd had time to come up with an excuse to get to my car and get out of town. I was going to ask Barry to drive me to my car under the premise I needed it for work. Hopefully, Jack would agree to let me get my car since he insisted I had to stay with him until the killer was caught, and he couldn't very well expect me to be stuck here without transportation.

Jack needed stitches on his shoulder, and Phil was going to drive him to the hospital. I figured that would give me enough time to get home, pack a bag, and hit the road. To where? I'd make that decision once I was on the road, but first I had to get to my car.

I was sitting on his couch, thinking about what I needed to do—where I should go, if I should call Bailey, and a million other things—when his voice broke my concentration.

"Babe, worrying about something you have no control over will accomplish nothing... Except frown lines you women are always complaining about." Looking at Jack and seeing his blue eyes twinkle at me, I tried for a smile I wasn't feeling and then nodded my head. Thinking now would be a good time to bring up the subject of my car, I took a deep breath and went for it.

"Jack, while you're getting stitched up, I need to get my car. Can Barry drive me to it?" Jack watched me for a moment then looked over at Barry, studied him, and said, "Stand up." Barry did as Jack asked, looking confused, as Jack walked up to him and looked down. He looked Barry over, and then spoke over his shoulder to me.

"Barry isn't tall enough to be the killer," Jack explained, and I jerked my head back, shocked he'd even considered Barry. Barry got angry, of course, then crossed his arms over his chest and glared.

"What the—you thought I was the killer?"

"No, but whoever this guy is has an obsession with Jenn, and you've been obvious about your feelings for her, so I had to be sure."

Barry's face turned red, and he looked away. I got embarrassed for him and felt the heat creep up my face. Jack was right, of course, but Jack being Jack didn't even try to soften his remarks, and that had to sting no matter who you were.

Barry turned back to look at me and then with a grin said, "Man would have to be blind not to notice you." I bit my lips to keep from laughing and crying at the same time. My life was a nightmare.

God, how had it come to this? Barry was a great guy, but he wasn't Jack. No man was, obviously, but it didn't matter that Jack was wonderful and that I was falling hard for him, because, after tonight, I didn't know if I would see him again.

"Are you done flirting with my woman? If so, take her to her car and make sure she gets back here in one piece." Barry nodded, wiped the smile from his face, and turned to me.

"You ready?"

"Yeah, but give me a second."

"I'll just wait by the door. Take your time."

Nodding, I turned to Jack and tried to keep my heart rate from racing. Jack didn't know it, but this could be the last time he saw me, and the thought I might never come back to this man was cutting me deep. Jack started talking first, so I bit my lips and listened, determined I wouldn't cry.

"I'll see you when I get back. It shouldn't take more than a couple of hours." Afraid I might cry if I spoke, I nodded I understood, got up on my toes and kissed him gently on his mouth. Jack didn't close his eyes, and neither did I. I wanted to take that with me and hold it close for when I was lonely or scared: his face, warm and loving looking down on me as I said goodbye.

"Goodbye, Jack," I whispered, and then turned to leave. Jack grabbed my hand and pulled me back. Both hands to my face, he crashed his mouth on mine, kissing me like he knew he'd never see me again. When he pulled back, he put his head to mine and whispered, "I'll see you when I get back."

All I could reply was "I'll see you soon,", because that was something I hoped would come to pass. The killer caught, women out of danger, and me returning to this life I'd started for myself. So I grabbed my purse and clothes and then headed to the door. When I reached Barry, I turned back to get one last look at Jack, one last memory to take with me in case I never returned. I smiled at him, and he grinned back before giving me a chin lift. I took a deep, calming breath, turned, and walked out the door and out of Jack's life.

***

a reason to breathe

Two hours later...

The lights of a highway patrol vehicle and its siren grabbed my attention as I was driving down the highway. I looked in my rear-view mirror and wondered if I'd been speeding. Pulling over, I put my jeep into park and waited for the officer. A nice-looking man about forty got out, walked up to my window, and tapped on it. I rolled it down a little, looked up at the man, and waited for him to speak.

"Are you Jennifer Stewart?"

My eyebrow reached my forehead at this stranger knowing my name, and I stupidly nodded the affirmative.

"Ma'am, I have instructions from the Gunnison County Sheriff's department to tell you, and I quote, "Get your sweet ass back to town or I'll tan your hide."

I cried out a laugh at the audacity of that man. I guess Jack found my note.

"You can tell the sheriff that I'm not coming back until the killer is caught. If I'm gone, he won't have a reason to kill."

"Ma'am, Sheriff Gunnison told me to tell you that if you were stubborn enough to disagree with this request, I was to handcuff you and bring you in forcefully for trespassing."

That got a gasp from me, and I narrowed my eyes.

"You wouldn't."

"Ma'am, if my woman was going off half-cocked, running in an attempt to protect others from a killer, I'd do the same thing."

"I'm not going off half-cocked! I thought this through

194

while in the bathtub."

Mr. Highway Patrolman shook his head and then looked to the heavens for patience.

"Ma'am, honest to God, you need to turn your vehicle around and head back to Gunnison. For all you know the killer is following you and you won't be safe from him alone on the road or anywhere else, for that matter." I sighed, exasperated, and thought to myself: *Why do all men think they can boss you around?*

"I appreciate your advice, officer, but I've watched my rear-view mirror, and no one has been following me." He shook his head again, obviously thinking I was a crazy woman with a death wish, and then moved as lights came up behind us. I looked in my rear-view and watched as Jack got out of his truck and walked towards my Jeep. *Shit.* The patrolman moved to him, spoke for a minute, and shook his head again. While I was contemplating whether or not I could outrun both of them in my jeep, Jack slapped the patrolman on the back, and the officer looked back at me again with little more than the male equivalent of *"Women, heaven help us." Well, hang around. You think I'm stubborn? You ain't seen nothin' yet.*

Jack watched him leave, then looked back at my Jeep, assessing the situation, or counting to a hundred was probably more like it. He looked back at his truck, then back at my Jeep.

Decision made, he walked up to my door, leaned down but instead of barking out an order he simply said, "Scoot over, babe, I'm driving."

I looked back at his truck and saw no one in the cab, so I asked, "What about your truck?"

"I'll get it in the morning. Now scoot over, I'm driving you back so you can't take off again." His tone was starting to change to frustrated, and I knew I wouldn't win this battle, so I unlocked the door and scooted into the passenger seat, feeling defeated that I hadn't escaped. Jack got in, buckled up, and started my Jeep, but before pulling back on the road, he turned to me and without any preamble laid down the law. The word *"brace"* flew through my mind when I looked at his face.

"You try and run again, I'll tan your hide. You think about doing anything that puts you in danger from here on out, I'll lock you up. You even think about investigating this killer another minute, I will put a bodyguard on you 24/7. You will do as I say, or I will arrest you. Do you understand me?" My hackles went up, but I kept my mouth shut... and then I didn't.

"You're insufferable," I hissed.

"Yeah? Good, means I'm doing my job."

"And what job is that, Sheriff?" He looked at me for a brief second and then let me have it for the second time.

"Keeping the most irritating, stubborn, and so damn sweet she makes my dick hard just thinking about her woman—a woman I've fallen for, I might add—safe. And if she thinks I'll just let her walk away from me, she's crazier than I thought... Safe. From. A. Lunatic," he growled and then, "That is my job, Jenn, so deal with it; and don't you ever get in your fucking car and leave again. Do you understand me now?"

Um, wow, this man of few words could really lay a string of them on you when he was motivated. Nodding my head in short quick moves—because really, after that, would you argue?—I opened my mouth to say I was sorry, but he interrupted me.

"Don't fucking say you're sorry," I closed my mouth, then opened it again, and he narrowed his eyes, so I froze.

"Swear to Christ, every fucking time you apologize...Every other woman I know would stand their ground just to fucking stand their ground, but you always fucking apologize." Confused, I started to defend myself, but he shook his head, raised a hand, and continued.

"And when you do, I want to rip your clothes off and fuck you till you say it again."

I bit my lip to keep from saying anything else because I wasn't pushing him any further. Would you? *We're on the side of the highway for God sakes; I don't want my butt on display.*

Jack watched me for signs I might lose my battle with keeping my mouth shut, and then finished his tirade while shaking his head, "Jesus, I fell for a woman who can admit when she's wrong . . . swear to Christ I didn't know they existed."

I rolled my eyes at him, but he merely glared back at me, so instead of verbalizing my thoughts, I kept them to myself. *On behalf of women everywhere, I will silently say, WHATEVER!!!*

Nineteen

This Hurts Me More Than You

Walking into the kitchen, the smell of coffee filling the air, I saw Jack leaning against the marble countertops, a look of abject concentration on his face. I moved to the cabinet, grabbed a cup, and then walked to the pot of coffee still brewing. Jack turned to me and studied my face. I knew he wanted to talk more about my leaving last night, but honestly, I was so stressed about this killer, I didn't think I could take another lecture from the man.

Jack came up behind me, leaned into my back, pushed me further into the counter, and then brushed his lips against my neck. Warm arms surrounded me and pulled me back into his hard chest. Standing here now, I wondered what I'd been thinking, leaving last night. *You hadn't been thinking. You'd been reacting.* Sighing, I laid my head back on his shoulder and drew strength from him.

"We need to talk about who this is, Jenn, and you're the only one who can fill in the puzzle pieces." I shook my head. No way. I didn't want to think about the fact that someone in my life, someone I had to know pretty well, was a killer.

"Jack, I'll make you a list of every man, woman, and child I know, but please don't ask me to figure out who, out of the people I know, I think might be a killer, because the answer is no one."

"Baby—"

"I'll think about it, all right? Just give me some time to wake up and then I'll think about it." Jack sighed in my ear, and I could feel him readying himself for battle. He needed information to catch this guy, but he also needed to keep me safe from the killer, so his burden as sheriff was personal as well. Rubbing his hands up and down my arms, he kissed my neck again, then moved to the cabinet and grabbed a cup, then the pot, and poured coffee in both of them. Blowing air across the hot coffee, his eyes met mine and held. I shook my head, then turned with the cup and headed back down to his bedroom.

How did I make a list that would point a finger to someone I knew? With all of the lists we'd made in the past few days, not once did I believe it could be anyone connected to me.

I thought about everyone I'd grown fond of since moving here and couldn't see any of them capable of murder. Maybe it's someone I interacted with, but hadn't given a second thought about. *Maybe* it's someone obscure like the dry-cleaning guy or the fry cook at my favorite diner? Still no names for a list, but feeling better about it being someone other than my nearest and dearest, I wanted to soak away my troubles. As I was heading for the bathroom, I heard my phone ringing, so I grabbed it off the bedside table and saw *"Mandy Calling."*

"Hey, girl."

"About time you answered."

"Sorry, it's been an eventful twenty-four hours."

"Heard about the break-in last night. Did the killer really go after Jack?"

"Yeah, he did, stabbed him in the arm. It was terrifying."

"No shit. I'm terrified and I wasn't even there." I moved to the bathroom and turned on the tub, pouring in my scented bath oil.

"Jennifer, I took your advice and have been thinking about the men who might have it out for Jack. I've got a list if you want to get together and look over it." That piqued my curiosity, and I walked back to the bedroom to make sure Jack wasn't listening.

"How many names are on the list?" I asked as I looked down the hall and saw Jack on his phone.

"Five. You want me to give them to you now?"

"No, I can't talk about it now; Jack's in the other room and he doesn't want me to investigate this guy anymore."

"No surprise there, Jennifer. Jack isn't gonna want you anywhere near this guy. Are you done investigating then? Do you want me to turn this list over to Lorraine?"

Biting my lip and thinking about how mad Jack would be if he knew I was still investigating, I almost answered her in a positive, but I felt responsible for the deaths of these women and if I could help find this guy, maybe I would buy some absolution for the part I inadvertently played in their deaths. Deciding I'd just have to be careful about my involvement, I checked one more time that Jack wasn't close and then closed the door to the bedroom and whispered to Mandy, "I'll meet you at The Bean in an hour. Call Lorraine and Ben for me and see if they can meet us there."

"Girl, you're gonna piss that man off...I love it. Keep him on his toes, Jennifer, he's not used to women, or men for that matter, ignoring his orders." I knew this firsthand, but it wouldn't stop me from doing what I needed to do to help find this guy. For some reason, I felt like I was the key, and that I was the only one who could stop him.

I hung up with Mandy, ran into the bathroom, drained the tub and took a quick shower. I'd just gotten my clothes on when Jack walked into the bedroom, looked me top to bottom, and asked with disbelief, "You think you're going somewhere?" I knew this would be difficult, so I lied.... right to his face, and let me tell you I was good at it...so good, I scared myself.

"I've got two events I have to cover today. The paper doesn't have anyone else they can send, and I can't lose my job, Jack. I'm taking Rick, the photographer, with me, and I'll come straight back once I'm done."

Jack looked like he was going to explode, so I grabbed my purse and walked quickly over to him, threw my arms around his neck, and kissed him till my toes curled. Before he could tell me to stay put like a good little girl, I rushed down the hall, leaving him dazed and confused.

***

Business at The Bean was slow, making it easy to grab a table in the back, away from prying eyes, and it gave me the advantage of knowing who came in before I was seen. If Jack or any of his deputies came in for coffee, I'd just duck into the ladies' room. Coffee in hand, Ben, Mandy, and Lorraine joined me at the table. Mandy pulled out her list, and we passed it around to each other.

"I see the mayor made the list," Lorraine laughed.

"He and Jack have dated the same women in the past and Jack, being the better man, always won out," Ben informed the three of us. Jack being the better man was an understatement of epic proportions. It had only taken one lunch with the illustrious mayor before I knew why his wife had left him.

"I can attest to the difference between them, but I can't see the mayor being the killer. Wouldn't he have shown signs by now? He's in a powerful position, and I'd think that would tend to lend itself to showing his weakness of psyche by now."

"What about Christopher Hartman? He was in a bad way when Kimberly dumped him to date Jack instead."

Mandy informed me that Christopher was the high school football coach and had been dating Kimberly for several months when Jack stepped up, and Kimberly stepped down from Christopher. I shook my head; I didn't know this man, had never met him, so there was no reason for him to be protective to the point of murder.

"Why don't you think it could be him?" Lorraine asked.

I looked around the table and decided I'd better fill them in if this meeting was going to be productive.

"The killer said something last night when he was fighting Jack, which leads Jack to believe that this killer may be obsessed with me. I don't know if it's true, but it fits, and I've never met Christopher Hartman."

Gasps and a grunt were heard around the table. I looked at each of them and continued, "We need to focus on men I know until Jack decides otherwise."

"Oh, my God, are you telling me this creep is killing women because he's in love with you and that he wants to kill Jack?" Mandy's pissed-off voice whispered across the table.

"That's what Jack thinks." I kept my eyes on Mandy and watched as her face got redder by the second, so I grabbed her hand and squeezed it.

"This is messed up, Jennifer. I can see why someone would fall in love with you, but kill people because of you? There's a special place in hell for that kind of fucked up." I was about to respond to Mandy when Lorraine nudged me, and I turned to her; my eyes went up when I noticed a tall figure behind her.

I met Jack's angry eyes and had the good grace to say, without him even saying a word, "Sorry."

Jack raised an eyebrow at that, and I smiled. He rolled his eyes to the ceiling, clearly asking for patience, and then grabbed a chair and sat down at the table.

"If you're going to lie, at least make it believable next time, *and* something I can't pick up the phone and verify, for Christ's sake. So what was so damn important that you had to lie, ignore my orders, and earn yourself a lockup in the county jail?" Wanting to point out that I'd never verbally agreed to this arrangement, since he wouldn't let me speak last night under penalty of punishment, I ignored his empty threat and turned to Mandy.

"Mandy made a list of all the men who are pissed at

you over women, and we're going over the list to see if I know any of them." Jack looked at me, then at the rest of table, *then* said on a growl, "Tell me you didn't leak confidential information to a member of the press?"

"I'm a member of the press, Jack."

"You're also a witness to the attack and were bound by the Sheriff's department not to discuss this with anyone." *Whoops.*

"Shit, sorry." Jack raised his index finger to stop me.

"Don't say you're sorry, not one more time."

I rolled my eyes and then turned to Mandy. "Show him the list."

Mandy handed the paper to Jack, and he stared at it a moment, finally took it and read the names. He pulled a pen out of his shirt pocket and added names, as well as marked out some of them. Curious about who he marked off and added, but not about to ask and get growled at again, I waited until he'd finished. Once he was done, he folded the paper up and then stuck it in his pocket.

"Hey, that's ours," I cried out, but Jack raised his finger and I bit my lip. He turned to Ben.

"Now that you know, can I count on you to stop meeting with Jenn and investigating?" Ben nodded once. Then Jack turned to Lorraine.

"Now that *you* know, can I have your assurance that you won't print a word of this until the killer is caught, and *you'll* stop meeting Jenn to investigate?" Lorraine gave a slow nod as well. Last, Jack turned to Mandy, looked at her and then shook his head.

"I know better than to ask you. You're as stubborn as she is." Mandy snorted and crossed her arms. *Then* he turned to me, cocked his head to the side and said,

"Your sweet ass is gonna look good in orange."

"You wouldn't."

"Told you last night I would."

"I don't believe you."

"Told Chad if you stepped out of line again, I'd arrest you."

"I haven't done anything wrong."

"You just leaked information to a member of the press, *after* you signed a confidentiality agreement with my office. I can and I will."

I watched his face for any signs he was bluffing, but didn't see any. *Shit.* I couldn't apologize again, because that would only piss him off. Looking around the table and then back again at Jack, I decided I only had one choice. So I jumped up and made a run for it.

***

"Let me go, Jack."

"Should have thought of this sooner. I can bring you to work every day, lock you up, keep you out of trouble, get my work done, and then collect you from the jail on my way home."

"If you shut that cell door, I swear I'll never speak to you again."

"Sweetness, that's not much of a bargaining chip you're offering."

"Jack, this isn't funny."

He shut the cell door and turned the key. Then he smiled, turned around, and chuckled as he made his way out of lockup.

"Jaaaack?" Nothing, no answer. I turned around, looked at the cell, walked over to the cot, and sank down on it. *He was just joking around...he'll be back.* I looked back the way he left. Still no Jack. I looked back at the cell, saw a metal tray with food and got an idea...

***

Jack's voice came over the loudspeaker. "Just so you know, I put you in isolation. No one but you can hear that racket you're making." I stopped banging the tray against the bars and turned my head towards the camera I'd seen in the ceiling. I tried to bring up some tears for effect and then, with broken words, pleaded my case.

"J... Jack, I'm sorry, I... I promise. OK?"

"Baby, this hurts me worse than it hurts you," he laughed.

With nothing else in my arsenal, I did the only thing left to me. I flipped him off. *Yeah, that showed him, Jennifer.* I heard Jack laugh louder over the speaker and then it went silent. I threw myself on the cot, looked back at the camera, and then stuck my tongue out for good measure. *Screw the killer... I'll kill Jack myself.*

Twenty

You're An Imposter

"You ready to go?" Lying with my back to the cell door, I was still trying to figure out how best to pay Jack back for my illegal, immoral, unnecessary, and completely embarrassing incarceration. This man had no limits to his bossy behavior, and as much as I liked him that way, I had to put a foot down.

No more. He can't tell me what I can and cannot do. We'll have a talk like the adults we are, and settle this once and for all.

With a game plan in place, I rolled over and gave him my best death glare. He didn't even have the decency to look just a little bit affected by it. *Clearly, I'm going to have to work harder than I thought about getting my dislike for my current situation across.* I rolled off the bed, walked over to him, and looked up. He put his hands on his hips and looked down. The stare down began. After about fifteen seconds, I caved.

"You ever lock me up again, I'll, I'll...Well, I don't know what I'll do, but you better believe it will involve pain." Eyebrows raised, he shook his head, then grabbed me by the waist and drew me to him.

"Baby, you broke my rules. I told you what would happen if you did; you wanna stay out of this cell, I suggest you start following them." I pushed at his chest, but of course he didn't budge. I felt my anger building, and he just stood there in his righteous state of manly know-it-allness. I wanted to scream...so I shrieked at him, and he grinned. I stomped my foot, and he laughed. If I'd had a gun, I would have shot him.

"You done?"

"No."

"I'm tired and I'm hungry. We're going out, so are you gonna keep this up, or do I have to gag you and carry you out of here?" Considering I didn't think he'd lock me up, I wasn't taking any chances, so I dropped my hands, huffed out a, "Fine," and he let me go.

Jack grabbed my hand and led me out of lockup, down several halls and toward the front. As we passed the room that housed dispatch, Barry walked out. Stopping to watch us heading in his direction, he shook his head and slapped Jack on the back as we passed, then turned his eyes to me and let me have it.

"You played me last night. I'd have never let you go back to your cabin if I'd known you were stupid enough to run."

Already pissed-off, his stupid remark opened the floodgates.

"Swear to God, all the men in this town were raised in the 1950s. Think women can't think for themselves or make decisions. Heaven forbid they think they have a mind of their own! One, I might add, that I've used without any of your or *your*," I pointed at them both "help up until this week... I'm sick up to here," I threw my hand up over my head for emphasis, "of the lot of you. I'm going home, and I will shoot the next man who drives up my mountain and knocks on my door."

And with that, I turned and stomped off down the hall, pushed through the doors, made my way to the lobby and out the front doors. When I got outside, I remembered I didn't have my Jeep. *Well, shit.* I turned around and saw Jack heading for the front door, and without thinking twice, I ran toward the side of the building as if my ass were on fire. As I turned the corner, I saw Ben drive down the street. *Thank you, God.* I jumped off the curb and ran right in front of his truck, throwing my hands out to stop him. He screeched to a halt, and I rounded the truck, jumped in the cab, and shouted:

"Drive!"

"Drive?"

"Yes, drive, now, foot to the pedal, pedal to the metal, D.R.I.V.E.... Now, go, go, go!" Ben looked at me like I was nuts, then, mumbling and grumbling, took his foot off the brake and drove...like the grandpa he was.

As he rounded the corner that took us past the station, I ducked down in the seat so Jack, who was searching for me while walking towards his truck and looking as if he was going to shoot someone, wouldn't see his escaped prisoner. Ben looked down at me but kept going.

"Take me to my Jeep, Ben."

"Jenny, he'll just find you like he did last night."

"Fine, he'll find me, but just take me to my Jeep. I've been locked up all day; I need some time to myself to think." Ben gave me the *"women"* look that all the men in this town had perfected, but he kept driving back to The Bean like I'd asked.

When we got close, I got my keys out of my purse, ready to storm out and then jump into my Jeep. Ben stopped by my bumper and turned to me.

"Jenny, don't you go off half-cocked like you did last night. Jack can keep you safe. You just need to let him." I sighed 'cause he just didn't get it.

"I'll remember that, Ben, and for your information, I'm not running. I just need to think, to breathe for a minute. I'm at the end of my rope. I need to decompress without over six feet of testosterone telling me what to do all the time." Feeling my chance for escape dwindling with each second that ticked by, I kissed him on the cheek and jumped out of the truck.

***

Checking my rear-view mirror all the way into Crested Butte, I decided I didn't want to go back to my cabin. I wanted to sit down, have a drink and just think. So I pulled onto Elk Street and headed to The Wooden Nickel, one of the original and oldest saloons in the town, and a favorite of mine. It had warm, dark wood walls, a bar that looked original and made you feel like you'd just stepped back in time, and an atmosphere that said "sit down and stay a while." But what I liked most of all were the friendly bartenders who made you feel welcome, but left you to it if you needed to be alone. I slid up to the bar, and Charlie, one of the regular bartenders, was there. He tipped his head to me and walked over.

"You drinking alone tonight?"

"If I can help it."

"Bad day?"

"Bad week."

"Same as usual?"

"That'll work, thanks Charlie."

"Honey whiskey, neat, coming up."

Closing my eyes, I let the sounds of the bar filter through my brain; glasses clinking, soft murmurs coming from the patrons, a jukebox playing in the corner. All sounds of just everyday simple and mundane. I came here for a new life and a little excitement. Hiking, that was my idea of excitement. Maybe horseback riding on the continental divides. If I had to write a list of things to make my life more exciting, I'm pretty sure being the obsession of a deranged killer would *not* make my top ten. But even as a child I tried to excel, so there you have it: I excelled at one thing...I could now check being the object of a killer's desire off my bucket list. *Guess I'll drink to that!*

"Honey whiskey neat... you want something to eat with that?"

"Yeah, burger and fries, please, Charlie."

"You got it." He studied me for a second and was about to say something, so I put up my hand.

"Trust me, you don't want to know."

"Oh, I'm pretty sure anything you have to say would be worth my time."

"Ha, you're funny, but really, even if I wanted to, I'm sworn to secrecy by confidential agreements."

"Ok, I'll leave you to it then, but anytime you need an ear, I'm here for you." I watched Charlie head to the kitchen to place my order.

Did he just flirt with me? He was a nice-looking man, and a little younger than me...Hmmm, maybe I should bring Mandy here and introduce them. I turned back to the large mirror behind the bar and looked at my reflection, not seeing anything that would drive anyone to kill.

"Ok, let's see if I can wrap my head around all this crap." *There's a killer, who for some unknown reason is angry, in love, or obsessed with me.* My mind wandered to all the men I'd met since arriving in Colorado, and I couldn't picture any of them being that unstable. The mayor came to mind, and I thought about how arrogant and full of himself he was, but a murderer? It didn't jive. He was organized, true, but there was an obvious part of his personality that all women with half a brain could see, and I didn't think a killer like this would be that openly douche baggy. In order to stay undetected, he'd have to hide his obsession, but the mayor let it all hang out. Most serial killers hid in plain sight, so let's assume he *was*, in fact, doing just that. Barry was too short; I'd just met Grady; Ben was too old, and Gerry was also too old. *Does the man I buy my coffee from even count as someone I know?*

"This is so damn frustrating."

"I'm sorry, were you talking to me?" Turning to the deep voice sitting two stools away from me, I saw a man with a bright smile and about ten years younger than me.

"NO, sorry, just thinking out loud."

"Damn, I was hoping your frustration was from not having spoken to me yet." I laughed at his bad pickup line and stuck my hand out to introduce myself.

"Jennifer Stewart, too old for you."

"Mark Sanchez, I'm all for cougars who like to prowl." We both laughed, and Mark scooted over one stool and lifted his drink in a toast.

"A toast to the beauty of age. It comes in all ranges, but who really gives a shit?"

I chuckled and clinked my glass to his. Age wasn't my problem right now; men were, and they were everywhere these days. Jack, Barry, Ben, the mayor... they were all telling me what to do or trying to point out my misguided ways. I didn't have time for this flirty man, but Charlie had just put my hamburger in front of me and I was hungry. So I grabbed the ketchup and covered my burger and fries with it, then proceeded to listen to this man flirt and try to convince me how good we could be together...at least for one night.

"Now that I've spent the past hour trying to convince you to run away with me, why don't you tell me what was so frustrating before?"

"Ah, well, that's complicated. Let's just say I've got too many men in my life and not enough bullets."

"Ouch, did I just put myself on that list?"

"The minute you said hello," I laughed. Leaning my head in my hand, I realized I hadn't actually thought about any of that crap while I'd listened and laughed with this man, so I nudged his shoulder, "You've been very good company I'll admit, so thank you for that. My head was ready to explode, and you actually helped."

"Ah, here comes the old brush-off already," Mark chuckled and emptied his glass.

"No, not a brush-off. Just a thank you. I'm not really

available to be swept off my feet, anyway."

"I see...Is it one of these men who's got a bullet reserved for him?"

"Oh, yeah." I emptied my own glass and looked around the bar, then back at Mark. I stood and put my hand out to shake his.

"Mark, it's been a pleasure meeting you, but I think home is where I'm headed. Enjoy your stay in Crested and don't forget to head over to Gunnison like I said." Mark pulled his wallet out and threw bills on the bar, then stepped back from his stool. "I'm gonna walk you to your car. It's the least I can do after the entertaining conversation."

"I won't argue with that. It's always nice to see gentlemen still exist." Grabbing my jacket and purse, we headed to the front of "The Nickel", as locals called the bar, and Mark grabbed the door, opened it, and the cold air hit me.

"Where are you parked?"

"Around back. If we take a shortcut through the alley we can get there quicker."

"Lead the way, fair maiden."

"Stopped being a maiden when I had my daughter twenty years ago, just so you know."

"What were you, ten when you had her? You don't look a day over thirty."

"Still trying to get in my pants, I see."

"Is it working?"

"Nope."

"The other guy's that good?"

"Nope, he's better than good. He's bossy, and, apparently, that does it for me these days."

We'd made it halfway through the alley when I heard footsteps behind us, so I turned my head for no other reason than I was curious who was there. I saw a figure in a black mask come up behind Mark, raise his hand high and then down, shoving a knife into Mark's back. Mark arched, tried to pull the knife from his back as I screamed, "Oh, my God!"

The attacker pulled the knife from Mark's back, and turned toward me, whispering, "He corrupted you. You're nothing but a whore now, just like the rest." Knife raised, his intent was clear: gone were his feelings of love, now I was his target. Suddenly, Mark tackled him from behind, sending the knife flying. The killer rolled and threw Mark off his back and stumbled to his feet. I backed up, keeping my eyes on him at the same time looking for anything to use as a weapon. Luck favored me at that moment as I saw a long board next to a dumpster about ten feet away.

Turning my body toward the dumpster, moving swiftly for the board, I saw the killer jerk my direction, babbling on like the madman he was.

"Thought you were like her, innocent and pure," he hissed out, still whispering. "Thought she had come back from the grave, that God had given me a second chance at love." He spit on the ground, spittle hanging from his mask. "But you're no different from the rest, whoring with the sheriff, whoring with this man. You're not my Annie. I should have killed you for impersonating her instead of killing those women to get your story." I was near the dumpster when his words stopped me.

"My story?"

"You wanted to be a real reporter, you whined and

cried you wanted to get out of working the events page. I gave you that, and you thanked me by being a whore."

"You're crazy! Oh, God, this isn't happening." My back hit the dumpster as the killer turned and picked up his knife. Mark was lying on the ground, barely moving, his face pale in the dim light of the alley. I reached behind me and searched blindly for the board, at the same time wondering why no one had heard me scream?

Finding the end of the board, I wrapped my fingers around it and pulled it up in front of me like a baseball bat, then moved out from the dumpster to keep from getting pinned.

"I'm sorry I upset you. I didn't know how you felt." My stomach churned at that apology; I was hoping to keep him distracted until someone came along. I remembered my phone in the pocket of my jacket, but couldn't hold the board without both hands. The killer ignored me and lunged with his knife held high. I swung and connected with his side. He grunted, and I jumped back out of the way of his knife when it came toward me.

"Help me!" I screamed, and took off running back the way we'd come, hoping to reach the end of the alley before the killer could recover. I made it five feet from the end when I was tackled from behind. He pulled my head up and slammed it down on the cobbled stone surface of the alley. Stars sprung to my eyes, but I heard a male voice in front of me shout, "What the fuck?!" and then the killer was gone. I heard his loud footsteps retreating behind me as the man who had shouted ran up to me and put a knee to the ground near my head.

"You okay? Mike, dude, call the police. Some guy just

attacked this woman." I tried to move, so he helped me sit up.

"Call an ambulance, there's a man in the alley who's been stabbed in the back."

"Holy shit, hold on. Mike, call an ambulance, some dude in the alley's been stabbed."

I pulled out my phone and handed it to him, unable to clear my vision enough to see.

"Check my call list, find the caller "Bossy," and hit redial, please." The Good Samaritan found Jack's number, and actually snorted when he realized there was, in fact, a caller named "Bossy," handed the phone to me, and then turned and ran down the alley to Mark.

I braced for the reception I'd get, but was surprised when Jack calmly answered, "You keep this up, and you'll live in that cell."

"Jack, the killer—" was all I got out.

"Where are you?" he growled.

"The Nickel in Crested. Jack, he stabbed a man."

"I'm ten minutes out, be there in five," he said and ended the call. My head was pounding, but I no longer saw stars, so I got up and headed back down the alley to check on Mark.

Lying in a pool of blood, but breathing, his eyes closed, but they opened when he heard me approach. There were several people gathered around him, so I stopped at his feet.

"You ok?" he grunted through the pain.

"I'm fine, don't worry about me."

"Was that one of the men you wanted to put a bullet in?"

I cried out a laugh that was thickened with tears and

nodded, "Yeah, definitely one I want to put a bullet in." Kneeling down, I got close to his face.

"You saved my life when you tackled him. I won't ever forget that," I whispered in his ear.

"I had to do something to get your attention away from the other men." I nodded and chuckled at his foolishness, then grabbed his hand and squeezed.

"An ambulance is on the way, you hang in there, ok?" His eyes lifted, and I could feel the energy behind me change.

Mark looked back at me and said, "Is one of your problems a pissed off sheriff?"

"Yeah, is he behind me?"

"Yeah. I have a feeling it's a good thing I'm already injured."

Before I could answer him or turn to Jack, an ambulance pulled in the alley, and the techs jumped out and headed to Mark.

Jack grabbed my arms and pulled me up and out of the way, then walked me over to the side.

"Talk to me," he seethed

"I came for a drink to think, had dinner. Mark—"

"He a *friend* of yours?"

"No, I just met him—"

"You picked him up in the bar," he hissed.

"If you'd let me explain, I'd tell you," I hissed back. Jack crossed his arms, and his pissed-off eyes met mine. He raised one eyebrow and waited.

"As I was saying, I was eating, Mark was eating, we were leaving at the same time, and since it was dark, he offered to walk me to my car. We made it halfway up the alley when the killer attacked, stabbed Mark in the back and then came after me. Mark got up, tackled the killer, and then I backed up, grabbed a board, and when the killer attacked again, I hit him in the ribs and took off running for help." I didn't think it was possible, but the whole time I was talking Jack got even more pissed off.

"Did the killer say anything?" he barked. Oh, yeah, he said a lot, and it made me sick to death to repeat it. Jack waited while I gathered my thoughts. Then he got tired of waiting.

"Talk to me, for Christ's sake."

"Fine, he called me a whore, said I was impersonating some woman named Annie, and that I should have died instead of those women he killed, for me, I might add, so I could have a story." Jack looked over my shoulder, studying Mark, then looked back and narrowed his eyes.

"Why'd he call you a whore?"

"Because I slept with you."

"Sleeping with one man doesn't make you a whore. Why'd he stab this Mark person?" I paused too long, and he narrowed his eyes even more.

"Fine, you win. Mark was hitting on me all night, and I told him it was a lost cause, that I was too old for him, but that didn't stop him from being charming and flirty. Clearly, the killer must have seen it, and when Mark walked me to my car, he assumed I was going home with the guy. Are you happy now?"

"Not in the fucking least, but we'll get to that later. So assuming that's the killer's reason for attacking you, he had to have been in "The Nickel", watching you. I'll have Barry talk with the staff and see if anyone remembers a man alone with eyes on you and your..." His eyes moved to Mark, who was being moved from the ground to a stretcher, and then came back to me. "...dinner companion we'll call him." Jack's jaw got tight as he searched my face, looking for what, I didn't know, but then his eyes stopped at my forehead.

"You hit your head?"

"Killer chased me and tackled me, then he slammed my head into the ground." Pissed-off Jack morphed into Concerned Jack when he heard this.

"Jesus, what am I going to do with you?" His face softened then, and he grabbed my neck and pulled me forward, kissing my head. He kept his lips there, and I wrapped my arms around his waist. The events of the last hour hit me once his strong arms circled me, and I answered his question while hanging on tight.

"Probably lock me up in a cell," I whispered in his chest.

"Tried that, and you see how well that worked."

"Yeah, you should probably just get used to the fact I'm not going to listen to you."

"Baby, figured that out five minutes after I met you."

"Then why'd you throw me in a cell?"

"I'm trying to contain you, keep you safe from yourself."

"I don't need saving from myself," I replied with the kind of indignation any woman in my position would have had. Jack searched the heavens for an answer, but not finding one. He looked back at me and let me have it. Swear to God, this man had a speech for everything.

"*You* need saving from your own innocence... the same innocence that attracted this killer in the first

220

damn place. Men will take advantage; women will take advantage; /intend to take advantage of all that is you. Mandy said you're a shiny new toy, but she's wrong. You have a bright light that shines from you and it draws people in. You have no clue how people see you, 'cause you've got your damn head in the clouds and don't see what's happening right in front of you." I was breathing heavy 'cause all that sounded nice in an insulting sort of way.

"I'm not naïve, Jack," I whispered.

"Innocent isn't naïve, Jenn. Innocent means you trust people to do as they say. You give yourself away without expecting anything in return, and you think of others before yourself. Innocent, as in untarnished by this ugly fucking world, and I intend to keep you that way. 'Cause honest to God, after all the shit I've seen in my lifetime, you're the closest thing to perfect I've found. So stop fighting me and let me protect your fucking light."

I felt my whole body fill up with something I couldn't put words to. It warmed me in a way that I hadn't ever felt, like Jack's words filled something that had always been empty in me. My head hit his chest again, and I nodded. Bossy was getting his way. No way could I pretend that meant anything other than he cared about me and would do anything to keep me safe. And at the end of the day, if someone cared that much and wanted to protect you, you had a responsibility to help them keep their promise. And Jack promised that if I listened to him, he'd keep me safe...So that's what I'd do. I'd listen to Jack...At least until the killer was caught.

Twenty-One

Poking the Viper

"You're just like the rest, a whore."

"No, please, I didn't know."

"You whored with the sheriff and now you're whoring with this man."

"No, leave him alone! He didn't do anything."

The man in the dark mask turned his back to me, reached for Mark's head and pulled it back. His knife slashed across his neck in a single slice.

As Mark's blood ran from his body in a river of scarlet, I screamed, "No!"

"No, Mark." I woke with a start, another dream about the killer never to be erased from my memory. I looked around, then turned my head to see Jack staring at me. I let out a breath and rolled to my side and looked at him.

"Hey," I whispered.

"Bad dream?" Jack replied.

"Yeah, the killer was after me."

"And Mark?" Jack's face told me he was pissed, but I wasn't sure why.

"Yeah, he was in my dream."

"Yeah, babe, I know. Been lying here listening to you

talk about him."

"I talk in my sleep?" Jack rolled to his back, looked at the ceiling for a moment, and then rolled back.

"Yeah, you talk in your sleep," he snapped. Realizing I'd said something he didn't like, I bit my lips to keep from asking. Jack watched my mouth, then looked to my eyes; he narrowed his and, without any segue, started in.

"You wanna tell me again exactly what happened between you and this Mark guy?"

I grinned at Jack; he was jealous. The green-eyed monster had bitten big bad Jack. If I didn't think it would piss him off more, I'd have laughed. Actually, on second thought, this could be fun!

"Not much, Jack."

"What does "*not much*" mean?"

"He flirted, tried to convince me I was meant for him even if I was older. Wanted to take me back to his hotel room, but I insisted I go home. He told me I didn't look a day over thirty and asked me if that would that get him into my pants." The longer I spoke, the angrier he got, which made me want to laugh even more. I swear I could actually see his face turn green.

"You think this is funny?" Jack sneered.

"Yeah, I do," I giggled, then threw my arms around his neck. Jack rolled me to my back and moved between my legs. I was smiling up into his face, but his was still hard.

"You don't test a man like me, Jenn."

Watching Jack's face, the angry scowl and ticking jaw, I realized I'd gone too far. My smile slowly fell, and he watched with satisfaction, having gained my full attention. I watched him closely as his face changed from pissed to serious, and I felt like a harpy who played with men for enjoyment.

"I'm sorry, Jack. Nothing happened, it was harmless," I apologized. I realized my mistake as soon as the words left my lips. Jack narrowed his eyes and then grinned.

"Did you just say sorry?"

"Yes," I whispered. Jack's face dipped to my neck; his teeth nipped at my shoulder, and then he kissed and tasted his way back to my ear.

"You're gonna pay for that and for trying to rile me up," his hot breath whispered in my ear, sending a warm feeling between my legs at the thought of how I'd pay.

"I didn't try, Jack. I succeeded," I answered, thinking I was right about teasing him to begin with.

"You like playing dirty," Jack whispered.

Extremely turned on at this point, I answered him by lifting my hips into his obvious erection and then followed that action by biting his neck.

"I'm going to teach you a lesson, Jenn," Jack groaned in my ear.

"What lesson would that be, Jack?"

"You dance with the devil, you pay the consequences. I've claimed you, and you're mine," he stated. "You don't drink with other men or flirt with other men, and I sure as hell don't want to hear you say another man's name in your sleep."

I ignored his comment and ran my hand down his back to grab his bare ass; I squeezed him, ran my tongue up his neck, and whispered in his ear.

"Sorry, won't happen again." Jack sucked a breath through his nose on *"sorry"* and slammed his mouth on mine. His tongue parted my mouth and then he bit my bottom lip, pulling back and then letting it go.

"I'm gonna fuck you into submission," he explained and I figured he could try, 'cause I sure as hell wouldn't stop him. Bucking my hips, I put my foot to the bed and rolled him to his back. Lifting the t-shirt up and over my head, Jack's hands came to my breasts, his thumbs grazing my tight nipples. I threw my head back at the sensations, while he weighed and played my breasts like a pro, pinching then rolling, until I was riding his stomach for friction. He moved to grab my waist, and I reversed my position, giving him my back. I looked over my shoulder, only to find Jack raising an eyebrow before he put his hands behind his head. *Such a cocky bastard.* I leaned over and, without any prelude, sucked his hard length into my mouth, taking him all the way to the back of my throat.

"Christ," Jack groaned, as my mouth slid back up his cock. I wrapped my hand lower on his length and pumped in rhythm with my mouth. His hips lifted as I came down, using as much suction as I could.

"My turn," Jack growled and grabbed my hips, pulled my legs out from underneath me and my dripping sex to his mouth. I paused my movements as his tongue found my clit, then moved in quick bursts, sending an electric shock through my body. Two fingers joined his mouth, and it was all I could do to remember what I'd been doing. I licked his crest, but then whimpered as Jack's fingers hit my sweet spot, making me buck. Next thing I knew, Jack had me on the bottom, and his mouth buried in my folds, licking, tasting and driving his fingers in until I clamped down around them.

"Ride that out, baby," Jack growled, and I did as he said while he pumped me over and over, bringing me back again to fall off the edge into erotic bliss.

Relaxed from the massive release, I couldn't raise my arms, but I didn't need to. Jack turned me onto my stomach, grabbed my hips and thrust in, seating himself and then rolling his hips. I found my arms again, pushing up and then back with each brutal thrust. Hands at my hips, fingers digging in, Jack slammed into me like he was branding me.

"You want it dirty and hard?"

"Yes, Jack," I answered, my voice barely heard above his breathing.

"Who do you belong to?"

"What?" I whimpered.

"Who." Pound. "Do." Slam. "You." Roll, thrust. "Belong to?" Jack demanded to know. That was easy to answer as far as I was concerned: Jack owned my body, and, what was becoming apparent to me, my heart.

"You, Jack," I acknowledged out of breath. He yanked me up so my back hit his chest, wrapped his arm around me and my head slammed into his shoulder. Warm hands moved from my hips, up my sides to my breasts, and then both thumbs and forefingers found purchase on my hard nipples, pinching hard and pulling, sending a shock to my core.

"Hold on, baby."

Shaking my head, 'cause no way could I last, but bossy Jack didn't like no.

"Almost there, hold on." It was too much of everything, his hands, his large size...I was overwhelmed with sensations, and I whimpered my regret. Jack knew how to bring a woman pleasure, and if he wanted me to hold on, he shouldn't be so damned good at turning me on.

I turned my head to find his mouth. His tongue dove deep, igniting me even more, and I exploded. I clamped down around his cock, and that was all Jack needed. He brought us both over together, grunting out his pleasure in my mouth, his arms tight around my waist, almost to the point of pain.

As we started our descent, Jack moved his mouth to my neck and breathed me in, while his thrusting slowed to a tender caress. His hands moved over my body, like a blind man trying to identify an unknown object, feeling his way, memorizing my curves.

With one last kiss to my neck, he fell back to the bed taking me with him, and then proudly told me:

"You're great with your mouth."

"Ditto," I panted.

Rolling off, I turned and laid my head on his chest, running my fingers up and down his stomach. Jack pulled me up higher, wrapped me up, and kissed my head. We were silent for a minute before Jack asked me what I knew he had to.

"Talk to me about what the killer said again."

Rubbing my cheek on his chest, I thought back to last night, closed my eyes and heard the killer's whispered voice in my head.

"He said he thought I was his Annie who had come back from the dead." Rising up on an elbow, I looked at Jack and asked, "Do you know anyone who's lost a girlfriend or wife named Annie?"

Jack was silent, thinking as he ran his hand over my hip.

"It's not ringing any bells, but this guy might not be from around here, so the death may have taken place in another state."

Nodding my agreement, I tried to think of anyone I knew who'd mentioned losing someone.

"You should call Ben and Gerry. They know everyone around here. They might know, or Lorraine."

"I'll call them once I get to the station...Now, let's talk about what you're doing today and where."

I thought about my schedule and remembered I was meeting with the organizers of the haunted house to take a tour for the article I would write. I looked at the clock and then bolted upright; it was already 7:45 and I was meeting them at ten.

"Shit, I have to get ready."

"Not until you tell me where you're going."

"I have an interview and tour of the haunted house. They opened it in the old gold mine. I hear it's really scary; you want to come, keep me safe from all the ghouls and goblins?" I giggled, and Jack grabbed my arm, pulling me back down.

"Did I tell you your giggling is a turn-on too?"

What? I'd been trying to stop from giggling around Jack all week. *Swear I'll never figure this man out. Giggling is a turn on; sorry is a turn on... I wonder if arguing is a turn on, because, if so, we'll never leave the bed,* I thought.

"I'll remember that," I answered, and bit my lip to keep from giggling. Jack grinned, and I melted, but then I remembered the time and pushed up. "Let me up. I have to get ready."

"I want you to call me when you get there and to call

before you leave. I want you to go straight to your office after, and then straight over to the station when you're done. I don't want you to come here without me, and I don't want you near your cabin until this guy is caught. If I figure this out while you're out today, I'll call you so you'll know to keep an eye out."

There was so much in that command to argue about, but I promised last night to follow his orders until this guy was caught, so I'd do that for Jack...even if it killed me.

Pushing up on my hands and then off the bed, I stared down at Jack for a few beats. Just like he and so many of the men in this town had done all week, I put two fingers to my forehead and saluted him.

"Smartass."

"Bossy."

Jack bounded from the bed, bent at the waist, and picked me up. Playfully, he smacked my ass and carried me into the shower... and I giggled the whole way.

***

"Grady, find Barry and Phil, we've got a lot to go over. Tell them to meet here in an hour for a meeting." I was heading out the door when I shouted at Grady, "And call Ben, Gerry, and Lorraine Beckett as well. Let's see if these old-timers know more than I do."

"On it, Jack," Grady replied and then headed back to his desk as I turned to make my rounds.

Arriving back at the station an hour later, I headed to my office and found the FBI profile on my desk. Sitting down with my coffee, I started skimming it. Our killer fell into the "Gain" category of serial killers. *Christ, these sonsabitches have different categories.*

"Based on the information you have given us and the evidence obtained, your killer is a white male, 25-55, maintains a job but unlikely to work in an office due to his tendency to fixate on women. He is need driven, for money, an object or person he sees as valuable. This person of interest will not be of financial means and more than likely lives in squalor. He has no problem making friends of his own sex, but will fixate on women he finds desirable. He may observe from a distance, but more than likely situate himself in a position of confidant with those he fixates on."

My heart started pounding when I read that last line. My eyes snapped to the clock, and I knew Jenn had left for the haunted house already. I picked up the phone and called her number, but got no answer. *Can't she follow directions for one fucking day?* Jumping to my feet, I grabbed my keys and gun and headed to my door. As I turned the corner, Grady was walking towards me with Lorraine and Ben in tow, and I lost it.

"Tell me you didn't do this to her," I shouted in anger, my hand going to my gun.

"What in the hell are you talking about?" Ben replied.

"I've got a profile in my hand that all but points to you. Now look me in the eyes and tell me you didn't do this to Jenn," I roared.

Keeping my eyes on him as I made my way closer, I was still trying to process if this gentle old man could do this to Jenn.

"Son, if you'd take the time to calm down you'd know it couldn't have been me. I've got arthritis in my hands, and if the guy you fought the other night was the killer, then I'm about 75 pounds too heavy. Now what in Sam Hill are you going on about?" Ben calmly answered.

I searched his face for the truth, and saw nothing to suggest he was lying. Taking a deep breath and trusting my gut, I turned to my side and indicated with my hand that they should enter my office. Once they were inside, I stood behind my desk and watched Ben as he helped Lorraine sit and then lower his own body slowly into the chair. Christ, there was no way this man could have attacked me.

I looked between the two of them and then asked, "Where's Gerry?"

"He's out on the river. Had a group come in two days ago and hasn't gotten back."

Deciding to move on and pick their brains like I'd intended, I didn't explain; I just started asking questions on the fly.

"You know anyone in town who was ever married or had a girlfriend by the name of Annie who died?" I watched as both of them thought, but neither seemed to hit on the name.

"What's this got to do with the killer?" Lorraine inquired.

"The killer went after Jenn last night, stabbed a man in the back. The killer indicated he'd lost someone close to him, and her name was Annie."

Shock and anger passed over their faces and then Ben jumped in.

"You said the profile fit me... What did it say that makes you think it was me?"

"Said the killer would be easy for men to like, and that

he either would obsess over Jenn from a distance, but more likely situate himself in a position of confidant."

"Can I see the profile?" Ben asked, so I handed it to him and watched his face as he read the same description as me. While he was reading, the color drained from his face.

"Merciful heavens," Ben whispered.

"Talk to me, old man."

"It can't be; he loves her..."

"Who loves her?!" I roared.

"Gerald... This is him right down to the living in squalor."

I closed my eyes, simultaneously feeling relief that we might have a name, pain at what this would do to Jenn, and sadness for Ben. *Jesus, he tried to give me advice and warned me away from Jenn.*

"His wife died," Lorraine whispered, disbelief written all over her face.

"He told you that?" I barked.

"Years ago, when he first moved here. I remember him saying he was escaping the loss of his soul mate. Said he had to get away from the memories. He even left a son to be raised by her parents." I turned to Grady and gave him a nod, indicating I wanted Gerry brought in.

"Ben, do you have Gerry's full name so I can run his information?" Ben, still lost in thought, looked up and answered me.

"Gerald Marcus Walker, age fifty-four."

"Gerry's fifty-four?"

"Years in the sun aged him ten years. We always joked about him looking my age and not his own. We even laughed...oh, God...we laughed when Jenn said we didn't make the list of possible killers because we were both too old. I didn't correct her because I knew he was innocent. I, I mean I thought he was...That son of a bitch!" Ben shouted. "He tried to kill my Jenny, he really tried to kill her?" he asked, confused, still trying to make sense of it.

He turned to Lorraine and in a voice full of pain tried to explain himself, like he thought that, somehow, we blamed him for Gerry's betrayal. "I promised I'd keep her safe. I spent sleepless nights watching over her before you came into the picture, Jack."

His last statement hit me.

"It was you in her window that night."

"Yes, dammit, it was me. I've worried about her since she moved here. She reminds me of my first girlfriend, the one who got away. Something about Jenny makes me want to protect her, so I'd go up in the middle of the night when I couldn't sleep and check on her. Then the killings started, so I went every night."

I studied him and asked, "You throw a bird through the window?" Ben's face grew angry, and I knew the answer to that question. I held up my hand to stop his outburst when Grady walked back in.

"Jack, called Scenic River Tours and they said Gerry hasn't been on the river since Tuesday."

I bolted from my seat and grabbed my gun, then handed Grady the paper with Gerry's name and said, "Run this." Then I grabbed my phone and headed down the hall towards the front of the station just as the mayor walked in with a council member.

"Don't have time for your bullshit, Mayor," I growled as

I made my way past him and to the front doors.

"I think you'll want to make time for me, Jack. I'm lodging a complaint with the City Council that you're ignoring your responsibilities as sheriff. Once that's done, we'll be appointing Grady as acting sheriff until we can review your case, which should be sometime in the near future."

I stopped, turned slowly to face this prick, and with controlled anger, told him exactly what I thought of his threat.

"John, be a man and accept when a woman thinks you're an ass. Don't run to your council members to eliminate the competition."

The mayor said nothing but turned three shades of red. I was done. I didn't give a shit, so I turned and headed to the door, but before I walked through them, I heard Grady address his father.

"I'll turn down your appointment, and if you force me to take it, I'll quit."

The doors opened behind me, and I moved to see Barry, Grady, and Phil all heading to their vehicles, all of us with one objective in mind.

Find Gerry.

I paused as I reached mine and gave them a nod, and then I climbed inside to find this sonofabitch and put the killing to an end. But first, I had to find Jenn and tell her a man she trusted and saw as family had betrayed her and had tried to kill her light.

Twenty-Two

Ghost Mine

"Shit, I left my phone at Jack's." Dumping my bag on the seat of my Jeep, searching, but finding no phone, I looked up at the old "Ghost Mine" haunted mine tour and saw several people waiting for me. Hoping Jack didn't try to call me while I was here, I took a deep breath to shake off the last week, grabbed my bag, got out of my Jeep, and then headed toward the waiting assembly of ghost and goblins.

"Are you Ms. Stewart?" a man dressed as a ghost miner asked.

"Yes. Are you Mr. Buckley?"

"Indeed. Pleasure to meet you. Thank you for coming and touring with us today."

"I've been told I'm a kid at heart, so it's my pleasure to be here. I love a good old-fashioned haunted house to get you in the mood for Halloween."

"We brought in the whole crew to give you the full effect and invited our families as well. One can't get into the atmosphere of the place unless there are plenty of people screaming."

Thinking I'd had enough screaming to last a lifetime, I smiled at the man and then pulled out my camera to take pictures of all the actors in their costumes. I had them pose in different positions, reminiscent of the old time photos. When I finished, I put my camera back in my satchel and slung it across my body, ready for the tour.

"Ok, Mr. Buckley, lead the way."

"Excellent. Places, everyone!" he shouted, and the group of actors headed into the mine to prepare for our tour.

I perused the crowd as I waited and saw many faces I knew, so I waved at them. Several teenage girls squealed as the line moved forward, and we had just started to move when I felt a hand at my elbow and turned to see Mandy standing there.

"Hey, what are you doing here?"

"Carla's brother works here and she invited me." I turned to the woman on her right and smiled. My attention was quickly captured by the screams already coming from the narrow tunnel of the mine.

"You're brave coming to this after the other night," Mandy whispered in my ear.

"Ha, not brave. It's called a paycheck."

Mandy chuckled, "Right," as the line kept moving. We entered the dark tunnel, and the air became much cooler. I shivered, wishing I'd brought a jacket. There were torches on the walls, throwing enough light in our path to see our feet, but giving the creepiness factor a boost. There was a turn in the tunnel and more screams were heard; a hand reached out from the dark and grabbed my arm, and I screamed, immediately jumping back into Mandy. She laughed in my ear, and it made me groan for reacting like a quivering child.

"*You* get in front of me if you think it's fun being scared." Mandy pushed past me, and I decided I was chicken enough not to care and grabbed the back of her shirt to hold on to. I saw a green glowing light up above and searched ahead to see if I could make out what was happening. All three of us jumped when something brushed across our legs, sending chills and thrills just like the flyer for "Ghost Mine" promoted through me.

"Shit, what was I thinking coming here?!" Mandy shouted over the haunting music and deathly cries emanating from the loudspeakers.

"Beats me, but you're not leaving me here alone!" I shouted back. Carla pressed in close behind me, and as the green light got closer, a ghost miner jumped out from nowhere, swung his pickaxe high in the air, and shouted in a dead voice, "This is my Mine. All who trespass shall die." I giggled at the teenage boy and his serious expression when a cold blast of air hit our necks, and we jumped again, screaming.

"Jumping Jehoshaphat," I screamed, pulling both women back with me further.

"Jumping what?" Mandy laughed.

"Whatever," I laughed.

Looking further down the tunnel, all I could see were girls screaming and people jumping, and I braced for what might be next. Someone pushed past us, shoving people out of the way, and I figured they had the right idea. Get out quick. *I really hate my job right now.*

More hands, more screams, men jumping from corners, women lying on floors bleeding, it was a frightening and nerve-racking culmination of sights and sounds that had me ready to leave.... Like, right now.

"You think this is almost over?" I whispered in Mandy's ear. Her shoulders shrugged with the unknown answer. I thought that if I kept my eyes on her back, I wouldn't see anything and therefore make it out without peeing my ever-loving jeans, so I did just that and focused on staring at a rose tattoo on her neck. A few nerve-racking turns later, there was a commotion in front of us, and we stopped. Some woman said hysterically, "That looks real, doesn't that look real?"

I turned to the right where she was pointing and saw a man lying in a vignette of barrels and cobwebs. The blood on the floor around him still seemed to be flowing, and I wondered how they got it to run out like that. As we pushed forward, watching, I was thinking that any minute the man would jump up and scream at us. As I passed the body, I saw movement from the corner of my eye and turned to see Gerry lunge from behind a barrel.

I stood stock-still and smiled at him. He hadn't told me he was working here. I noticed he had fake blood on the front of his t-shirt, and I wondered why he wasn't in costume. He was heading right for me, so I waited for him, when his hand rose from behind his back, and I saw the jagged knife he was holding. I felt my face fall a split second before my brain interpreted what was happening.

Gerry screamed, "Whore!" and quickly ran towards me.

A hand from behind me grabbed my arm, and a panicked Mandy screamed, "Run, Jennifer!"

cp smith

***

"This isn't happening," I chanted as I ran down the tunnel, the screams of those behind me echoing around me, keeping me company. Jesus, what was happening with my friends?

Mandy had shoved me forward and screamed, "Run!" then turned towards Gerry like some sort of bodyguard. I'd turned back to get her when Gerry punched her in the face, sending her falling to her knees. Men who were near tried to stop him and I saw more than one get stabbed in the arm for his trouble. Gerry was trying to pull away when he turned his head toward me, and I felt the ice-cold fury in his face run through my blood. That's when I knew he wouldn't stop until he was free and had buried that knife deep in my chest. I had to save others from his wrath and avoid any more bloodshed, so I did as Mandy said: I ran, praying it would draw Gerry after me and leave those behind safe from harm.

I'd guessed correctly. I heard his feet pound the rock ground in pursuit, but I didn't chance looking back to see how close he was. There were more people up ahead, and I screamed, "Move, hide!" but all I got in return were a few screams and giggles from girls who thought I was part of the entertainment.

"Oh, God, where's the exit?"

I could hear him getting closer when an opening in the tunnel came up, so I darted left down an unlit corridor and slowed my pace, hand to the wall guiding me. I realized my mistake immediately, though. I should have zigged when I zagged...Left took me further into an unknown tunnel when forward would have taken me to the exit. I stopped and listened, trying to keep my breathing quiet. I plastered myself against the wall, praying I'd been far enough ahead that Gerry didn't see my wrong turn. That's when I heard the footfalls and knew he was coming. Without any choice, and praying someone got to the exit and phoned Jack, I kept moving forward.

***

I should have called Bailey this morning. I could have told her I loved her one last time. I can do this, I can do this. Don't make a noise and hide when you can. Simple, really.

I kicked a rock, sending it flying across the floor, and then it went silent. Holding my hand over my mouth to keep from crying out in frustration, I listened but heard nothing. Had he turned back?

"I heard that, whore. I'll find you, and when I do, I'll send you to hell with all the other whores. You're nothing like my Annie. I can't believe I fell for your temptress ways."

Shaking in terror and in shock that my friend, a man I considered family, was a maniac, intent on ending my life, I took a deep breath and let it out slowly. Inch by inch, I moved down the side of the wall, careful not to kick any more rocks.

I moved my foot an inch more to the right, and I felt the ground disappear from under it. Grabbing hold of the rough wall, I stopped myself from falling. Reaching around with my foot, I felt the ground until I found the edge of the opening, so I dropped to my knees, and crawled forward, searching for a way across. Scared I'd have to turn around, I heard footsteps coming and panicked. I was trying to stand when a light from a cell phone hit my eyes, blinding me.

Gerry roared, "Time for you to die, whore!"

Oh, God, I was trapped. He ran straight at me, and I didn't have time to react. Petrified and without thinking, I stepped back and lost my footing just as he reached me. The ground disappeared from beneath my feet as Gerry hit me, and we both fell.... and fell.

***

"Swear to Christ the woman can't listen to a simple request to stay in touch for more than a minute." I was racing down the highway to the abandoned gold mine, because the one time I needed that woman to have her phone on her, I'd found it sitting on my kitchen counter. I could feel the tension of the past week riding up my neck, but I ignored it and put my phone to my ear and called the station.

"Sheriff's Department."

"Amy, call Grady and the boys and tell them I'm headed to the old gold mine haunted house. I'll be out of range soon, so if they need me, they'll know where to find me. I'll call in as soon as I'm done and let you know where I'm headed.

"Will do, Sheriff."

I threw my phone on the seat and thought back over what Ben had said. Christ. Jenn had sat there with that bastard, talking about the killer, and he'd played along, never giving anything away. I punched the steering wheel with my palm, wishing I had Gerry's neck between my hands. He'd murdered four women in his demented approach at winning Jenn's love. How a man's mind could turn that sick was beyond me, but I'd seen enough in my twenty years as a cop to know that, as sick as he was, there were more out there just like him, some of them maybe even worse.

My phone started ringing, and I looked at the screen. An unknown number scrolled across, so I picked it up, thinking Jenn had borrowed someone's phone and was finally calling in.

"Jac...hel...Ja...r you there?" I heard what sounded like Mandy coming broken across the line and then it went dead. Prickling ran across my spine, and I hit redial and listened to the phone ring on the other end.

"Jack, are you there?"

"I hear you Mandy, just barely."

"Old gold mine.... Gerry.... knife." And the line went dead again. I felt a cold sweat break out across my forehead and didn't want to think about what it meant that Mandy was calling instead of Jenn. I pushed the accelerator to the floor, grabbed the CB and prayed I wasn't out of range.

"Base, this is Gunnison, come in."

"Base, this is Sheriff Gunnison, come in." The CB crackled to life, and a faint voice came across the wire.

"Base to Gunnison, we hear you, Jack."

"Find Grady and the boys, and get them out to the old mine haunted house. Repeat, the old mine haunted house. You copy that?"

"We copy that, Sheriff. Contacting now."

I dropped the handheld and drove faster. Within five

minutes, I saw the sign for the old mine coming up on my right. I took it too fast and fishtailed, straightened out, and gunned the gas. The road was bumpy, and the contents of my cab went flying as I raced towards the mine. As I neared the entrance, I saw a large group of people standing around and others sitting or lying down on the ground.

Mandy ran towards my truck, while I scanned the crowd, looking for Jenn. I threw the truck in park and jumped out of the cab as Mandy reached me, screaming:

"Gerry's the killer, he's in the mine with Jenn! He chased her down an unmarked path and neither has come out."

My breath caught on her words, but I quickly shook it off, grabbed her arm, and pulled her with me as I moved towards the entrance.

"Someone needs to show me where they disappeared." A man in his forties moved forward, so I stopped and looked toward him.

"You know the way?"

"Yeah, I saw her turn down the passage, and he followed her. We have two men at the entrance in case he comes out."

"You didn't go in after her?" I thundered and grabbed the man by his shirt.

"You let a defenseless woman be chased down by a man wielding a knife?" I hissed, and the bastard had the decency to go pale. I grabbed his arm and hauled him with me to the entrance, then shoved him in and on a shout threatened, "You haul your ass down this tunnel to where she disappeared like your life depended on it, 'cause if any harm has come to her, I will personally rip you in half."

He didn't hesitate; he turned and started running. I pulled out my flashlight and gun, then followed close on his heels. After a few minutes of running, we came up on what looked like a body on the ground, and I hesitated, afraid it was Jenn.

"He's dead. We checked him already but didn't want to move him."

I shoved him forward, and we picked up the pace. I had my gun drawn, ready for anything, praying that we'd round a curve, and I'd find that bastard standing in front of me so I could empty my magazine into him.

Within a few minutes, we came upon two men who were standing at the entrance to a dark tunnel, holding metal pipes in their hands. I tamped down the disgust I felt, knowing Jenn was down there fighting for her life, and these so-called men just stood there and did nothing. I recognized both of them, but didn't have time to shove my boot up their asses for being less than men.

"How long have they been gone?"

"Forty minutes, hour tops," one said. Without another word, I turned with my gun and flashlight held high, sweeping back and forth as I quickly made my way down the corridor, praying I wasn't too late.

***

No sign of struggle anywhere, so I kept moving. Knowing Gerry would see me before I could see him, I kept my finger on the trigger instead of the safety position, ready to fire if I saw the whites of his eyes.

Still nothing. Where the hell are they?

Something dark opened up before me; it was a sinkhole in the floor of the tunnel. I scanned for a way around it and saw none. How had Jenn gotten around this in the dark? *Jesus.* Fear hit me, and I ran to the edge and pointed my light down. Twenty feet down, I saw Jenn lying unconscious, not moving.

I shouted, "Jenn!" and dropped to my knees to get a closer look. There was a foot near her head, so I pointed my light over and saw Gerry, knife embedded in his chest, no movement, just stone cold dead. I shone my light back on Jenn and watched for movement. I was holding my breath, paralyzed, thinking she was dead, but then I noticed her chest rise and fall.

"Jenn, can you hear me?" Nothing.

"Baby, open your eyes," I pleaded. Nothing. I watched her, trying to decide how to get her out. No phone would work in here, and it was too deep for me to reach her and carry her out. I needed the fire department, and I needed them now. With one last look to assure myself she was breathing, I knew I had to run back the way I came and get help. Then I'd come back, climb down in that pit and hold her until help arrived.

***

I reached the end of the tunnel, running faster than I had in years, to find none of the men waiting for me. Too worried to give it a second thought, I followed the lights down to the exit and walked out into the light. My eyes were trying to adjust, so I pulled my sunglasses on to see, and was headed toward my truck when one of the men from the tunnel came into my view. Without even thinking I grabbed his shirt, shoved him back, and punched him in the jaw.

"You left her to die!" I thundered at the three of them, my worry for Jenn multiplying ten-fold the longer I was away from her. With no time to spare, I turned my back on them and ran to my truck.

Screw the mayor. He wants my badge, he can have it. All those men deserved that and more. I didn't have time for this shit. I needed to get Jenn help and I needed it now, so I moved to my truck, opened the door and grabbed my cell.

No. Fucking. Bars.

I grabbed my CB and, with a prayer to God, turned it on.

"Base, come in."

"Base, this is Gunnison, come in."

Nothing.

I was ready to shoot every man who was standing there out of frustration, when I heard a faint crackle.

"Sheriff?"

"Base, do you read me?" No reply.

"Base, if you read me, I need Fire Rescue to the mine. I've got an injured woman in a twenty-foot hole, and a dead body to retrieve. Over."

I waited, and then, as if my prayer had been answered, I heard, "Affirmative. Fire Rescue on the way, Jack. Over."

"Thank, Christ." I turned to the back of my truck, opened the tool chest and pulled out my rappelling gear, first aid kit, and more flashlights. I heard vehicles approach and looked up to see Grady, Barry, and Phil pull in, so I moved to them quickly and brought them up to speed. Barry grabbed his rope and started heading to the entrance.

I turned to Grady and Phil, and with a quiet calm I didn't' feel, ordered, "Check these people for injuries, and then get them out of here. Mandy can stay, but the rest, especially the men, I want them gone. Secure the crime scene in the tunnel and have Mandy direct Fire Rescue to the tunnel entrance when they arrive."

Both nodded, and with one last look at them, I turned my back and headed to the entrance, praying to God I wasn't too late.

Twenty-Three

Drunken Stupor

"Jesus, Jack, how far did she fall?" Barry asked when we reached the edge of the pit.

Too far. I needed to get down to her now. I didn't answer him, because it didn't matter, so I ignored his question and dropped my rope and pack, then shone a light down on my girl to make sure she was still breathing. When my light hit her face, her eyelids twitched, reacting to it hitting her face. Relief hit me like a punch in the gut, and all I wanted to do was climb down in that hole and bring her out. But I couldn't risk a possible neck or back injury being exacerbated by moving her.

"I'll tie off and you can lower me down."

"I think you should lower me down, Jack; I'm lighter, and you can hold me easier." I didn't have time for this. I wasn't gonna play this game with him. He wanted to be near her because of how he felt; I got that, but there was only one of us going in the pit, and it wasn't him.

"I'll tie off and you can lower me down," I repeated, ending the discussion. Our flashlights were putting off enough light for me to see him look down at Jenn, worry etched on his face. *Jesus, this guy's in love with her.* I didn't need this. I didn't want to see it; the irrational side of me wanted to punch him in the face for having feelings for her, so I turned from him and tied the rope off around my waist, then slapped him on the back to get his attention and handed him the rope.

"Let's take this slow and easy. I don't want to land on her."

"Right," Barry replied, his mind still on Jenn, so I pushed him back, drew up the slack and got his attention.

"I need your head in the game, Barry. I can't help her if you drop me." Barry nodded and handed me the first aid kit. I slung it over my shoulder and waited for him to tighten his grip on the rope. I leaned back, and started walking my way down the side of the wall as Barry slowly lowered me down. When I reached the bottom, I untied the rope and moved to Jenn.

"Jenn, baby, I'm here. I got you, you're gonna be just fine," I whispered in her ear. I felt for her pulse; it was weak, but there. Shining the light down on her, I checked her front for injuries. I couldn't find any, but there were scrapes on her hands and face. I gently felt around her head for any lacerations that needed my attention and felt something wet at the base of her skull. I pulled my hand back and saw blood, so I inspected it further and found a large gash just behind her left ear.

A rock nearby had blood and tissue on it, and I knew she'd hit it when she fell. Careful not to move her neck, I dug through my first aid kit, finding gauze and a roll of tape, then applied pressure to the wound to stop the bleeding and taped it in place.

Pulling a blanket from the bag, I tucked it around her

to help fight off shock, then grabbed her hands and started rubbing them together to warm them up, watching to see if she responded. Nothing. No movement. Determined not to think about why she wasn't responding, I pulled out a normal saline solution IV and an oxygen tank from my kit and began the process of starting an IV.

Finding a good vein in her hand, I cleaned it with betadine, popped the cap off the butterfly needle and gently inserted it into her vein. Tapping off the needle and looping the IV tubing, so it wasn't caught and ripped out, I shone my light around me, looking for something to hang the bag on, and found a large jagged rock protruding from the side of the wall.

"Jack, is she responding at all?" Barry shouted from above.

"Not yet," was all I could give him, and kept working.

IV and oxygen in place, I looked at my watch, noting it had been twenty-five minutes since I'd called the station, so Fire Rescue should be arriving any minute. With nothing to do but wait, I talked to Jenn, hoping my voice would get a response

"You know, when you walked up at that second crime scene six days ago, I thought you were the sexiest woman I'd ever seen. Then you opened your mouth." Watching for a reaction, hell, praying for her to sit up and argue with me, I kept going.

"You acted all tough and sure of yourself. Christ, that was sexy too. Didn't know it then, didn't see it until I confronted you at the paper that same day. But you're not tough...no, you're not tough at all, you're a fighter. Fight for what you want, for those you love. Fight for the right to be who you want to be; you even fight for the right to fight. So I'm asking you, right now, to fight. Don't let that sonofabitch win."

Still nothing, so I lay down next to her, gathered her in my arms as best I could, and then put my mouth to her ear and whispered, "Fight for us, baby."

***

Five minutes later...

"Jack, Rescue's here." I leaned up, kissed Jenn's head, and looked up. Light shining down from above blinded me, so I covered it with my hand and watched as an extension ladder came over the edge. One by one, three EMTs came down the ladder. I jumped up, helped them with their equipment and then stood back and watched as they assessed her. They checked my IV site, collared her neck, checked her pupils, slid a flat board under her, and then moved her to a recover basket. They strapped her in, hoisted her up and out, and not one damn time through all of that, did she move.

"Sheriff, this guy is dead," I heard someone say from behind me as I watched Jenn rise to the top. I turned my head and, not giving a shit, said, "Good". Then I walked to the ladder, climbed up and out, grabbed my pack, jogged over to Jenn, and held her hand. I didn't let go until they closed the doors on the ambulance and left me waiting outside the mine.

***

"There is swelling on her brain, a cerebral edema. We

need to manage the swelling and bring down her temperature by administering Mannitol*. I'm also going to put her on a respirator to make sure she's getting enough oxygen to her brain," Gill Harrison, the county ER doc, explained after they ran a battery of tests on Jenn. Closing my eyes at this news and praying yet again that God would answer, I shook his hand and pulled out Jenn's phone, looking for the contact information for Bailey Stewart. *Christ, what a way to meet her daughter.*

Ten minutes later, after listening to tears and a promise to be on the next plane out, I hung up with Jenn's daughter and smiled. Like mother like daughter. Once Jenn was better, and we had her back on her feet, something told me I'd have my hands full with the both of them. I couldn't wait.

I looked up as Ben and Lorraine came rushing in, panicked as they came straight to me.

"How is she?" Ben asked.

"She's in a coma due to swelling on her brain. They're treating it with medicine, both cold and oxygen."

"Merciful heavens," Ben whispered, and Lorraine grabbed his hand and patted it before leading him to a chair and sat him down. I watched as she took care of Ben and for the first time, it registered that those two seemed to be closer than I remembered. The elevator opened, and Barry, Grady, Phil, Mandy, and a slew of people dressed in period costumes and fake blood walked out and right to me. Another ten minutes passed during which I brought everyone up to speed. The doc told me I could go in and sit with Jenn once they had her stabilized, so I stood at the entrance to ICU and

252

waited.

"Sheriff Gunnison," I heard a nurse call out. As I walked toward her, she said, "Follow me," and then led me down the hall. She stopped and let me enter in front of her. I sucked in a breath when I saw Jenn's tiny body in that big bed. There was a machine breathing for her, a water blanket to bring down her temperature, and IVs in her arms, sending fluids and medicine to heal her swelling brain. Pain hit me in the gut, and I moved to a chair, pulled it over to the side of the bed, and sat down. I grabbed her hand, closed my eyes with my head to her hand, and prayed like I'd never prayed before.

***

"Come on, Jennifer. Enough with the sleeping already, it's only six days until Halloween, and I need you to help me come up with a sexy costume to make all the boys at school drool."

Coming out of the fog, I heard what sounded like my daughter chatting away. My mind seemed sluggish, and I couldn't think long enough to respond to her. My dreams were getting more lifelike as of late. Jack talking about being a fighter. Barry talking about getting coffee and apologizing for acting like an ass. Ben crying, saying he didn't know and to please forgive him, and now Bailey, who was off at school, wanting me to wake up.

"Enough is enough, mom. I lost dad, I am not losing you, too. So pull up your big girl panties and wake up, dammit."

"Don't cuss, it's not ladylike," I whispered. My throat

253

was so dry. I tried to lift my hand, but it felt too heavy; I wiggled my fingers, and they felt tight, like I'd been working too long in the garden and dried out my skin from working in the dirt. In fact, my whole body seemed tight and achy.

"MOM!" I heard Bailey scream. Flinching at her voice, my head felt full, and I decided I'd tied one on and was just now waking up from a drunken stupor.

"Bailey, don't scream. My head hurts," I replied, my voice sounding louder. I tried to move my arms again, and they rose and then fell.

"Don't move. I'll get the nurse," Bailey replied, which I thought was odd. *What the hell is she talking about, the nurse?*

There was a rustling in the room and then a noise that sounded like a shower curtain being pulled back. A moment later, a warm hand touched my arm, and I jumped from the sudden contact. Opening my eyes, I could make out someone standing there. My vision was blurry, though, so I blinked several times until I saw Jack's smiling face looking back at me.

"Welcome back," he whispered, but that just confused me more.

"Did I go somewhere?" I asked him.

"Yeah, baby, you went to sleep for about a week." I snorted at his joke. That must have been some bender I went on. Trying to remember the last thing I did, the only thing that came to mind was a hot body, strong arms, and a fantastic orgasm.

"Did that orgasm you gave me knock me out for a week?" I giggled. Then I heard a cough and a woman's voice I'd never heard before saying, "Sheriff, if you'll excuse me? I need to get in here and take her blood pressure." I looked around the room and realized I was in a hospital room, and that's when I started to panic.

"What's wrong with me? Did I get sick? Did I wreck my Jeep?"

The nurse's face leaned into me. Smiling faintly, she shook her head. "You took a tumble down a hole and you needed rest to get better."

I lay there, trying to remember falling, but nothing came to me. Only Jack and great sex. I bit my lip and concentrated on remembering anything as Jack leaned into my ear from my other side and whispered,

"Sweetness, I'll explain it all once you're better. Just concentrate on getting stronger."

"Ok, Jack," I whispered back and leaned my head into his.

Then I heard Bailey laugh, "I like him, Jennifer. He knows how to shut you up." Looking towards my mouthy daughter, I smiled.

"Bailey, how long have you been here? When are you going back?"

"Got here a week ago, Mamacita. Been hanging with Jack here and his wild bunch of deputies. I'll leave when you're ready for me to and not a day sooner."

"But your classes..."

"Got permission from my professors to follow the classes online to keep up, and they're giving me extra time to make up my assignments. So don't sweat it."

"So you're here until I'm better?"

"I'm not going anywhere before you can walk and talk and boss me around."

"Awesome." *I think my recovery period just got longer.*

"I hear our patient is awake," said a balding man with sharp blue eyes and a round belly. I turned to him and smiled. He took the chart from the nurse and read it, then signed it and stuck out his hand to me.

"Dr. Harrison, pleasure to finally meet you. Your daughter has been regaling us with stories of her childhood and the supermom that you are."

"If any of the stories were embarrassing, they were all lies," I replied sleepily and yawned.

"Looks like you're tiring out already, but that's to be expected. Give it a couple of days, and you'll be feeling more like yourself."

"Is there anything still wrong with me?"

"Nothing time and rest won't heal, so take it easy. No getting riled up, just rest and more rest." I nodded my head and put it back on my pillow. I felt Jack grab my hand and raise it to his mouth for a kiss. Bailey watched and smiled a sweet smile, then looked at me and winked. I felt my eyes getting heavy, and before I could say anything else, I drifted off into slumber.

***

"Time to die, whore!"

Gasping for air, I tried to get Gerry off me; we were falling, oh, God...

"No, NO!" I shouted, arms thrown out to stop the knife from stabbing me in the heart. I felt strong arms wrap around me, and I fought, trying to get away when I heard Jack in my ear. "I've got you. I've got you. You're safe."

I stopped struggling, and then everything came back to me at once. Gerry, the tunnel, the knife, the falling down a dark pit... I even felt the impact at the back of my head pounding with the memory. The shaking hit like a tidal wave, reminding me of when I gave birth to Bailey. Everything shook that day after delivery, and this was the same. I couldn't control it if I tried. I grabbed Jack's arms and hung on, burying my face in his neck. Without asking, he climbed in the bed, lay down next to me, pulled me back into his chest, and just held me while I shook and cried.

"You remembered?"

"First time I wished I couldn't."

"You want to talk about it?"

"God, Jack. I've never known terror before. You watch those horror movies and yell at the heroine to run faster or don't go back into the house, and you think that if you're in the same situation you wouldn't make those same mistakes, but you do. You run down the wrong tunnel and fall into a hole."

"It's over and you're safe," Jack insisted.

"He was my friend," I said on a cry and let the tears fall, gulping huge breaths. Jack drew me closer, and I continued to cry. I cried for the friend I thought Gerry was, for the women who died because of me, and because I just needed to let it out.

"He was no friend, baby, and he doesn't deserve your tears. He died a coward, lived his life less than a man, and gave up a son to hide his own pain. He should have moved forward, taking care of what was his and finding another good woman to love instead of worshiping a woman who was dead. That's on him, not you. You can't blame yourself for his actions, and you can't help that you're the most amazing woman I've ever met."

Thinking about his words, I let them sink in. My crying now under control, I wiped my face of the tears and agreed with him.

"Ok, Jack."

"That's twice you've agreed with me since you woke up, and if I didn't like it so much, I might call the doctor in to give you another battery of tests." I giggled at that and Jack squeezed me.

"Baby, what'd I say about giggling?" he purred in my ear. That got me laughing, and I said without thinking, "Sorry."

"Jesus, this is gonna be a long recovery," Jack growled in my ear. So I giggled again, and Jack decided he'd get even by smacking my ass. Bailey walked in on the smack, raised an eyebrow, but then she grinned and laughed, "You go, Mamacita." *Can you die from blushing?*

Twenty-Four

Conniving Ways

"Bailey, turn that down," Jack shouted from the kitchen. I smiled to myself as I lay in bed, listening to Jack and Bailey fight over the noise level of the TV. The theme song to "Sons of Anarchy" was playing loudly down the hallway, and I knew that Bailey had won.

It'd been one day since I was discharged from the hospital, Jack insisting that I recoup at his house so he could help Bailey take care of me. I didn't tell either of them I felt fine. Just a little tired and sleepy still, but no more so than if I'd had stayed up all night, working on a story, and needed coffee to get through the day.

It had been a week and a half since I'd fallen down that hole and Dr. Harrison said I'd recovered quickly because of Jack's pre-hospital presence of mind to start an IV and oxygen on me; all were parts of the therapy they'd prescribed for the brain swelling I'd endured.

Jack was making soup, home on his lunch hour from the station, and Bailey was supposed to be working on a paper she had to turn in once she left for South Bend and college life at Notre Dame. I heard the doorbell ring and then voices. I tried to hear who was at the door, but Jack's bedroom was at the back of the house.

"Mom, can Ben come in and see you?" Bailey bellowed down the hall.

Thinking about what Ben had lost and also the guilt he seemed to be carrying around with him, I answered immediately. "Sure, send him back." Straightening my blanket and propping pillows behind my head, I waited for Ben to make his way down the hall.

I heard a knock on the door before it opened a bit and Ben ask, "You decent, Jenny?"

"Come in, Ben, it's fine." Ben entered and smiled, and then moved to the bed to sit on the edge near my legs.

"I just wanted to check on you, make sure you were doing ok."

I didn't hesitate: I moved forward and wrapped my arms around his big neck and tried to reassure him that I was fine. Shocked, but fine.

"Ben, I'm all right. I'm feeling stronger every day, and the doctor said if I'm up to it, I can go back to work at the beginning of next week."

Ben slowly wrapped his arms around me and patted my back, saying, "Good, good. That's good to hear, Jenny girl."

I held him for a moment and decided I needed to address the elephant in the room. Ben's friendship with Gerry had lasted a long time, over twenty years, and he had to be feeling used and lost just like I did.

"Ben, please don't blame yourself for Gerry's actions. He fooled all of us, and even though he was a monster in the end, maybe it was more of a sudden snap and the person you were friends with just got lost in there."

"Always looking for the good in people, even when they murder five people. This is why I kept an eye on you. You're too sweet for your own good."

Rubbing tears from my eyes, I saw Jack at the door, and he looked amused.

"What?" I sniffed, searching for a tissue.

"Nothing, babe. Just wondering how many men are gonna fall in love with you before you notice."

"What are you talking about, Jack? Honestly, you talk in riddles sometimes." Jack barked out a laugh and moved farther into the room.

"Just pointing out that Ben here sees what I see: he saw your innocence and sweetness and fell for it too. Lucky for me, he's too old, so he fell in a fatherly way."

"I keep trying to tell you I'm not naive, and certainly not innocent. My twenty-year-old daughter in the other room proves that."

"There she is."

"There who is?"

"My Jenn. Ready to fight with me over anything. It's good to have you back." I narrowed my eyes at him, and he smiled.

I rolled my eyes and looked at Ben. "You see what I have to put up with?"

Ben looked between Jack and me and smiled. "I'd say Jack is right: you're just fine."

Honestly, men stick together tighter than women do.

"Whatever," I replied, and both men laughed.

***

"I'm bored," I whined in the phone.

"I can hear that," Jack replied, *all* but ignoring me.

It was day three since my release, and bed rest was

for the birds. With the exception of hot sex, I'd insisted the only fun I was having had been tormenting Jack and Bailey by ordering them around just for the hell of it. Watching them try and bite their lips to keep from yelling at me, because everyone knows it's bad manners to yell at a sick person, was fun. *Yeah, I know, childish, but still fun!*

"Jack, are you listening to me?"

"If I say no, will you hang up and let me get back to work?"

Oh, no, he didn't?

"*Sorry* I bothered you. I'm sure someone else will talk to me. Oh, look, the mayor's been calling me. Bye, Jack."

Yeah, that was childish, but I was so bored. Sitting there, looking around the room, I decided enough was enough. I was going out. Screw Jack and his "stay in bed or else" orders. Bailey was out, I was home by myself and I craved human interaction.

My phone buzzed a text message, so I looked and saw it was from Jack. I swiped the screen, read it, and laughed.

Babe, ignoring everything but the "sorry". See you tonight.

Well, now what? I needed to either wash my clothes and haul them back up to my cabin, or haul them up to my cabin and then wash. While pondering this dilemma, my phone rang, and I pounced like a puma.

"Hello."

"Hey girl, you done healing?" Mandy's cheerful and much needed voice rang out.

"Yes, but if you tell Jack or Bailey, I'll deny it."

"Gotcha, mum's the word. So if you're feeling better,

you wanna grab some lunch?"

No sweeter words had ever been spoken.

"Sounds good, but can we do it in CB? I need to haul some of my stuff back to the cabin to get ready for work next week."

"Works for me. We can go to McGill's for lunch." I hesitated when she said that, and she caught it immediately.

"Jesus, Jennifer, I'm such an ass. Forget I said that."

"It's fine, it's fine, I can't avoid it forever. I haven't been there since everything happened...In fact, I don't even know if Ben goes there anymore."

Deciding to meet this head-on and rip it off like a Band-Aid, I replied with more conviction than I had before, "McGill's it is."

***

"So what will it be?" Rosie asked us.

We'd arrived at McGill's, and when we walked in, I tried not to look over at Ben's normal spot, but being a glutton for punishment, I did.

It was empty.

Sadness ran through me when I turned and headed to the table. I looked at Mandy, she looked at me, and we grabbed a chair and sat down.

Band-Aid ripped off. Rosie brought us menus, and we ordered our lunch.

"Turkey Club for me," Mandy said to Rosie.

"I'll have the chicken salad, please."

So here we were, sitting at Ben and Gerry's table, and nothing bad happened...

Then my phone rang. I looked and saw it said *"Bossy Calling."*

Yikes.

"Hello."

"You wanna explain to me why you're not at home?"

"Mandy called and we went to lunch."

"You wanna explain to me why you're not at home?"

Apparently Jack was on repeat. Two could play that game.

"Mandy called and we went to lunch."

Jack sighed. I smiled. *See, it's fun.*

"You wanna explain why you aren't resting instead of being out running around?" Jack asked through his teeth.

"I called you, and I told you I was bored. I rested in the car while Mandy drove, and now I'm resting in a chair at McGill's waiting on my sandwich, *and* I will still be resting while eating that sandwich."

"You trying to test my last nerve or is this just your general disposition when sick?"

I thought about that, and I wasn't actually sure to be honest, so I answered truthfully.

"A little of both. Did you need something or is this just your general disposition when you're bossy?"

There was a pause; then he barked out a laugh.

"Christ, if that doesn't turn me on too."

"What? I didn't apologize."

"No, you just know how to push my buttons, and you do it without a care in the world about how pissed off I'll get."

This was true.

"That's true.

"No *sorry* for making me mad?"

"Um, no, because I'm not."

Jack sighed and then moved on.

"You gonna be out all day?"

"Probably not. I don't want to overdo it."

"Then I'll see you tonight."

"Sounds good."

"Later, babe."

"Later, Jack."

"Jesus, it's like listening to an old married couple," Mandy laughed.

We were laughing as Rosie walked up with our food, and I looked up and saw Ben walk in with Lorraine. He looked right at me and smiled, then brought Lorraine over and joined our table. We looked at each other with sad smiles and then moved on.

"So, Lorraine, you and Ben dating now?" Mandy asked around a bite of sandwich. Lorraine smiled a crafty smile and Ben coughed.

"We've been getting to *know* each other better, yes."

"I'll bet," Mandy mumbled in her napkin. I coughed, Ben looked to the ceiling, and Lorraine chuckled.

"Let's just say the plumbing is in order."

I choked down my bite, Mandy hooted, and Ben excused himself and went the men's room.

"Spill," I whispered when he was out of hearing range.

"Man spent all those years eating like a hippie, and the good foods he grew, taking care of his body, paid off. I am *just* as satisfied at sixty-eight as I was at forty."

I sat back, mouth open, and then turned to Mandy, who had the same expression on her face.

"Close your mouths or flies will get in," Lorraine

laughed.

"You're a dirty whore and I want to be you when I grow up."

Lorraine burst out laughing at Mandy's declaration, and I still sat there trying not to think about the fact that Ben and Lorraine were, um, having sex, doing the nasty, hitting the business. Pondering this, I wondered who was on top, and the image of Lorraine riding Ben and shouting "yee-haw" while he slapped her butt hit me. I closed my eyes to get *that* image out of my head when Ben walked up.

I knew I couldn't look him in the eyes, so I stood up and said, "Excuse me." I ran to the bathroom and laughed my ass off. 'Cause, honestly, it wasn't funny—it was awesome—but I knew them, and I didn't want to know that, so I needed bleach and I needed it now!

Five minutes and a shit-load of tissue paper to dry my eyes and wipe my smudged eyes free of makeup later, I walked out to the table and found Lorraine on the phone. She had a pen and notebook out and was writing furiously while replying to someone.

She hung up, turned to me and announced, "Some idiot is robbing the credit union and has hostages. The sheriff's department's been called in, and Bob wants me down there to cover the story."

I didn't even think; I stood up and said, "Let's go." Then I grabbed my purse and turned to Mandy.

"You wanna come or do I need to catch a ride with Lorraine?"

"Hell yeah, I'm coming. I'm not missing this."

We all jumped up, threw money on the table and headed to our cars. Lorraine and I discussed how to

266

approach the story, then jumped in our vehicles and headed off down the highway. It wasn't until we were almost there that it occurred to me that Jack would be there and probably unhappy to see me. Oh well, he needed to get used to it because I had every intention of moving my way up the editorial page at the paper, and, hopefully when Lorraine retired, win her spot.

We reached the credit union twenty-five minutes after the first phone call, and found the sheriff's department had cordoned off the streets two blocks in both directions from the bank. Lorraine and I got out and headed to the barrier with our press passes around our necks, and our game faces on. Grady was standing guard, and when he saw us walk up, his jaw got tight and he shook his head.

"I got no comment, ladies."

"When can we expect a comment?" Lorraine asked.

"Sheriff won't make any comments until this standoff is over."

"So it is a standoff?"

"I'm not commenting."

"Gosh, I hope no children are inside," I innocently said to Lorraine. She gave me big eyes and nodded in return.

"Gunman let them go ten minutes ago," Grady explained quickly to alleviate my worry.

"So there *were* children inside? Where are their mothers?"

"Still in there."

"Poor things they must be so scared. Do you need help with them?" I asked, using my best *mom* voice.

"Got them in the diner with some uniforms. They might need a woman's touch, though."

"Are they talking?"

"I told you I couldn't comment on anything that's happened, Jenn."

"Of course, Grady, I'll leave you to it. I'll just head over to the diner and see if they need help with the kids. Anything I can tell them to ease their fear?"

"Tell them we're talking with the man who's holding their mothers and that the sheriff will make sure they come out unharmed."

"Thanks, Grady. Will you call ahead and let them know we're coming?"

"Sure thing, Jenn."

I nudged Lorraine, and she came with me, whispering, "You're good. I'd love to see what you'd drag out of him if he had permission to talk."

"Like taking candy from a baby," I laughed.

We entered the diner two blocks down and found three children aged six to nine, all looking scared, and it tugged at my maternal heartstrings. Lorraine and I sat down in the booth with them while two highway patrolmen stood guard. Two boys and one girl sat with coloring books and stuffed animals the patrolmen kept in their cars for just such an emergency, and they froze when we sat down.

"Hi, I'm Jennifer. I just wanted to check on you and see how you're doing."

"Is my mommy coming out soon?" the little girl asked.

"I'm sure your mommy will come and get you just as soon as she can, sweetie."

"Is the man with the gun still yelling at her?"

I looked at Lorraine and then back at the little girl; she reminded me of Bailey when she was just a baby. I stroked her hair, hoping that would make her feel safer, and asked, "What was he yelling about?"

"He said he needed money and to put it in a bag."

"Was he mean to anyone?"

"No, he just told everyone to get on the floor, and then when we started crying, he let us go. Said he couldn't think with the crying."

"Don't know why everyone was so scared. It's just a fake gun anyway," one of the boys piped up.

"Why do you think it's fake?" Lorraine asked.

"It's an air gun. They have orange tips so the cops will know they aren't real. He'd covered it with tape so you couldn't tell, but I was standing right next to him when he pulled it out, and some of the tape was loose and you could see the orange."

I looked back at Lorraine and nodded toward the patrolmen; she got my meaning, stood up, and walked over to talk to one of them.

"You're a smart kid. I'm Jennifer. What's your name?"

"Timmy, but I like Tim. Sounds more grown up."

I smiled at how cute he was and then turned back to look at Lorraine and the patrolman. He was talking into his handheld. Figuring Lorraine had it from here, I raised my hand to the waitress and when she approached, I ordered Hot Fudge Sundaes for the table.

Twenty minutes and three messy faces later, I watched as Grady walked into the diner and then over to the table.

"Your mothers are fine. If you're ready to go, I'll take you to them."

All three the kids jumped up, and little Allison grabbed my hand, dragging me with them. Timmy and Tommy—

brothers—held hands as we left the diner and walked down the street to a holding area for the sheriff's department. Lorraine was in-tow, talking in her handheld recorder, detailing the *"Long steps as the frightened children were returned to the safety of their mother's bosom."* A little dramatic for my tastes, but I was sure she'd work it like she always did.

Grady walked behind the barricade, allowed us to enter, and when the women looked up from talking with Jack, they jumped up and raced to the children, who in turn ran to them. Lorraine spoke furiously in her recorder, not missing a tearful touching moment, while I got choked up and watched. Then I looked at Jack.

He narrowed his eyes at me and growled, "Follow me," as he passed me. I hesitated for a brief moment because A) I would miss what was happening, and I loved a great happily ever after story, and B) because he might throw me in a jail cell again.

I squared my shoulders and turned, head held high, and passed Grady who laughed, knowing what was coming. I gave him my *"What?"* look, and then followed Jack around the corner of the building. When we were out of earshot and sight, he grabbed my arm and pushed me back into the wall, pinning me with his body.

"You should be resting, but instead you're at *my* crime scene talking to *my* witnesses without *my* approval, which, I might add, I *will* be talking to Grady about your manipulative ways, thus putting a stop to any further conniving on your part. So ask me, Jenn, why do I wanna fuck you instead of arrest you and tan your hide?"

"Why do you want to fuck me instead of arrest me,

Jack?" I breathed out.

"'Cause the idiot had a fake gun, and when we confirmed it, I walked in there and took him down. Half the town was in the credit union, including the mayor, and when I walked in there and took the guy out, it put an end to whatever fucked up ideas the mayor had about taking my badge. But mostly, your interference got those mothers out of there and back to their kids, and *that's* worth you not staying at home resting, so *that's* why I want to fuck you instead of arrest you."

"I'm sorry I tricked Grady."

"No, you're not."

"Ok, I'm sorry you're mad."

"No, you're not."

"Ok, I'm not sorry you're mad, or that I tricked Grady, but I am sorry you don't know whether to fuck me or arrest me."

Jack's eyes went dark and he moved closer to me.

"I know exactly what I'm gonna do to you. Right now, I'm gonna kiss you, and tonight I'm gonna fuck you and spank that sweet ass of yours for disobeying me once again."

I rolled my eyes, because honestly, where did men like this come from? Then I answered Mr. Bossy Badass Sheriff, 'cause I really wanted a kiss.

"Whatever, kiss me already. I have a story to write." Jack grinned, leaned in, bit my lip, and then thoroughly rewarded me for my conniving ways.

Twenty-Five

Harry Potter

I was pounding hard into the tightest woman I'd ever had. She was dripping wet, soft like silk, and tasted sweet like honey.

"Jesus, you're tight, never felt anything like it," I hissed as Jenn's back arched, and I covered her mouth on the moan escaping her. Swear to Christ I'd never had a woman like her. I could bury myself deep all night and never get tired. I'd brought her to orgasm twice already and wasn't finished.

"You like it rough, baby?" Jenn whimpered her reply like I knew she would. I was playing her body like the priceless instrument it was, and the rougher I was, the more turned on she got. Her breathing was accelerated; her moaning was getting louder, and I knew she was moments away from exploding. I was holding off; I wanted her putty in my hands. One leg wrapped around my back, the other tangled around my thigh, I thrusted hard again and felt her tighten and then spasm around my cock, milking me. I watched her eyes roll back, and that about sent me over the edge. *She's fuckin' beautiful when she comes.*

The male instinct to claim kicked in and my thrusting

became more brutal, neurons were firing, and they said one thing only: Mark her, claim her, and make her mine.

"Jack, honey, I'm gonna go again, oh, God."

That hit me in the balls, and I squeezed my eyes shut, concentrating on not losing it before she came. My thumb found her clit, and I rolled it. She ignited again, and that was it; I couldn't hold off another second. I thrust twice more, and then buried my cock deep in her walls and emptied myself into her as if it was the first time I'd ever come. I moaned deep in my throat as my mouth found her neck. I had to mark her. Teeth sinking in where her neck joined her shoulder, I rode out my release, thinking I could die now and not regret my life for one second. Christ, but I was gone for this woman.

Nuzzling her neck, tasting and kissing my way back to her mouth, needing to taste her one more time, I took it and tangled my tongue with hers while I slowly finished thrusting into her heat.

"Wow, that was unreal," she whispered, and I grinned on her mouth.

Every fucking thing about this woman turned me on, turned me inside out, hell, turned me on my fucking head.

"You better believe it," I smirked.

"Full of yourself and bossy," she giggled.

"Confident in my abilities is more like it."

"Where I'm from it's called arrogant."

"Where I'm from it's called being a man."

"Lucky me," she sighed, and I rolled to my side, tucking her into me. Then I remembered I owed her a swat for disobeying me, so I smacked her ass, and she yelped.

"That will leave a mark," she cried out.

"You're lucky I didn't smack both sides."

"You take your job as my oppressor too seriously."

"I take my job as your man extremely serious and the sooner you start listening—"

She cut me off, grinning huge and rolling her eyes, "Jack, it's cute you think you'll ever be able to tell me what to do, really. It entertains me daily," she laughed.

I sighed and shook my head. Her inability to see that I would win, I *always* did, was almost as cute as her trying to ignore my orders. And for some damn reason, I wondered if her dead husband had the same problem.

"Why are you scowling?" Jenn whispered in my ear. I looked down at her and for the first time realized she'd loved another man. I knew she'd been married, but we'd never really talked about it, so I'd forgotten. Now I remembered, and it was like a punch in the gut that someone else had held her heart.

"Did you love him?" For some insane reason, I needed an answer to that question.

"Who?"

"Your husband. I know you had to get married, but did you love him?"

She paused; her eyes unfocused as she thought about the question, and she smiled.

"Yes, I loved him. He was my best friend."

That sucker punched me, and before I could recover she continued, "I don't think I was in love with him like you're supposed to be when you marry someone, but he was funny and easygoing and a great father. It was no hardship being married to my best friend."

The breath I'd held since she'd spoken released, and

I breathed deep. Relief for some inexplicable reason coursed through my body and I knew right then that I'd fallen in love with her. The thought that another man might have held her heart the way I wanted to had gripped mine until she released it with her words. Christ, I sounded like a damned Hallmark card at the thought of possessing her heart.

I rolled into her and ran a finger down her jaw until it found her lips and pressed into her mouth to keep her from talking.

"You're mine now. I'm sorry he died, sorry Bailey lost her dad, but I'm not sorry it brought you here to me."

It was a shit thing to say, but I didn't care. She belonged to me now, and if he rose from the dead tomorrow, I'd kick his ass back to Kansas.

Jenn stared at me for a moment, the wheels of her mind turning, and I wondered what she was thinking. She opened her mouth and then closed it, hesitant to say something, then, like always, she came right out with it.

"Doug was a good man. He gave me Bailey, and I will always love him for that and miss his gentle spirit and sense of humor. But I'd be lying to myself if he knocked on my door tomorrow—I'd be thrilled he was alive, of course—but it would be a lie to go back to him.... Since I've met you, I realized I was settling."

"Are you saying you're not settling now?" Her hand came to my face, and I kissed her palm.

"No, I'm not settling. What can I say, I have a thing for bossy."

"Then I guess we're made for each other, baby. 'Cause you don't listen for shit, and that turns me right the hell on."

She giggled, and I felt that in my bones. How this tiny woman could bring me to my knees baffled me, but I sure as hell was gonna enjoy finding out why she did.

***

It was Sunday morning. Jack had the day off and was making pancakes. With Mandy's help, I'd hauled most of my clothes back up to my cabin two days earlier. Bailey was staying until Halloween. She'd decided to spend the holiday with me when she heard about the fall festival and costume party they put on each year. Jack was going to drive me up to my cabin after breakfast so I could settle in and relax before I jumped back into work tomorrow, so Bailey and I spent the morning browsing the internet, deciding on which costumes to wear.

"Mom, you should go as a sexy pirate or vampire. You've got the tits and ass for it."

"Bailey, I was thinking more along the lines of something scary." She looked at me in horror and shook her head.

"No way. It's the one time of the year you can almost go naked in the streets and get away with it, Mom. You have to do something sexy...You know, to hold Jack's attention."

"I don't know, Bailey. Oh, wait, show me that Harry Potter one again." Bailey rolled her eyes and scanned back; but then her smile grew.

"I like it, Mamacita...Very you."

"You think Jack will like it?"

"I think Jack will hate it."

"Good, then it should do its job."

Bailey burst out laughing as Jack walked into the room, took one look at us, and narrowed his eyes. How he could tell we were up to something I'd never know, but in the short time he'd been around us, he'd learned to read us like he'd known us for years. *I'm so not seeing good things for my future.*

***

Breakfast over, dishes washed, it was time to head back home. After a week at Jack's, it would be great to be home, but I'd miss waking up to him. Bailey was meeting me there after she headed to the costume shop to pick up what we needed for the party in two days' time, so it was just Jack and me heading up the mountain.

I was watching the scenery pass by when Jack's phone rang.

"Gunnison." Jack answered. I was half-listening when I heard Jack cuss. Seeing as he cussed a lot, I didn't pay attention until I heard him say, "Did you contact Buckley?" Buckley was the last name of the man I'd met that fateful day when Gerry's life ended. Mine almost did, and our town was rocked by the news that one of their own beloved members was a killer. So I listened, but couldn't figure out what was happening.

I'd no sooner given up when Jack said, "Was the mine tour a total loss?" I watched as Jack's jaw tightened and then wondered what had happened at the Ghost Mine. "Roger that, I'll be there in an hour. Just dropping off

Jenn at her place." Jack hung up, dropped his phone on the seat, and turned to me.

"Somebody set fire to the mine tour. Total loss. Fire department's there now." I wasn't sure how I was supposed to feel hearing this, so I said nothing.

"You ok?" Jack asked.

"I think so; it wasn't a place I wanted to go back to, but it's a shame for the Buckley's after all their hard work."

"Was planning on spending the day with you, but I have to head back and handle this."

"Don't worry about me. I've got a ton of laundry and work I need to do before tomorrow."

Jack grinned at me, and I thought that was odd, so I asked him, "What's so funny?"

"Nothing, just not used to a woman who doesn't throw a fit when I get called out." *Score one for Jenn!!!*

"Oh, well then, smile away." And he did. He also grabbed my hand and held it on his lap the rest of the way to my cabin. *Nice.*

***

"Mom, they only had that costume in a size smaller than you wanted," Bailey shouted as she entered my cabin.

"Did you get me something different?"

"No, I got it. It will just be shorter and show more cleavage than the larger one."

"I don't know, Bailey. That might be pushing it for someone my age." She actually snorted when I said that, then pulled out the costume and threw it at me.

"Try it on. I got my legs from grandmother, but yours are smoking hot. I say if you've got it, flaunt it."

Looking down at the scrap of fabric that constituted the costume, I had second thoughts on the whole plan of making Jack burning mad, which equaled him taking it out on me in the bedroom. I'd still have to go out in this, which meant be seen in it, and I was thinking my butt hanging out wasn't worth my reward.

"Just try it on, Mom. You'll see." I looked at Bailey and figured *"what the hell?"* So I headed to the bathroom and put it on.

Yup, I'm gonna wish I'd kept my mouth shut.

Boobs showing, ass covered by a half inch of fabric, but at least there was a cape. I walked out to show Bailey, and she was standing there talking to Mark. I was shocked to see him. I'd been so busy recovering from my own injuries I'd forgotten about him. Bailey was flirting per usual, and before I could turn around and duck back into the bathroom, he looked up and grinned.

"Well, looks like I came by at the right time."

"Uh, hi, hi...Sorry, I'm just gonna go change this."

"Don't change on my account," he laughed. Seeing my robe hanging on the dining room chair, waiting to be washed, I grabbed it and threw it on.

"Mark, what are you doing here?" Realizing that was blunt and rude, I apologized. "Sorry, that was rude. I'm just surprised to see you. I figured you'd have gone home by now."

"Got discharged a few days ago and wanted to come by and see how you were doing."

"How did you find me?"

"Googled you."

"I'm on Google?"

"Good lord, Mom. For a reporter your computer skills

a reason to breathe

are severely lacking."

I ignored Bailey and moved toward them.

"So did you heal, any lasting injuries?"

"Yeah, nothing permanent except a broken heart." Shaking my head at his ridiculous remark, I laughed. He was extremely charming, and he knew it. I guess that's why I'd enjoyed his company that night at The Nickel.

"I'm sure you'll recover just fine. Are you heading home soon?"

"Yeah, in a couple of days. Have some things to take care of first, and then I'll head home."

"You want to stay for some coffee or hot chocolate?" Bailey jumped in, and I realized I'd forgotten my manners.

"Sorry, do you want some coffee?"

"No, I can't stay. I just wanted to pop by and say hi. I'm glad to see you're doing ok." He turned to make for the door, and I followed him out to the porch.

"Thanks for stopping by, Mark. It was nice to see you again and know you're doing well."

He turned to me and studied me for a brief moment and then said, "Oh, what the hell," and he grabbed my face and kissed me.

I was stunned and frozen, my eyes open and eyebrows up in shock. I didn't even move my hands, and since my non-movement didn't say stop, he tried to wrap me up in his arms; of course that was the moment that Jack decided to pull into the driveway.

I heard the crunch of rocks made by his tires and then Bailey said, "Oh, shit,"

I tried to push back, but Mark had my arms wrapped up against me. But then he heard the truck door slam, and was pulling away from me when he was yanked back, and then shoved into the side of my cabin.

"You got two seconds to explain why you had your lips on my woman," Jack seethed.

"Jack, he was saying goodbye, and he wasn't thinking. He's leaving, just let him go," I begged. Jack looked at me with fire in his eyes.

"Who is he to you?"

"This is Mark, the man who got stabbed by Gerry."

"Why do I get the feeling you left something out about what happened in the bar?"

Before I could answer, Mark jumped in, "I apologize. I didn't mean to step on any toes. I'm leaving in a couple of days and just wanted to say goodbye, honestly," he wheezed out.

Jack's forearm was pressed into his neck; then he moved it to Mark's shirt and spun him from the side of the house to the steps and gave him a shove. Mark spun around as he walked to his car and apologized again.

"I'm sorry, Jennifer. I meant no harm. I just had to know if there was anything there."

"Just go, Mark. I'm glad you're fine, take care."

He moved to his car, and Jack watched him the whole time. I didn't know what to do, so I stood there and waited. When Mark pulled out, Jack turned to me and looked down. I held my breath, waiting for him to bellow at me, but he just studied me for a moment. His hand came up and cupped my face, his thumb moving across my lips like he was trying to smear the kiss off them. I didn't know what else to do so I bit his thumb. His eyes narrowed and went dark, then he sucked in a breath and laid down the law for the millionth time since

I'd met him.

"No one touches these lips but me, do you hear me?"

"Ok."

"I don't want to see that guy within ten feet of you again."

"Ok."

"I find out he's been around when I'm not here, I'll find him and beat the shit out of him."

"Ok."

He looked at me again for a moment, studying me, then he continued, "And from now on, you do as I say, no arguments."

"O...hey, nice try, but I'm not that—" Jack swooped in and kissed me. His hands were in my hair, then running down my back, pulling me closer. He deepened the kiss, his tongue staking his claim and *that* kiss took away any lingering memories of another man's lips. Jack pulled back and scanned me from head to toe, while my head spun, and then he tilted his head amused.

"Knew you were trouble the first day I laid eyes on you."

"I knew you were bossy the minute you opened your mouth," I responded.

"Babe, answer me one thing."

"What?"

"What the hell are you wearing?"

Twenty-Six

Celebrating

Three days later....

"You're moving in with me."

"I'm what?"

"Woke up three days in a row without you in my bed after having you there a week. I'm too old to play games, so you're moving in with me," Jack ordered over the phone.

Jack and I had been spending what time we could with each other, between his job and mine. Lunch here, dinner there, hot after dinner sex, before he had to leave since he was on call for the evening. He'd had a fire at the Mine, an elderly man who walked away from an Alzheimer's ward to find, and he was still dealing with the aftermath of the bank robbery. After seeing each other daily, it was an adjustment for me, and clearly it was an adjustment for him, 'cause now he was ordering me to move in with him.

"Jack, be reasonable. We've only known each other three weeks. We don't need to rush this."

"Jenn, I don't need another day to know I wanna build something with you, and I'm not doing it living separate lives. You're moving in. Call Ben and tell him you'll be out within a week so he can start looking for another tenant." Before I could even respond, he hung up. I was learning that when Jack wanted something, he said what's gonna happen, and if you didn't agree, he walked right over you. This was gonna be one of those times. Since I kinda loved his bossy ways, and I was sure I kinda loved him, I picked up the phone and called Ben.

"Hiya, Jenny, what's up?"

"I'm moving in with Jack. He told me to tell you I'd be out in a week."

"Took him long enough. I didn't think he'd let you leave once you were discharged."

See! Men totally stick together!!!

"Do *you* boss Lorraine around like this?"

"Hell no, she wears the pants and I'm fine with that." I could totally see that.

"Glad it works for you, Ben, and thanks for understanding. Talk to you later."

"Call me if you need help moving."

"Will do, thanks."

I hung up and looked around my cabin in the mountains and was sad to think about moving. Realizing I had to pack everything for the second time in five months, I groaned. Bailey walked in from outside, and I blurted out, "I'm moving in with Jack." She looked confused by my outburst, then it hit her. First, she smiled, then she laughed.

"I knew that costume would work." Smiling at her excitement, I laughed when I thought about Jack's reaction when he'd asked me what I was wearing. When I'd told him I'd been trying on the Halloween costume Bailey bought me, he quickly turned to her, and, I kid you not, said, "You're grounded."

Needless to say, he expressed his extreme displeasure with my costume. He said he was working the event and under no circumstances was I to show up in that, and if I did, he'd tan my hide. To which I laughed, thinking he was funny for trying to tell me, yet again, what to do. So I'd nodded and mmhmm'd while he carried on about how he'd have to shoot anyone who looked at me, and did I really want to risk the lives of every man in the county?

The discussion ended with Bailey saying she'd return the costume for something else, but Jack didn't catch the gleam in her eye. When she returned the next day with a new costume, it was worse than the first. I was now going as a sheriff; Bailey thought that was appropriate, but I didn't think this was standard issue. The black shorts covered less butt cheek than before and the top only covered half my boobs. And that wasn't good, 'cause they weren't itty-bitty cups. Spiked black boots and a ball cap with aviator glasses rounded out the stripper gear, and I just knew Jack was gonna explode... *(Insert evil laugh).*

See why I missed my daughter? She rocked. She was my best friend, and I wouldn't change a thing about her.

She pulled me out of my head when she said, "Daddy would have liked Jack."

"They're nothing alike. Why do you think he would have liked Jack?"

"'Cause he would have enjoyed watching Jack try to boss you around, knowing it wouldn't work. Dad always said to try and stop you was a waste of energy, 'cause you couldn't be harnessed. He said you were like a wild mustang."

God, that made me sad, thinking about Doug, and how much he was missing out on Bailey's life, and how much Bailey was gonna miss her dad in the future, then she rocked me again.

"You'd lost that after he died. You were cautious, like you forgot you could do anything you put your mind to. Jack brings out your fighter instincts. He's good for you; you're *you* around him."

A knot formed in my throat; my eyes got wet, but I was determined not to cry because my daughter thought I could do anything. So I tucked that memory away for another time.

"Who wouldn't fight with that man? Seriously, you've seen him order me around. He's a throwback to the cavemen days."

We both laughed, then Bailey gave me a hug. "I'm happy for you, Mom. You deserve forever with a man you love and who loves you." *Like I said, she rocks.*

***

Two hours later, I was at my office, starting my article on the upcoming Halloween Festival, when I heard Bob call my name. Looking over my computer screen at my editor, he raised his hand to indicate he wanted me to come to him. Grabbing my notebook and pencil, I headed to his office, wondering what crafts fair or bake sale had called in for coverage.

I entered his office, and he pointed to a chair in front of his desk. Sitting, I waited for him to take a seat, and when he did, he floored me. "Lorraine and I have been discussing her cutting back at the paper. She wants to spend more time with Ben while they're still young." He laughed and then continued, "So she's asked to take over your position in events."

"What?"

"I'm moving Lorraine to events and moving you to editorial."

"What?"

"Lorraine will finish up the Halloween Festival piece, and I want you to concentrate on the new casino that's attempting to move in. We need a human-interest piece on this, and why it will change the area for good or bad. Research any states whose economy is dependent on tourism, see if the areas have had a rise in crime, also if the funds dumped into their economies were worth what they had to give up."

Still in shock, I grabbed my notebook and started scribbling furiously while he spoke. Half listening and half wanting to do back flips with a half pike, I kept my cool.

When Bob finished, I looked up and, with a serious reporter face, said, "I'll get right on it, and thanks for the opportunity, Bob."

"Thank Lorraine. She told me I'd be an idiot to keep you on events. Said something about you having the sheriff's department wrapped around your pinky, and if you could do that, you could sweet talk anyone for information."

I made a note to hug Lorraine and buy her a gift, but only nodded once and replied, "Yes, sir." Then I turned and exited his office. I hurried to my desk, grabbed my phone and dialed Jack.

***

I walked into "Mike's Burgers" and scanned the restaurant, looking for Jack. He'd had time for a quick bite when I told him the good news. "We're celebrating, meet me at Mike's," was his bossy reply, so here I was looking for Jack, who hadn't arrived yet. Deciding to grab a table, I told Shirley at the counter to give Jack the heads-up when he arrived.

Looking for privacy, I spotted a booth in the corner and headed over, passing tables and booths filled with locals. I waved hi and went to sit down when I heard giggling from one booth over. Turning my head, I found three sets of women's eyes on me. I'd never met these women, so I wasn't sure who they were, and what was so funny. I looked at my jeans, then at my boots to see if I was trailing toilet paper. I found nothing to be hilarious, so I ignored them and sat down.

"You're that reporter, aren't you?" a buxom blonde inquired. Something about the way she said that reminded me of someone, but I couldn't put my finger on it, so I stood and walked over to her table and put out my hand.

"Jennifer Stewart, nice to meet you."

"We've met, or I should say we've spoken on the phone. You called to warn me I might be a killer's next victim."

Since Jack had called me and put a stop to my phone calls, I'd only gotten in touch with one woman that day: Amber Welsh, the only one Jack said hated him. *Dammit, today has been a great day so far.*

I smiled as genuinely as I could and replied, "Amber, right? Nice to meet you."

"Have you taken my advice and dumped Jack before he dumps you?" Why had I introduced myself? I should have known she was trouble from just looking at her.

"No, I'm still seeing Jack."

"You mark my words: you'll be history in a month."

"I'll keep that in mind," I answered as diplomatically as I could. She actually rolled her eyes at my answer, and that pissed me off. I decided an escape was the best course of action for now, so begged off with, "Nice to meet you, but I'm on a short lunch hour so I think I'll just go order from takeout," and then turned to the front when Jack walked in. *Shit.*

Jack saw me, smiled big, and headed my way. I didn't know whether to move to him, stay still or go sit down, so I went with greet him.

As I reached Jack, and before I could say anything, he shouted behind him, "Shirley, two specials and two pieces of your chocolate cake. We're celebrating."

Damn, escape was fading fast. I looked for another table on the other side of the room and found one, so I grabbed Jack's hand and tried to head toward it, but Jack pulled me back.

"You forget something?" he asked me, smiling.

"What?"

"Haven't seen you today, and you're movin' in, so give me a kiss, baby."

I melted when he said that—who wouldn't?—and without even caring who saw, I rose up on my toes and kissed him. Jack wrapped me in his arms and then deepened the kiss. It was hot, so hot I forgot where we were. When he pulled back and smiled at me, he whispered, "Hi."

"*You're* moving in with him?" I closed my eyes when I heard Amber's accusatory remark. Apparently leaving out that tidbit during our conversation pissed her off. Dammit, this was supposed to be a celebration lunch, not a bitch fight. I could feel my temper rising, so I counted to ten.

"Amber," Jack answered her question with a warning.

"*You're* moving in with him?" she repeated in a tone that screamed disbelief. The anger I'd been holding off by counting came back, and I reacted.

"You heard him, I'm moving in, and I won't be moving out."

Jack wrapped his arm around my chest and pulled me back as I leaned forward. Amber narrowed her eyes, and then gave me a once-over like she was trying to figure out what I had that she didn't. "Brains," I wanted to shout at her, but bit my lip.

Jack barked, "Move on, Amber; we're here for lunch. Don't cause a scene."

"Don't cause a scene? You mean like the one you just caused, sticking your tongue down her throat, rubbing it in my face."

"Christ, Amber, I didn't even see you, and if I had, I wouldn't have cared. You don't ping on my radar, haven't in over two years."

Amber sucked in a breath, hell, I sucked in a breath, but she was getting what she deserved. Her eyes got wet, and I heard Jack mumble, "Shit."

Deciding it was time to end this, I opened my mouth

to apologize for any discomfort she might have endured seeing us together. Why, I don't know; it must've been that damn golden rule my mother ingrained in me—"do unto others"—that made me feel guilty when her eyes teared up, but before I could say sorry, Jack must have felt it coming and whispered, "Don't," in my ear. I understood why when Amber opened her mouth again, and let it rip.

"Shannon wasn't good enough, I wasn't good enough, Naomi and Shannon both got killed because of this slut, and now you're moving *her* into your house? Is that what I'm hearing? All the women you've had in your bed and *this*," she waved her hand up and down, indicating all of me, "is what you finally fall for? Really?"

"I didn't just hear you call her a slut," Jack growled.

"Believe it," she hissed.

I was too busy wondering what "this" meant to retaliate. I was shorter than all of them by 3-4 inches; I didn't have big hair, my boobs weren't *that* huge, and my IQ notwithstanding, they weren't *that* different from me. In fact, since I was smarter and not a bimbo, I figured that gave me one-up on them, so that being the case, I was pissed right the hell off. Figuring everyone else let it all hang out, I decided it was my turn.

"Didn't you get the memo? Jack decided he prefers brains *and* booty." I heard Jack chuckle, but I kept going. "So move on, get over it, and check the attitude, then maybe you won't scare off the next guy.... and in case you're not clear on what I just said, I'll dumb it down for you: fuck off."

Amber reacted quickly, screaming, "You bitch!" and then lunged for me. Jack yanked me behind him and put up a hand to stop her before she reached me. In an angry voice he barked, "Stand down, Amber, or I'll cuff you."

Everyone in Mike's had gone quiet as they watched this play out, and I'd come this close to sticking my tongue out at her, but thankfully, came to my senses and bit my tongue.

"Fine," she hissed, then dramatically turned with a flip of her big hair and made her way to her friends standing at the door.

Without another glance in her direction, Jack grabbed my arm and marched me to a table in the back. He sat me down, and when he joined me, I couldn't help myself: I started laughing.

"You find that amusing?"

"Yes," I replied, still laughing, and he shook his head and grinned.

Shirley showed and saved the day when she placed two specials on the table. Burgers, rings, two chocolate milkshakes, and two chocolate cake slices, that all guaranteed I'd need a larger pants size by the end of the day. Jack raised his milkshake, so I lifted mine, too. He toasted my job, our moving in together and "finally" as he put it, "Meeting and falling for a woman who was smart-tongued enough to put that bitch in her place." So I drank to that. Who wouldn't?

Twenty-Seven

Witches Ball

Halloween....

"An invitation to the Witches Ball." The Gunnison Halloween Festival was set for 5 P.M.in the town square, and this invitation was for seven. It was Thursday, Halloween day, and I couldn't wait to celebrate with the rest of the town tonight. Bailey was leaving tomorrow morning to go back to South Bend, and Jack was working the Festival, so Bailey and I were painting the town red, or black and orange since it was Halloween, and I was stoked. Looking at the invitation for a return sender, I didn't find an RSVP. Strange. I was just about to toss it when Bailey walked in, and I showed it to her.

"Cool, we should go. It must be a private party."

"I wish I knew who left it. If you want to go, I should find out if they need us to bring food, and I should pick up a bottle of wine for the hostess." Growing up, my mother always said, "If someone goes to the trouble of hosting a party, you should always offer to bring food and never arrive without a hostess gift." I'd always abided by that rule and never arrived invited to a social gathering without a bottle of wine. Making a mental note

293

to call Lorraine since she probably knew who was hosting the party, I turned to the coffee pot and started looking for my coffee.

I'd spent the last two days packing for my move to Jack's, but we were both too busy to haul the boxes down the mountain until this weekend. Maneuvering my way around stuff and finding my coffee and two coffee cups I hadn't packed yet, I flipped the switch and turned to Bailey. "What are you up to today?"

"Depends. What time are we going into town?" Bailey inquired while I tossed bread into the toaster.

"I need to work on my Casino article, so I'm just staying home today. We can head in and be at the Festival when it starts. You're all packed to leave tomorrow, right?"

"Packed and ready. I think I'll head over to Crested first and do some shopping before we get ready. You need anything while I'm there?"

"Nope, I just need quiet and an internet connection."

"Is Jack meeting us there?"

"No, he's working the Festival."

"You mean he won't be walking around with us, his gun drawn, threatening men who look at you?" she laughed. She was clearly enjoying Jack's possessive nature and, based on the costume she picked out, liked poking it as well. I laughed at her nonsense and poured our coffee. I'm sure Jack was just exaggerating when he went on about me wearing a revealing costume in public, and if he wasn't, I guess we'd find out tonight.

***

"Mom, can you hook this for me?" I finished clasping the buckle on my boot and stood up, looked in the mirror and laughed. I was so getting thrown in jail.

Bailey entered my bedroom, stopped, whistled, and then said, "You better hide Jack's gun." She was not wrong; in fact, she was so not wrong I considered changing. This outfit might be poking at Jack a little too much.

Throwing that idea aside for now, I moved to Bailey, and she spun around so I could hook her necklace. She was wearing a less revealing cowgirl outfit, but not by much. Thankfully, the skirt was longer than my shorts and her boobs were covered. The overall look was flirty, but not risqué. She'd left the slut look to me.

"I'm having second thoughts about this outfit," I announced while trying to cover my butt.

"No, you look hot, Mom. It's perfect and Jack will love it."

Thinking she really didn't understand Jack, I explained, "Jack will love it in private. It's the public part that concerns me." My bravado about wearing whatever I wanted was faltering the closer we got to leaving. Jack was gonna go ballistic, I just knew it, and more to the fact, I didn't think I was that comfortable showing this much skin, either.

"Nope, you're not changing. This is a statement to Jack that you will always do as you please, no matter how much he yells."

"Says the girl who is flying out in the morning and won't be here to endure his anger," I laughed.

"You rock the outfit, you're wearing it, so grab your coat and let's go."

I looked in the mirror one last time, felt like making the sign of the cross to prepare myself against the up-coming war with Jack, and then grabbed my coat and purse. As I made my way to the front door, I snatched the Witches Ball invitation and a bottle of wine. I'd called Lorraine to ask if she knew who was throwing the ball, and she informed me it was quite an honor to receive the invitation and that it was hosted by a group of town leaders. "Only the who's who of Gunnison got invitations," she'd replied, so I figured, with my new position at the paper, I shouldn't decline. So I bought wine and planned to make an appearance after enjoying the festival.

We headed to my Jeep, and for some reason, as I climbed in, I felt like I was heading to my doom. Chuckling for being so dramatic, I pulled out and turned my Jeep toward Gunnison and my first Colorado Halloween.

***

Gunnison business owners had pulled out all the stops. Each business was decorated to the nines with a ghoulish atmosphere, and there was plenty of candy for the goblins and ghosts. The bars and restaurants were open and thriving, tourists and locals all getting in the spirit of the holiday. Partiers were decked out as vampires, witches, the boys from Duck Dynasty. Bailey and I fit in and we had a ball. The sheriff's department had barricaded the ends of several blocks so no cars could pass through, allowing everyone to mingle in the streets. With my hat and aviator glasses on, most I knew didn't recognize me, and that afforded me the luxury of being seen by the deputies and Jack from a distance, but not having a badass sheriff breathe down my neck. I heard lots of comments like "You can cuff me anytime," and "I'll break the law if you haul me to your cell."

Food and drink flowed and we saw a few fights between teenage boys, but all in all, the festival seemed to be a success. It was nearing time to leave to head to the Witches Ball when my phone rang, illuminating, *"Bossy Calling",* so I answered it.

"Hello."

"Where are you? I thought you'd have made it here by now."

"We've been here a few hours, but we didn't want to bother you," I lied. Truth was if he didn't see me, he couldn't yell.

"I'm taking a break, you wanna meet up?" *Oh, lord, decisions, decisions.*

"We're getting ready to leave. We got invited to the Witches Ball." There was a pause and then an angry Jack spoke.

"You're not going," he snapped out.

"What?"

"I said you're not going anywhere near that fucking ball."

"Can you explain to me why, or is this just your general response to anything I want to do?" I replied, getting angry myself.

"I can give you two reasons."

"And they would be?"

"One, the mayor organizes that party and he will be there," I heard from behind me.

"And two, you're not going anywhere else in that costume except straight home," he barked as I turned around and looked up. *Shit!*

Hands on his hips, glaring down at me, his eyes raked over my body, and his jaw got tight. I could tell he was about to blow, but unfortunately for a drunken guy who walked up, slapped my ass, and shouted, "I want to confess, torture me, and I'll tell you where the body is buried," he let loose on him instead.

It all happened quickly. Bailey started to laugh—she's twenty, everything is funny—the drunk threw an arm around my shoulder, and before I could remove it, Jack's head spun around in a move comparable to the "Exorcist"; his eyes rolled back in his head as he lunged for the guy, grabbed his arm around my shoulder, and pinned him to the ground. He looked back at me and spoke through gritted teeth.

"Put your coat on and cover yourself. Then get your ass home before I kill someone."

I went to say something, but he cut me off, "It doesn't require a comment. Just put your coat on now," he barked.

I still didn't move, 'cause his bossy had stepped up to a whole new level and moved right on to jerk. I narrowed my eyes, and he watched me get pissed as he stood with the drunken guy, holding his arms behind him.

Again he ordered, "Put. Your. Fucking. Coat. On. Now."

Bailey grabbed my arm and broke my stare, whispering, "I think you better put your coat on."

I was trying to decide if doing as he wished was giving in, allowing him to dictate me, or if giving in was just the right thing to do since it bothered him, when I heard him count.

"One, two—"

"Are you counting down?" I hissed.

"I get to five, and that coat isn't on, we got problems. Three—"

"You are *not* counting down as if I were a child."

"Four—" I looked at his eyes, and he paused to see if I would comply. I could tell he wanted me to disobey. Insufferable man. So I decided to spoil his fun and put my coat on. He didn't grin in victory, though, but remained angry.

Jack was still holding the drunk and pulling out his cuffs when I decided it was time to go. I put my arm through Bailey's and pulled her with me; then I gave Jack an *"I'm not speaking to you"* look as Bailey and I headed off toward my Jeep.

"Straight home," I heard Jack call from behind me, but that hit me wrong, so I turned back to him, and he raised an eyebrow in question.

Since I was a good twenty feet away, and he couldn't reach me, I felt bold and replied, "Don't wait up, Jack. I have a ball to attend." With that parting shot, I turned and kept on walking, *quickly* I might add, since I was only brave when there was a good distance between me and Jack.

Bailey leaned in and whispered, "I think the costume pissed him off."

I rolled my eyes at her intuitiveness and laughed, "Yeah, it pissed him off, and then he became a jerk and pissed *me* off. Pissed I can handle, but jerk? Not so much."

Bailey turned around to see if Jack was following us

and then turned back and said, "That Mark guy is behind us." I looked over my shoulder, and he raised a bottle of beer at me.

"Walk faster," I begged, and we picked up the pace. I didn't need him mixed in with the already bad situation. I just kept walking, dragging Bailey with me, and when I saw my Jeep, we double timed it and got in.

"Witches Ball or home?" Bailey inquired.

"Honestly, I was tired and thinking home before Jack went all he-man jerk on me, so now I say Witches Ball just out of protest."

"Awesome. That's the spirit, Jennifer. Show him who's the boss."

I smiled at my daughter and her skewed view of Jack and me. She'd learn just as I had: that there was only one person wearing the pants in this relationship. I was just trying to ignore the fact.

***

Staring up at the huge luxury cabin decked out in orange and black twinkle lights, Bailey whistled. I just stared in envy. A two-story log cabin that looked like it belonged on the cover of a magazine stretched out before us. Wrap-around decks on both levels were filled with people in all sorts of costumes.

Bailey whispered, "Wow," and grabbed my hand. She tugged me up the front steps and into the foyer. Inside, the furnishings screamed money: western and cabin décor that was tasteful and staged to an inch of perfection, proving that sometimes money *could* buy happiness. It. Was. The. Bomb. Huge, but comfortable, not ostentatious, more Ralph Lauren meets Gunnison. The party had all the trimmings: champagne fountains flowing on both levels, tables covered with food, chefs manning the stations carving prime rib, while bowls of shrimp, pâté, canapés, and crab legs stared back at us. Never had I been to a gathering like this, or seen a spread of food like this. To say I wanted to pull out my phone and snap a picture to post on Facebook, stating, "You won't believe where I am" was an understatement. Bailey read my thoughts and snapped a picture; she posted it, tagging my name.

"Shall we?" I asked my daughter, the table of food laid out in front of us.

"I suppose you could twist my arm," Bailey laughed and then grabbed my hand, and we hit that table like a cow to a trough. In other words, we loaded up.

Moving through the crowd, I observed who was here and kept an eye out for the mayor; Jack may not want me here, and truth be told, I didn't want to have to deal with the mayor either, but I figured I could avoid him with this many people if I kept my eyes open. Standing off to the side, we people watched. Bailey and I loved to go to the mall when she was younger and watch the people, making up identities for them.

"Two o'clock, pudgy man with the blond bimbo. I say he left his wife at home and picked up a hooker for the night."

I turned my head to the right and spit out my drink when I locked eyes on Bob, my editor, and Amber Welsh. Bailey laughed out loud at my display, pounding my back as I choked on my drink. My luck was not shining on me this night. Amber heard the commotion and turned her head. Recognition hit her, and I saw her look around for Jack. I had a very bad feeling that, when she didn't see him, round two was approaching, and without Jack here to hold me back, I might not hold my tongue. And with my boss standing at her side, I really, *really* needed to hold my tongue.

Using my head for once, I grabbed Bailey's hand and started walking towards the staircase, Bailey laughing as she followed.

"Wait, do you know them?" she asked.

"That's my boss and the bimbo is an old girlfriend of Jack's. She doesn't like me, as in she hates me, so let's go downstairs," I replied, moving fast down the stairs. When we got to the bottom and turned the corner, I ran straight into Mayor Hall. *Swear, if I didn't have bad luck, I'd have no luck at all.*

"If this is what the sheriff's department is hiring these days, I'll make sure to increase the budget for more."

Bailey, being my daughter, of course sensed he was a player the minute he opened his mouth.

"You must be the mayor. Jack's mentioned you," Bailey interrupted.

"And you must be Jennifer's daughter. You're just as beautiful as your mother." John's eyes made their way to her chest, then her legs, and I instinctively stepped between them, grabbing her arm and moving her out of his line of sight.

"Mayor, how nice to see you again. Thank you for the invitation." John leered at me, his eyes now moving to my chest. He tried to put his arm around me, so I stepped back and right into Amber Welsh. *Fucking, fucking hell.*

"I see while Jack is working, you're out enticing all the other men in Gunnison. I knew when I laid eyes on you in Mike's you were a slut."

I sucked in a breath, and then heard Bailey do the same, and before I could shove the pointed toe of my boot up her ass, she stepped in. *Oh, dear lord, I hate when Jack is right. I shouldn't have come.*

"Bailey," I snapped and grabbed her arm before she defended my honor. She turned back to me, pissed the hell off, and I couldn't blame her, but I needed to defuse this situation now.

"Get our coats, ok? I'll be right with you." Bailey looked between us both and relented. She nodded and headed for the coatroom at the front of the house.

I turned to John and Amber and, speaking through my teeth, said, "Pleasure seeing you both, as always. If you'll excuse me, we'll just be leaving."

Without a backward glance, I turned in the direction my daughter went. I'd only made it three steps when I bumped into someone. Stumbling back, I turned my head and smiled.

"Fancy meeting you here," I laughed.

"Follow me. I saw the altercation and know a shortcut."

***

Finally finished for the night, I headed to my truck. I had a wayward woman to find, and I'd better find her ass at home if she knew what was good for her. My phone buzzed in my pocket, so I grabbed it and saw it was Bailey calling. *If she thinks I'm letting her off the hook for that stripper outfit she put her mom in, she better think twice.* If she wasn't heading back to school, I'd tan both their hides and ground her for a month, but then again...

"Tell me where you are, and I'll consider not grounding you for a month."

"Jack, oh, God, Jack, please help me. Mom's missing."

Twenty-Eight

BOLO

"Jack!" Bailey shouted when I arrived at the mayor's house. She was waiting for me on the front steps, so I climbed out of my truck and watched as Barry, Grady, and Phil pulled in next to me. When I reached Bailey, she was a bundle of nerves, shaking and crying, so I grabbed her and held on while she buried her head in my chest. "Bailey, I need you to talk to me so we can find Jenn."

She pulled back, wiping her face with the backs of her hands. She nodded and took a deep breath.

"Mom and I were people watching; I commented on some blond bimbo, and she panicked when the woman looked at us, and then hurried me downstairs to get away from her. She's some ex of yours."

"Amber?" I questioned, and she nodded.

"When we got downstairs, Mom ran into the mayor; he was putting the moves on Mom, and she was trying to move away when Amber came downstairs, saw the whole thing and called Mom a slut. So I got pissed, and Mom told me to stop and to go get our coats. She said we were leaving, and that's the last time I saw her. She never came looking for me, and now I can't find her anywhere."

I looked over at Grady and the boys and ordered, "Search the grounds, inside and out," then I turned back to Bailey. "You said someone saw her walking with a man?"

"When she didn't come for me, I went looking for her, found the mayor and asked where she went. He said she was chatting with some man and left with him."

I felt my anger spike at the thought of Jenn talking with another man, but shut it down; I didn't have time to react. I needed to keep my head on straight and look at the evidence. Jenn wouldn't leave her daughter stranded for a man; something wasn't adding up, and I needed to find John and make him talk.

Inside the mayor's house, I noticed no one had stopped with the festivities. A woman was missing, and everyone was drinking and eating like nothing had happened. I felt my temper spike higher and looked around for John. I caught a glimpse of him with Amber in the corner and headed their way. When I reached them, Amber turned to me and sneered, then with her claws bared, attacked.

"Heard that slut of yours left with another man, abandoning her daughter just to get laid? You sure know how to pick 'em, Jack."

"Considering Jenn's the best thing to *ever* happen to me, by a *long* shot, I'd say that's a compliment." Amber flinched and turned her eyes from me. My bulls-eye had hit dead center, so I moved on like she wasn't there.

"Mayor, Jenn's missing, and you're the last person who saw her. You wanna fill me in on this man she was talking to?" His arrogant demeanor turned cold and calculated as he responded, choosing his words carefully for maximum effect.

"Jack, be a man and accept when a woman leaves you high and dry for another one. Don't use your authority as sheriff to eliminate the competition." The mayor openly laughed, repeating my own words from two weeks before. And it took everything I had not to touch him. But then I decided, fuck it, and lunged, shoving him into the wall. I pressed my arm into his throat, cutting off his air, and got right in his face.

"Jenn is missing; she didn't abandon her daughter. Now tell me who the fuck she was talking to, or I'll arrest you for obstruction of justice."

I kept my forearm on his throat and watched as he looked around, and then I noticed the silence. The room behind us had gone quiet; we had an audience, and I didn't give a shit if it got me answers, so I didn't back down. John looked back at me and raised his shoulders in a shrug, answering my question, but giving me nothing.

"Never seen him before."

"You got a description; hair color, eye color, height, weight, tattoo, anything that will lead us to him?" I ordered.

"Average height, average weight, dark hair, decent looking, wearing jeans and a white t-shirt, not in costume, no visible tattoos and from the reception she gave him she knew him." That piqued my interest.

"You could tell she knew him?"

"Yeah, she said, *"Fancy meeting you here.?"* I pushed off John, glaring, and turned to Bailey, who'd been waiting and watching the whole time.

"Bailey, did Jenn indicate she knew any of the people here?"

"No, we hadn't been here that long. We got food and were just people watching." Her head jerked, and she looked at her phone, reading something on the screen, a puzzled look on her face.

"What is it?" I ordered, noticing her confusion.

"I posted a pic on Facebook of the food table, and a friend just posted a response, asking, *"Who's the creepy guy staring at you?"*

I moved to her side, ordering, "Show me the picture, honey." Bailey went to the camera function on her phone, found the picture and then blew it up so we could look. A picture of a table filled with food was on the screen and you could see a man staring across the room in the background; it looked like he was staring right at the camera. Dark hair, jeans and a white t-shirt, and the look on his face was one of longing. He looked familiar, but I couldn't place him.

I grabbed the phone and shoved it in the mayor's face. "You know him?" John looked at the picture, then back at me and nodded.

"That's the man she left with."

I shoved him back in disgust before I drove a fist into his face, and turned to leave. Grady entered on a run. I moved to him and snapped, "Talk to me."

"Got a witness out back who says he saw a man carrying a woman to his car, silver sedan, and Wyoming license plates. Said he thought she was drunk and even helped the man put her in the car. Description matches Jenn. She was out cold, and they put her in the back seat so she could sleep it off. Left heading north about an hour ago."

Christ, north led to highway-50 which took you to the interstate, and that meant he had an hour's head start and could be anywhere by now.

Bailey heard the conversation and broke down. I didn't have time to comfort her; I needed to hit the road, and I needed to do it now, but I turned to her, pulled her in my arms and held her tight for a minute.

I whispered in her ear, "I'll find her, I promise you. I will find her," then I kissed her head and turned to Grady. "Keep an eye on Bailey for me. I'm heading out and I'll call in the state police. You take Bailey to the station, and I'll keep in touch."

Grady nodded once, moved to Bailey and put his arm around her. She face planted into his chest and then broke down. The sounds of her cries sent me off as I exited the house to find Jenn.

"This sonofabitch is dead," I mumbled to myself as I threw open the door to my truck. I saw the other door open, and Barry climbed in.

"Just fucking drive, Jack," Barry snapped, not waiting for a response to his presence. I nodded once, started the engine, and grabbed my handheld, calling the station.

***

Hang in there, baby, I'm coming, I thought as I accelerated onto the highway and headed west on 50 that would take me to interstate 70. Wyoming was north, so my instinct said that was where he was going. Sirens blaring, speeds hitting 100, I kept my eyes peeled for a silver sedan with my woman in the back seat. I'd radioed the station and told Amy that when Grady got there, he needed to take Bailey's phone to one of the computer guys, have them clean up the picture, and put out a BOLO (be on the lookout) with the guy's picture and description of the car over the wires. Who was this guy? How the hell had one tiny woman attracted two whack jobs in five months? *Someone knows this bastard. If Jenn knew him then maybe Ben knows him as well?*

I pulled out my phone and dialed Ben while trying to stay on the road at my high rate of speed. Ben answered on the third ring, sounding tired and confused.

"Jack, this better be good!"

"Jenn's gone missing, Ben. Some guy snatched her from the Witches Ball. I need you to go to the station and look at this guy's picture and tell me if you know him."

I heard Ben's breath catch, and he whispered, "Missing?" He recovered quickly, though, and continued, "I'll be there in forty minutes."

I hung up the phone without another word, pushed the pedal to the floor and kept driving into the night.

***

One hour later....

"Base to Gunnison, you there, Jack?"

"Base, this is Gunnison, talk to me."

I was still heading north, pushing my truck's speed and praying like hell for a break. Barry kept an eye out and spoke with the state police as I barreled down the highway, hoping I wasn't going the wrong fucking direction. This guy had an hour's head start, but I was convinced he wouldn't want to bring attention to himself by speeding. With the posted 55 miles per hour, because of the hills and two lanes the highway narrowed to, if he was on this road, I'd catch him by doubling my speed.

"Jack, Ben Gates was here and looked at the picture. He was positive he knew the guy and made a phone call. We just confirmed the suspect's name is Charles Marcus Walker. Jack, we ran his name: he grew up in Wyoming, moved here three months ago, and his father was Gerald Marcus Walker. He's been bartending at The Wooden Nickel for the past six months."

"Son of a bitch!" I roared. That whacked-out fuck had borne a whacked-out son. It was like a damned horror movie with Jenn starring as the damsel in distress running for her life. Only this time, she was passed out cold in the backseat of the car at his mercy, and I didn't have a fucking clue where they were.

Breathing fast and trying to concentrate, I weighed my options. Turn back and start over, or keep driving north and pray I wasn't wrong? Barry was staring out the window, his eyes searching, saying nothing. I put the handheld to my mouth and, going with my gut, responded, "Understood, base. Traveling north on 50, will update you in an hour."

I kept driving, searching, Jenn's face in my head, thinking about her laugh. The look in her eyes when she was pissed, that brilliant light that shone from her face and drew people in. I was so lost in my thoughts that I missed the vibrating of my phone. After the third time, I picked it up and saw "Jenn Calling" on the screen, and I almost wrecked in my haste to answer.

"Jenn!" I shouted.

"Jack, oh, God, Jack...Help me. I was kidnapped and I'm in the back of a car."

"Where, baby? Tell me where, and I'll come get you."

"He stopped for gas. The sign says Clinton's Truck Stop."

"Good girl, I know the place. I'm just a few miles behind you. Can you stall him?

"I'll try, but I can't move very well. He drugged me." My jaw clenched when I heard that. This guy was dead. No reason to apologize for thinking it. I'd kill him, pure and simple.

"Swear to God, I'll rip his head off when I get there. You hold on, do you hear me? I'm coming, Sweetness, I'll find you."

I waited for a response but didn't get one. "Jenn?" Dead air, she was gone. I didn't know if she hung up, or if he found her phone. All I knew was I needed to get there. I grabbed my handheld and called base.

"Base, this is Gunnison, come in."

"Gunnison, this is Base."

"I need you to call the state police and tell them we have a kidnapped victim in the back of a silver sedan, Wyoming license plate, at Clinton's Truck Stop outside of Delta on highway 50. Suspect is considered armed and dangerous. Last-known was two minutes ago. Tell them we've had contact from the victim, and she is attempting to stall him until help can arrive. Male suspect is wearing jeans, white t-shirt and has dark hair. Victim is wearing...shit...Victim is wearing a stripper's costume, with the name Sheriff on the back.... And tell them to bring some clothes for her as well."

"Roger that, Jack, contacting now."

I heard Barry chuckle and speared him with a "don't fucking test me" look. He threw his hands in the air, and I turned my head back to the road. I heard my radio crackle to life and then dispatch reported:

"Gunnison, this is Base. We have two highway patrols in route, and they're two minutes out."

"Roger that."

I saw a sign up ahead that said gas next exit, Clinton's Truck Stop, and I relayed it to dispatch.

"Base, I'm coming up on the exit for the truck stop in one mile. Tell patrol to come in quiet. I don't want him to run if he hears the sirens."

"Roger that, out."

I took the exit and could see the lights of the truck stop up ahead. My heart was thundering while I looked at all the cars at the pump. Red, blue, where the fuck is the silver sedan?

"There!" Barry shouted and pointed to the last pump closest to the truck stop. I pulled in behind it and threw my truck into park. Reaching under my seat for my weapon, a 9mm Colt Defender, I checked my rounds, flipped the safety off and then opened my door. Barry had done the same and was now exiting his side of the truck.

I walked up slowly, looked in the back of the car, and saw the hat and glasses Jenn had worn lying on the seat. I looked up and saw two patrol cars coming in fast, but not hot. I pulled my badge out of my pocket and flashed it as they came up on the car. They nodded, and I pointed to the truck stop indicating they were inside.

Both cars drove to the front of the building, and I motioned to Barry I was going around back to make sure he didn't get away with Jenn through the back exit.

Once everyone was in place and any customers who were trying to enter were sent back to their cars, I put my radio to my mouth and clicked three times to indicate we were going in on my three. I counted down and then pushed the button and held it, commanding "Go, go, go."

Twenty-Nine

Seal the Deal

I'd had to disconnect my call to Jack. Charlie had finished at the pump and was making his way to the driver's door. Remembering how I got here, I wanted to scream at myself.

Charlie had told me he knew a short cut out of the Mayor's house, so I'd stupidly followed him since the coatroom was by the front door and we were in the back. He'd taken me down a hall, and as we came to a door at the back, he opened it and gestured me through. As I walked out the door, I felt a sharp pain in my neck as Charlie wrapped an arm around my waist. I felt the night sky start to spin and my eyelids get heavy. I tried to speak, but my tongue felt thick. When I tried to take one step to move away, the lights went out.

Next thing I knew, I woke up in the back of this car and tried to work out where I was. Charlie had been behind the wheel driving, humming, and I'd panicked at first, not knowing how long I'd been out. I could feel my phone tucked into the back of my tight shorts and knew I'd have to stay calm and wait for the opportunity to use it. We'd driven a while longer when Charlie pulled off the highway and into this truck stop, mumbling about being better prepared.

That brought us to now. Charlie was back in the car, and I'd made my call to Jack and he'd said to stall him, so I had to think of something in order to do just that. Charlie turned to check on me and was surprised when he saw I was awake.

"Charlie, I have to use the bathroom."

He looked out the window of the car and surveyed the area, then looked back at me and said, "I wasn't going to put this on you until we got home, but if you need to use the bathroom, I need to know you won't run." I didn't know what the hell he was talking about. Put what on me?

Charlie got out of the car, went to the trunk and opened it. A few minutes later, he crawled in the back seat with me. I tried to move back from him, but my arms and legs were still sluggish. He looked over my body, Bailey's ridiculous stripper costume showing entirely too much of everything, and I felt dirty, like his eyes were touching me in private places they shouldn't. I held back a shudder and tried to remain calm, but after Gerry and his knife attack, I'd long since passed being able to stay calm. The memory of it was too strong, so my tears started to fall and my breath accelerated. Charlie reached out, grabbed my foot and pulled it across his lap. I squeaked at the sudden movement. Reaching into his bag, he pulled out a black ring with a blinking red light and opened it like a bracelet. It hit me what it was, and I tried to pull back my foot, but he grabbed hold and wrapped the cuff, used for keeping track of inmates, around my ankle and locked it. Then he pulled out a remote and flipped a switch. The red light on the bracelet went green, and then he turned to me and without any remorse said, "I've wired this bracelet with C4. If you run, I'll blow you up." *Oh, shit, oh, my God, oh, God, oh, God, oh, God.*

"Why, why are you doing this, Charlie?"

"Because I love you."

He smiled at me as if he'd just given me flowers, not an ankle bracelet armed with explosives. My heart was beating out of my chest, and I didn't know what to do. Jack said stall; Jack would know how to handle this, Jack would kick his ass for me.

Holding on to that thought, I took a deep breath and said again, "I need to go to the bathroom, Charlie."

He nodded at my request and opened the door, put his hand out to me and pulled me out of the car. I stumbled a little on my feet, so he put the remote in his pocket and then picked me up like a bride on her wedding day and carried me across the parking lot. He went into the truck stop and didn't stop until he got to the ladies' room. He knocked on the door, and when we got no answer, he opened it and carried me inside.

"I can take it from here," I told him. I did need to pee and I wasn't about to do it in front of him.

He put me down, cupped my face with his hands and then leaned in and tried to kiss me. My head snapped back, trying to avoid the kiss, but he just pulled me harder to him and slammed his mouth down on mine. I pushed back hard against him and stepped back, wiping my mouth.

He leered at me and hissed, "You'll learn to accept me, Jennifer. You'll learn to love me just like I love you."

"Charlie, I don't understand why you're doing this? I

don't even know you other than having a drink at the Nickel."

"Like father like son. Gerry fell in love with you and I did, too."

"Gerry's your father?" I whispered in shock. The look on Charlie's face turned to one of disgust.

"That man may have fathered me, but he wasn't my father. He abandoned me thirty-three years ago to live with my grandparents. I was raised with the back of a hand by an angry old man who hated me."

For a moment in time, I saw that little boy who'd been abandoned, crying for his mother who was dead. Crying for the father who couldn't cope with the loss and finding no comfort, only pain.

The mother in me reached out. I put my hand on his shoulder and softly tried to reason with him. "Charlie, forcing me to love you and taking me away from my daughter isn't the answer to your pain. I would have listened if you needed to talk. I'm your friend."

Sadness filled his eyes, and he whispered, "I just want someone to love me." I nodded my understanding. Didn't we all want to be loved?

"I'll be your friend, Charlie, and I'll help you find someone to talk to, but you have to let me go. You'll only make this worse for yourself if you don't."

He looked like he was battling with his sense of right and wrong when I heard a noise outside in the store, and then angry voices shouted, "Down, down, everyone down!"

Charlie's moment of reflection disappeared immediately. He grabbed my arm, spun me around, and then pulled out the remote.

He moved to the door and opened it a crack, then closed it and put the remote in my face and growled, "Not a fucking word out of your mouth or I'll blow the whole place up."

I didn't have time to respond before he opened the door and pulled me through it and further down the hall. He found a door that led to a storeroom, moved us inside, locked the door, and then pulled me to the window. He was looking around for something before he moved to a shovel, came back to the window and smashed it. I could hear the voices getting closer and just as the knob on the door was jiggled and banging started, Charlie grabbed my waist, picked me up and pushed me through the window, then followed after me as I heard the door behind us burst open.

"Jenn!" I heard Jack shout as Charlie yanked my arm and started running toward a row of semi-trucks lined up for fueling. He kept running until we'd made our way to the other side and out of sight from the building. Charlie stopped, looked around and saw a truck pulling to a stop, waiting on the traffic to pull out and ran toward it.

The truck was the size of a dump truck, but the back was open. Charlie lifted me inside and then pulled himself over the back just as the truck pulled out onto the highway. As I felt the truck pick up speed, he shoved his body over mine to keep me still.

So close... Jack had been so close to helping me, and now we were on the move again. I didn't know if Jack knew I was gone, saw what happened and was right this moment following us, and since I didn't know and was scared to death, I lost my ability to think clearly and started struggling to get free. If I were going to die, I'd die trying to get back to my daughter.

"Don't move," Charlie growled, but I ignored him. I reached up and clawed his face, causing him to pull back in pain. I struggled under him to break free and got to my knees. I tried to crawl forward so that I could bang on the window of the cab, hoping the driver would stop. I got up in a crouch, but the truck hit a bump, and I fell back into Charlie, causing the remote that he'd been holding to fly across the truck bed. Charlie was on his back, I was lying on his stomach, back to his front, so I brought my arm up and slammed my elbow into his stomach, knocking the wind out of him.

With all the movement in the back, the truck started to slow and then I heard them: the sirens from behind us. A spark of energy hit me. I rolled off Charlie and tried to stand up and move toward the remote. I got within a foot of it when the truck slammed on its brakes, and I went flying forward, slamming into the back window and falling on my ass. I heard cars screech and looked down to see the remote in front of me. I grabbed it, then turned to Charlie and saw him stand up; he bent down and picked up a pipe, raised it over his head and moved toward me.

Paralyzed with fear, I didn't move, and as his arms came down, aiming the pipe at my head, I screamed, "JACK!" I didn't hear the word leave my mouth because the sound of a gun being fired filled the air. Charlie looked shocked when the bullets hit him in the back. He looked down with a questioning look and then dropped the pipe, crumbled to his knees and fell on top of me.

"JENN!" I heard Jack shout, but I couldn't move

because of Charlie's dead weight.

"Jack, get him off!" I shrieked, closing my eyes to his dead ones staring back at me. I felt his weight move from me and opened my eyes to look up at Jack's worried ones, giving me a once-over.

"I've got you, baby," Jack whispered as he picked me up and drew me into his arms, holding me tight. I buried my head in his neck and sobbed great, ugly tears as he rocked me back and forth.

"Jack," I whispered, "there's a bomb on my ankle."

Jack's head snapped back, and he replied, "What the fuck?"

"Charlie put C4 in an ankle bracelet to keep me from running. I'd really, really like for you to get it off me right about now," I whined.

Jack looked down at my leg, and I handed him the remote. He studied it for a moment then looked back at my ankle. He moved his hand up my leg to the top of my boot and unbuckled the straps, then, just as calm as if he was saying "pass the salt, please", he said, "Pull your foot out, baby."

I looked at the boot then wanted to kick myself for not thinking of that first. I wiggled my foot until it came loose, and I pulled my leg from it.

Jack stood with the boot and handed it off to a highway patrolman, instructing him to be careful and to call in the bomb squad. Jack turned back and helped me stand, I pulled off the other boot so I could walk.

I noticed Jack was looking me up and down and he barked, "Barry, find me a fucking blanket or coat."

I'd forgotten about the stripper costume, but Jack, clearly, had not. I leaned into him on weak legs, and without a moment's hesitation, he picked me up and carried me to the back of the truck. He jumped down, landing on two feet, and without breaking step, moved to his truck, put me in the cab, and climbed in, turned to me and pulled me back into his arms.

"Jack, Charlie was Gerry's son."

"I know."

"How'd you know?"

"Bailey took a picture at the party and he was in it. Called Ben, and he recognized him from the Nickel. Called the Nickel and got his name, then ran a check on him."

I burrowed deeper into his body and said, "He thought he was in love with me. He needed help, Jack...his grandfather beat him the whole time he lived with him."

"Seems everyone who meets you falls in love."

I looked up at him and saw his face was warm, a small smile on his lips. Then he made my heart skip a beat when he continued, "I know I fell the moment you opened your mouth."

"Jack," I mouthed since I had no voice. My heart was pounding, and a lump had formed in my throat.

"Love you, Jennifer. Don't know what I'd have done if something happened to you."

I shook my head to stop the tears from falling, then lunged into him and buried my face in his neck. Too many emotions were coursing through me. I wasn't looking for love when I moved here, but I sure as hell found it, and after kind, gentle and sweet Doug, I knew what I felt for him was just a shadow of what I felt for Jack.

Jack completed me, made me whole, and sparked a desire in me that I didn't know existed. So with no voice to express my own love, I moved to his ear and whispered, "I love you too, Jack."

Jack's hand came up to the side of my head and cupped my face, tilting it back. His eyes had gone dark, his breathing deeper. He leaned in and brushed my lips, his tongue tasting them. I opened for him, and he deepened the kiss, pulling me harder into his body.

Time stood still while I poured the love I had for this man into the kiss, trying to express the depth of my emotions. The kiss went hot and wild, my hands moving up the back of his shirt, clawing his back lightly with my nails. Jack moaned into my mouth, then broke the kiss and put his forehead to mine.

"Jesus," Jack choked out and buried my head in his neck, holding me tight.

Someone knocked on the window, and we pulled apart to see Barry standing there with a blanket. Jack rolled it down, grabbed the blanket from Barry, and I leaned over to the window.

"Thanks, Barry."

"Glad you're safe, Jennifer."

"Thanks for coming to the rescue."

Jack interrupted by growling, "For Christ sake, cover yourself before I shoot Barry too."

Barry chuckled at Jack's possessiveness then moved off to talk with the highway patrol.

I hadn't known for sure who'd shot Charlie, but now I did. I searched Jack's eyes to see if he was hiding any pain from killing the man, but only saw the irritation caused by my outfit.

I leaned in and asked, "You okay?"

Jack's eyebrows drew together in confusion.

"About shooting Charlie. If you need to talk, I'm here for you."

His face warmed, and he kissed my lips quickly then answered, "He drugged you, stole you from me, scared you, scared Bailey, threatened to blow you up, was going to kill you with a pipe, *and* I have no doubt got an eyeful of you in that outfit... So, yeah, I'm fine. I'd shoot him again if I could, but that's frowned upon in a law man. Apparently, sheriffs aren't allowed to overkill."

I didn't know if he was serious or joking to lighten the mood of a shitty night, so I kept my mouth shut by biting my lip. Jack saw it and stared, then looked at me and smiled. *I'm thinking he was serious.*

I was just about to say something when his radio crackled to life.

"Gunnison, this is Base, come in."

Jack grabbed his handheld and answered, "Base, this is Gunnison."

"Jack, Bailey wants to know if you have her?"

I was so caught up in everything I'd forgotten to have Jack call Bailey. Damn.

I grabbed the handheld from Jack and replied, "I'm here; I'm fine. Tell Bailey she still has to go back to school tomorrow, and that we'll be home in a few hours. Oh, and tell Bailey I'm picking my own costume next Halloween."

I turned to Jack and smiled. He threw his head back and laughed. Then he pulled me to him.

"I'm picking your costume next year," he demanded. I looked at his smiling face and thought about his possessiveness. Deciding it was sexy just like his bossy, I shrugged and answered him, "Ok, Jack."

"How do you feel about going as a pregnant woman?"

"I'd prefer going as something scary."

"I'll rephrase that. How do you feel about being a pregnant woman next year?"

I considered his words, understood the change in his sentence and froze.

I looked up and asked, "You want me to *be* pregnant, not *dress up* as a pregnant woman?"

Jack smiled at me and said, "She finally gets it."

I started breathing hard, a little freaked out to be honest, and then I thought about being a mother again. The thought of having Jack's baby made me feel warm and happy and I started to smile.

Jack saw my face change and whispered, "The thought of you carrying my child is sexy as hell, and it'd beat that costume you're wearing right now by a mile."

Staring at his smiling face, I envisioned a little boy who looked like Jack running around my house, dark hair, blue eyes, following Jack around, wanting to be just like his daddy, and I knew my answer.

"Ok, Jack." Just like that, no doubt in my mind.

How we'd ended up talking about having kids after I'd been kidnapped only weeks after having been attacked and put in a coma, was beyond me, but nothing since we'd met had been traditional or normal, so why not?

"Ok?" he questioned.

"Ok, but under one condition."

"What's that?"

"I don't want to be an unmarried woman when I get

pregnant again."

"You asking me to marry you?" he smiled.

"No, I'm telling you to marry me," I explained.

"Look who's bossy now?" he whispered as his mouth came to mine. Right before he kissed me, he whispered again, "Marry me, baby?"

"Ok, Jack."

"That's my girl. Now kiss me and seal the deal."

So damn bossy.

Epilogue

Three months later...

"Bob, I'm telling you, the trail leads back to the mayor."

You could have slapped me and I wouldn't have felt it when I made the connection between the fires at the old mine and the new casino proposal. Bob, my editor, gave me an assignment to investigate the new casino proposal after promoting me to Lorraine's position. He wanted me to find out about other small communities and how it affected them and their economies, as well as their crime rate. In doing so, I called the developers of the casino, and by sheer luck, ended up talking with someone who was chatty; they told me that the land they were looking at for the casino was the land around the old gold mine. As you can imagine, having been attacked there was followed by a mysterious fire caught my attention. My spidey senses kicked in, and I looked into the owner of the mine. I found out that the mayor purchased it from the family who owned it a month after the fire and was now looking to make some serious dough on this deal.

If I was right, he used his position as mayor to not only negotiate this deal, but also to find out what property they wanted. And *then* he lucked out by a mysterious fire that made it possible to purchase that very land? It smelled of scandal; it reeked of corruption and it screamed of arson for the sole purpose of purchasing the property for a song. *Wait until I tell Jack . . .*

***

One month later...

"You fucking bitch!" the mayor roared in my face. My article about what I'd uncovered had gone to print the night before, and all of Gunnison was waking up to find their mayor a suspect in the arson at the mine, *and* that he was an opportunist of his own making. By allegedly setting the fire, he was able to take advantage of the owners because the fire had made the mine unsafe, and the owners didn't have the money to exact repairs.

The story went like this. The casino was interested in the mine, but the owners didn't want to sell. A mysterious fire destroyed the mine, making it unsafe and expensive to rehab for the owners.

In stepped Mayor Hall: "I'll buy it from you and preserve the history," he'd told them, but he had no intention of doing so. I found out through communications with the casino owners, that he intended instead to bulldoze the mine and sell it to them for a song.

That brought us to now and the enraged man in my face.

Everyone at the paper got quiet, and I was so shocked by his anger that, for once, I said nothing.

"I'm suing this paper, I'm suing you, and if you think

the sheriff won't see his termination for investigating this bullshit, you're sadly mistaken. I will bury you both."

I heard Lorraine on the phone, whispering, as I kept myself on the other side of my desk, afraid the control he was holding on to might snap.

He leaned into my desk and hissed, "You're through in this town, Mrs. Gunnison. You, and your brute of a husband."

Did I mention I'd gotten married? Jack wasn't kidding when he said "marry me", and he wasn't kidding when he said he wanted a baby. It had been four months since Charlie abducted me and, since then, Jack had hauled me to Vegas where we'd gotten married with Bailey, Grady, Mom, Dad, Jack's mother, and Ben and Lorraine all in attendance. Neither of us wanted any fuss. So one month later, instead of the traditional Thanksgiving, we all flew to Vegas and had a short wedding at Cupid's Chapel, then had a long weekend of gambling and shows. Well, the rest of our wedding party did. Jack and I surfaced once for a Garth Brooks show, 'cause honeymoon or not, it was Garth, and I wasn't missing out on him.

Anyhow, back to our story.

The mayor ended his threat by taking his hand and swiping it across my desk, knocking everything to the floor, and then prowled around the desk. I backed up and put my hands up in front of me to keep him back. I heard running in our direction but kept backing up, tangling my foot with my chair sending me to the floor just as Jack rounded my desk.

And since I'd informed him two days prior that we were having a Halloween baby, he kinda lost his shit when he saw me fall.

Jack grabbed the mayor, threw him to the side, reared back his fist, and nailed him right in the jaw. Then he followed with a leg to his stomach, bringing the mayor to the floor and he was out cold. I was trying to get to my feet to stop him, but he turned to me, picked me up, and put me gently in my chair. He proceeded to look me over, searching for injuries.

"I'm ok, Jack."

"How hard did you fall?"

"Jack, I'm fine. I took spills with Bailey; my pride is bruised, not my body."

Jack took a deep breath then leaned his forehead against mine.

"I wanted to kill him when I saw you go down."

"You may have, because he's not moving," I replied as I looked at the mayor lying on the floor.

Moments later, the mayor started moving and then rolled to his back, trying to breathe through the pain. His eyes finally opened, and he turned his head to Jack and sneered, "You're finished. I'm pressing charges for assault; I have a room full of witnesses, and the council will have no problem with my recommendation after this."

Lorraine walked up about then, looked down on the mayor with a look of disgust, and informed John how it really was.

"You threatened and advanced on a pregnant woman, causing her to fall. You continued to advance on her, even after she was down. I have no problem telling the council that a man protecting his wife, or a sheriff protecting a defenseless pregnant woman, was well within his right as a husband or a Sheriff."

When Lorraine finished her speech, Bob stepped up.

"I didn't see anything. Sorry, Mayor."

"I don't have my glasses with me today. Sorry, Mayor. I didn't see anyone beat the shit out of you with one punch," our print editor, Thomas, laughed.

Grady, who had come with Jack, was standing to the side with his arms crossed over his chest, scowling at his father. He stepped up and helped John off the floor, and then pulled his arms behind his back and stated, "You have the right to remain silent—"

"What the fuck are you doing, Grady?"

"Reading you your rights. We have a warrant for your arrest. Got it this morning from Judge Thompson. We found the evidence you started the fire at the mine in your barn, you stupid sonofabitch. Anything you say can and will be used against you in a court of law," Grady continued as he walked his father out of the newsroom and out the door.

"Wow, that was freaking awesome," I whispered to my husband who'd been watching the whole thing, scowling with rage.

"Yeah," was all Jack grunted, then he turned back to me and ordered, "Want you home in bed resting after that spill you took."

My guy was so cute. I was heading home anyway, so his bossy didn't bother me; not when it was wrapped up in love and concern for his future son or daughter.

"Ok, Jack."

"You need me to drive you home?"

"I think I can handle it," I smiled. This was going to be a long eight months if he reacted like this with every spill

a reason to breathe

or stubbed toe I got.

***

Three months later...

"Mamacita, I'm home," Bailey shouted as she flew through the front door, Grady following in her wake with a huge grin on his face. Did I mention that during my kidnapping, Grady took care of Bailey and they made a connection, one that was still going strong seven months later? You'd have to forgive me—pregnancy hormones—and my memory wasn't what it used to be. They were adorable together. Grady was a badass in the making; give him eight more years until he hit thirty, and I guaranteed he'd be uttering monosyllabic sentences and he and Jack could sit around grunting "babe, yup" and "babe, nope" to answer every question ever asked of them.

"Oh, my God, look at your cute little Buddha belly," Bailey squealed, rushing forward. I was three and a half months along but it looked more like six. I was keeping a surprise from Bailey until she was home for the summer. Twins. God had a sense of humor.

For the first time since I'd met him, Jack was speechless when I'd told him. He just looked at my stomach and smiled. We didn't want to know the sex of the babies, or if they were identical, until they were born, so instead of coming up with a single girl's or boy's name like most pregnant couples, we had to come up with two of each to cover our bases.

Bailey got down on her knees and whispered to my

stomach, "Hey, little bro. I can't wait to meet you."

"What makes you think it's a boy?"

"Please, would Jack's loins produce anything but?" *She has a point there.*

"Well, now that you're home, you can help us pick out names. I need two of each."

"Cool, I'll pull up names on the web, and we can write down what we like, but why two?"

"Because we're having twins," I beamed.

Bailey threw her head back and laughed, "Of course you are! Jack got his way with this as well. He wanted two kids, so he got two in one go."

Jack walked up as she was laughing and wrapped his arms around my belly, kissing my neck, and then whispered, "Your daughter has me figured out. When will her mother accept I get my way in all things?"

"Her mother knows it; she's just fighting it."

"Losing battle, just saying," he replied in my ear. Bailey was watching us, smiling, and then she teared up.

"You guys are so cute together. I just love how much you love my mom, Jack," she cried. Jack moved to her and wrapped her up in a hug, and she buried her face in his chest.

I knew there would be moments that Doug's death would hit her hard. Luckily, she had Jack in her life as well, and he took over the role of "head of the house" and "protector of his women" as if he were a seasoned pro. No one had better mess with his girls. Ask Grady: he'd had the "I'm watching you" talk from Jack already. For a man who'd never been married, he was a great stepfather and husband, and most of all, a great best friend. We only fought when I didn't agree with him, which happened more often now that I was pregnant. Jail time had been threatened if I carried anything heavier than a pillow...Men forgot that before modern medicine came along, women plowed the field and only stopped long enough to push out the baby; then, with baby strapped to their chest, went back to plowing the field. (Ok, a bit of a tall tale, but not by much.) However, like Jack said, he got his way in most things, and since it meant I could sit with my feet up, who was I to complain?

***

Five months later...Halloween

"Mom, please try to get along with Jack's mother." Mom had flown in from Florida to help me with the babies. My due date was three weeks away and since I was carrying twins, my doctor had put me on bed rest for the last two months of my pregnancy to keep me from going into pre-term labor. Twins liked to come early, and anything beyond thirty-six weeks was considered a bonus. I was in week thirty-seven, and everyone was staring at me, waiting for me to burst. Jack's mother, living only a county away, drove over every day to help. And since this was her first grandchild, she was anxious and excited and tried to help out as well. My mom being my mom obviously thought that "this is my daughter, I'll take care of her" and she kept arguing about how Susie, Jack's mother, was doing things.

"I get along fine with her. She just doesn't know how we do things, and I didn't want her to make more work for you, that's all."

I lifted an eyebrow at her.

"Mom, it's just towels. She can fold them any way she wants to."

"They take up too much space the way she does it," Mom explained.

I looked at her, then back at my mother-in-law who was sitting on the couch, looking pissed off at being told, "You're not folding them right, Susie," and I threw up my hands. I was too exhausted carrying around all this weight; my feet were swollen, my back hurt all day, and I was just plain tired of being pregnant, but it was Halloween, and I wanted to sit on the couch and watch the kids come to the door and get their candy. So out I came from my bedroom to find Susie and Mom sniping at each other about how to fold a towel.

And don't get me started on mealtime...I hid in my room when it was time to decide what's for dinner and who's cooking it. *Thank God, there are two babies.* Wars have started over who held the baby next and for how long.

I sat down, grabbed the bowl of candy, and started digging through it. *There better be my favorite candy in here, or there'd be three angry ladies in this house.*

The doorbell rang, and I heard a little girl's sweet voice saying trick or treat.

Whoops, I have the candy.

I pushed off the couch and waddled my way to the door. When I arrived, I found a cute, blond, blue-eyed girl with an angelic face.

I leaned over and said, "You're so pretty, are you a princess or a fairy?"

Angelic child moved closer and said, "I'm a princess. Are you dressed up like a pregnant woman or are you pregnant?"

Smiling, I thought back to the year earlier when Jack had asked me to be a pregnant woman for Halloween and here I was, just that.

I leaned in and said, "Pregnant with twins. You want to feel? They're kicking." Her eye's got big when I took her hand and put it to my stomach where baby A was kicking. Her angelic face grew in awe, and she smiled.

"Cool, huh?"

"Way cool," she replied.

I handed out her candy and waved goodbye as she made her way back to her mother. I turned to the couch and I'd only taken two steps when a sharp pain hit my lower stomach and I felt liquid rush down my leg. I shouted out in pain and bent over as my mother and Susie rushed to me.

"My water just broke."

"Sweet baby Jesus in a manger," my mother replied.

"I'll call Jack," Susie shouted and then headed for her phone. I breathed through the contraction, still bent over, and when it finished, I stood up and walked down the hall with my mother holding on to me.

Once in the bedroom, I headed to the bathroom and stripped out of my maternity clothes and got in the shower.

I had three more contractions while cleaning up, but the hot water helped relieve the pain. I was just getting out of the shower when Jack burst through the door, looking anxious, so I smiled at him.

"Can you believe it? They're being born on the night

segmentheadcp smith

"Jesus, what are you doing in the shower?" Jack growled.

"My water broke, Jack, so I wanted to get cleaned up."

"Christ," he replied as he grabbed my hand and helped me to the bedroom. Mom was standing, ready to dry me off and help with clothes, and Susie was getting my bag together.

"I'm giving you five minutes to get dressed, then I'm carrying you outside and to the truck."

"Whatever," I muttered, feeling more pressure than before. As I got my bra and panties on, another contraction hit me, and I reached for Jack.

He grabbed my hand and whispered in my ear, "Breathe, sweetness, I got you."

"Jack, we need to go, I feel like I need to push."

"Is that bad?" he asked as his face paled.

"It's not bad if you're in a birthing room with a doctor, but at home with no one to help deliver your babies, it's not good." I'd no sooner got that out when another contraction hit.

"Oh, dear, the contractions are right on top of each other; we need to hurry," Susie implored.

"Too late," I snapped and sat down on the bed.

"I'll carry you, let's go. Get her bag, Mom, we're leaving now."

"Oh, God, too late, Jack, I have to push. Mom, call 911."

"I'll get you there, baby, just hold on," Jack bossed.

"Jack, honey, you're not getting your way on this one. Help me lie down." Jack just stood there staring at me, working this problem out in his head.

337

"Jack, I swear to God I'll find your gun and shoot you if you don't move and help me," I hissed and then another contraction hit, and I screamed, "I hate you, I can't believe you talked me into doing this again." Deep breath in, let it out slowly, "No, don't touch me," deep breath in, let it out, *forget this*, panting now. "Now's... oh, God, now's not the time to be touching me if you want to keep your balls intact."

"Swear to Christ, Jenn," Jack growled, then picked me up and laid me on the bed. I'd only got my bra and panties on, so Jack pulled them off and then covered me with a blanket.

"Everything's always a drama with you!" he shouted.

"What?" I hissed.

"We met during a murder, *drama*. You get attacked, *drama*. You get kidnapped, *drama*. You get assaulted by the mayor, *drama*. Can we just bring our babies into this world without drama?" he shouted louder.

"Are you seriously shouting at me while I'm in labor having *your* babies because they decided to come quickly?"

"Yeah, no, yeah... Christ, where's the fucking ambulance?" he roared at the room and no one in particular. I started laughing, and he looked at me like I'd lost my mind.

"Jack, baby, you need to breathe."

"I'll fucking breathe when the fucking ambulance is here and takes my wife to the fucking hospital to have my babies where she fucking belongs and not a fucking minute sooner... Jesus, why's the room spinning?"

"Jack, sit down, you're breathing too fast and making yourself dizzy."

Jack looked at me then looked at the bed and sat down, putting his head between his legs. I grabbed his hand and squeezed when another contraction hit me. The pressure to bear down was so great I had to, because not doing so went against nature.

Panting, and "hee hee who'ing," I cried out as Jack held my hand, saying, "Just hold on, please Jenn. Don't push, the ambulance is coming."

"Jack, you gotta look and see if I'm crowning."

Jack looked at me, then at my belly, looked back at me, and then something shifted. He went from scared husband to sheriff and trained medical tech. I didn't know if he'd ever delivered a baby before, but he was quickly gonna find out if he was up for the job.

"Mom, go open the door and wait for the ambulance. Valerie, get me the clips we use on the potato chips and a pair of scissors, towels, baby blanket, and the nose sucker in the baby bag."

Then he turned to me and said, "Don't you push unless I say so, do you hear me? If you're not dilated enough, you'll rip your cervix."

I nodded at my take-charge husband and felt calmer already. Experienced or not, he seemed to have it under control.

Jack lifted the blanket and looked between my legs, and I heard him say, "Shit."

"Don't cough, sneeze, or breathe." Then he bellowed, "I need that stuff right fucking now."

A contraction hit me, and I screamed, "Jack, I gotta push!"

If I wasn't clear on this already, not pushing was like telling your body not to breathe; it was a reflex, my body pushed, and I kept breathing, trying to stop, but it wasn't working. I screamed out in pain and frustration as Mom ran into the room and handed the stuff to Jack.

Jack lifted the blanket, and I screamed again, "I can't Jack, I can't hold off, oh, God."

"Push, baby, I got you, I got you, push."

Mom grabbed my hand and helped me lean forward; she counted to ten while I pushed, then I took a deep breath and pushed to ten again.

Jack shouted, "Stop pushing," and then grabbed the nose sucker, and I heard him suction. I felt like I was splitting in two when he finally got up in the middle of the bed and with both hands grabbed the baby's head and said, "Give me one long hard push."

I drew in a breath and pushed right through the pain, then pushed to bring my baby into this world and finally lay eyes on one of them.

Jack grunted, and I could feel him pulling on the head then turn the shoulders, and with a gush, I felt the baby swim out.

I waited while Jack did whatever he was doing, but I kept chanting, "Is he ok, is she ok?"

I saw Jack clamp the umbilical cord with the potato chip clips and then heard the scissors snipping.

"Jack, why isn't he crying?" I'd no sooner asked that when I heard a smack and a wail, and then Jack finally looked up.

"Meet Keller, baby... you gave me a son," he choked out as tears ran down his face.

Mom was standing next to Jack, smiling, as he handed her Keller, and she wrapped him in a blanket, before handing him to me.

Instant love so strong it overwhelms your heart hit me, and when I looked into those baby blues, I prayed they'd be like his father's. Dark-brown hair, tons of it for a newborn, and he was big. Bigger than I thought for a twin, because he had to be six and a half, maybe seven pounds. Tears ran down my face as I kissed his little head and breathed him in for the first time.

Susie rushed in, screaming, "The ambulance is here," and she raced over to look at little Keller.

I felt another contraction and cried out, "Take the baby," as baby B decided it was time to make an entrance. Jack was scowling and ordered, "Jenn, the baby's turned, don't push."

I breathed through the contraction, trying to stop pushing, when an EMT rushed into the room. Jack briefed him on my condition and then moved aside and took my hand.

"Mrs. Gunnison, don't push, the baby has breached, and we need to get you to the hospital."

I nodded my understanding, and he stood and started an IV. Another tech brought in a stretcher and transferred me onto it, then took me out to the waiting ambulance. Jack crawled in the back holding Keller, then my hand, as we rushed down the road to the hospital.

I had three more contractions on the way, breathing and cussing at Jack, who grinned while looking worried at the same time. We made it to the hospital in record time where I was unloaded, taken to the ER, and informed that since the baby was breach, they needed to perform a C-section immediately.

Rushed from the room with Jack at my side, and

Keller handed off to the nursing staff, who placed bracelets on both Jack and my wrists for identification and security, we had to part company to get me ready for surgery and for Jack to change into scrubs.

"I love you, Jenn. I'll be in there shortly," Jack whispered to me.

"I love you too, Jack," I whispered back, exhaustion finally hitting me. Another contraction came, and I whimpered.

"Time to go, Mrs. Gunnison. Sheriff, you can step in here to change and we'll be back in a moment to get you." Jack leaned in and kissed my forehead, holding still for a moment before moving back. He grabbed my hand and held it until he had to let go, and they wheeled me through the birthing room doors.

***

Two hours later...

"The doctor thinks they're identical," Jack told Bailey over the phone, grinning like the new Dad he was. I could hear Bailey laughing over the phone and smiled down at the two little boys in my arms. There was no doubt in my mind they were identical, and there was no doubt in my mind they looked just like Jack. *God help me; I'll have a long road ahead of me if they're just as stubborn and bossy as their father.*

"Ok, Bailey, love you, Princess. See you soon."

Jack started to call Bailey Princess after he found out I was pregnant. I didn't know if knowing he was going to be a father kicked in his paternal nature, but as far as

Jack was concerned, Bailey was his and I loved him even more for it.

Jack moved from the chair and came to the bed. He looked at his sons, Keller and Kaiden, and leaned down, kissing both their sleeping heads.

"I can't believe you gave me two sons," he said with a hard edge to his voice.

"Are you disappointed one wasn't a daughter?"

"Hell no. I got a daughter already, and now she has two brothers to kick Grady's ass if he gets out of line," he announced with conviction. Hearing that, confirming what I already knew in my heart, made tears well in my eyes.

"Thank you, Jack."

"For what?"

"For loving me, for giving me a family again, and mostly for loving Bailey like your own."

Jack studied my face, his eyes warm and bright; then he came closer and kissed my forehead, my nose, and my lips.

"Thank you for giving me what I thought I'd never have."

"A family?"

"A reason to breathe."

Bonus Scene

Motherhood the second time around was far from easy. You'd think, since I'd been through it once already, that it would be a piece of cake. Maybe if they weren't from Jack's loins that would be true, but Keller and Kaiden were their father's sons. Meaning they ignored me, did what they wanted, ordered me around, and shook their heads when I tried to argue with them.

Having two little Jacks in the house along with dealing with the big, bad original, you'd think I would run screaming for the hills. However, just as it was with their father, I was helpless at first sight to do anything but fall in love with them. And just like their father, they were possessive of my time and brooded when I left them alone for too long. Just like they were doing now after returning from a long weekend in Alaska for Jack's cousin Max's wedding.

Jack and I had taken the trip without the boys, leaving them here with their big sister. They, of course, were making me pay for abandoning them for a few short days. Keller and Kaiden were now three, and they weren't precocious little boys who drew on walls and gave me sloppy kisses, but future lawmen in the making. They scowled at me when we arrived home as if I had been a bad mother. Then they proceeded to let me have it just like their father did when he thought I'd gone too far with a story. I had no doubt that if they could have put me into timeout, they would have done it; such was the heinousness of my crime by leaving them behind. What made it worse was they didn't even blink an eye at their father for leaving. Instead, they'd run to him while glaring at me all while verbally abusing me with, "We told you not to leave," at the top of their little boy lungs. I gawked at them while Jack picked them up, chuckling at their reception. He mumbled, "You'll get used to her not following instructions." This was because when we tried to leave three days earlier they had, in fact, shouted, "You aren't leaving, Mommy!

Honestly, when he'd left the room with the boys and they'd looked back and given me two fingers to the eyes as if saying, "I'm watching you," I wouldn't have been surprised.

Now, I was at home with them, and Jack was at the office. They were giving me a good taste of their cold shoulder. Currently sitting at the table eating their lunch, they would talk and yell at each other, but they would barely look at me. Done with being ignored, I sat down with my own sandwich and decided it was time to reason with the two. I'll remind you that they are their father's sons, so reasoning isn't exactly the word I'd use, more like creative manipulation in order to bring them around to my way of thinking. Not that it's ever worked with Jack . . . but they're three, and there's a first time for everything.

"If you two will stop being mad at me for going on a very short trip, Mommy will first take you to the park and then let you visit Daddy at work."

The boys turned and looked at me, then looked back at each other, and I watched their beautiful blue eyes sparkle with excitement as something unspoken passed between them.

"Ok, Mommy," they both replied, smiling.

Huh, that was easier than I thought.

"Then finish your lunch and we'll head into town when you're done," I told them, smiling now that my little men were happy with me again.

An hour later, we were in the park, and I sat on the park bench where Jack and I had spoken four years earlier when I'd first moved to town. I kept an eye on the boys as I worked on an article for the paper about the new principal, who had been hired to replace the retiring Principal of Gunnison High School. The new guy, one Sam Steele, was forty-five, divorced and quite a handsome man with broad shoulders, a head of thick light brown hair, and stunning green eyes. I'd met him once to interview him for the article, and I'd also soon heard that all the single women between the ages of thirty-five and forty-five were chomping at the bit for an introduction.

As I watched the boys swing, a shadow blocked the light of the sun, and I looked up to find Sam Steele standing there smiling down on me.

"Hello, Mr. Steele,"

"Sam," he answered.

"All right," I replied. "How are you settling in over at the high school?"

"Your former principal ran a tight ship. My transition with the staff in preparation for the new school year has been easy," he responded, taking a seat next to me.

"How do you like our fair city?"

"Can't complain. The welcoming committee has been more than...welcoming," he smiled.

"I've heard. You're a shiny new toy," I explained, then laughed because I knew how he felt. Small towns don't get many newcomers, so when they do, and especially if they are single, they get a lot of attention.

Sam chuckled in response as I looked back at the boys to make sure they were still behaving themselves. They'd stopped swinging and were now running towards me.

"Are those your boys?" Sam asked as he watched them approach.

"Yeah," I smiled, but then frowned when I saw the look on the boys' faces. They were scowling at me again. Clearly, they were going to hold on to this grudge longer than I thought.

When they made it to the bench, they immediately grabbed my hand, saying, "We want to go see Daddy."

"Oh, ok, well, it was nice to see you again, Sam. Let me know if I can assist the school in any way. Maybe if I lend a hand now, you'll overlook the two hooligans when they grace your halls," I laughed.

I'd barely gotten that out before the boys were pulling me down the sidewalk towards Jack's office, so I waved at Sam as he smiled.

When we entered the reception area, the boys took off down the hall as I greeted Dorothy, the receptionist. I took off after the boys, expecting them to head towards Jack's office, but I found them begging Barry to show them one of the isolation cells instead. He shook his head no, but then they leaned up and whispered into his ear. He laughed at the boys while I stood there wondering what in the heck they were about.

"Come on boys, let's go find your father," I told them, but Barry shook his head and buzzed the boys through, so I followed them.

We walked the long hallway down to a single cell that they only used for dangerous criminals so they wouldn't be around the general population. I had seen this cell up close and personal when Jack and I had first started dating, and the boys had heard the story about how their father had locked me up.

"Is this the cell that Daddy put you?" Kaiden asked.

"The same one," I informed him.

They walked into the cell, so I followed them in and just as I cleared the door, they darted behind me and grabbed the cell door and closed it.

"Boys, what are you doing?" I cried out as I moved to the door and tried to open it. They smiled their impish little smiles, then turned around and took off running down the hall.

"Keller, Kaiden?" I shouted at their retreating backsides watching as they were buzzed back through the door.

"Barry," I shouted at the camera in the ceiling, hoping he was watching from his position in the control room. Nothing.

Not about to panic that I'd been locked in the cell yet again, I walked to the cot and sat down until help arrived. I knew the boys would run straight to their father, so it was just a matter of time before Jack came and let me out.

Five minutes later, I heard the door buzz open, and in

walked Jack holding both boys' hands.

"It's about time," I hollered.

When they reached the cell, I expected Jack to laugh and open the door, but all three of my men stopped and crossed their arms, staring at me.

"Open the cell, Jack," I demanded.

"Did you sit on our bench and laugh and smile at another man?"

"What? Where did you—"

"Yes or no, Jenn?"

"You set me up," I gasped at the boys.

Everyone who knew Jack knew he was possessive and easily jealous where I was concerned. He kept it in check enough that it didn't annoy me, but I had no idea the boys had figured that out.

"Baby, answer the question," Jack grumbled, but there was a bit of a twinkle in his eye.

"I can't believe you boys set me up," I repeated.

Keller and Kaiden's little faces pulled into grins that matched their father's, and I knew then they were getting back at me for leaving. So I crossed my arms and glared at them both just as I would Jack, letting them know, in no uncertain terms, that they could not order me around.

"Boys, it looks like your mother needs time to think about her answer. Who wants ice cream?"

"You wouldn't!" I shouted.

"Babe, I would."

"I'll never speak to you again."

"Sweetness, that's not much of a bargaining chip." Then he looked down at the boys, put his hands out in high five, and, after celebratory slaps, all three of them turned on their heel and headed for the door.

"Boys, I'm... I'm so sorry I left you behind. I promise, ok? I'll never leave you again," I whimpered, hoping my sad voice would appeal to their love for me.

Jack stopped when they reached the door and looked back at me, smiling, and then he called out, "Baby, this hurts them more than it hurts you, promise."

And then they were gone.

Books By CP Smith

Reason Series

a reason to breathe

a reason to kill

a reason to live

Stand Alones

Restoring Hope

Property Of

FRAMED

Made in the USA
Monee, IL
29 January 2024

52593229R00197